MW00769573

This is a work of fiction. All characters and events are either a product of the author's imagination or used fictitiously, and any resemblance to real people or events is entirely coincidental.

SERPENT'S MARK

Cover art by Beth Alvarez

Edited by Savannah Grace Perran

First Edition: March 2020

ISBN-13: 978-1-952145-03-2

SERPENT'S MARK

BOOK ONE OF THE SNAKESBLOOD SAGA

BETH ALVAREZ

For the posse

CONTENTS

A RUNE

THE CEREMONIAL CLOTHING NEVER FIT HIM. DAEMON SMOOTHED the ornate robes and the midnight blue fabric pooled around his toes. He understood the ruin-folk had little to offer, but that didn't quell his irritation. Everyone in the underground had gathered for this ceremony. The least they could have done was ensure he was presentable. Instead, only the tips of his clawed hands and feet—both marred by glittering green scales—remained visible, while the rest of the outfit threatened to swallow him whole.

The fit was no different from the rest of his life. Pieced together from the scraps others left behind, a shamble everyone pretended was acceptable as they pushed the unsightly patchwork out of sight. His unwillingness to pretend alongside them was what landed him in this situation in the first place. In spite of what he was, the ruin-folk offered an opportunity for something better than patchwork. He supposed he should be grateful. Even if it meant wearing oversized robes.

"Lord Daemon," a soldier called from his chamber's doorway, "it's time for the ceremony to begin."

The robe would have to do. Daemon adjusted his plain metal mask before he turned toward the man. The soldier shuddered at the sight. Daemon pretended not to notice. He couldn't blame the man for his discomfort. Behind the mask, Daemon's violet eyes glinted, their unnatural glow and slit pupils hinting at the foul magics responsible for his existence. And then there was the small matter of his corrupted body.

As Queen Lumia's right hand, her followers respected him. But he had limited contact with the army outside of the skirmishes they faced together, and he was as uncomfortable socializing with the soldiers as they were with him.

"Her Majesty doesn't like to be kept waiting," the soldier said as Daemon slipped past him.

"I know." He expected reprimand for it, too, but he felt little guilt. If they wanted him to be prompt, they should have provided clothing he could walk in without stumbling. As if to confirm the thought, Daemon's claws caught on the robe's hem as he strode forward. He stifled a growl.

A handful of men waited in the hallway outside his quarters. They fell in step around him as he started down the twisting corridor to the throne room. It wasn't a long walk, but it wasn't one he'd been looking forward to, either. His heartbeat thumped a hard, unpleasant cadence in his ears, but he willed his breath to remain even.

He'd heard whispers of this blood oath, though no one mentioned what it would be like, and every tale of its purpose was different. Either way, it didn't sound pleasant, and that was all he knew.

Regardless, Queen Lumia said the oath would cement his place among her people. Daemon didn't mean to doubt his queen, but after twenty-five years among the ruin-folk, he wasn't sure anything would. They'd been wary of him when he'd joined their ranks, and they were not prone to change. Daemon suspected little here was.

Though a large network of tunnels connected the palace and its hidden city to the outside world, the world seemed to stay just that—outside. The black stone palace stood underground;

far from the feuding Eldani and Giftless men that claimed the surface of Elenhiise island. The tunnels doubled back on themselves so often only a seasoned explorer might have found the people living in their depths—or someone like him, who had stumbled over the Underlings by mistake five pents prior.

After today, he'd be an Underling, himself. A pitiful name, though whether they'd thought it up on their own or adopted it from the Eldani on the surface, no one seemed to know. Daemon saw little that distinguished them from the rest of the island's inhabitants, though living in caves seemed justification for the title. The label stuck in his head and warred with the name of ruin-folk they seemed to prefer. That he still never knew which name to use solidified the lack of belonging he always felt.

A large tapestry hid the passage's end and a soldier held it aside for the group to pass. The bright illumination of the great hall made Daemon wince and blink, and a moment passed before he could see. Dust and flakes of brittle cloth fell as the tapestry dropped back into place behind them. Everything here was old; it was a wonder the whole place hadn't fallen apart from age alone. That was one thing Daemon could say about his robes. They may have belonged on a man twice his size, but at least they were new. Mindful of the trailing hem, he pressed on.

For the first time he could recall, fires blazed in the large iron braziers between black stone pillars, the ruddy light refracted in the hollows and recesses of the ribbed ceiling that arched far overhead. Crystal skylights might have let in sunlight if not for the rumbles of thunder that echoed in the skies. The firelight danced over the friezes of serpentine creatures that lined the tops of the walls, lending them the illusion of movement. Daemon tried not to look. Had the palace not been ancient, he might have suspected those sculptures were there for his discomfort alone.

Though the throne room was at least thirty yards from end to end and twenty or so across, it held but a fraction of the Underling hordes. This ceremony had been a long time coming and, as festivities in the underground were few, it had been eagerly anticipated by peasantry and soldiers alike. People pressed to the very edges of the room and excitement hummed in the air.

Beyond the spectators, a worn red carpet ran the length of the hall, from massive double doors to the steps of the throne's ebony stone dais. Daemon had expected they would enter through the doors instead of the side passage they'd taken. The crowd shifted to clear a narrow path for his retinue. No one stood on the carpeting, though people sat along its edge. Once Daemon and his escort reached it, the path to the throne was clear. The queen waited ahead, and her delicate lips twitched into a smile when she met Daemon's eyes.

Youthful and golden-haired, Lumia appeared as gentle as her throne was grim. Her fingertips traced the thorny shapes of the throne's blackened iron arms and she shifted on a velvet cushion more threadbare than a queen should have allowed. She rose as he approached and, even with the dais beneath her, he had little more than to raise his chin to look her in the eye.

People filled the empty space behind them. The soldier that led his escort climbed the dais and dropped to one knee before the queen to offer an engraved iron collar on upraised palms. She took it and waved him away as she cast Daemon an expectant glance. He waited for the other men to take their places before he knelt at the queen's feet.

"You kept me waiting," she murmured.

"My apologies, my queen." His voice echoed, tinny, behind his metal mask. "I was delayed during my return from the surface." He lifted his head as she placed the collar around his neck. It snapped shut with a clack, the iron cold against his skin. He swallowed.

Each of the four soldiers of his escort produced chains from somewhere within their armor. Each affixed one end of their chain to one of the throne's legs and coiled the excess length on the ground. Then they moved back, loose ends in hand, ready for the ceremony to begin.

Lumia patted the side of Daemon's mask and chuckled. "Don't fret, my love. Your ordeal will not be long."

Unsettled, he clenched his jaw as she straightened with a grand flourish of her arms and greeted the gathered masses with a brilliant smile. A reverent hush fell over the crowd.

"My friends," she started, voice sweet as it carried to the far reaches of the dark room, "it is not often that I am gifted with such a servant as this. For years, you have witnessed his loyalty. He strives alongside us, aiding our growth, bolstering our strength as we prepare to rise anew."

She turned and took the chains from the soldiers at her heels. The men retreated to join the crowd.

"In years past, you honored him with his name: Daemon. Today, he shall take the oath to make himself your blood, your kin, your kind." She fastened the loose end of a chain to his collar with each word. The fourth chain, she held.

"It is in him I see our chances for survival. This is your brother in arms, your comrade. Not of your flesh and blood, not of your world, but destined to be a hero among us."

A roar of approval swept through the crowd as she looped the final chain over the back of the throne, tying him close. Daemon licked his lips behind his mask and gazed up at her as she eased into the throne again. He had expected the crowd, but he hadn't expected the chains. The entrapment made his skin crawl.

"I have chosen him to become my champion," Lumia continued, a glitter in her cold blue eyes. Her smile set him on edge. "Not only for his courage or strength, though they are admirable qualities. Not only for his cleverness or the cursed appearance for which the surface world shuns him, but for all the things that make him what he is, and for all that his union with us shall bring. May he become an invaluable part of our family." She patted the throne beside her. "Lay your hand upon the arm of my throne."

Daemon shifted to her side, never rising from his knees, and rested his left hand against the cold iron. The skin of his upper arm rose in gooseflesh and he fought back a shudder. A soldier knelt at Lumia's other side and presented a dagger with intricate patterns inlaid in its hilt. She drew the dagger and brandished it before Daemon's mask. If the room had been quiet before, now it grew deathly still.

"My pet, as every soul in this room will tell you, our society is formed by trust, not power. Those bonds are represented by your chains." She rested the tip of the dagger atop his hand and turned it so the width of its blade ran parallel to his fingers. He tried not to move. "You must place your trust in our forces to ensure your survival, though your instincts may scream otherwise. And because these men shall have trust in you, you must not abandon them. Our strength is in our solidarity. What say you?"

The watching crowd grew still. Daemon met her eyes without wavering. "I stand with you."

"And you have. But you are not yet one of us, though you have lived among us. If you truly wish to stand with us, be a part of our people and help lead us to glory, you must swear fealty. As my champion, you must swear it on your blood." Lumia's blue eyes gleamed with the final word. "Do you trust me, Daemon? Will you place all faith in me?"

Daemon shifted beneath the weight of hundreds of unfamiliar eyes that scrutinized his position at their leader's side. He hadn't felt so much an outsider since he'd first fallen into the catacombs beneath the ancient ruins.

Lumia stroked his taloned fingers with her free hand as if to soothe him. With the dagger pricking at the back of his hand, that seemed impossible.

He clenched his teeth behind his mask and silenced the protests that rose in the back of his mind. This was what he wanted, wasn't it? To be accepted? To belong? His voice came as little more than a whisper, hoarse in his throat. "I swear, on the blood that flows through my veins, to place all loyalty and trust in my queen."

A metallic clang ripped through the stillness as the dagger struck the throne and a tingling shock lanced up his arm. Heat bloomed in his hand, then searing pain, and Daemon gasped a moment before he could make a sound. His fingers flexed before he could stop them. His hand writhed beneath the dagger that pinned it to the throne. A low, gurgling hiss escaped his throat and red light flooded the inside of his mask as his magic reacted to the pain. It surged within him, a mindless instinct that struggled against his control.

Lumia laughed and jerked the blade free. Thick, black ichor rolled down the blade and collected in a droplet at its tip.

"You gave me your trust and I betrayed you." Challenge flashed in her eyes. "Would you trust a wicked queen again? Could you? Would you dare?"

He tried to pull his hand away, but she caught it and held him in place, her palm over the sticky wound in his hand. He couldn't tell if the crowd cheered or jeered. Grimacing behind his mask, he tried to still the trembling of his arm.

"Come now, love," she purred as she dangled the dagger over their hands. She turned the pommel between her fingers. "Will you trust me again?"

Pain throbbed with every beat of his heart. His eyes settled on the black blood that trickled down the twisted throne and he swallowed hard, his mouth gone dry. "Keep your hand there and I will."

Lumia dug her nails into his wrist as she drove the dagger down. Her face remained perfect, still, oblivious to the pain as the blade tore through her flesh and sank into his. Daemon choked back a shout before it could escape, but he couldn't help the strangled whine as she drew the knife back out. Her blood was hot, too hot, searing the wound in his hand.

"Pain means nothing to me in the face of glory, my pet. I do not fear it as you do." She smiled and tilted the dagger to point its tip at his face. "Do you think yourself foolish now? Or perhaps too trusting? What ought trust be, between a queen and her champion?"

Daemon grimaced and clawed at his arm with his free hand. His head spun; he blinked hard to try and still it. Something hazed his vision and he couldn't tell if it was smoke from the braziers or pain that clouded his senses. "Not..." It was a struggle to speak. He felt faint, though not from the injury or bleeding. It was the way her blood stung his flesh, burning as it mingled with his. Trails of black and crimson trickled down the arm of her throne to stain the floor beneath it. The copper scent of blood filled his nostrils, acrid and nauseating. "Not this."

Lumia's expression never wavered. The thud of her dagger came accompanied by the crack of shattering bones. "That's not a very good answer, my love." She pushed the dagger down harder and Daemon howled in pain. He slumped against the throne, his steel mask clanging against it and making his ears ring.

"Let me go!" he gasped.

"You are sworn to me, Daemon," she announced. The icy tone of her words stung. "You are bound to me as my champion, to uphold my word and my law. On the mixing of our blood, you have sworn this to me."

His resistance faded with each moment of pain. His lungs burned and his chest heaved. Unable to form words, he swallowed thickly and leaned forward until his mask rested against the arm of the throne. He didn't see her withdraw the dagger to ram it through their joined hands one last time, but the crunch of bone elicited no more than a groan. Exhaustion seeped throughout his body and it was all he could do to remain upright. He did little more than grimace as she wiggled the blade free one last time.

"It is done!" She held the dagger high overhead and the room roared in response.

Daemon drew back his hand the moment it was free, cradled

it to his chest and stared at it in disbelief. The wounds were sealed, flesh and bone mended, though the pain lingered. Thin lines of intersecting scars formed a rune where the injury had been. He made a fist and rubbed the fresh scar with the palm of his other hand. Blood made it sticky, but the pressure eased the pain.

Lumia's lips curved into a contented smile and she ran her fingers through his hair as he sank to the floor. "We will put you on your own throne yet," she whispered.

She loosed the chains from his collar as she raised her voice for the gathered people to hear. "You now bear my mark. The mark of your new family. Now and forever, you shall see that as the mark of your queen."

A low and wondering murmur rolled through the crowds in place of the cheers Daemon expected. Lumia stifled a sound of displeasure in her throat. The queen, too, had expected cheers.

The throng parted and Lumia lifted her chin as a small figure passed through the crowd. When he came close enough to be recognized as a sentry, she scowled.

The sentry muttered apologies as he shoved past the people clustered nearest the dais, daring to step onto it before he dropped to his knees in front of the queen.

"Your Majesty," he gasped, struggling to catch his breath. "The scouts have reported someone in the ruins, approaching where one of our tunnels empties into the—"

"How could you let that happen?" Lumia snarled. "Who has gotten through? Why haven't you killed them?"

The sentry flinched and bowed his head. "Our orders were to avoid engaging any threats, my queen."

She snorted in disgust. "Who gave you these orders?"

"You did, my queen," the sentry said, apologetic, all but groveling before her. "It's only a mageling, run away from the temple, but—"

"What a failure you are!" Lumia spat. She brandished her dagger, its blade marbled with blood. "The lot of you make note

9

of this: there is no tolerance for incompetent fools in my house!"
A cry of pain punctuated her words as she delivered a kick to the
sentry's jaw and he toppled backwards onto the floor. She flung
the dagger at him but missed flesh by inches. The blade skittered
across the stone and people recoiled as if it were a serpent. A
handful of men moved to help the sentry to his feet, though no
one dared speak. Lumia wheeled in place and Daemon flinched
as she leveled a finger at him.

"You," she snarled. "These fools look a threat to our home
full in the face and run to have decisions made for them. Their
wasted time puts all of us in danger. Our secrecy is our safety.
You've sworn yourself to serve me. You will go. You will clean
up this mess. Do you understand?"

Daemon swallowed. "Yes, my queen." He bowed his head as
she removed the ceremonial collar from his throat. Relief flooded
him and he breathed deeper. His heart still hammered, and a
hint of pain pulsed behind his eyes, but he was free. He stood
and shrugged out of the lavish decorative robes. The ornate
fabric slid to the floor and he righted the plain clothing he wore
underneath.

"And as for that wretch," Lumia raised her voice as she
settled on her throne again and dangled the collar from her
fingertips. "Feed that pathetic excuse for a soldier to my pets."
The collar clattered against the floor.

"No!" the sentry cried, scrambling backwards as the armored
soldiers advanced on him. "No, please!"

Cringing, Daemon pushed through the masses and toward
the main doors. The crowd closed behind him and he did not
regret that he would miss the gore of the sentry's demise.

2

A RUIN

"BOTHER," FIRAL SIGHED. HER AMBER EYES FLICKED TOWARD THE darkening sky, barely visible through the leaves fluttering with the wind. Only a moment ago, sunlight danced like golden butterflies across the papers in her lap, wings flitting where the leaves permitted. Now raindrops changed written words to blotches and thunder rumbled in the distance. Firal swept her papers into her arms before they could be ruined. Hurrying to her feet, she hugged her studies to her chest and bowed her head against the rain. The cobblestone path through the garden already glistened with water, slick beneath her steps.

All she'd wanted was a moment to study outside the noisy dormitory, and now it seemed even the weather was against it. Of course, the weather had been fickle lately. It wasn't surprising that it would begin to storm just as she sat down.

Scattered drops became a downpour and she broke into a run. The doors of the temple's dormitory were only a few steps ahead, standing open beneath the awning to welcome the cool breeze that accompanied the storm.

A figure stepped into her path.

Firal grimaced, halted mid-stride and lifted a vicious glare to the young man most students referred to as the Archmage's pet.

"Ran!" she cried, clutching her precious papers to her chest in a vain attempt to shelter them from the tropical rain. "Get out of the way, before my homework is ruined!"

Lomithrandel was the only part-time student ever admitted to the temple, for which many magelings held him in silent contempt. Unusually well-built for an Eldani man and standing a full foot taller than she did, he made an intimidating adversary. His blue eyes danced with mischief as he looked down at her, a broad smile on his lips. He didn't even acknowledge the rain. "I've been gone for days," he said, sarcastic complaint oozing from his tone. "Is that all the hello I get?"

Firal crinkled her nose and darted toward the awning behind him. He shifted to block her and she glowered. "I didn't bid you farewell, did I? So I have no need to greet you." She lurched forward and dug her shoulder into his stomach. Much to her pleasure, he winced and moved aside. She stomped past him and into the empty main hall of the dormitories.

"Well, then!" Ran rubbed his stomach with one hand and grinned as his good humor returned. "Why don't you go ahead and say goodbye now, so that you can give me a proper greeting when I come back?"

Firal patted her blurred papers with the sleeve of her green robes. It did nothing to help; her clothing was just as wet as her notes. "I haven't the time." She thrust her homework into his hands so she could wring out her ebony hair. "I need to get my studies out of the way."

"Studies." He frowned, paging through the soggy papers. He tilted his head, trying to puzzle out the blotches that had once been words. "That's all you ever do. You take this training far too seriously."

"And you take it far too lightly," she snapped as she finger-combed her hair away from her face. "Gaining admittance to the temple in the first place is no small feat for most magelings, mind you. It's difficult enough to find time for my reading without your interruptions. Give me those." She sniffed and shook water from her hands before she snatched the papers back. "You're soaked too, you'll make the ink run."

"I don't think it can run any more than it already has." Ran eyed the dark blotches on his hands and shook his head before he slid his fingers through his tawny wet hair. The ink left several dark streaks and Firal made a face.

She could not understand why the temple had accepted him, though there were a number of rumors. The most popular of which claimed the Archmage had been paid an impressive sum of money to accept him as a student when his Gift was discovered. Ran did, at least, seem to be quite inclined toward magecraft, though he was rarely around for classes. He had a terrible habit of disappearing for anywhere from days to weeks on end.

"Are you all right?" He waved a hand before her eyes. It took a moment for Firal to realize she was staring at him and he was staring back, a strange look on his face.

She flushed and tucked in her chin to hide her annoyance. "I have to get to my room." She started toward the east hallway in a rush. Ran made no effort to follow.

The dormitories within the large, curved stone building were separated by sex, the east wing housing female students and the west wing housing male. The upper floor was home to most of the faculty. There were far fewer male students than female, though just as many men as women were born Gifted. Young men were simply more likely to pursue mundane careers, settling as blacksmiths or even farmers. As far as Firal knew, Master Nondar—her favorite teacher and the one in charge of her training as a healer—was the only man among the Master mages who resided in the temple.

The small dormitory room she claimed as her own was equipped to house two students, though it was rare for anyone to be saddled with a roommate. Accommodations easily outnumbered magelings, though she'd heard their numbers had been more plentiful in the beginning. Fewer mages applied for admittance to the temple every year.

Firal paused before her door and exhaled hard. Her shoulders slumped as if to shed her frustration as she pushed into her room. With the way the building's wings curved back, none of the rooms were quite square. Hers faced the main courtyard of the temple and was wider at the far end. The furnishings were simple; mismatched beds stood more or less in the far corners of the room with a recessed window between them. One wide desk with a single chair sat beneath the window and a deep trunk for clothing rested at the foot of either bed. The other two corners of the room hosted a full-length standing mirror—a clear display of the temple's wealth at its founding— and a small table with another chair.

Firal left her ruined papers on the table as she made her way to the window to close the shutters. Then she peeled her training uniform off over her head and draped it over the back of the chair to dry. In spite of the luxury of mirrors in the dormitory, the temple did not have the resources to issue more than one uniform to a student, and she would need hers again for classes tomorrow. The simple robe's color was faded, but she was proud of what it stood for. Mages, while representing their craft, wore colors to distinguish their rank within the temple. There were six ranks of color, each showing a different level of proficiency. Her green robes marked her as a fourth-rank mage, and a band of color for each rank she'd graduated marked her upper sleeve: gray, lavender, and yellow.

Her underthings were damp, too, she noted with a frown. She stripped out of them, folded an arm across her full bosom and cast a glance toward the shuttered window as if she expected it to fly open before she retrieved fresh clothing from her trunk. With Ran in the temple, she never knew what to expect. But the window remained closed and she donned her underthings in peace, topping them with a simple yellow dress that was a little tight in the bodice. She sucked in her stomach to do the laces up the front.

While not exactly plump, Firal was stocky in build and lacked the willowy grace of her counterparts. Her hips were too wide, her chest too deep and breasts too full for her hand-me-down clothing to be comfortable, and the tropical heat turned her long hair into an unruly frizz of curls that spilled around her pointed ears. She didn't think herself unpleasant to look at, but if nothing else, she knew her fiery amber eyes were lovely.

She tucked her hair behind her ear with one hand and freed her necklace from the bodice of her dress with the other. It was nothing special, a white-on-blue relief of a seven-pointed star with a ring around its center—the Eldani kingdom's crest. But it was all that her mother, a court mage, had left her. She'd been told her mother's rank was the only reason she'd been accepted as a student at the temple. At times, she thought that meant she was wrong to begrudge Ran his special treatment. Then again, she was expected to attend all of her classes. He was not.

Firal ran a thumb over the embossed pendant before straightening the chain, settling it around her neck again as she sat down at her desk. Her mother's legacy was a lofty one to live up to, and there were times she doubted she would. Few mages were granted the honor of serving the king.

The rain did not stop until after she'd rewritten her homework on dry sheets of paper. She would have to remember to demand Ran replace what had been ruined. The temple was some distance from the nearest market, making decent paper hard to come by. Not to mention the expense. She hoped leaving the blotched papers in sunlight later would bleach them enough that they could be reused.

Firal's stomach grumbled, reminding her of the time, and she cleaned her quill pen and corked the ink bottle before she started for the dinner hall.

The temple courtyard had been transformed by the rain. Pools of muddy water collected on the stone paths and droplets glittered on garden plants like gems in the light of the setting sun. Lamps lit the large communal hall nestled in the northwest corner of the temple grounds, giving it an inviting glow. Light streamed from the wide windows and the open double doors.

The dinner hall was a beautiful structure, built with a high ceiling and open rafters. Aside from the many tables and benches, it was home to the kitchens and a number of storerooms. The interior walls of the building had been whitewashed recently—an event Firal recalled clearly, as Ran had dumped a pail of whitewash down her front—and it made the room feel bright and airy.

The temple was home to perhaps five hundred students, and another hundred instructors and workers. From the din of voices that crashed over her the moment she set foot inside, Firal imagined most were already gathered to eat. Preferring quiet, she settled at the first empty table she found. As soon as she sat, a service-woman deposited a tray heaped with food before her. Firal no more than touched her fork than the cheerful voice of her dearest friend rose behind her.

"Eating alone again?" Kytenia asked teasingly. She still wore her robes, and Firal suspected she'd stayed with Master Nondar for extra drills. Kytenia shared her healing affinity and had been studying at the temple for nearly four pents, and while her yellow robes marked her a rank beneath Firal, she was quite skilled for a half-blood.

"Of course not." Firal nibbled the crust off a piece of bread and gestured for her friend to sit. "I was waiting for you. I hope you haven't spent half an hour trying to find me in the crowd this time?"

Kytenia laughed and put her plate on the table across from Firal. Half-bloods were often referred to as awkward and uncouth, but Kytenia was tall, slender, and moved with the grace of a dancer. Save her less-pointed ears hidden by her orderly brown curls, there was nothing to betray her human heritage. "Actually, I just caught you out of the corner of my eye as I was sitting down. Have you seen the other girls? I haven't been able to catch anyone since Master Nondar wanted me to repeat that splint-setting exercise after class. There are rumors from the capital and I hoped we could speak." She heaved a sigh and bit into a slice of buttered bread.

Firal shrugged and picked at the edge of a pastry on her plate. The dinner hall was too loud for comfortable conversation and she leaned closer to be sure Kytenia would hear. "I haven't seen any of the girls. I did see Ran, though, when I was coming in from the rain."

"Oh, he's back again, is he?" Kytenia wiped the corner of her mouth with a fingertip. Her wide green-hazel eyes sparkled with mirth. "I'm sure Master Nondar will be after him for missing classes again. Did he ask for tutoring? Or did he want copies of your notes this time?"

"No," Firal snorted as she tucked her pastry into a hidden pocket of her skirt. "And it's good that he didn't, seeing as the rain ruined them all while he was blocking the door."

Kytenia gave her a curious look. "Not hungry?"

"I am, but I have a lot of notes to rewrite. I'll need to find somewhere quiet if I'm to get anything done. With that beast back on temple grounds, I never know what will happen when I'm trying to study." Firal shuddered.

"Off to your little retreat again, then?" Kytenia rolled her eyes. "If that's the case, you won't get much studying done. I'm not distracting any Masters for you to sneak out this time."

"I don't expect you to." Firal took a few bites of the boiled yams on her plate and pushed her food around as she gulped them down. "I don't see what the problem is, honestly. The Masters spend an awful lot of energy hammering old folktales into our heads. They'd be better off focused on teaching our craft."

"Maybe they're superstitious, maybe they're not." Kytenia shrugged and swiped a forkful of yams from Firal's plate. "Either way, you know how I feel about you wandering off in that place, folktales or otherwise. Even if it's not haunted or anything, I'm sure you'll break an ankle trying to climb over everything that's fallen down."

"I'll be careful, I promise." Firal stuffed her mouth with the last of her meal before she rose from the table. Aside from Kytenia, there was no one familiar in sight. Relieved she wouldn't have to escape Ran's antagonistic antics twice in one day, Firal patted Kytenia's shoulder affectionately on her way out.

A short detour to her room let her pick up her cloak, lantern, and the small satchel that hung from the desk chair. The satchel was always ready for expeditions, filled with papers, sticks of graphite, and the leather-bound notebook Master Nondar had given her on her birthday. She settled it at her side and slung her cloak around her shoulders on her way outside.

The Kirban Temple had been built right on the edge of a massive structure the rest of the world called the Kirban Ruins. Firal didn't know whether the ruins had been named after the temple or the temple after the ruins, but she did not particularly care. Magelings were not to leave the temple grounds without a Master to escort them, and anyone who asked to be taken into the ruins would have been thought mad. As far as Firal was aware, Kytenia was the only one who knew of her affinity for the place.

Thick clouds masked the darkening sky again by the time Firal reached the hedgerow at the edge of the gardens, though their pale underbellies made rain seem unlikely. The mage-barrier, the invisible wall of magic used to keep outsiders at bay, waited just beyond the hedges. She drew a breath and held it as she shoved through the dense bushes. A sharp prickling coursed through her body as she moved past the hedgerow and barrier and ceased the moment she stumbled into the field between the temple's grounds and the thousand crumbling stone entryways of the ruins.

The soft carpet of grass tickled her sandaled feet and a breath of wind ruffled her cloak and skirt as she hurried across the open space to dart inside. She always felt safer once she was in the ruins. As risky as Kytenia made Firal's exploration sound, the only real danger was being caught by the Masters. The ruins were a refuge against the bustle of magelings and the persistent tingling sense of magic that pervaded the temple.

A labyrinth of concentric circles, the ruins sprawled across nearly a quarter of Elenhiise Island, and close to a third of the Eldani kingdom. Once strong walls now crumbled, and mossy stones lay strewn across the unkempt corridors. Night insects whirred in the tangled undergrowth. There were large trees farther in, but only a handful of saplings grew in the grassy outer rings of the structure. Despite her years of exploration, Firal had never reached the big trees—a testament to the size of the place. Even when looking out from the temple's central tower, the ruins joined with the horizon before their middle could be seen.

A number of legends surrounded the ruins. Having lived in the temple for as long as she could recall, Firal had heard plenty of them. Most tales were filled with beastly creatures and wars against the Eldani, and the stories had been used to frighten her before bed when she was a child. She still remembered most, though there wasn't a single tale she liked to recall.

Firal cast a glance behind her and pulled her cloak farther over her shoulders. From where she stood, the entrance she'd taken appeared little more than a dark sliver. She waved a hand over her lantern and a flame sprang to life within it. Using magic for such frivolities was disallowed, according to her teachers, but she saw no reason to carry flint when a simple gesture and the barest hint of concentration could serve the same purpose. Then again, misuse of magic was the least of her concerns, given that the ruins were forbidden in the first place. If she were caught, the punishment for her exploration would be much harsher than the punishment for improper use of her Gift.

Stepping over a tangle of vines, she crept around the first

turn in the hallway she'd chosen and squealed when she walked face-first into a sapling no taller than the walls. In all the time she'd spent in the ruins, she had never memorized more than a few of the roofless hallways, though she had mapped many of them. The labyrinth was too vast, its pathways twisting back on themselves like a serpent. Every so often, she encountered surprises such as this. Firal pulled away from the tree and grimaced when her necklace tangled in its branches. The necklace popped against her skin and she felt the chain go slack.

"Lovely," she muttered. She caught the pendant with a sigh as the broken chain slid from her neck. Her fingers curled around the stone as she considered it. Worn as her dress was, she didn't trust the pockets hidden in its skirt. She had mended holes in their corners too often. Instead, Firal took her leather journal from her bag and tucked the necklace into a pocket in its cover. It would do for now. She clapped the book shut and tucked it back into the top of her satchel as she started off once more.

Now and then she paused her exploration to crouch with her book and take notes against her knees. Her personal notes meant as much to her as her studies, and mapping the ruins was her only real hobby. She noted each turn she took and compared them to the paths she'd plotted out before. Occasional dead ends forced her to turn around. It was difficult to see how the corridors fit together, and while she had larger sheets of paper back in her room to copy her findings onto later, the smaller maps in her journal left her feeling as lost as a blind merchant's ship.

The rising soldier moon, Ithi, cast a weak glow through the clouds and its position indicated an hour or two had passed. The tiny flame in Firal's lantern seemed inadequate against the dark, but the farther she traveled, the more familiar the path seemed. She tucked her journal into her satchel, lifted her lantern overhead and pressed her fingertips upon the grainy surface of the weathered stone wall. Positive the little nook she often hid in to study would be waiting just ahead, she picked up her pace, rounded the corner and froze when the empty air of another long corridor greeted her.

Firal stepped back to review the path she'd just taken. "Strange." The walls looked just like those that framed her usual spot, a comfortable little cranny made by a fallen wall. Had she missed a turn? Or had she just been exploring the ruins long enough for everything to start looking the same?

The wind stirred the leaves of a sapling behind her, and the sharp breath Firal drew made her unpleasantly aware of the tight bodice of her ill-fitting dress. She laid a hand flat against her middle, just beneath her breasts, and willed the flame in her lantern to grow a little brighter. Thinking of the old myths put her on edge, like a child afraid of the dark after a frightening story. Shaking her head to scatter the thoughts, she tightened her grasp on her lantern.

The farther Firal went, the taller the stone walls were. The growth underfoot seemed almost manicured, though there were still fallen stones scattered in the grass. Her hand shook and her lantern rattled. She inched closer to the wall and pressed her palm against it to keep her balance on the uneven ground, and her footsteps grew more cautious. There was a gap in the wall up ahead, but it was different from anything she'd seen before, framed by an archway with the unmistakable appearance of a great creature's mouth. Hanging moss drooped from its top and created the illusion of jagged teeth. Firal leaned around the corner and lifted her lantern to peer inside.

It was not another hallway. The yawning gap was an alcove with a low ceiling, and stairs of black stone descended into the earth before her. It delved deeper than the feeble light of her lantern could reach. Somewhere far below, she swore she heard the patter of some tiny creature's feet. Firal swallowed hard. "They're just stories," she muttered as she fumbled for her journal and a stick of graphite. The ruins were manmade, but that did not mean they were inhabited. Still, her fingers trembled as she drew out the lines her path had taken. She marked the location of the entrance at the end of the corridor and drew a rough outline of what it looked like on the opposite page. The architecture was something she could research later.

Jamming her graphite into her bag, she turned back and collided with a shadowy shape that hadn't been there before. Her eyes darted up. A glowing pair of crimson lights seared the darkness, only inches from her face.

Firal shrieked and reeled backwards. She stumbled over the uneven ground and fell. Stars exploded in her vision as her head hit the wall behind her. The high, shattering peal of her lantern's glass hovered right on the edge of her senses. The flame extinguished before she could see the figure in front of her, a black silhouette that loomed between her and the cloud-hazed sky.

"If I catch you in here again," said a masculine voice, with an odd timbre like a feral growl, "I promise you won't get a second warning."

Firal's vision doubled as she slid to the ground against the wall. The dizzying stars in her sight faded and consciousness slipped away.

3

VISITOR

Birdsong and sunshine flowed through the open window, though the cool breeze carried the scent of coming rain and the distant sound of thunder. Firal groaned, blinking against the light and fighting the haze of sleep that clouded her mind.

"Waking up, are we? The Archmage isn't going to be pleased when she finds out where you've been." Ran clicked his tongue in disapproval.

Firal grimaced and forced her eyes open. She was almost surprised to see her room. Ran sat in a chair beside her bed, hunched over a book he'd taken from her desk. The door stood wide and a tray of breakfast waited on the table across the room. She clenched her jaw. "The Archmage isn't going to find out."

"Oh, come now. Nothing escapes her eyes. And after that little event last night, I'm sure she's already heard." Ran leaned back in his chair and frowned. The look he gave her made her suddenly aware she wore nothing but smallclothes beneath the worn sheets.

"What are you doing in here?" She clutched the sheets to her chest and then drew them up over her shoulders. "This is the girls' dormitory!"

"There aren't any rules saying I can't be in here, just that the

23

door can't be closed." He glanced toward the doorway, disinterested. "Kytenia asked me to stay so she could get something to eat. She sent that tray over there, too, in case you woke."

"Kytenia?" Firal eyed him with suspicion. "Why was she here? What happened?"

Ran snorted a laugh as he clapped the book shut and tossed it back onto her desk. "That's what everyone else wants to know. A man in a cloak carried you to the middle of the courtyard, left you on the ground, and disappeared into the ruins before anyone could catch him. The most popular rumor is that he was a scorned lover. Or an Underling, among those who believe in them." A spark in his blue eyes gave him a mischievous air, which was only strengthened by his smirk. "You know, leaving temple grounds without a Master is against the temple's rules."

"What would you know about temple rules?" Firal spat back. She twisted the edge of the sheets between her fists and wished she could twist his neck instead. "You don't follow any of them!"

"Well, I'm exempt."

"What is that supposed to mean?" Her brow furrowed. "No one is exempt from the Archmage's rules."

He flashed her a broad grin. She hated it when he did that. It made it that much harder to ignore the fact he was almost charming. When he didn't answer, Firal snorted and shook her head.

Though she'd spent her entire life in Kirban, Firal couldn't recall having actually seen the Archmage. The woman only left the temple for the most important occurrences. The rest of the time, she locked herself up in the top floors of the tower that stood in the very center of the temple's grounds. Supervision of the magelings was left up to the Masters, but severe misconduct was punished by the Archmage herself. The thought of being expelled made Firal shudder.

"Aren't you missing class?" she asked, changing the subject.

"I know you probably can't afford to miss this morning's lessons."

Ran shrugged and scratched his chin with his thumb. "Oh, there's no class today."

"No class? They never cancel lessons. Even in the worst weather." Thunder sounded, as if to underscore her statement. Firal glanced toward the open window and fought the compulsion to close it.

"They do when the king pays a visit." Something lingered in Ran's voice, something she couldn't quite put a finger on, though she could have sworn it was dismay.

"Very funny," Firal said. "The whole temple would be in an uproar if something like that happened. The Masters would be falling over themselves."

The corners of Ran's eyes pinched and his cheer evaporated. He pushed himself out of his chair and started for the door. "You're supposed to stay in bed today, but I'm sure the girls will fill you in later. He's here to see the Archmage. The rest of the temple is just sort of waiting to hear what all this is about." He paused by the doorway. "I'll let Kytenia know you're awake. She'll be glad to hear it. I'm sure she'll be full of questions."

Firal groaned as he slid out the open door and disappeared. She was unsure what to think. While Ran was a mischief-maker and a perpetual thorn in her side, she didn't think him a liar. But what reason would the king have to visit the temple? To her knowledge, he never had before. At least, not in her lifetime. The mages offered invaluable services to the kingdom. Their ability and expertise was treasured in everything from counsel to agriculture. But the king had built the temple as a gift to the Archmage and her Masters, and beyond its founding, he had shown little interest in the establishment.

Thinking gave Firal a headache. She rubbed her temple and winced when she discovered a sizable bruise on the side of her head. What exactly happened last night? She thought of Ran's goading and scoffed. A scorned lover? That was laughable.

Firal sucked in a breath and thrust herself from the bed. The sunshine had disappeared, so she closed the window first and then hurried to the door to push it closed. If Ran was to be believed, there was an entire day ahead with no classes to fill it. Injuries aside, it was a perfect opportunity to catch up on her studies. She was a little unsteady on her feet, but there was no reason to waste time now that she was awake. Whatever had happened in the ruins, it had cost her a night of study.

Moving the chair at her bedside back to its place at her desk, Firal caught sight of the book Ran had been reading. She paused. An Underling, Ran said. It should have been no surprise to see he'd picked up an old storybook about them, kept on her desk since childhood. She'd never been able to get rid of a book; he must have figured its presence meant she believed the old tales. She had half a mind to break something over his hard head.

Ran was only trying to scare her. But she couldn't remember anything about that silhouette, save those red, glowing eyes. The memory of them made the hair stand on the back of her neck. Firal shook her head, opened the book and settled in her chair as she paged through it.

The illustrations inside were fanciful, to say the least. Drawings of hunchbacked brutes and monsters driven to caves beneath the island centuries ago decorated the pages. None of the illustrations portrayed ordinary men. Firal had seen no more than a silhouette and those crimson lights, but if the shape of him hadn't convinced her he was a person, his voice certainly had. She studied the images of troll-like monsters labeled *Underlings* across several more pages before she snorted and clapped the book shut. There were more important things to worry about.

Firal's satchel hung over the back of her chair. She assumed Kytenia had ensured it made it back to her room. The book about Underlings went back on a stack of volumes borrowed from the temple's library while she rooted in her satchel with her free hand. Her brow furrowed when she realized her journal wasn't there. The vague memory of dropping it flashed through her mind and she cringed. With her broken necklace hidden within its cover, everything that was important to her—memories, notes, research, and otherwise—was inside that book. If it had been rained on...

Firal scanned the room twice before she found her faded green training robes folded atop the chest at the foot of her bed. She recognized Kytenia's handiwork and would have to thank her later. If it rained much more before Firal could retrieve her journal, all her pages of thoughts and drawings of the ruins would be illegible. Yet it would be safer and easier to sneak out of the temple's grounds after dark. She mulled things over as she dressed.

If she could not find her journal or if it had already been ruined, then the notes inside needed to be replaced now. Without them, she could barely remember what was on her impending tests. Kytenia could help with that, and if Kytenia wasn't in the library, she would be in the dinner hall. Firal chewed her lip a moment or two before she decided. Her studies had to take precedence. She'd visit the library first. If luck was on her side, everything would be undamaged after nightfall.

Firal craned her neck to look for her sandals. They weren't on the floor and weren't under her bed, either. Grumbling softly to herself, she added a stop by the temple's storerooms to her mental list and stalked out of her room barefoot.

The temple grounds were all but empty, the ominous clouds in the sky enough to keep the other magelings indoors. The teachers and staff, Firal presumed, would all be occupied by their guest of honor. That was, if the king really was visiting. She sniffed at the idea and wrinkled her nose as she tip-toed through a puddle. The water was clean and warm, but still unpleasant against her bare feet. The Archmage's tower loomed above her, its yawning windows reminding her of mournful eyes. She squirmed beneath their accusatory gaze and hurried to the doors at the foot of the tower.

The first floor of the Archmage's tower was a library. Most days, its doors stood open, welcoming anyone to explore. For the doors to be closed on rainy days was not unusual, but when Firal pressed her hands to the seam where the great doors met, they didn't budge. They'd been bolted, or barricaded; whatever one did to lock doors of that size.

She frowned and lifted the edge of her robes as she stepped back over a few puddles. There was a smaller entrance on the far side, in the temple's gardens. Perhaps it would still be unlocked. It was best to fetch the books and start on her own. Though Kytenia was good at reciting points from their lectures by memory, she was pitiful about taking notes. Firal padded to the far corner of the tower and hesitated when she caught the sound of voices and the sharp clang of metal striking metal. Slowly, she peeked around the corner into the gardens.

In the center of the circular patio beneath the fruit trees, Ran held a sword locked against that of an unfamiliar man. "You're welcome to try it, but I could just slide to the right and run you through before you regain your footing."

"You couldn't either!" the stranger protested, though he gave a wry smile. He did not waver beneath the press of Ran's sword. Instead, he stepped forward and forced Ran back.

Firal's brow knit in a mix of curiosity and confusion. She leaned against the corner of the tower, watching them move. Both men were untidy, apparently having been at their sparring match for a while. But Ran's opponent still seemed fresh and vital, moving with a lithe grace that didn't befit his solid-built warrior's body. He was handsome, though his features were harder than those of most Eldani men. Judging by the fine blade he held, Firal pegged him for a king's guard. Perhaps Ran had been right about that visit, after all.

Step by step, the man pushed Ran back, tossing his head once to throw disheveled sandy-blond hair out of his face.

"I could always just pull a dagger and stab you while my

blade has yours pinned." Ran smirked, though he gritted his teeth. "I foresee you losing, either way."

"Foresee my foot!" the man said.

Ran's laugh cut short as he failed to see the sweep of his adversary's leg in time to dodge and his feet were knocked out from under him. He fell backwards and hit the stone with a thud and a splash.

Firal burst into laughter, applauding the poor landing as his opponent brought the tip of his blade to Ran's throat.

"I tried to warn you," the man chuckled. He cast Firal a sideways glance before he lowered his sword and offered a hand.

Ran groaned at the gesture but accepted the help. "And here I thought I was the one fighting dirty."

"No one fights entirely fairly, boy." The swordsman jerked his head in Firal's direction. "Who's this? Friend of yours?"

"Not sure that's what I'd call her." Ran drove the tip of his sword between the cobblestones and let it stand, brushing in vain at the muddy splotches on his pale blue mage's robes. How he'd ended up a rank above her, she would likely never know. "That's Firal."

The corners of Firal's mouth twitched upward at the introduction and she strode to the edge of the patio to offer a curtsy. "Sir."

"So you're Firal." The stranger gave Ran a thoughtful look and cleared his throat. Sword still in hand, he strode forward, dipped in a graceful bow and took her hand to place a gentle kiss on her knuckles. "It's a pleasure to meet you, at last."

"At last?" She gave a thin laugh and avoided eye contact. His eyes were a vibrant green, not an unusual color among her people, but they had a piercing intensity that made her uncomfortable. She swallowed. "Surely you don't mean he's spoken of me."

Ran waved a hand and scoffed. "Cut it out, there's time for

that later. Firal, this is Kifel. And if you'll excuse me, I believe I'd like a rematch."

"Oh, come now, he obviously has far more experience with a blade than you do." Firal gave Ran a disdainful look as he jerked his sword from the cobblestones. "Have you even picked up one of those before now?"

"He has a few times, but he doesn't spar often enough. In fact, I'm fairly certain anyone could best him." Kifel turned and offered the hilt of his sword to Firal. She blinked in confusion.

"She'll just hurt herself," Ran muttered.

"Or perhaps she'll hurt you. Besides, I think it best if you have a match with someone who shares the amount of battle experience you have." Kifel smirked as he pressed the sword into Firal's hands and closed her fingers around it. The black hilt looked and felt like twisted glass. Red gems set in the pommel and cross guard gave it a ceremonial look.

"This is a fine weapon, I really shouldn't..." she trailed off, wincing at the weight of the blade in her hands. She could barely hold it up.

"Same experience? Hardly." Ran shifted his sword in hand. "Sparring or not, I practice daily."

"But you've never fought against an opponent that actually meant to kill you." Kifel stepped behind Firal, placing his arms beneath her arms and hands atop her hands. "Here. Like this. Set your feet apart, otherwise one swing of this weapon will throw you off balance. You don't want to fall on your own sword." He nudged her bare heels with the toe of his boot to settle her into a ready stance.

"I can hardly lift it, how am I supposed to swing it?" Firal's grip on the hilt tightened until her knuckles grew white. Only Kifel's hands over hers kept the sword from quivering with the tremble in her arms.

He drew the sword back and guided her through the first swing. "You let the blade move itself, you just guide it. Once you set it in motion, the weight of the blade will finish the swing."

Ran met her weapon and deflected it effortlessly. Feigning disinterest, he retreated a step.

"Good start," Kifel said. "You seem to have more strength in your right arm, so put your left to the front. You want the power of your dominant arm behind a thrust, or it won't pierce armor. Use the strength of your shoulder and your upper body, not your arm." He released her hands and drew back her shoulder before allowing her to make the jab. The sword sagged at the end of her arm's reach.

"Perhaps you'd be better off teaching her to lift a sword before trying to teach her to use it," Ran teased as he nudged the tip of her blade away with the flat of his sword.

Firal's nose crinkled and she jerked the sword sideways in a clumsy sweep.

"Hah!" Kifel gestured to the thin slice through Ran's robes, not far below his waist. "Better mind your tongue. If she'd been any closer, that might have changed your lifestyle permanently."

Firal flushed, but couldn't help laughing at the horror and disgust that flitted across Ran's face. Kifel only grinned as he took back his sword and sheathed it at his side. The gems glittered with the movement and Firal followed it with her eyes.

"Thank you," she murmured. "You're a good teacher."

Kifel made a small sound, more acknowledgement than agreement.

Ran rolled his eyes and dragged the tip of his sword against the ground. The metal squawked as if to protest the treatment. "What about my rematch?"

"As much as I've enjoyed our playtime, I'm afraid our rematch will have to come another day. I have important business to see to while I'm here and I've spent enough time dallying." Kifel gave him an apologetic look. The glance he spared for Firal seemed weighted with something else. She shifted and turned away. He bowed his head in farewell before turning on his heel and disappearing around the corner of the Archmage's tower without waiting for a response.

Unsettled, Firal worried her hands. "What was that all about?"

"Don't know." Ran shrugged and rubbed the broad side of his sword against his boot to remove more dirt from its tip. "This is his sword, though, so I suppose he'll be back." He fingered the hilt of the blade thoughtfully and turned it over several times before he hefted it up to rest it flat against his shoulder. "You stayed awfully composed through all that. I'm impressed."

"I'm not afraid of wielding a sword," she said, a stubborn set to her jaw.

"I didn't think you were," he laughed. "I just don't think I'd have kept my composure so well, getting my first lesson in swordplay from the King of Elenhiise, himself." He patted her shoulder and brushed past as the words sank in.

All the color drained from her face.

4

BORDERS

THE TOP FLOORS OF THE ARCHMAGE'S TOWER WERE BRIGHTER AND airier than any other buildings in the temple. Kifel couldn't say he cared for it. The lack of glass in the tall windows made him nervous. He'd never realized the difference it made to be walled in, to have even a transparent barrier to keep one from falling. Of course, he'd also never realized he was afraid of heights. He tore his eyes away from the windows lining the far wall as he reached the Archmage's office. Her door was always open. She never seemed to fear interruption.

"There's some story floating about the temple that one of your magelings escaped. That she went through the ruins and a stranger brought her back." He tried to sound nonchalant as he leaned against the doorway with his arms folded over his chest. She had known for a full day that he was coming, but she didn't even look up from her desk when he spoke.

"The mage-barrier surrounding the temple is meant to keep people out," she said, her response crisp and cold. "Not keep them in. It's the duty of the Masters to keep their pupils in line. What a mageling does in their free time is no concern of mine."

He found it amusing how her appearance matched her chilly words. Envesi, Archmage of Kirban Temple, had once been a handsome woman; he'd been there to see it. Her face and body remained youthful, but time wielding great power had given her an air that made her seem ancient. Her long hair cascaded in white waves, her skin pale as ivory and her eyes frosty blue. Mages didn't age the way other Eldani did. No one seemed to have a clear understanding of it, not even the mages themselves. Wrinkles were common enough, but more than anything, he thought they grew paler. As for how old she truly was, Kifel could only wager a guess. Older than he, in any case. The skill she commanded would have taken centuries to learn.

"A poor way to look at it, if you ask me." Kifel raised a brow when she gave him a dark look. Anyone else would have been groveling in his presence. He knew better than to expect it from Envesi—in private, at least. In public, she knew her place. Still, her lack of respect incensed him.

Envesi dropped her quill into the inkwell close at hand and dusted sand over the wet writing on the pages spread before her. "Have you only come to criticize, or is there a more important reason for your visit today?"

"I wanted to discuss my plans the upcoming solstice festivities, but there seem to be more pressing issues at hand." He clasped his hands behind his back and strode forward at a leisurely pace. "It's come to my attention there have been a number of raids on small border villages between the ruins and Ilmenhith, particularly those too small for a guard station. Men from the east appear to be crossing into our territory to help themselves to supplies and livestock. Surely you haven't forgotten your part of this arrangement? I finance your temple and you keep an eye on the border?"

"Is there no better way to keep an eye on it than to have mages stationed along its edge?" Envesi gave him a grim smile. "Of course, I don't have enough Master mages on hand to accomplish such a thing. Aside from teachers, all the temple's Masters have been sent to the chapter houses in the cities, and even then the chapter houses are barely staffed. If we were allowed the resources to train more magelings, perhaps things would be different, but we can only support so many with how the weather has affected the harvests. Shipping food from the mainland is expensive." Her eyes narrowed. "Besides, you oughtn't speak as if I do nothing for you. There is plenty else we've arranged that I've upheld quite well."

Kifel's jaw tightened. "Is lack of resources the reason you struggle to supervise your own temple grounds? How am I to trust you to watch the border if your students are running off? I spoke with Lomithrandel. He was the one who mentioned the rumor."

The Archmage paused. "It will be dealt with, my liege."

"You may wish to see that your Masters mind what they're telling magelings, as well. One of the stories is that the girl was brought back by an Underling."

"The fancies of magelings are hardly the fault of my faculty. You know how children are," Envesi sighed with a wave of her hand. "They'd do well to keep their heads out of the clouds. No sense wasting time on folktales."

"Indeed," he murmured, his eyes drifting toward the tall windows. A thin shadow of gray hung far to the east, though the sky overhead was still relatively clear. The suggestion he did not provide her with enough resources was spurious, but Envesi was right about one thing. It was hard to predict what the weather would do anymore. It made things difficult for more than just the farmers. "Tell me, how is the training of your weather mages coming along?"

"Training goes as well as can be expected. I have several Masters pursuing such studies." She shuffled her papers into order and piled them neatly at the side of her desk. "Of course, we would do well with more mages in Master white. Masters can either pursue such fields, or they can train new mages. They cannot do both."

He watched as she tucked papers into labeled volumes. What the Archmage studied in her own time was of little interest to him, but he had sent several requests for things he wished to have mages investigate. All of those subjects were peculiarly absent from the books on her desk. The absence of weather studies bothered him most, considering Envesi had mentioned the lack of food herself. If the unusual weather continued to cause crops to fail, the trouble of feeding the temple would pale in comparison to feeding the kingdom. "Perhaps you ought to consider holding skill evaluations early so you can raise more magelings to Master, then. I've seen several students wearing the blue."

"Including that boy you're so fond of." Envesi glanced up. Her blue eyes chilled him to the bone.

"I don't know any mages well enough to be so bold as to suggest one." He made a point of changing the subject; he wouldn't let her needling jabs pry anything out of him. "Will you be able to spare your Masters for the solstice? I assume you have read the correspondence I sent you."

The Archmage brushed wrinkles out of her stark white robes as she stepped away from her desk and moved to one of the glassless windows. "You will have the whole of the temple at your disposal. But I suggest you not become used to such a luxury. We have work to do. We cannot cater to such trivialities on a regular basis."

Kifel fought a rising prickle of irritation. A king's orders were hardly trivial, but he'd long since learned that rank held little sway over the opinions of mages. She was unwise to insult him, but only a fool would do anything to draw a Master mage's ire. "I'll trust you can assign Masters to oversee the matter, then. I'll leave that in your hands." He started to leave, then paused inside the doorway. "Do remember to take care of that little problem with the ruins. I can't abide having that get out of hand. The border is to be closed both ways, after all."

"It will be done, my king," Envesi replied impatiently.

He turned away, but not before he caught an irritating look of satisfaction at his retreat wreathing itself upon her face.

FIRAL GRUMBLED IN FRUSTRATION, PULLING AT HER WILD CURLS AS she pressed her back to the wall. She'd walked the dinner hall three times over, surveying the crowd gathered for the noontime meal. "Hasn't *anyone* seen Ran? It would be a lot easier to avoid him if I knew where he was."

"If word got around that you were trying to hide, he'd probably show up." Kytenia finished her pastry and licked her fingers clean. She had taken to following Firal some time ago, though she wasn't helping the search. "What are you hiding for, anyway? Or do I dare ask? It sounds more like you want to give him a piece of your mind."

Firal sighed and gave her hair one last tug. "He just let me embarrass myself this afternoon, that's all. Ran could have at least told me who we were talking to before letting him teach me to use a sword, blight him."

"Language," Kytenia chided.

Firal huffed. "Sorry. But you know he gets under my skin like no one else."

Kytenia arched a fine brow. "Care to elaborate on what happened?"

"Not in front of everyone in the dining hall, no." A flush rose into Firal's cheeks and she rubbed at her face with the sleeve of her robes.

"All right, then. Later. Can we sit down and get a real meal now? If Ran were still here, you would have found him. We can go to our rooms for you to fill me in after we're done. Besides, that will give us time to talk about the solstice." Kytenia gestured to a table nearby as the seats around it emptied. The two of them barely settled before a woman came along to clean the table and serve them.

"What about the solstice? Is something going on?" Firal poked at the vegetables on her plate with a fork.

"Oh, Shymin told me all about it." Kytenia grinned. As

empty as the dormitories were, Shymin and Kytenia had made the decision to be roommates on their own. One glance made it obvious the two were related, though no one had ever seen reason to inquire as to how. Most of the temple's magelings didn't speak of family or home, as those phases of one's life were meant to be left behind. Clinging to the old was seen as a sign of weakness, so perhaps it was out of respect that no one asked.

"And?" Firal eyed her expectantly. "What did she say?"

"Patience, patience! Let me chew, at least," Kytenia managed around a mouthful of food. She held up a hand and swallowed with a grimace. "The Masters haven't issued a formal statement on it yet, but everybody expects one before nightfall. Rumor has it, the king visited to invite the whole temple to the masquerade they hold in the palace every year."

Firal stared. The summer and winter solstices meant little in the tropics, but they were the only events celebrated in both the Giftless and Eldani kingdoms. They were a big to-do among commoners and nobles both, but from the stories she'd heard from the Masters, nothing compared to the grandeur of celebrations in the capital. Firal had long dreamed of visiting Ilmenhith for her own reasons. She'd spent her life studying in hopes of being assigned to the capital's chapter house, or perhaps even the king's personal cabinet of mages. If her mother really had been a court mage, a chance to speak to the mages in the palace presented an opportunity unlike any other.

But she was a mageling, and magelings were not invited to the palace.

"There's no reason for the temple to be invited," Firal said. "I don't see why the king would visit just for that, besides. He could have sent a carrier pigeon. It seems like a waste of time. Ilmenhith is what, three days from here on a fast horse?"

Kytenia shrugged. "I wouldn't know, I've never been there. I doubt he rides, though. Court mages are the most powerful there are, and the king has an entire council of them. I'm sure he just has them open a Gate. There's no sense in walking if his mages can send him directly."

Firal's shoulders slumped. "Maybe Ran has someone Gating him around too, considering how fast he disappears when he's in trouble."

"You know," Kytenia said, pointing skyward with her fork as she finished chewing, "Marreli mentioned she thought he was sneaking out of the temple grounds to get around some of the rules."

"Really?" Firal rolled her eyes. "I can't imagine why anyone would think such a thing."

"You just be glad they don't say the same thing about you." Kytenia lowered her voice as a serving woman paused to deposit mugs of cider on the table. "I'm surprised there aren't already rumors flying about you and Ran."

Firal's jaw dropped. "I can't believe you just said that!"

"He is a very attractive young man, you know." A sparkle lit Kytenia's eyes. "I wouldn't mind sneaking out with him, myself. Men like that don't end up at the temple very often."

Shuddering, Firal reached for her mug. "I'm certain there are better looking and kinder men about. And a lot more accessible than Ran will ever be."

"Well, that's fine by me. If you're not interested, it just means I'll have less competition after we become Masters and have time for such things." Kytenia smirked and tucked her fork into her mouth.

"Not everyone becomes a Master, Kyt." It wasn't something Firal liked to consider, but she wouldn't deny the possibility. Though the strength and ability of mages varied widely, the temple sorted them into six ranks. Each rank was identified by color, each mageling issued a colored training robe for their level of command over magic. Gray mages were the lowest in rank; the rest wore lavender, yellow, green, blue, and white. White was reserved exclusively for Masters, who had reached the pinnacle of their ability and were able to perform certain tasks without assistance. Being a green-rank mage, Firal didn't know what those tasks were, but apparently they demanded enough respect that even non-mages didn't dare clothe themselves in white.

Firal drained the last of her cider and put her mug aside as she stood. After a pause, she snatched a roll from her plate and tucked it into the hidden pockets of her robes. "Besides, graduating a rank is several years off for either one of us. I do not now, nor will I ever, believe a man is worth waiting years for."

"You're not going out again, are you?" Kytenia stuck out her lower lip in an exaggerated pout. "Rikka was hoping we could get together and discuss our dresses for the solstice."

"Rikka will be all right waiting until the week's end. We won't have any classes then and we can fuss over dresses and jewels all she wants." The words came out sharper than Firal intended. She softened her tone as she added, "Besides, I won't be gone long. I must have dropped my journal last night. I'm just going to get it back. My necklace is in the pocket of the cover and you know how much it means to me."

Kytenia leaned back and gave her a somber look. "Aren't you worried about running back in there after what just happened?"

"I got spooked in the dark, that's all. I tripped and hit my head." Firal shrugged stiffly. "The worst that can happen is I stumble and twist an ankle, or maybe break a bone. Really, Kyt, you shouldn't worry so much."

"And you should worry a little more! Aren't you at all concerned about how you got back here? I really don't think you should be running off alone."

"You could always come with me, you know." Firal shrugged again when Kytenia said nothing. "Well then, your loss. I suppose I'll be going alone after all. Just don't gripe at me about it, since I invited you along." She patted Kytenia's shoulder and took another roll to eat on the way out of the dinner hall.

Outdoors, thin shafts of sunlight filtered through the clouds and glinted off the flooded stone pathways and courtyards.

Droplets on hibiscus blossoms shimmered like molten gold all along the path to the gardens. Firal trailed her fingers across the blooms and watched the droplets fall. The rainy season had gone on too long. The nights were a little too cool, the days a little too muggy. The rain patterns made no sense, either. Storms brewed from nowhere when there wasn't a cloud in the sky. It was said that enough mages with the right affinities might be able to alter the weather, but her Gift was focused elsewhere. Rain was none of her concern.

She hurried through the gardens, anxious to press past the mage-barrier and get into the ruins before the midday meal was over and the temple's grounds filled with people once more. Water dripping from the garden's fruit trees left dark splotches on her robes and made her regret that she hadn't brought her cloak. She had almost reached the hedges at the edge of the garden when a sharp whistle from one of the cherry trees stopped her in her tracks.

"Sneaking out again, are we?" Ran's words sounded playful, though when Firal's eyes swept up toward him, his expression was serious. He swung his dangling legs, shifted against the tree's trunk and tried to look disdainful. "It hasn't even been a full day. I would have thought you'd have the sense to wait a bit before trying that again. The whole temple is talking about you."

Firal gritted her teeth and leered at him, her shoulders bunched with agitation. "Here I was hoping you'd left."

"I started to leave, but I changed my mind. There are interesting things happening here today." He slid to a lower branch and lingered there a moment before he jumped to the ground. "Really, though. With all the rumors flying after last night, the Archmage is going to have her eye on you."

"With the visitor she's got today, somehow I think I'll be the least of her priorities." She folded her arms over her chest and glared. "The visitor you might have warned me about, mind you."

Ran chuckled. "I did warn you, remember? I told you he was

here when we were in your room. Either way, I'm surprised you're going back at all, after yesterday. You're lucky you didn't end up staying in the infirmary." He straightened his blue robes and fingered the slice their sword match had left in the front. He was too tall for the robes to fit properly. The hem reached no farther than his knees. With the belt he wore around the middle and the boots and trousers underneath, it looked more like an oversized tunic than a mage's robe.

A frown worked its way onto her face as she watched him fuss with his clothes. "How exactly did I end up in my room?"

Ran's brow furrowed. "You don't remember?"

A hint of uncertainty crept into Firal's expression. He almost sounded concerned.

"You must have hit your head harder than I thought," he murmured. "It's bad enough that people are talking about that whole Underling—"

"I don't believe in those fairy tales," Firal spat, her amber eyes flashing. She planted her hands on her hips. "And frankly, I'm tired of hearing everyone talking about *rumors* today. I didn't get myself back to the temple, fine. I'll accept that. But someone brought me back. Someone who knew I was out there to begin with, and knew where to take me."

Ran tugged at his sleeves and avoided her eyes. She almost enjoyed seeing him squirm.

"Listen," he started slowly, "I'm just trying to help. You can live in your own little dream world for as long as you want, but you're better off doing it here. One of these times, reality will catch up with you. There are all kinds of dangerous things in there. Snakes and scorpions and deadly spiders, not to mention the walls falling."

"If you think you're scaring me, you're wrong." She tossed her head and started toward the edge of the gardens again.

He raised his voice to call after her. "And there are beasts in there that can do things you couldn't even imagine; not in your most frightening dreams. If you think I'll risk myself to get you out of there again, you're mistaken."

"You?" Firal paused mid-stride and looked over her shoulder. The ice in his expression startled her, and it took her a moment to find her voice again. "You brought me out?"

"Why are you going back in there?" he asked with an edge in his tone.

One more step carried her through the hedgerow and the prickling mage-barrier. She glanced back again and set her jaw in defiance. "I dropped something last night. I won't give up until I find it. I'm not afraid of that dilapidated mess, I'm not afraid of those old wives' tales, and I am most certainly not afraid of you."

"Perhaps you should be." The words came out frosty, a steely gleam in his blue eyes.

Firal bit her tongue to still it as she turned away. The open space between the temple and ruin was vacant, but she scanned the temple to be sure no one was watching. Then she sucked in a breath, hitched the hem of her robes up around her calves, and hurried into the passage of the ruins she'd taken the night before. There, she paused just long enough to shake out her robes and glance back.

The gardens behind her were empty, but out of the corner of her eye, she caught a glimpse of blue robes as Ran disappeared into the ruins some short distance away.

5

A RAID

THERE HAD BEEN A TIME WHEN TRADE WAGONS ROLLED OFTEN through the small border village of Charth, but territory feuds between Giftless and Eldani lands brought commerce to a standstill. A muddy pit replaced the market square. Narrow roads lined with simple houses branched from it in equally simple rows. Daemon was pleased to see the longhouses and barns behind the houses were full to bursting. Crates of goods they'd been unable to trade sat in the open.

Whether or not the place was ripe for the picking, he was not pleased with the orders that brought him here. Daemon wasn't fond of raids. He hadn't approved of it and certainly hadn't expected to lead it. The task was beneath him, but since the order came directly from Lumia, he could only assume it was some sort of test. He resisted the urge to shake his head. Violence would hinder them in the long run. Even so, he couldn't deny that they couldn't wait for a better plan. His people were starving; before him was food. The best his men could offer him was a few quiet hours he could scout and prepare, and he would simply have to hope it would be enough.

Women spread laundry on ropes between houses and the steady thud of an axe sounded nearby as a farmer chopped firewood. The lack of trade made Daemon doubt they'd had recent visitors, but no one paid any mind to a lonely stranger roaming the streets. His mask might have drawn attention, so he kept his hood up and his head bowed just enough to hide it.

He enjoyed watching the village at work, finding the everyday monotony pleasant. This was the life he dreamed of. In time, perhaps his people would find it. Clinging to that hope, he moved on.

Though small, the village hosted an inn. A promising sign. If they were equipped to receive guests, Daemon's presence was less suspicious. If he could convince his men to wait until evening, perhaps he could meet merchants and farmers and negotiate trade over a drink.

A child's shout gave him pause and Daemon stepped aside as a handful of children ran by. One flung a worn rag doll into the air and he watched it land in the middle of a muddy rut in the street. Glancing after the children as they vanished around the corner of a house, he crouched to pick it up and wrung water from the doll's skirt.

It didn't take long for the owner to present herself, lagging behind the group, sniffling and wiping her eyes. She kicked the ground as she shuffled toward him.

"Is this yours?" He straightened the doll's yarn hair with one gloved hand and tried to make his muffled words sound friendly. Befriending her worked to his advantage. Children often made the best guides.

"Yes, sir." The girl bobbed her head and inched forward with outstretched hands. She studied him as she might any other stranger, in spite of the thick brown cloak drawn around his shoulders and the featureless steel mask that concealed his face. Her expression didn't change when he laid the doll in her hands. "Thank you, sir."

"You're welcome." He brushed his dark hair back from his mask and rested his elbows on his knees. He always found the judgment of children interesting. When he greeted them at their level, they never seemed intimidated. Even with his mask. "She's too pretty to go in the mud, wouldn't you say? It wasn't nice of them to throw her. You'd best let her sit in the sun to dry where she won't catch cold."

"I will, sir." She sniffled, rubbing her nose with a sleeve, and looked down at his bandage-wrapped feet as he stood. Her nose wrinkled, but she said nothing.

Daemon started across the empty market with an easy stride. There appeared to be a barn ahead; he hoped to peek inside. Livestock fared well in the grassy ruins, when they could obtain animals.

The girl fell in alongside him, taking two steps for each of his. "What's your name?"

"I haven't got a real one." He gave her a glance. "You may call me whatever you'd like. What's yours?"

"Lea. This is Cara." She hugged the doll tight to her chest. "Cara says thank you for saving her from the water."

He chuckled but didn't reply, focusing on the village as he walked. It was a barn. Sheep, judging by the bales of wool stacked inside the door. The supplies were satisfactory, and few village men appeared armed. Though Daemon hoped to stay his soldiers, he had to prepare for the worst. With so few guards present, it would be a clean raid. With fortune, it would be the last.

Horns blared from the western edge of town and Daemon spat a curse. They'd been spotted. He'd told the men to stay farther back, to linger near the edge of the ruins.

Perhaps it wouldn't be so clean a raid after all. His mouth tightened as the city's few guardsmen scrambled for weaponry.

The girl at his side cried out at sight of the swords and hid behind his cloak. Daemon turned in several circles before he caught hold of her and crouched at her side. "Lea—"

"Let go! The bad men are coming!" She clutched her rag doll to her chest and strained against his grasp.

So it wasn't the first time the village had been raided. He'd known this was a mistake.

"Listen to me, Lea. I need you to do something." Daemon kept his voice calm as he pulled a small object from beneath his cloak. Before she could reply, he pressed the cool stone crest into her hand and closed her fingers around it. It was a feeble attempt to establish a connection, but now it was the best chance he had. "This is very important. Hang this on your door as soon as you get home. It will keep your family safe as long as all of you stay inside. Do you understand?" He met her gaze and, as frightened as she was, Lea couldn't seem to tear her eyes away. Not for the first time, he wondered if it was just the appearance his snake-slitted eyes that held people fixated, or if it was something more.

The girl's lip trembled, but she nodded. She didn't stir a step until he released her arm. He moved back as the plaza flooded with farmers and blacksmiths brave enough to draw weapons and fight. Then she fled, and he frowned as a woman swept the child into her arms and disappeared among the throng.

Daemon skirted the edge of town, but watched the village defenses assemble. Their numbers weren't impressive; his hundred men on the other side of the hill would flatten any opposition that rose against them. He left by the city's eastern side and gave the village a wide berth as he moved toward his soldiers.

His men loomed at the top of the hill to the west, perhaps a half mile from the town's edge. He wasn't pleased they had defied his orders to remain hidden. His frustration grew when he saw them watching the villagers bolster their meager defenses.

The entire rank straightened when he appeared in their midst, perhaps conscious of defying his orders. Some nameless soldier stepped forward with the reins of Daemon's black warhorse, the only steed they'd brought. Daemon's eyes narrowed as he took the reins. An unfamiliar horse lingered at the rear edge of his army.

"What are your commands, sir?"

Daemon turned his head just enough to see the captain he'd left in charge. Davan was a good man and a good soldier, one of few who had taken to his new leader without complaint. Thus far, Davan was the only officer he trusted.

Daemon moved his horse's reins from one hand to the other as he shrugged out of his worn cloak and brushed at the black-and-gold dress armor and cape underneath. He peeled off his gloves and replaced them with gauntlets from his horse's saddlebags. The custom armor left his talons exposed. "Who moved the men up the hill?"

Davan hesitated. "Not all are used to following your lead yet, sir." He cast a glance toward the second horse. "Some still cling to the old."

Clenching his jaw, Daemon tightened the straps on his gauntlets. He didn't need to look again to know what Davan meant.

Tren Achos had served as general of Lumia's army for close to two decades. There was a time when Lumia favored the man, thought to place him on a throne beside her, but Daemon's presence had changed many things. Tren's interference wasn't surprising, but it was a frustration.

Daemon couldn't fault his men for accepting orders from the former general. The title had been his for mere days, and he was still unproven. Perhaps Lumia meant the raid to be his proving ground.

"See to it the news is repeated, then," Daemon said. "They're under new leadership."

"Aye, sir," Davan agreed. He pressed a knuckle to his forehead in the salute common in the Underling army and slipped away.

Daemon's mouth took a grim set as he watched the captain go. Davan's deference was appreciated, but coming from a single soldier, it meant little. Grateful for the mask that hid his expression, Daemon let his eyes sweep back toward the village.

Had the child not indicated Charth had been raided before, the organized group the village put together would have betrayed it. The village men settled into tidy ranks along the main street. A man in armor stood before them, presumably giving orders in his aged but shining steel. Despite their valiant effort, their defenses were almost nonexistent. It was pitiful, and it twisted Daemon's stomach in unpleasant ways.

Strife had become commonplace in the borderlands, and Daemon was certain it was one of the reasons Lumia had chosen Charth. The history of border raids gave his men the benefit of anonymity, though the idea of their raid being blamed on Giftless bandits left a sour taste in Daemon's mouth.

"They're ready, my lord," Davan prompted softly.

Daemon exhaled and gripped his horse's reins a little tighter as he faced his small army. "It's been a while since raiders came this way," he began, his voice level. The men quieted. The weight of their eyes on him did not make it any easier to speak. "What we need should be in the storage sheds and barns. Leave the houses alone unless we can't get what we need elsewhere. Burn the storage buildings after taking what is needed, we don't want them to know which supplies we're after. Kill only those necessary. Spare the children and elderly."

It felt strange to give orders; he'd never led before. He couldn't afford to let them think he was weak. And he couldn't let their judgment influence Lumia's opinion of how much power he could be trusted with. He knew too well, now, how far she would go. Metal rasped as he rubbed the back of his gauntleted left hand with the palm of his right. The new scar in his hand still ached. He shook his head and grasped the pommel of the warhorse's saddle to heft himself into place.

"And what of the women?" It was hard to tell where the question came from, though a few of the soldiers closest to him snickered.

"We're not here for prisoners." Daemon tightened his hold on the reins as he settled on his horse. "In and out. Do nothing to make yourselves memorable. Remember, they're to think we're border raiders from the east."

"Yes, sir!" The shout came with laughter, but the acceptance of his command was repeated by the hundred men behind him.

Daemon adjusted his mask as he drew his sword and raised it high. The small army readied themselves with a rattle of weapons and clank of armor. He twisted the sword in hand and pointed the blade to the horizon and the village ahead with a cry that signaled those behind him. It was answered by an eager scream from a hundred throats.

With a thundering of feet, the gray sea of armor surged forward.

Daemon's mount tossed his armor-plated head, whinnied, and danced as his rider held him back. Daemon waited a heartbeat, expecting Tren to pass him. He glanced over his shoulder and spat a curse as he realized the other warhorse was gone. He could only hope whatever contradictory orders the man had given wouldn't cause more trouble. Gritting his teeth, he let the reins slack.

Head freed, the great black warhorse flew forward through the masses of men and left the front line behind. Hoofbeats fell in rhythm with the pounding of Daemon's heart. A surge of adrenaline and the cheering screams of his army stilled his conscience and the final pulls of doubt.

The raid had to happen. It was best for his people, best for his army.

It was best for him.

Blood spilled as a raking sweep of his sword took the head of one of the city's sentries, and the body crumpled into a useless heap on the ground.

Then the wave of soldiers behind him crashed down on the village.

Shouted commands became gurgling cries as the village's defenders fell. Underling soldiers streamed past the bodies and the looting began.

Men rolled barrels from a nearby shed and tossed sacks of goods from another down the street. Near the edge of the village, raiders piled the spoils on a stolen wagon bed, its team of horses having panicked and broken free. Daemon left his horse beside them in hopes the lone warhorse would be enough to drag it to the ruins. He couldn't see how far it was to the labyrinth's walls; smoke poured from buildings and left a gray haze in the air.

Men shattered the doors on houses and dragged out baskets and crates of foodstuffs. Daemon hacked his way through a thin line of men blocking the road, working toward the center of the town. The sound of mothers and children screaming seemed dim in his ears, buried beneath the crackling crunches of wood and bone. Metal rang above the choked cries of men as they fell. The village defenders fell into clusters to better their odds.

Then, swallowed by the heart of it all, Daemon saw nothing but war.

It was exhilarating and terrifying. He gasped for breath as he watched another man drop. Rivulets of blood flowed down his sword. He shook droplets from the blade as he wheeled to drive it through another man's chest. A weapon fell from the man's hand before he ever had a chance to raise it. Battle was heady; the blood smelled sweet, intoxicating. Power burned in him like it never had. He wanted more.

A sword whistled as it tore through Daemon's cape. He bared his teeth behind his mask, growling as he spun, and slammed the back of his gauntlet across his attacker's face. Another guard rushed him from the side and Daemon winced as the tip of the guard's sword chipped at his mask. He knocked the blade aside with his own and delivered a swift kick to his assailant's chest, driving the air from his lungs and sending him to the ground.

The first man came at him again and Daemon barely had time to bring his sword around. The blades clashed and when the man stepped back to swing again, Daemon dropped beneath the sword's reach and struck the man's knee. The villager collapsed with a cry of pain.

Adrenaline pounded through Daemon's veins. He fed off it, thrived. His blade hungered; Daemon was eager to satisfy. He spun as the guard he'd kicked to the ground found his feet again. He took the man's sword arm with a single sweep and his head with a second. Blood made his blade's hilt slick. The force of his swing carried him around and he drove his sword through the chest of the man with the wounded knee.

More blood! The craving burned in every inch of his body. Daemon's eyes flashed red, blazing behind his mask like fire. The streets boiled with madness, the few remaining village defenders struggling to escape. One lashed out at Daemon as he passed and Daemon reacted before he knew he'd moved. His gauntleted knuckles smashed into the would-be soldier's face. The exposed talons of his other hand dug into the man's stomach and rent him from navel to throat. The man choked and staggered on his feet for a moment before his eyes glazed and he collapsed.

Breath came ragged, searing Daemon's throat. His gaze shifted to his upraised hand, the blood on his fingers, the bits of flesh and gore that slithered down his arm. The enraged color faded from his eyes and left them a dull violet as his hands began to tremble. His brow furrowed. What had he done?

His eyes slid to the corpses that surrounded him, Eldani and Underling alike. What had he done?

He felt his strength waning. He clawed the mask from his face, desperate for air. The wind hit his bare skin like ice.

He fell to his knees and retched.

6

MARKET

Though she searched for hours, Firal never found Ran's path. She was positive it had been him that slipped into the ruins. She'd spent more time looking for him than looking for her journal. She found neither, and Ran hadn't turned up in the temple for classes the next morning. Several days crawled by without him surfacing again.

Firal frowned in thought, her quill pen beating a quiet rhythm against the paper before her. A blotch of ink grew larger with every tap. Surely someone knew where he'd gone; perhaps one of the older Masters. The trick would be finding someone willing to talk to her about the matter, and finding a way to phrase the question without incriminating herself.

"Firal!"

The thud of Master Nondar's fist against his desk jolted her attention back to the classroom. Firal swallowed hard, fumbled with her pen and gave her near-blank paper a panicked look before she met his glare.

"Awake, are you?" Nondar adjusted his spectacles with a gnarled hand. "Good. You stay put. The rest of you are dismissed." He eased himself back into his chair.

Firal shrank in her seat as a flush rose into her cheeks. A few giggles reached her ears as her classmates gathered their papers and laid them on the Master's desk.

Nondar's eyes remained fixed on Firal while the other magelings filed out of the room. Kytenia paused at the door to give Firal a wistful—or perhaps disappointed—look before she disappeared. Once the magelings were gone, Nondar sighed and looked over the mess of papers. Firal tried not to watch. Her gaze settled on the empty desk two rows over and she wondered again where Ran had gone. Why warn her away from the ruins, only to go there himself?

"Ah, Firal. What am I to do with you?" Nondar studied her in burdened silence, then went on when she didn't reply. "You know I find you a good student, when you're paying attention. But it seems you've become more and more addled as classes have gone on." He clasped his hands together and rested them against the edge of the desk.

Firal fidgeted with her blank assignment and bowed her head. She liked Nondar, withered and old and cross as he was. A scolding from him stung more than she expected. The fact that he was the only half-blood Master had always intrigued her. His eyes were the same pale blue of all Masters, rimmed with black ink to mark his rank as leader of the House of Healing. But unlike most other mages, he showed his age clearly. Deep wrinkles furrowed his darkly tanned forehead, and his retreating hairline drew extra attention to the creases. His mouth was set in a tight expression above a well-groomed—if very long—beard, and his shaggy brows knit together in a look of concern. Magic slowed aging, sometimes dramatically, but the more diluted the Gift, the less effect it seemed to have. Firal couldn't help but wonder what Kytenia would look like when she was Nondar's age.

"I'm speaking to you, dearest," Nondar said placidly.

Firal tucked in her chin. "I'm sorry, Master. I'm just distracted today. I won't let it happen again."

"Which is what you said the last time, and also the time

before that." He gave a halfhearted chuckle and the corners of his eyes crinkled with his resigned smile. "You are fortunate I am familiar with your usual academic performance. Tell me, child, what's on your mind?"

She hesitated, wringing her hands. Part of her wanted to spill everything. Nondar had always been the father figure in her life, not simply because they shared an affinity for healing. But she did not know if he had noticed the sideways looks and whispers that filtered through the classroom when she entered, and drawing his attention to the rumors about her own escapades would have been unwise. Instead, she cast another glance toward Ran's conspicuously empty desk a few spaces away. "I was hoping Ran would be in class today. I thought I saw him going into the ruins several days ago and I haven't seen him since. I wanted to speak to him. I think he was angry at me."

"Angry? Goodness me, that would be the day." The old Master shook his head and rubbed the swollen joints in his hands. He gestured toward the papers strewn across his desk. "Would you pick those up for me, child? My arthritis is acting up after this morning's rain. It's an unusually wet season."

Firal bit her lower lip, but nodded and strode to his desk. "Where does he go whenever he leaves the temple?"

"Lomithrandel travels frequently between the temple and his home." Nondar frowned and his eyes narrowed until they almost disappeared amidst wrinkles. "Of course, only the Masters who work with him directly are privy to his particular circumstances, but surely you understand that he is...special, shall we say."

"How do you mean, 'special'?" Firal gathered the papers and winced when one slit her fingertip. "Ow." She slid the injury into her mouth and sucked to relieve the sting.

Nondar did not reply right away, massaging the knots in his hands and staring into the distance. Eventually, he sighed. "As much as I would like to tell you, dearest, it isn't my place to do so. I oughtn't speak of it."

"Why not?" She tried not to sound disappointed.

"The Archmage takes things said about him as a personal affront. I'm afraid I cannot speak of that further." He took the ream of papers from her and tapped them against the edge of his desk to settle them together. "But then, you seem to be the closest friend he has. If you are gentle about it, I wouldn't be surprised if he told you of the matter himself. His Gifts are unusual and should be treated as such. But I will say no more than that."

His closest *what*? Firal could have choked. "You must be mistaken," she protested. "Ran is the most popular young man here. I barely know him. He hardly has time to speak to me."

"Popularity has nothing to do with friendship, child. Just because many pine for him doesn't mean he has friends. You, child," he said, leveling one thick finger at her nose, "you see him for the person he is. That sets you apart."

She harrumphed. "I don't see him as anything but an annoyance."

Nondar let out a rasping guffaw. "Yes, perhaps so." He reclined in his chair and slipped the stack of papers into a drawer. "Now you'd best run along and join the others. If the lot of you are to meet for a trip to the market this afternoon, you won't want to miss the outset. You won't be allowed to leave on your own. I trust you shall pay better attention in tomorrow's class."

"Of course, Master. Thank you." Firal gave a quick curtsy and a nod of appreciation before she hurried to the door. The thought to ask when Ran might be back tickled her thoughts and she turned to ask, but stopped when she saw the troubled frown that twisted Nondar's mouth. Another time, she decided, and hastened to meet her friends.

THE SUN HAD ALREADY PASSED ITS PEAK WHEN FIRAL RUSHED TO HER room to change out of her training robes. She hadn't missed the look she'd gotten from Kytenia when she was held after class. They'd only just discussed the afternoon's market trip that morning, and Firal was already late. She laced the bodice of her dress in a hurry and gathered her things, then opened the door. She yelped in surprise when she found Kytenia on the other side, her fist raised to knock.

"Brant's roots!" Firal clapped a hand to her chest and sucked in a sharp breath as her heart settled.

"Oh. Sorry." Kytenia flashed her a sheepish grin and lowered her hand. "I was just coming to see if you were ready. I wasn't sure how long Master Nondar would keep you. The others are already waiting with a Master who's agreed to escort us."

"I'm ready now," Firal said, though nerves put an anxious flutter in her belly.

The formal invitation for the magelings to attend the solstice masquerade in the palace had come that morning, and the temple had been in a tizzy ever since. Firal had no doubt the market would be chaos; she'd seen more than one doodle of a dress on the papers she'd gathered for Master Nondar.

Firal was eager to visit the palace, herself, though for more personal reasons. For what might as well have been all eighteen pents of her life, she'd hoped to visit the king's court and learn what became of her mother. She had pinned her hopes on her studies. Now the chance to bypass decades of struggle dangled before her, an irresistible morsel on a string. She gazed back into her room, pensive.

Kytenia didn't seem to notice. "Let's go, then. Have you got your money? Hurry and fetch it, if you haven't."

"I have it." Firal pulled the door shut behind her. Though the others planned for their dresses, Firal had more practical reasons to visit the market. Replacing her lantern came to mind—as well as the papers she doubted Ran would pay for. She touched a hand to the small purse hidden in her skirt's pocket and weighed it in her fingers.

A mageling's income was meager at best. Firal's was limited to a few coins earned here and there by running extra errands for Master mages. The idea of purchasing expensive fabric and a seamstress's services was less than pleasant. Her life savings amounted to little more than a handful of copper pennies and a few silver coins she'd received as gifts from her teachers throughout the years. She hated to spend what little she had, but a trip to the palace demanded she look as if she belonged.

"So, what did Master Nondar say?" Kytenia asked, looping her arm with Firal's. "Is everything all right?"

"Everything's fine." Firal was surprised by that answer, herself. Her disastrous trip to the ruins seemed to have been forgotten, perhaps because the gossip had died down following news of the solstice. She hoped it hadn't been long lived enough for the Masters to take notice. "He just wanted to make sure I was paying attention."

Kytenia gave her a suspicious glance, but said nothing else as she led the way to the temple's main gate.

The group that waited for them was small, but Firal was glad to see the cluster was composed of only her nearest friends and Master Alira. The gates stood wide open, as they often did. With the mage-barrier that kept unwanted visitors at bay, the gates were largely for show. Half the temple wasn't even walled in.

Master Alira watched the two of them approach with a neutral expression, though it was easy to tell she had not agreed to take them out of a desire to visit the market. Nondar had likely asked her to travel with them in his place. Firal could imagine no other reason a mage of such high rank would agree to escort them. Alira's eyes had not yet changed to blue, but she still painted them with the patterns of black ink that marked her as Master of the House of Fire. Unsurprisingly, the pattern she'd chosen mimicked flames.

"Sorry we're late, Master." Kytenia lifted her skirts as she hurried toward the group.

Alira frowned, but started down the road without a word.

Her white robes swirled around her ankles. For a moment, Firal felt as if she should add her own apology. It had been her fault they were late. But the other girls—Rikka, Marreli, and Shymin —moved to greet them with bright smiles, and the urge to apologize subsided.

"I heard Nondar kept you after class. Did he give you a scolding again?" Rikka's blue eyes sparkled as she nudged Firal with her elbow. She stood out among the other magelings, milky pale and freckled instead of tan, her hair so vividly red it was almost pink in the sunlight. Any time she smiled, it looked like trouble. Now was no exception.

Firal nudged back. "That is none of your business."

"He likely just slapped her hand with a ruler and called it a day." Shymin flashed a sarcastic grin over her shoulder. As expected, Shymin and Kytenia fell in step together. The two of them looked quite alike, though Shymin was a bit leaner and a bit taller, and her face was just a hint more square. But her hair was the same curly brown and her eyes the same snapping hazel.

Marreli giggled, but said nothing. Firal didn't expect more than that. The youngest of their group, with a round, cherub face and her hair in braids, Marreli was also the weakest mage. A decade after she'd been accepted into the temple, she still wore gray robes. She made up for her lack of power with cleverness in how she used it, though her head was often too far into the clouds for her clever solutions to come in a timely fashion. Even now, she appeared lost in a daydream, playing with the end of one dark braid and gazing at the sky.

Firal listened as her friends settled into cheerful banter, though her eyes swept toward the nearby ruins. The market excursion was important, but she couldn't forget her necklace. Once she made it to the palace, she was certain she'd need her mother's pendant to gain the attention of the court mages. Fighting twinges of uncertainty, she walked.

The road that ran from the temple to the market was rarely

used. It narrowed to little more than a trail of hard-packed dirt once they passed the hedge walls of the temple's gardens. Untended grasses grew tall to either side of the path, allowing only enough room for the group to walk two by two.

There was little of interest along the road once they moved beyond the ruins. During Firal's childhood, a number of farms had dotted the countryside. After heavy rains became commonplace and the good soil washed away, civilization began to move with the farmers, settling in temporary-looking villages of thatched buildings and canvas tents. The only permanent structures were guard garrisons and the chapter houses that belonged to mages, and there were neither near the temple.

As they walked, the other magelings chattered about colors and styles and fashion, discussed which seamstresses were best, and debated which merchants they thought they could persuade into giving them better deals. Disinterested in the subject, Firal let her attention wander instead.

Now and then the group passed fallen blocks or pillars alongside the path. Judging by the markings etched into their surface, Firal thought they had once been used as distance markers. The weather had long since rendered the markings indistinguishable. She trailed her fingertips over the face of a pillar as they passed. The shapes and hollows were familiar. Some corners in the ruins bore similar marks. The observation returned her thoughts to the events of the past few days, and Firal grimaced to herself.

The longer she thought about all that had happened, the more she thought her irritation with Ran was unfounded—or at least misdirected. She was confident she had every right to be angry he'd let her fumble through a lesson in swordplay with the king, but she'd let that anger overshadow the weight of what he'd done for her.

Firal had gotten herself in trouble and been hurt in the ruins. Ran had rescued her, and the longer she stewed over it, the more she suspected he'd concocted the Underling rumors himself.

Kytenia was right; Ran was a handsome young man. Firal had no doubt rumors involving *him* would have drawn unnecessary ire from her peers. For some reason, he'd chosen to try and protect her, and she'd shouted at him in return.

No matter how it stung, Firal owed him an apology and her gratitude.

When they arrived at the market, the sun's light was fading and the afternoon's heat had begun to give way. The market roared with activity, catching their small group and washing it into the sea of strangers.

The other girls seemed perfectly at home amidst the teeming masses. They slipped between booths, wagons, market stalls and the crowds with an ease Firal envied. She'd never thought herself clumsy, but her skirts caught on carts, loose nails, belt buckles and the boots of passers-by. The gap between Firal and her companions grew and she struggled to close it.

The market itself seemed foreign after the years Firal had spent in the temple. She'd ventured there with other Masters— Nondar sent her to buy fine paper for his office twice a year— but twice a year hardly fostered familiarity. Narrow stalls that were little more than wooden frames draped with thick canvas crowded the twisting streets, interspersed with larger tents that had three sides rolled up to capture the soft, pleasant breezes that came with the evening. Carts filled with baskets of fruits and baked goods roamed the dusty roads, and the crush of people grew so thick that Firal feared she might suffocate among the pressing bodies. Her heart thundered in her ears as nerves twisted her belly into knots.

Ahead, Master Alira's white robes flashed between the skirts and boots of shoppers. She had stopped. Beside her, Kytenia bounced on the tips of her toes and waved an arm. A moment later, she wiggled her way out from between a pair of arguing women directly in front of Firal.

"Come on," Kytenia said as she took Firal by the arm to

hurry her along. "Rikka's found her favorite seamstress. We'll need to be measured before we can buy cloth."

"Measured?" Firal squeaked, squeezing her eyes shut and shielding her face as Kytenia dragged her along so forcefully Firal was sure they would barrel into the other pedestrians.

Instead, a cool shadow enveloped them and the crowd seemed to disappear. Firal cracked one eye open, then the other, and sighed in relief. Aside from her companions, the seamstress's tent held only supplies. A large cutting table rested in the middle of the tent, stools and wooden boxes and dress forms of all sizes around it. Colorful cuts of fabric and bright spools of thread piled high atop the shelves that framed two walls. Judging by the rough-hewn boards behind them, the seamstress had occupied this space for a long time.

Rikka already stood on top of a wooden box, her arms spread. The seamstress circled her with a measuring tape, taking notes on a pad of the thinnest paper Firal had ever seen.

"I've already been measured," Shymin said when they approached. "I always thought taking measurements would take longer."

"Well, she does it all day. You're bound to get fast that way." Marreli stood beside the cutting table, playing with one of her dark braids as she inspected ink drawings illustrating the latest fashions across the island and the mainland. Her brow crinkled with thought.

"Where's Master Alira?" Kytenia asked.

Rikka made a face and fought to keep from fidgeting. "She stopped at the papermaker. She'll catch up with us once she's done."

"I needed to go with her," Firal sighed as she moved in line to wait her turn. "The last of my paper got wet."

"Really?" Rikka gaped. "We're here to get dresses for the solstice masquerade, and you're thinking about homework?"

"What else would she think about?" Kytenia teased, and a hint of color touched Firal's cheeks.

It didn't take long for all of them to be measured. The seamstress labeled each set of numbers with their names and the style of dress they'd chosen, along with the amount of material they would need. When she took Firal's name, the seamstress paused. But she said nothing, her eyes narrowed as she wrote it down, scribbled something out, and added a note to the bottom of the paper.

"Take these to the third cloth merchant down the main road and he'll give you a discount," the seamstress said as she passed out their papers and settled on the stool behind her cutting table. "Just remember to bring them back with you so I won't have to measure again. I'll close shop an hour after the lamps are lit, so hurry along."

Kytenia led the way this time, while Marreli latched onto Firal's arm to keep her from falling behind. Other familiar magelings swirled in the crowd as more parties arrived to shop. Firal couldn't help but wonder who else had been invited to the solstice masquerade. The temple's mages would attend, but had any commoners been invited? She hadn't heard. A few wistful faces on passers-by made her doubt it. Mages were a class of their own.

"Oh." Firal leaned forward so Rikka, who was just ahead, could hear her. "If the solstice ball is a masquerade, shouldn't we look for masks?"

"Not here," Rikka called over her shoulder. "The nearest place you could find a mask maker is in Wethertree. We'll have to get masks when we arrive in Ilmenhith."

Firal almost groaned. With as chaotic as the small market was, she didn't want to imagine what shopping was like in the capital.

"Here," Kytenia called. They had stopped outside the fabric merchant's tent, where racks of bolts and stacked rolls of cloth created makeshift walls. Rows of racks and tables piled high with cloth waited inside the large tent. The merchant's desk sat square in the middle of it all.

"Welcome," the merchant called, waving them inside. His colorful robes were loose and airy, well suited to the heat, and his smile was warm and friendly. "Who sent you?"

"Just ask if you need any help," Kytenia murmured at Firal's ear before she joined the merchant. She raised her note and pointed at the numbers, her low question lost in the racket of the market behind them.

Firal blanched. She was as useless and out of place in a fabric shop as she would have been helping the seamstress with their dresses. She brushed her fingers over a nearby bolt and stared at the patterns. All her clothing was provided by the temple. She'd never purchased anything for herself. What did one look for in fabric? Against the back wall, Shymin fussed over a flaw in the middle of a panel of silk, while Marreli cooed soft sympathies. Rikka already had something tucked under her arm.

"Do you see nothing you like?" The merchant sucked in his paunch and squeezed through the narrow space between his desk and the shelves to join her.

Firal flushed and clasped her hands behind her back. "I don't really know what to look for."

"There's something for everyone. Sometimes you don't choose your goods, your goods choose you. Let me see the note your tailor gave you, eh?" The corners of his eyes crinkled with a smile as he held out his hand. "Perhaps I will have a suggestion for you."

She eyed the merchant doubtfully, but passed him the note. He studied it for a time, scratching his chin with fat fingers. Then he grinned, the white of his teeth a stark contrast to his dark skin.

"Ah, yes! Yes, your goods are all ready." He squeezed behind his desk and squatted to remove something from underneath the counter.

"I beg your pardon?" Firal blinked in confusion, uncomfortably aware of the way the other girls stared at their exchange. When the merchant stood again, he held a thick

66

package wrapped in brown paper and tied with twine. He pushed it toward her, and Firal raised her hands and stepped back.

"You must be mistaken, sir," she protested. "I haven't ordered anything."

"No, no, I remember quite clearly." He tapped his temple with a forefinger and then ticked the same finger at her. "Don't argue, it has all been paid for and you must take it. The receipts are drawn, and if you refuse, I will have to give it to your friends."

Her mouth worked wordlessly. The merchant took it as acceptance and thrust the package into her arms.

"It's a very good choice," he reassured her. "The finest quality I offer. You will be pleased. And tell your friend thank you for me again, eh?" He gave a hearty chuckle and reached for a bolt one of the girls had left on his counter.

Kytenia grabbed Firal's arm and pulled her to the open front of the tent, a look that was half wonder, half scolding on her face.

"Your friend? What in the world, Firal?" Kytenia whispered. Her eyes dropped toward the package in her friend's arms. "What is he talking about?"

"I don't know!" Firal whispered back. "I don't even know anyone who would have the money, except—" Her eyes widened and she stopped short. A crimson shade crept into her cheeks.

"Except who?" Kytenia eyed her.

Firal swallowed hard. It had only been one quick lesson in swordplay. Surely he wouldn't have even remembered her name.

"What's going on?" Rikka nudged Firal's shoulder as she joined them. "Someone bought your cloth?"

"Do you think it was Ran?" Marreli asked as she appeared at Rikka's elbow.

"I doubt it," Firal said. Then again, perhaps it had been Ran. Master Nondar had just spoken of special cases and how he must have considered her a friend. Perhaps Ran had gleaned some sort of knowledge about the king's plans for the solstice ball before the rest of the students. His latest disappearance would have given him time to visit the market. It almost made sense, but where would he have gotten the money? Firal took another step away from the tent to give herself space to think.

"I doubt it was Ran, I don't think he knew she would need it. Come on, Alira will expect us to be with the seamstress." Shymin started down the street, seeming to expect they'd follow.

The other magelings arranged themselves behind her and trailed along like chicks behind a mother hen.

Firal studied her toes as they walked. "Kifel," she managed.

"Who?" Marreli asked.

"I think...I think it was Kifel." Firal's stomach gave an uncomfortable flutter. "I didn't realize when Ran introduced us. I'd never heard anyone refer to him as that. I didn't know he was the king until later, and—" She croaked as her voice failed her.

The procession stopped and all of them turned to stare at her.

"What?" Rikka asked.

"I met him the other day," Firal added lamely.

Kytenia's jaw went slack. "The king?" she repeated. "King Kifelethelas?"

"I told you, I didn't know it was him!" Firal blurted. "I just ran across them while they were practicing with swords, Ran didn't even tell me who he really was until afterward!"

"Ran was practicing sword-fighting with the king?" Marreli gave her a skeptical look.

"Firal, you didn't tell us about this!" Shymin cried. "Tell us the whole story!"

Grimacing, Firal hugged her bundle to her chest as if she could hide behind it. The crowd felt too close again, and the sense of suffocation returned. "Look, can we talk about this later? We're right in the middle of the market, and Alira will be waiting."

"Fine," Kytenia sighed. "Let's finish here. When we get to the temple, we can go back to my room. We can sit and talk there."

The room Kytenia shared with Shymin was far enough back in the dormitory that it was unlikely anyone would notice if they were up late. Chances were, once Firal shared her story, they would be.

———

"OUCH." SHYMIN SCRUNCHED HER NOSE AND FLICKED ASIDE THE rock she'd found in her sandal. "You know, this whole solstice thing had better really be something. My pocket hurts from all that spending, my feet hurt from all that walking, and my ears hurt from listening to everyone else complain!" She brushed out her skirts as she hurried to catch up with the others.

It was well after dark, and all the girls dragged their feet. Mage-lights glowed above the temple in varying colors, suspended in the air without anything to hold them.

"Oh come on, Shymin. I don't want to hear it." Kytenia shifted her paper-wrapped bundle in her arms. When the other girls had gotten cost estimates from the seamstress, Firal thought it looked as if their eyes might fall from their heads. Kytenia was the only one of them who could do needlework with any sort of skill, and had elected to sew her dress on her own. There wouldn't be enough time for the rest to learn before they had to travel.

Firal, of course, had no need to learn. The girls—including Firal herself—had been scandalized to learn the seamstress's services were already paid for. The style of Firal's dress, too, had been chosen for her. And while her stomach twisted at the idea that the merchant could have sent her off with the gaudiest cloth he had to offer, she had been pleasantly surprised when the seamstress opened the package. The bundle contained lengths of the finest silk any of them had felt, cuts dyed the richest red and deepest black Firal had ever seen.

The girls picked at her the entire walk home, trying to pry out the rest of the story she'd started in the market street, but

Firal stayed tight-lipped and intended to remain so until they were outside of Master Alira's presence.

When Alira stopped the temple's main gate to dismiss them, each of the girls gave the Master a grateful bow and a murmured thank-you. The Master waved the five of them off with an irritated expression. Firal figured they should appreciate the silence. Master Alira was not known to be amicable and Firal did not know how the woman had been convinced to take them shopping.

The girls managed to keep from asking questions on the way into the dormitory. As soon as the door closed behind them, Shymin spun to face Firal. "So?"

Kytenia settled on the edge of her bed, put aside her package of cloth and retrieved a basket of colorful thread and embroidery floss from the floor. She looked up, a sparkle in her eyes.

Firal shrank. "So what?"

"So tell us, now that we're alone!" Rikka crossed to the desk under the window and pulled out the chair. She turned it around to sit on it sideways with one elbow propped against the back. "Why would the king spend a small fortune on silk for your ball gown before we ever got to the market?"

"Is it true he's a widower?" Marreli asked. "Maybe he's looking for a new queen."

"Hush!" Kytenia glowered. "Let Firal talk."

Firal blushed and sank to the floor as her friends turned expectant eyes toward her. Shymin and Marreli joined her, and everyone leaned in. She recounted the story and the strange way the king seemed to regard her, and the mage-lights over the temple extinguished themselves long before the girls finished their questions.

7

RANK

THE NAUSEA DID NOT SUBSIDE. IT HAD TWISTED DAEMON'S STOMACH since the village surrendered. If anything, seeing the village men throw down their weapons and plead for their lives had made it worse.

Davan had been the one to find him, maskless and retching, and pulled him to his feet. He'd been the one to order anyone who surrendered be spared, though he'd claimed the order came from Daemon's mouth. Daemon appreciated the captain's support, but it had driven home how unprepared he was to lead.

It wasn't supposed to end that way. He was supposed to have connections in the village, to have earned enough trust to open avenues for future trade. Instead, he'd only managed to protect one family. Raking his claws through his hair, Daemon hung his head. For the dozenth time in an hour, he regretted having immediately returned to the underground.

Lumia paced her quarters, circling between her dressing table and the bed where he sat. "There's no shame in inexperience, pet. Every warrior has to take a life at some point. You should be proud that you succeeded in taking so many without losing your own." It didn't show in her movement or tone, but Daemon could tell from the pinched neutrality on her face that her patience was growing thin. "Besides, you shouldn't punish yourself for giving them what they deserved."

He shouldn't have expected her to understand. In the heat of the moment he had relished the bloodshed, but the guilt that weighed on him afterward was immeasurable. Even the guards that met them in battle had hardly been trained. It wasn't a proud victory; it was murder. But the dead would get no sympathy here, and neither would he. He swallowed angry words before they could leave his tongue and searched his tangled thoughts for something calmer to say.

"They didn't deserve to die. They were only peasants. Farmers." Daemon doubted that made any difference to her. His claws traced over his mask, though he did not remove it. Instead, he buried his masked face in his scaly palms. He felt Lumia climb onto the bed and he cringed when she draped her arms around his shoulders from behind. Her fingers toyed with the laces at the front of his tunic.

He batted her hand away. "I shouldn't have let the situation grow the way it did. I let it get out of hand." Idly, he wondered if she had ever even experienced guilt. "We should have gone in the night, raided in shadow and left before they knew we were there."

"Do not mourn for them, my pet." Lumia pressed soft kisses to the back of his neck while she traced swirls on his sleeve. "If anything, you've done them a favor by freeing them of this miserable island. And now you know what you are capable of! You've seen the power you can have over men. Just imagine what it will be like when an entire kingdom is yours to command."

He grunted and twisted as if to shrug her off.

"Besides," Lumia sighed, "would things be any different if you hadn't joined me?" She reached around and touched the back of his hand. Her fingertips lingered over the scar there for longer than he liked.

"Yes." Daemon pulled away from her affections.

"You were built for war, Daemon." Her voice hardened. "Your creator wanted you for your strength and that alone. The mages only wished to take advantage of you. They never saw there was a man trapped inside that body. They never even tried to see there was a mind."

He turned his head and glared at her with one baleful violet eye.

"You are not the cold-blooded monster they wished you to be. You're stronger, better. Better than them. You are perfect, my love." She pressed her cheek to the back of his shoulder as her hand slid around to reach for his mask. He caught her by the wrist and she wriggled her fingers with a smirk.

"I'm not in the mood for games," he growled.

"And I am not playing," she replied. "Stay loyal, pet, and I will give you power. All you are owed and more. If they wish to see a monster, then that is what we shall show them. A beast, a monster, a tyrant king." She laughed, the sound all too pleasant for the weight of the things they discussed.

Daemon thought of pushing her away. Lumia was the one who had ordered him to lead the raid; the blood should have been on her hands, not his. But then his thoughts turned to the shackles that mages had threatened him with years before, and the memory scattered whatever feelings of rebellion had stirred. "I am loyal," he managed, though he had to force his voice to remain steady. He'd heard the oath from other men countless times, but saying the words himself nearly made his tongue curl. "I am an obedient servant. I will do as my queen commands me."

Lumia smiled, a cold gleam in her eyes. "The raid was your first test, pet. You've proven your worth better than I could have imagined. You now lead all my armies," she whispered, nestling her face into his dark hair and breathing deeply. "My General Daemon."

The words made him shiver. She chuckled.

Uneasy, he turned his head. "There is another matter I

wanted to address, about Tren—" he started, but her finger pressed to his lips beneath his mask. It took effort to restrain his frustration, but he knew better than to disobey.

"Come, my pet. That's enough talk for tonight." Curving her body against his, she pulled him between the crimson silk sheets of her bed.

KING KIFELETHELAS LEANED BACK IN HIS CHAIR, STROKING HIS CHIN as he read the missive a second time. The crest that had accompanied it lay on his desk. It wasn't even a decent quality of jade; there were too many inclusions and striations of other stone. Its front bore a crude carving that resembled a scorpion, the back etched with lettering from the mainland. It was a design he'd seen many times in Alwhen's markets before the border between kingdoms was closed, and it had remained popular among more rebellious Giftless factions. Its arrival in one of his border villages was troubling enough.

At least the letter wasn't difficult to understand. Likely penned by a border sentry, it contained none of the fancy wordplay officers used to make themselves sound clever. If the information within it was correct, there wouldn't be anyone of higher rank still living to send the message.

Armored men had ransacked the border village of Charth and slaughtered peasants and soldiers alike. That was all it said. Border skirmishes were not unusual, but a raid of the violent extent described in the letter was something Kifel couldn't recall happening before.

Weary, he rubbed his eyes. Had it even been a week since he'd left the Archmage's office? He'd already sent word to the rest of the border outposts and received messages in response from each. Not a single border station had seen an army move in from the east. But the very edge of the ruins sat, unguarded, on Giftless lands. The ruins, where tradition and legend deemed the land sacred. Where neither he nor Relythes, the king in the east, could claim ownership. Where they couldn't have any eyes.

The temple was as close to the ruins as it could be. Founded partially under the pretense of training mages to serve both kingdoms on the island, it had been Kifel's way of putting eyes where he wasn't supposed to have any. But those eyes were not looking where they should, and if Envesi would not uphold her half of the bargain, why should he support the temple? Mages were useful, no doubt, but there was no reason they couldn't be trained in the chapter houses scattered across his lands. Kifel twisted the missive into a roll again and took the jade crest from the table as he cast a glance to the page by the door.

"Send word to the court mages," Kifel ordered as he pushed himself from his chair. "Have them prepare a Gate to Kirban Temple immediately."

The boy nodded and scurried away before Kifel reached the door.

The halls of Castle Ilmenhith loomed empty ahead of him, though the solstice would see the palace filled to bursting with nobles, mages, and soldiers. Reservations for the traveling mages would have to be made with the inns ahead of time, he reminded himself. The missive and crest in his hand soured his mood, but he couldn't allow them to distract from the menial tasks that still required his attention.

The crackling portal was waiting when Kifel arrived. He kept a room set aside specifically for Gating, a small parlor with a stone archway constructed in the middle. All unnecessary, the mages assured him, but it gave him peace of mind to see such powerful magic worked in a controlled environment. An image of the temple library filled the archway, almost too crisp to be real. Half a dozen mages in blue-trimmed white stood in a half-circle around the back of the Gate, their heads bowed. He needed more court mages, as well. Kifel mentally added them to the list of necessities.

"Follow me and restore the Gate from the other side after I

pass through," he ordered as he braced himself for the short trip. "I shouldn't be gone long."

Moving through a Gate was always disconcerting. It seemed like there should have been some sort of uncomfortable tingle or prickle as he passed through the portal. From what he understood, that was precisely what mages felt. With no awakened Gift to speak of—ironic, for the king of the Eldani—Kifel felt nothing at all as he stepped from his palace to the temple's library. Traveling such distance in a single step was unnerving in its own right, though the way it made the hair stand on the back of his neck was the least of his concerns.

The library was empty, which was fortunate enough, given that he was hardly in the mood to deal with unwanted attention. Kifel had asked more than once for an anchor point to be placed in the Archmage's office. More than once, the request had been ignored. Without an anchor, a Gate could only be passed through in one direction. If cooperative mages could be found at a destination, Kifel typically relied on them to return him to the palace. With his temper on edge, he trusted only his own mages. They followed him through the portal and arranged themselves in the library to wait.

The trip up the stairs to Envesi's office was short. Her door stood partway open to let a breeze circulate through the upper floors. Kifel didn't bother to knock.

If Envesi noticed his presence, she gave no indication of it. She didn't look up from the papers that covered her desk, her quill scratching tidy notes on the edges of a page. Kifel's jaw tightened. He crossed the room in broad strides and cast the jade crest onto her notes. Its edge knocked the quill from her hand.

"We only just discussed the border, and today I receive word that one of my outposts was ransacked by men pouring from the ruins you're supposed to be guarding." He kept his words as neutral as he could, despite the itch of irritation that crawled between his shoulder blades. "Aside from rather interesting timing, given our last conversation, is it not concerning to think an entire army of raiders could slip past you without notice?"

Her eyes did not leave the papers. For a moment, he wasn't certain she even saw the crest. The long silence that met his question fueled his agitation. Little quirks were still what bothered him most, but her skill at ignoring him was rising quickly through the ranks.

But the Archmage did move, eventually, resting her elbows on the edge of the table and steepling her fingers together. "Are you sure of it?"

The question made Kifel snort and he gestured to the carved disk on the table. "What do you think?" he almost snapped. "There's only one way they could have gotten onto my lands without notice."

Envesi arched one fine white brow as she took the emblem and turned it over in hand. "There's no mistaking what happened, I only ask why you think negligence on the part of my mages caused it."

"I trust my subjects." Kifel's eyes narrowed. Regardless of what power she had, he was king. She would do well to remember his rank. "And I trust my soldiers. If what they're saying is true, then it means the situation here has already gotten out of hand."

Her thin lips twitched into a frown and the Archmage laid down the carving. She tucked her hands into the wide, snowy sleeves of her robes as she folded her arms over her chest. "What is it you are accusing me of, my liege?"

"You swore to me that if anything happened, you would let me know." His voice went cold and his emerald eyes hardened. "I consider this something, Envesi. I would like to know why you've said nothing to me. You stay here for a reason, and if you cannot keep matters under your thumb, I will not hesitate to find someone else to watch over this mess of a temple you started."

"Did it ever cross your mind that I could be unaware of the situation?" She gave a slow shrug, leaning back in her chair. "I am not omnipresent, Kifel. Do you wish me to stare out the windows all day, or study matters you place on my desk?"

"I do not allow you to run this temple and be *unaware*. You know the reason you were given this land. You know why you have the funding you have. I need someone stationed outside the ruins, to keep an eye on matters, to keep me informed in case something like *this* happened." His tone dropped low. "This problem is of your creation, mind you."

"I fail to see how a mere band of thieves could threaten our king." Envesi did not roll her eyes, but Kifel thought she looked close to it.

"You are treading a fine line, Envesi." He took the jade crest from the table and absently slipped it into a pocket. "Now prove you have a handle on the situation, or I will handle it myself, if I have to tear down half the ruins to do it. Fail me again and you lose everything. Understand?"

Envesi bowed her head in some mockery of graciousness. "As you wish. These bandits will be brought to accord."

"I am in need of more court mages, as well." Now that he thought of it, it had been several years since a new mage had joined those at the palace. Where she sent all of them after they graduated, he didn't know.

She visibly suppressed a sigh. Good of her to mind her manners for a change. "The students you have entrusted to me are being given the finest training possible. Several will be ready to graduate within the year. Though I ask more time to rein in your favorite student before I turn him loose in your armies."

"Granted," Kifel nodded, though the single word carried a bitter undertone.

"I am grateful, Your Majesty." She rose from her chair to sweep into an elegant bow. "Rest assured, you will not be disappointed again."

Kifel eyed her for a long moment, his fingers tracing the twisted hilt of his sword. His hand stilled when he caught himself doing it. "Good," he said, finally. "See to it I'm not."

He felt the weight of Envesi's eyes as he strode out of her tower, and he could not help the grim expression that drew itself upon his face.

LUMIA WASN'T CERTAIN WHERE DAEMON WENT TO SLEEP, AS HIS quarters were usually empty, but she didn't care. Before his hand had been branded, there was the possibility he would try to escape. Now, she doubted he could. The mark she had given him granted her more control than he realized. It was not the first time she'd formed a blood-bond, though she was inclined to say it was the most fulfilling.

She found him fascinating. Daemon was a far cry from being human or Eldani, though his effort to hide scale-covered flesh when not in her presence didn't escape her notice. He had the form of a man, at least, and when he bound his hands and feet in wrappings and found a way to conceal his claws, he might have passed for one. In the privacy of her chambers, though, she savored everything that made him different. She enjoyed the unnatural strength in his body, reveled in how powerless he made her feel beneath the crushing weight of his form. Only rarely was she left unsatisfied when he excused himself from her chambers. He had not disappointed tonight.

Lumia lounged in the chair at her desk after he took his leave. She could feel him, though faintly enough to know he was no longer underground. The dim pulse of his presence grew weaker still as a stronger, nearer presence took precedence. Their bond let her know who approached before the door opened, though the angry, heavy booted steps in the hallway were enough to tell her that. A saccharine smile curved her lips as she trained her eyes on the books spread across the desk.

"*General* Daemon?" The words were half demand, half growl.

"A pleasure to see you, Tren, as always. News certainly travels fast, doesn't it?" Lumia ran her fingers down the ragged

79

spine of a book and chuckled. "Did he tell you himself, or did you have an ear pressed to my door?"

"You're making a mistake," Tren snarled. He stopped only inches behind her chair.

"Well, I didn't ask for your opinion, did I." She craned her neck to look at him over her shoulder. "Goodness, Tren, learn to give people chances."

His breath hitched as he inhaled and his fingers curled around the hilt of his sword. "I am the only leader your army needs. My word should be enough. No chances, no outside trust. *It* is an outsider and a risk, whether or not you'll admit it."

"He was an outsider, but he has never been an *it*. Mind your temper, or you'll be doing worse than losing rank to him." She picked up a book and paged through it with feigned interest. His anger simmered in the back of her mind. It was entertaining to fan the flame.

"I don't care if you're queen of the ruin-folk, the Eldani, whatever it is you want to become." Tren shook his head and set to pacing. "You're being foolish and I won't stand for it. I won't let you risk what we've built by putting that *thing* into *my* position of command!"

"Daemon is perfectly responsible," Lumia replied calmly. "He has a home among our people and he's trained for strategy and combat."

"This raid was his first actual combat experience, and we all know how well he handled that."

She scoffed. "Don't pretend I can't see your jealousy. He's younger, stronger, more talented. Our people fear and respect him. You might have sway over the rabble, but the respect the officers had for you has been waning for years."

That needled him. Lumia sensed more than she saw the way his shoulders bunched and his step faltered.

Not yet satisfied, she pushed a little farther. "You're jealous of my plans to put him on a surface throne instead of you, is that it?" A demure smile flitted across her features as her eyes skimmed him from head to toe. "Or is it simply because I could never look at you the way I look at him?"

Tren had appointed himself as leader of her army long before she made use of him. With his squared jaw and strong features, and his dark hair and coarse goatee trimmed close in a soldier's style, he still looked the part. It was clear that heading an army was not enough to satisfy him. Her eyes settled on the scar in his hand; a different mark than what Daemon wore, but her mark, nonetheless. He'd sworn a blood oath to her as well, though she suspected he meant to defy it.

"I wouldn't want it," he spat, shaking his head in disgust. "Your affection for him is sick."

Lumia rose and brushed past him on her way to her bed. "He's grown a lot since I first caught him trespassing here, you know. Not that I expect you to know what he is."

"A monster," Tren said.

The corners of her mouth twitched, but she wouldn't give him the pleasure of getting a rise out of her. "The mages may have discarded him for the way his form was twisted, but he is well worth our time. He's only beginning to make his abilities blossom as they should, no thanks to those Gifted wretches set up on our borders." She snorted. "Daemon's power does not know the limits that I do. His is raw chaos. Unfathomable, perhaps limitless. With time, he could become the greatest mage to ever walk the earth."

A look of disbelief worked its way across Tren's face, followed by deep thoughtfulness. He lifted a hand to stroke his beard. "A war machine," he murmured slowly. "Which means..."

"That the stories of the ancient mages are true." A devious spark glittered in her eyes. "So please, offer him a little more respect. He is on our side, after all. My plans and purpose remain true to our cause. I simply see no reason not to use their own tools against them."

His eyes narrowed as he digested the new information.

"Now," she sighed, gesturing to the door. "I grow tired. I'd like to sleep. Run along. Perhaps sharing your words of experienced wisdom will help keep Daemon's new power from going to his head."

Tren gritted his teeth, but he still bowed. "I will see to it, Majesty." He clutched the hilt of his sword tight enough to turn his knuckles white and murmured in tones only just audible as he made for the door. "Rest assured, I will."

His anger tickled in the back of her head, and Lumia smiled.

8

LEASH

"Did you know two blue magelings quit the temple last week? Two! Can you imagine studying that long, only to give up one rank before Master?" Ran shook his head. The motion cast his sandy-colored hair into his eyes. He brushed it back, irritated. Even when he scowled that way, Kytenia found him charming. "No patience for decent opportunities to come along," he muttered.

"Oh, and you're so comfortable waiting for opportunity to present itself?" Kytenia lifted an eyebrow and smiled at him. He gave her a dirty look and she returned her attention to the task at hand. Little jobs like mending were something she enjoyed. That she was doing it for Ran was just a bonus. Kytenia's cheeks reddened at the thought and she tried not to look at him again.

She'd been surprised when he'd caught her after class and asked her to mend a tear in his training uniform. Having spoken with Firal the night before, she knew what it was from, and she struggled to hide her amusement.

"Quit looking so serious." She tugged the new seam a little tighter. "You're so much better to look at when you smile."

Ran snorted and his scowl deepened. "Are you done yet? I'm going to be late if you don't hurry up."

"I wasn't aware there were going to be more classes today." Kytenia did not hurry, and instead maintained a steady pace of small, even stitches. She barely glanced up when a scullery maid passed by. The dinner hall had cleared out after the meal. Aside from the few maids gathering dishes, they were alone.

Ran shifted on the table he used for a seat and let his eyes wander. "Not classes. Evaluations. They're holding them early for higher-ranking students. From what I gather, the stress from evaluations is why magelings are leaving."

"It sounds like the Masters are being more aggresive than usual this year," Kytenia said. "Maybe they'll hold early evaluations for the lower ranks, too." Ran's blue robes in her hands were a harsh reminder of his place above her in the temple. If his evaluations went well, a yellow mageling like her would be far beneath his notice. She changed the subject.

"I've heard the Masters are planning to allow a break after the solstice. Do you have plans to visit home?" The needle pricked her finger and she winced.

"That depends," Ran said slowly. The way his brows drew together gave her the impression the words were a burden. "On how evaluations turn out, that is."

"What do you mean?" Kytenia sucked her finger until the pain faded. "Will your parents be displeased if you don't pass with flying colors?"

He scuffed the toe of his boot against the floor. "Actually, passing is what I'm afraid of. If I do too well, the Masters will graduate me out of the temple before I'm ready to leave."

Surprised, she let her needle grow still. "Why wouldn't you want to get out of here? There's nothing I'd love more than to graduate and go back home. I could set up as the village healer like I've always planned. It would be wonderful."

"Because if I graduate, I have to go home for good. Not that staying here is much better." It was hard to tell if the sour note in his voice was despair or irritation. He didn't speak of home

often, but it was clear he didn't regard the place with the same love Kytenia felt for hers.

She let the conversation drop, knotting the thread and cutting off the excess before returning his robes. "All done."

"Thanks." Ran held up the garment to inspect it. Apparently satisfied, he pulled it on overhead and settled it on top of his plain tunic and trousers. The robes weren't tailored, and were not particularly flattering to anyone. His was much too short; the sleeves ended closer to his elbow than his wrist. It looked odd. Kytenia itched to offer adjustments to correct the fit, but if he was in a hurry, now was not the time.

"Good luck with your evaluations. I hope you fail." She cringed at the way the words came out, but he laughed.

"It's an odd desire, I know. I'm sure you'll hear how it turns out later." He flashed her a grin that made her blush. "And thanks again, Kyt. I owe you one."

She laughed and waved a dismissive hand as he started off at an easy pace, but her smile only clung until she was alone in the quiet dining hall.

Kytenia had never devoted a lot of thought to the ranks held by her friends. Firal was a rank above her. Ran was two. What would happen to their friendships when they graduated out and became Masters, scattered to the winds or put in positions of power over those they'd grown up with? Fraternization between magelings and Masters was forbidden. Would simple conversation become a thing of the past?

Unsettled, Kytenia bowed her head and set to collecting her things.

———

As much confidence as he put on, Ran couldn't recall a time he'd been more reluctant to cross the temple courtyard. The wide doors of the Archmage's tower stood open to the unusually pleasant day, but he stopped outside them and peered up the side of the tower. He already knew the Archmage meant to pass him to the next rank. That wasn't the problem. He was more concerned with finding a way to stay in the temple. Not only because he didn't want to go home, as he'd told Kytenia; more than anything, it was because he knew he wasn't ready.

Out of all the temple's magelings, Ran was certain he ranked among the strongest. But despite his strength, his grasp of power and his technique wielding it left much to be desired. His knowledge was piecemeal, his power out of control. Had he been present for more lessons, perhaps that would have been different. Yet the Archmage wouldn't have called him for an evaluation if she didn't mean for him to graduate, indicating she cared little about his actual skill. His stomach twisted and he swallowed hard against the knot in his throat as he crossed the threshold into the tower.

The first floor was pleasantly bright, despite its lack of windows. Ran wondered how many more chances he'd have to linger there. Low rows of shelving invited him to hide. The soothing scent of old books mingled with the fragrance from fresh-cut flowers from the gardens and he breathed deep. The library had always been his favorite part of the temple. Now, standing just inside the doorway, he feared this visit would be his last.

He'd always known his position in the temple was precarious, and that the Archmage would find some way to use his Gift against him. Tradition dictated he shouldn't have been allowed enrollment at all, unless he sacrificed the other half of his life and focused solely on magecraft. But his power was too dangerous to leave untrained, though he snorted at the idea it was trained at all. Ran knew just enough to pose a threat to anyone who crossed his path, but not enough to realize his full potential. He had long suspected the Masters kept it that way on purpose. Some treaty to harmonize the halves of who he was, perhaps.

A staircase in the far corner led to the second floor, where more books waited. Ran scaled past them and climbed through floors that hosted offices, research rooms, studies, and the personal chambers of some of the oldest and highest ranking Masters. The doors that led to the Archmage's office stood open in anticipation of his arrival. He grimaced when he saw her on the other side.

"I haven't all day," Envesi said, a curt edge to her voice. "Come in, so I can get this over with."

Ran forced himself to stand up straight, but kept his eyes focused on the floor as he stepped in and shut the doors behind him. "I am ready to be tested, Archmage."

She sneered. "Your false humility is insulting. Stand still, I don't need to see your abilities to gauge them."

He stopped in the center of the room and clenched his hands to fists at his sides as the Archmage circled him. He sensed the flow of power in her; her strength was exceptional, her presence almost overwhelming. It made him uncomfortable and he resisted the urge to shift.

"I've been watching you," Envesi said as she paced around him, her hands clasped behind her back. "You show no outward signs of growth. Your hair does not fade. Your eyes are not those of a mage at your level." She made a small, disapproving sound in her throat and continued her circling. "If you wish to channel it with ease, you shouldn't be reluctant to let the power flow."

"Even if I allowed it to bleach my hair and eyes, would you really want a show of my power this early on?" He tried to keep it from sounding like a challenge. Though the temple offered him many privileges, she was his superior and demanded respect. At least, whenever she was within earshot.

The Archmage's silvery-blue eyes narrowed. "Do you even know the measure of your strength? Do you know its limits? Your power is unrefined. You have not chosen a direction to grow."

"I saw no need." Ran lifted his chin to stare straight ahead. "Not every mage finds a specialty within their element. I see no reason to restrict myself to one skill." The greatest Masters did not limit themselves, and he'd always assumed them right. Why ought a mage with an earth affinity restrict themselves to dirt and never touch stone? Why would a mage with an air affinity stir the clouds in the sky, but never think to move anything else with their power? He could imagine no greater waste.

"Reasonable, but it does not exempt you from selecting an area to pursue as a specialty, and it does not explain why you fear your own strength." She stopped before him and grasped his jaw. Her fingers dug into his flesh as she forced him to tilt his face down and look her in the eye. Her power gave the impression she had greater stature than what she actually possessed. The look on her face told him she didn't like being reminded it was an illusion. "You're young and your power is raw. You still require a good deal of training and refinement to be useful, but as I intended, your strength already surpasses that of some of our Masters. You need only be brave enough to unleash it."

"I'm not afraid," Ran said.

A smile played upon her lips. "Aren't you?" She released his chin and chuckled to herself, gesturing to a chair as she returned to her desk. "Sit down, child."

He didn't need to be instructed twice, seating himself as Envesi took a small vial from her desk. She held it to the light, tilted it and watched the glass gleam.

"The time will come when our mages are hailed everywhere, recognized for their power. Already we are respected in both kingdoms on this island, given special privilege because of what we do. Soon, we shall spread that authority to the mainland, as well." The Archmage smiled, though the expression was cold. "In you I see the fruition of my best laid plans. To see you as strong as you are now, as raw as your ability may be, is an interesting reflection of all we have accomplished."

"What you've accomplished?" Ran asked. "Or what you haven't yet?"

Her jaw clenched and she curled her fingers around the vial as she stalked toward his chair. "I grow tired of playing the king's political games. I have my own duties and I am not here to hide his mistakes." She caught hold of his hair and pulled back his head to peer into his vibrant blue eyes.

He stared back, defiant.

"Do not lose your fire, my child," she whispered as she raised the vial. "That anger that simmers inside you will be the source of your power."

Ran didn't have time to blink. Stinging droplets poured into one eye and then the other, blacking out his vision. He stifled a shout, his fingers digging at the seat of the chair. She held him fast, forcing him to keep his head back. He struggled to blink the ink away. Tears welled in his eyes before he finally squeezed them shut.

"Good boy." She watched in satisfaction as the black drops rolled from the corners of his eyes and left dark trails in their wake. She dabbed away the excess ink with a stained cloth and blew gently to dry the markings before she allowed him to sit upright.

"What was that?" Ran snapped. His hands went to his face as he fought the impulse to rub his smarting eyes. His vision was blurred, but he glared nonetheless.

"Graduation, my child. As a Master assigned to the king's court, you may use your magic however you see fit. Only the Masters of the affinities and the head of the court mages hold rank over you." Envesi smiled grimly. She pressed the ink vial into the palm of his hand and closed his fingers around it. "You may choose your own markings. I suggest a great deal of practice before you present yourself in public. With time, you will grow used to the sting."

Ran's face twitched into a scowl. With how badly his eyes hurt, he doubted that.

The Archmage stepped back and flicked her fingers toward the door. "You may now return home."

BETH ALVAREZ

"I don't want to go home." The burning in his eyes lingered long after the shadow of the ink was dispelled from his vision.

"Why? Do you not wish for freedom?" The Archmage's expression was more challenge than question.

Ran hesitated. His gaze from her face to the vial of ink in his hand. "I'm not ready to face him."

"I see." Envesi cut a path to the tray-laden table against the wall. "Do you wish to stay here, then? We've always been happy to make exceptions for you." She moved a polished silver cup to the edge of the table and filled it from a matching coffee pot.

"Because of my power?" The words bubbled on the tip of his tongue like acid. "Is that why you'd keep me here? So that you might use me?"

The Archmage thunked the coffee pot against the table. "Do not challenge me, boy. No matter how strong you think your magic, you cannot stand against me. You are a tool, nothing more. Do not let your upbringing convince you otherwise."

"You insult my strength and my family." Ran's shoulders tensed as he rose from his chair. "Interesting."

"I may insult you as I wish. Don't you remember who brought you here? Who gave you permission to break every precedent the Masters set? It was not your noble father, I can assure you that." Envesi rolled her eyes and almost laughed. "I refuse to tolerate ungratefulness. Rein in your tongue, boy."

"Have I not done everything you asked of me?" Frustration made his throat grow thick and his voice climbed in volume. "I've learned everything the Masters offered! Isn't that what you wanted?"

"Please." Envesi took a long sip of her coffee. "I merely hoped for a powerful soldier. You deliver in all the wrong situations, and my recent dealings with Kifel leave me with no patience for an impudent whelp who is not even of Eldani blood."

The insult cut deep and Ran's power stirred with his rising anger. He caught it and struggled to contain it. Magic was

90

sensitive to emotion, and she was right; anger did fuel his strength. He refused to let it rule.

"Very well," Envesi said, the curl at the corner of her mouth indicating she'd enjoyed his brief struggle. "You wish to stay here? So be it. You have not outlived your usefulness. From this moment forward, you shall consider yourself leashed." Her cup clicked against its saucer, crisp and final. "You will play the part of lap dog for your beloved king, but remember who holds your lead."

The suggestion that lurked between her words fell on him like the kingdom's weight. From any other mouth, that order would have bordered on treason. Mages were afforded a great deal of power, but spying on the king? Ran bristled, but forced his expression to remain neutral. He'd gotten what he wanted. Permission to stay. Everything else could be dealt with later. He slid the ink vial into a hidden pocket in his robes and bowed his head. "Understood."

Envesi waved a hand toward the door. "Now get out of my sight."

Gritting his teeth, Ran offered an insincere bow and excused himself from the Archmage's office. His eyes still burned and his new role scorched his stomach like ice. He walked faster to escape the tower and clawed his blue robes off over his head.

THE GROWL OF DISTANT THUNDER MADE FIRAL WINCE. UNDER normal circumstances, she wouldn't have been concerned, but each untimely rainstorm reduced her chances of finding her journal still intact. This was her third excursion in effort to find it, and she'd resigned herself to the knowledge that her book would not outlive another storm.

Her mother's pendant was another story.

While she tempered her expectations, Firal couldn't shake excitement over the impending trip to the palace from her head.

A chance to speak to the court mages was a chance to get answers no one in the temple could provide. But without her necklace, she had nothing to support her claim her mother had served as part of the king's court, nothing to convince the court mages to give her the information she so desperately sought. The journal could be replaced, but she needed that necklace, no matter what.

Clouds had drifted in from the horizon, covering the sky in a blanket of soft gray. The position of the sun had grown hard to distinguish, and the biting edge to the breeze indicated the rain would be cold. Firal shrugged her cloak forward and hugged it close around her shoulders. She tried to recall the twists of the hallways, but the corridor she was in looped back on itself and made it difficult to keep her bearings. In passing, she considered climbing on top of a wall for a better view of where she was going, but she doubted the walls could support her weight.

Although the walls throughout the ruins had decayed, the worst of the damage seemed to be at the edges. The farther she went, the more solid they appeared. A few walls still lay crumbling, the stone covered in moss and lichen or swallowed by ferns and creeping vines. Deeper in, the plant life was more vibrant. Vines and bushes bloomed with oddly shaped flowers, and colorful hanging mosses dangled from the tops of the walls. A fully-grown tree loomed over the ruins not far ahead and, despite the coming storm, its presence piqued her curiosity. Firal was familiar with the saplings that grew in the outer rings, but she'd never seen a mature tree.

The plants that choked the path tripped her as she tried to get past them and she leaned against the wall to free her sandal from a tangle of vines. The unbeaten path bulged where the tree's knobby roots pushed through and the walls buckled where the stones had been displaced. Brushing dirt off her hands, Firal crept around the corner toward the tree.

An elliptical room opened before her and her breath caught. Despite all her exploration, she'd never found any rooms. Broken pillars indicated there had once been a ceiling. The tree replaced it now, growing in the very center of the space. Its canopy was flat on the underside and gave it the distinct look of a mushroom. Rounded fruits the size of eggs hung from its branches, their rinds a varied sprinkle of purple and blue among the leaves.

The tree itself was massive. Three men with fingertips touching would not have been able to encompass its trunk. Odd scrolls of unfamiliar lettering were burned into the bark just above the roots, wrapped around the trunk in a lazy spiral that reached toward its crown. Firal crept closer and laid a hand against the markings.

"It says, *'From roots and bark to leafing tips, all echoed in this seed.'* It's incomplete. I suppose there was no room for the whole poem."

Firal started and wheeled to face the doorway.

A man in leather armor leaned against the wall with arms folded over his chest. The hood of his dark cloak was drawn, his shadowed face further hidden by a mask that was little more than a shapeless scrap of metal.

"I'll give you a moment to tell me what you're doing here," he said, voice icily calm. "Answer well and you might get a chance to run."

"I—" Firal stumbled back against the tree. "I was just—"

"Time's up." He pushed himself off the wall and reached for the battle-worn sword at his hip. "And here I was kind enough to give you a warning. I told you not to come back." The dark eyes of his mask flickered to life, glowing brilliant crimson. The sight sparked memory and Firal went pale.

The moment he stepped forward, she bolted.

Firal scrambled past the swell of the great tree's roots and ran for an opening on the far side of the room. Screaming would do nothing. Running was her only option. Her feet beat against the uneven ground, her heart drumming against her ribs. Lightning crackled overhead, blinding her, making her footsteps falter. She stifled a cry and struggled to regain balance, silently cursing her curiosity as she skidded around the first corner. She should have left before the storm.

"You can't outrun me!" the stranger laughed behind her. "But go ahead. Run, like a scared little rabbit!" His voice carried on the wind as the sky opened and torrential rains crashed down.

Firal jerked her cloak forward against the beating rain. The thunder made her heart skip. Flashes overhead illuminated the rolling clouds as they darkened to black. Storm winds roared over the roofless corridors, whipped back her hood and lashed her dark hair about her face.

He clawed his way up to stand atop the crumbling walls. "You'll only prolong the hunt, little rabbit. Keep running, I'll trap you either way!"

She darted left into a curved hallway and threw a glance over her shoulder, just long enough to catch sight of him on the wall. The air grew green, the rain like needles on her skin.

The deafening boom of thunder rang in her ears as vibrations shook pebbles loose from the walls. Firal shrieked and threw her arms overhead as a decaying wall began to slide.

Her pursuer leaped down and hit the ground hard. A hand snatched hold of her arm and he threw her down so forcefully, she cried out when she struck the earth.

Stone cracked, a low crunch beneath the high-pitched whine in her ears. He dropped to his hands and knees and braced himself above her. The otherworldly light in his eyes flickered and faded.

She folded her arms over her head as he fell beneath the crushing weight of the collapsing wall and the rubble swallowed them both.

The earth beneath them groaned, and everything faded until only darkness was left.

9

QUEEN

"GET UP."

Firal groaned and pulled away from the hand that jostled her shoulder. She was cold. The damp stone against her cheek was colder.

"Get up," the voice above her growled. He shook her again.

Dizzy and disoriented, she struggled to open her eyes. Where was she?

Wherever it was, the darkness was oppressive. The air was thick and still, heavy with humidity and the smell of mustiness and earth. Shutting her eyes against the blackness, Firal pushed herself up. A slimy film covered the floor, sticky beneath her hands and knees. The cold made her limbs stiff. Sitting upright took some effort.

A pair of dimly glowing violet lights appeared next to her and she shrieked. A leather-clad hand clapped over her mouth to silence her.

"Shh!" The hiss was close enough that she felt the warmth of his breath spill from behind his mask. His glowing eyes turned toward something she couldn't see and his gloved fingers pressed against her mouth hard enough it hurt. She squealed in protest and flailed at him in the dark. Her knee struck something, yielding a grunt.

"Quit moving," he commanded.

Firal glowered in what she assumed was his direction, but stilled. His hand over her mouth eased and he looked away again, listening, though she didn't know for what. The occasional *plink* of dripping water was all that broke the silence. Seeming both satisfied with and disappointed by the quiet, he turned his attention to her again.

Firal's eyes widened when his gaze locked with hers. It was strange enough that his eyes glowed and stranger still that the centers were slit like a snake's, but strangest was the way the varying shades of purple in his eyes seemed to swirl and twist. She shuddered, but couldn't bring herself to look away. The slow shift of color proved mesmerizing in the dark.

"Relax." He drew his hand from her mouth. She heard him shift with a soft grunt of pain, then felt him ease down to sit beside her. "I hoped you'd learn your lesson after the first time I tried to spook you out. I suppose I was wrong to assume you would."

"Spook me out?" Firal repeated, her voice thick with disbelief. "I thought you were going to kill me!"

"Well, I don't think that's in my best interest." He moved farther away from her, his breath labored. "Make light."

"What?"

"You're a mageling, aren't you? Make light," he snapped. "Use your powers."

Firal hesitated a moment before she decided not to argue. Her hands explored the slimy ground until she found a small, elongated piece of stone and curled her fingers around it. Magelings were not permitted to use their Gift outside of controlled practice sessions within the temple. Though she wasn't against sneaking an occasional flame for her lantern on her own, she was reluctant to break the rules now that a stranger bade her do it. But wherever they'd fallen, it was so dark she couldn't see anything but his strangely illuminated eyes. A light would help. If she was going to escape from whatever this place was, she didn't have a choice.

Warmth blossomed against her palm and a red glow outlined her fingers. Firal opened her hand and the stranger beside her twisted away from the light with a sharp growl. She squinted against the mage-light and waited for her eyes to adjust. When they did, she yelped.

They sat in a vast crypt. Row after row of carved stone sarcophagi filled the room, more standing upright along the walls with bones piled between them. A thin, white film floated atop shallow water pooled in the crevices and hollows of the floor.

One of the sarcophagi lay in pieces where stones had fallen through the ceiling, presumably along with the two of them. Bones and copper coins mingled with the dark shards of sculpted stone and paler rock from the ruin walls. Firal's eyes drifted to the vaulted stone ceiling that arched overhead. A single hint of light shone between the broken branches, stone, and what she thought were tree roots that sealed the gap they must have come through. She only vaguely recalled falling. The hole they'd come through was a good twenty feet up, and smaller than she'd expected. It was a miracle she'd landed without breaking any bones.

The sound of movement beside her drew her attention. She turned and squealed when she discovered her attacker only inches away.

Firal scrambled backwards, pushed herself to her feet and clung desperately to the tiny mage-light she'd created. "Stay back!"

In spite of his mask, the look he gave her was clearly skeptical. "Really?"

He had pulled up his hood and was struggling to loosen the straps of his leather armor. He sucked in a hissing breath every time he jostled his leg. Dark liquid plastered his trousers to his calf and his sleeve to his arm, both on the same side. He had taken off his gloves, and what lay beneath made her stomach flop.

Four-fingered hands, scaled and tipped with claws. They made the memories of childhood stories and the spook-tales of Underlings come flooding back.

"Who are you?" She held the light before her as if it were some sort of weapon, something she could deter him with. Never mind that he'd asked her to make it.

He'd produced a knife from somewhere and used it to tear strips from the bottom of his cloak. The scent of blood tainted the air. He stifled a curse as he wrapped the makeshift bandage around his arm and struggled to knot it one-handed. "My queen calls me Daemon."

"Your queen?" Her brows lifted. Both halves of the island were ruled by kings who had no queen. "What queen?"

"I think that's enough questions," Daemon growled, struggling to get up.

She retreated as he moved, but his leg buckled and he abandoned the attempt with a sound of discomfort and frustration.

A low, frustrated huff escaped him. "Come here, mageling." It was less of a request and more of an order, but Firal did not budge.

Her eyes drifted over him, from his plain metal mask to the claws that tipped his three-toed, too-reptilian feet. Unconsciously, she tightened her hand around the mage-light.

"What's the matter?" he taunted. "Are you afraid of me?"

"Why wouldn't I be?" she replied hoarsely. She had spent her whole life listening to myths about Underlings and other inhuman creatures that walked like men, had read of them in the books kept in the temple library, but she'd never believed they were real. Her mouth had grown dry. She swallowed and forced herself to go on. "You threatened to kill me."

"Kill you?" Daemon laughed aloud, an odd gleam in his

illuminated violet eyes. "I did nothing of the sort. I said I would hunt you and trap you." A note of dry humor colored his voice.

Her eyes drifted toward the ceiling again. "Well, you've done a good job of trapping us both." The mage-light in Firal's hand reached much farther than a flame could have, and though the room was large, most of it was visible. An open doorway waited at the far end of the room. She turned toward it, holding the light in front of her.

"Wait."

She scowled over her shoulder. "What do you want?"

"To be able to stand would be nice." He laid a hand against his thigh, clearly wanting to move but dreading the pain it would cause. "I think I broke your fall a little too well, and broke something else while I was at it."

Guilt pulled at her for just a moment. Then his scales glinted in the light and her queasy fear returned. "I have no reason to help a monster like you." Proud of how venomous the words sounded, she lifted her chin and strode toward the doorway.

"Firal," he called after her.

She froze at the sound of her name. He knew her? How? She'd never spoken to this creature before. He'd known she was a mageling, but anyone who was Gifted could sense the presence of another mage.

Her stomach dropped as she realized she could feel Daemon's presence behind her. She hadn't noticed it before, distracted by her discoveries in the ruins. Now that she focused on it, his Gift swelled in her senses, betraying immense raw power. A chill rolled down her spine.

A soft rustle reached her ears. "Ahem. *Today I found strange writing on a wall. The letters were filled with moss and hard to read. I almost hated to scrape off the growth, as it feels wrong to alter anything I find in this most sacred place.*' Sacred, really?" Daemon chuckled. "Ah, there are drawings, too. Not much of an artist, but no one is perfect. Let's see. '*When I left the dinner hall this afternoon, it was raining. That was no surprise, but coming back to my* room to find the temple's new chickens loose in it certainly was. I suspect that Ran—'"

"Give that here!" Firal wheeled just in time to see him snap the plain leather journal closed.

His eyes gleamed behind his mask. "Heal me. Then we'll discuss you getting this back."

Her hands curled into fists at her sides as she resisted a scowl. Fed by her anger, the mage-light in her grasp glowed so brightly that it outlined every bone in her hand. The idea of helping him, even being close to him, made her sick. But he had her journal, and with it, her pendant. She saw no other options. Mentally cursing the predicament she'd landed in, Firal opened her hand to hold up the mage-light and returned to his side.

Despite the mask he wore, she was positive Daemon smirked when she knelt beside him. Loath to touch him, she let her hands hover over his bloodied shin for a moment before she forced herself to lay her fingertips against the sticky cloth of his pants. Healing was dangerous; it drained both the healer and the patient, and it was best to wield the power with extreme care. The magic that flowed through her was little more than a trickle at first, a hint of tingling warmth that seeped down her arms to spill into his body, but when it met and twined with his energies, she gasped at the way it magnified.

His torn flesh burned in her senses—it and the shattered bone in his leg, which bound itself together faster than she'd thought it could mend. Firal had healed a number of her fellow students as part of her training, but she'd never seen a reaction like that. Weariness hit her like a wave and she forced herself to abandon the effort.

"Dear journal, today I met a real, live Underling. He was big and scary, but my poor, tender little mageling heart wouldn't let me walk away," Daemon goaded.

Firal gritted her teeth, clenched a fist and slammed it into his shin. He almost doubled over in pain. Smug satisfaction welled in her chest. If used in time, magic could heal even the most grievous of wounds, but the pain often remained.

"You rotten little chit!" he spat, his slitted eyes flaring crimson behind his mask.

She recoiled, though she regained composure quickly when he didn't lunge after her. "You're healed, now give it here," she ordered. The command came out strong, but Firal tucked her dark hair behind her pointed ears and fussed with the laces that ran up the front of her bodice. If she didn't keep her hands busy, she was certain they would shake.

"I said we would discuss it." His voice carried an edge that matched his acid glare. "After that, I'm not sure I want to be so accommodating."

Firal clenched her jaw. "Be that way, then!" She whipped around and stormed toward the doorway again. "Stay there and rot while you wait for the pain to subside."

"You don't want to go that way."

Ignoring him, she continued on with the mage-light held out before her.

The corridor beyond the doorway was relatively clear. A few pebbles and flakes of stone dotted the damp floor, but little else. The walls on either side were a mixture of gray and black stone that glittered in the light. The floor was uneven, buckling and rising before dipping into shallow puddles. Silt stirred in the water as she sloshed through them, her legs too short to span the pools.

It didn't take long for the corridor to branch into countless hallways. The number of doorways was enough to make her head spin. Firal picked which to take at random, but tried to keep her path to a zigzag. Minutes dragged into what must have been an hour, and the mage-light grew dim. She replenished its magic more than once.

Eventually, she heard the echo of a large room. Eager to escape, she picked up her pace. Her enthusiasm faded when her hurried footsteps carried her into the great crypt again.

Daemon climbed to his feet, though it took him a moment to gain his balance. Evidently, the pain had begun to subside. "Back so soon?"

Firal resisted the urge to glower. "You think you'd do any better?"

"I'm fairly certain I will." His movement was languid and careful. He favored his newly-mended leg and likely would for some time, unless he found a way to dull the pain.

Reluctantly, she trudged toward him. "Where do we go, then?"

"We?" He stifled a laugh. "What makes you think *we* are going anywhere?"

"Because I'm the one with the light."

He regarded her silently for a long moment, then gave a quiet harrumph. "Fine. The corridor at the end of the room, to the right. Since you have the light, you'll lead the way."

"Very well," she agreed, though her mouth pressed into a frown. She wasn't entirely sure she wanted him behind her. Even in a weakened state, he was probably far stronger than she. But she was faster, and she set off at a brisk pace she knew would give him difficulty, slime and gravel crunching beneath her feet.

Now and then she paused and looked back, impatient. Daemon shuffled along quietly, leaning against the wall for support. He gave directions to guide the twists and turns they took, though sometimes he had to pause and think before he chose a direction. It did little to instill confidence that he really knew where they were going. Not that Firal trusted him, anyway —she had merely accepted her odds of escaping the maze-like tunnels were better with his help. Beyond that chase through the ruins aboveground, he hadn't done anything threatening. She suspected that between the mage-light and the healing she'd provided, she'd made herself useful enough to be safe.

"So, an Underling, is it?" Firal broke the silence, her words colored with too much indifference to be natural.

"That's right." A hint of pride touched his voice and he

straightened when she glanced back. "Faithful servant and general to Lumia, Queen of the Underground."

She could have groaned. It was bad enough that she'd lost her journal and her mother's pendant, worse that she had gotten lost while looking for them. But to fall into some long-forgotten maze of a tomb alongside an Underling? Silently, Firal berated herself for dismissing the old stories. More often than not, frightening tales were based on something worth fearing. *And he's a general,* she thought, biting her lip. Of all the monsters to be trapped with, it would happen to be one with rank and power.

The hall branched in multiple directions. She stopped in her tracks and stifled a sigh. She raised the mage-light, but its cool illumination revealed no hint what waited ahead. "Well, General Daemon, where do we go now?"

"Just Daemon will suffice," he replied curtly as he limped forward to peer through each doorway. "I hate titles."

Firal stepped aside to let him look. "And yet you're so willing to flaunt that you have one." But if he really was a general, why was he out in the ruins on his own? Generals belonged in war rooms or planning tents, surrounded by officers in tidy uniforms. She twisted a curl of her black hair between her fingers.

"That's not flaunting, that's informing. Come on, it's this way." Daemon jerked his head in the direction he'd chosen. His limp grew less evident as he took the lead.

"Have you ever been in these catacombs before?" she asked, unable to mask her doubt.

If the question bothered him, he didn't show it. "No."

"Then how do you know we're going the right direction?"

He halted just long enough to press a clawed hand to the wall. "Look." He wiped over the surface of the stone. Dust and grit flaked away to expose delicate etchings so worn, they were almost invisible.

Squinting, Firal held the mage-light closer. "What is that?"

"The closest thing to a map you'll get, in the ruins. Your

efforts to draw a map of the place have been valiant. Some drawings in your book are close. But the only real way to get around?" He tapped the etchings with a claw before he continued down the hallway. "Learning how to read these."

Firal did not follow. Instead, she held her pebble light closer to the wall and touched the symbols, her brow furrowed. She had paid utmost attention to her surroundings in the ruins. Surely she would have noticed if there were etchings in the walls above ground. She'd only seen something like them a handful of times, carved into corners where corridors intersected. "And on the markers along the path to the market," she murmured to herself. The markings did appear similar. Perhaps he was right after all.

"You coming?" Daemon's voice scattered her thoughts. He was some distance ahead by now, and the mage-light barely illuminated his figure.

"Coming." She recharged the light once more and hurried after him.

"How long have we been walking?" Firal groaned, rubbing her eyes. The mage-light in her hand had grown dim again. Recharging a light took little power, but she wasn't sure she had the energy—or the concentration necessary—to spare.

"How long have you been whining?" Daemon retorted, though he paused to lean against the wall and let her catch up. Even with the lingering pain he must have in his leg, he had better endurance than she did. She'd let him take the lead some time ago.

More than once, Firal had thought about trying to ease his pain. He hid it well, but after extensive healing, he had to be just as tired as she was. Despite the edge of irritation in his voice, she thought she heard a hint of sympathy for her weariness.

Firal rubbed her cold arms and frowned when it didn't make

her goosebumps go away. Elenhiise was a tropical island; it was strange to be cold. But then, being in the winding corridors of the underground was a new experience. It was wet, musty and, now that she thought about it, frigid. At least, in comparison to the temperatures she was used to.

Undeterred by his sarcasm, she persisted. "How much longer until we get out of here? I'm tired and it's freezing down here. Do you even know where we are now?" She was well aware the onslaught of questions sounded like more whining, but she no longer cared. "Can't we sit down for a bit?"

"There's still a ways to go. But I'd be happy to stop if you'd like me to warm you up a bit." His luminescent eyes raked over her from head to foot and narrowed with an unseen smirk behind his mask.

Firal gaped, folding her arms over her chest and shuddering. "Keep moving."

"Then quit complaining." Daemon shrugged.

She dropped her eyes to her toes as she scuffled forward. Her feet were sticky and numb from sloshing through slimy, icy puddles, and the constant rubbing of her sandal straps had given her blisters. The edge of her skirt was damp and dirty and stuck to her ankles when she tried to walk. The weakened mage-light in her hand began to flicker.

"Fix that," he said.

"I can't." She held out the little rock at arm's length. "You do it, I'm too tired to focus."

Daemon paused where a new pathway opened to the side. "I can't."

Firal raised an eyebrow. "You're Gifted, but you can't even make a simple mage-light?" If that was the case, it was laughable. Even the temple's least skilled students were capable of creating lights.

"That's not what I meant." That he didn't sound offended caught her off guard. "I can't do it because I've never been shown how. You know how magecraft works."

He had a point, but Firal wasn't about to validate his thoughts. Some mages could fumble their way through tasks by following an example, studying the flow of power in someone else as they worked. Others stumbled into the knowledge of how to wield their power in a few rudimentary ways on their own. Both developed clear pathways for the torrents of power to follow, but without a mentor, it was difficult to learn how to further access and expand those paths. A teacher was necessary to understand the nature of the magic in their blood.

And heritage *was* a concern. Until she'd sensed the Gift within him, Firal had assumed only the Eldani were Gifted. It was well known that humans never were. Daemon did not seem to be either, and so she didn't know where he fit.

"It's too bad they don't accept the likes of you into the temple." She lifted her chin. "If you can't figure out how to make a mage-light after seeing me recharge it this many times, then you're hardly a mage."

Daemon snorted. "Oh, is that the reason they wouldn't accept me? I would have thought it was because nobody believes Underlings exist."

She bit off a retort and flicked the dimly-glowing pebble at him. "Here."

His reflexes were good; he snatched the stone out of the air and rolled the stone between his green-scaled fingers before letting it settle in his palm. "What?"

"Charge it."

"What?" he repeated. "I just said—"

"All you're doing is transferring a bit of your energy into it. I felt you reinforcing my healing with your strength when I mended your leg. This is the same thing." She lifted the damp hem of her skirt above her ankles and tip-toed closer. "Feeding power flows to someone else's healing can be a challenge. If you could focus your magic enough to do that, I'm certain you can make a simple light."

Daemon hesitated, but said nothing. He turned the pebble over with a claw. Its light pulsed as it faded.

Magecraft was a fickle thing. Though it was called magic, Firal had never been certain if that was the right term for it. It was energy in its purest form, able to be shaped and molded to the user's will, with the assumption that the user knew how to manipulate it—and how to seize it. The ebb and flow of magic was everywhere; everything that existed contained potential energy, and that shifting tide was the reason they called the power *flows* to begin with. The trick was to harness it and redirect those flows into a manifestation of one's intentions. But energy was to be borrowed, never taken. Consuming all of something's potential power was dangerous, and the risk of something being unmade was too high a price for power.

She watched Daemon closely, gaining the distinct feeling that he frowned, though she couldn't see his face. Perhaps the healing had been different. He'd felt what she was doing and fed her raw power, nothing more. Mages could not heal themselves, and she hadn't felt him trying to manipulate her power once it poured into him. He would have felt the energy move through her each time she'd recharged the light, but without being connected to that stream, perhaps he didn't know how to mimic it on his own. The longer he stood in silence, the more amused she became.

"I can see perfectly well in the dark," he said at last, catching hold of her hand and pressing the pebble into her palm. He twitched his cloak forward over his shoulders and stalked off into the shadows.

Firal hurried after him. "Wait for—" Cold hands burst from a dark side passage and wrapped around her arm. She shrieked and the dimly glowing stone fell from her hand as the soldier twisted her arms behind her back.

A second soldier emerged from the shadow and strode toward Daemon. "We've been looking for you for hours, sir. Is everything all right?" He offered an arm.

Daemon pushed it away. "Fine, though I can't imagine why it took you this long to find another entrance."

Firal writhed in her captor's grasp. The man covered her mouth with a gloved hand before she could shriek again.

"What do we do with the girl, sir?"

Daemon studied her, the strange light in his eyes seeming to dim. "Bring her. We'll take her to Lumia and decide what to do with her after that." He turned and jerked his head in the direction he meant them to go.

Firal's heart plummeted.

"Yes, sir," the men echoed in unison, following Daemon's lead. Their hold on Firal's arms tightened and they marched her onward, into the dark.

THE PASSAGES GREW WARMER AS THEY TRAVELED AND THE GROUND underfoot went from slick and clammy to bone dry. Firal did not know what to make of the change. Nothing on the island was particularly dry, save the temple's library. A team of Masters supervised the environment the books were kept in, protecting them from humidity and decay. Somehow Firal doubted the place they were headed was under the influence of cautious temple mages.

She had struggled and shouted until her throat ached. Eventually, the soldiers and Daemon tired of shushing her. Once her throat turned raw and her voice raspy, she'd given up. Defeated, Firal shuffled along between her captors. Her blistered feet were rubbed raw, the dust underfoot a faint but constant sting in the wounds.

She could no longer see Daemon leading the way. The soldiers carried no light, and the glow of his eyes had vanished some time ago. From time to time she thought she heard one of the soldiers brush a hand against the wall. She assumed they were checking the directional engravings on the walls. Had anything been visible, she would have tried to commit the marks to memory.

Though the air grew fresher as they ventured onward, knowing they would emerge somewhere unfamiliar provided no comfort. The two soldiers spoke now and then, but the words were in a harsh, guttural language Firal couldn't understand. One pulled her hair and made a sound of disgust. Both of them laughed and, though she couldn't understand what they'd said, she felt a flush rise into her cheeks.

"That's enough," Daemon barked. "Just walk."

His voice startled the men to silence. A moment later, Firal stubbed a toe on the bottom step of a stairway and yelped in surprise. The stone floor of the passages they'd ventured through had borne dips and ridges, but she hadn't expected a staircase. Her captors shoved her forward and she stumbled. How was she to climb stairs in utter darkness? Firal bit her lip as she slid a foot forward to scout out the first step, then a second. It wasn't until they reached the top that she noticed the light.

The walls and floor were pure black, cut and carved of solid stone so there were no seams. A chilly blue light gleamed somewhere far ahead, reflected on the glassy, polished walls. It was bright enough for her to see Daemon's silhouette, now just a few paces ahead of them.

"Come," he said.

The soldiers urged Firal into motion again.

Few and far between, peculiar torches mounted on the black stone walls offered those tiny flickers of blue light. Firal studied the first one they passed. It behaved like some sort of magic, though she couldn't sense any hint of energy. There was no flame and no warmth, and Firal was not certain the torches were even wood. The glowing end provided feeble, icy illumination that made everything look just as chill as the air. Not that there was much to see. Every hallway and door looked the same as the last, plain and black, though remarkably well-crafted. It was dismal, to say the least, yet it held a proud beauty. Never had she imagined there could be anything like this below the ruins.

The more doorways they passed, the more Firal noticed the little details she'd first overlooked. The coarse grain in the lacquered black wood stood out, as did the web-like metal sconces that held the torches. Even the dark stone of the floor was unusual, shining black and specked with ashen flakes. Firal had seen stone like that before, though a small piece, in possession of one of the Masters. A particular sort of obsidian, she recalled; she knew little about it beyond its name, but the glittering flecks of gray-white made her imagine smoldering motes of ash trapped within the black glass. That a Master had seen fit to keep it meant it was something important.

The puzzle began to come together. It wasn't just a maze or labyrinth they walked through, nor an underground extension of the ruins she knew. They walked inside a palace. The realization had only just cemented itself when one last turn put them before a pair of large black doors, ornately carved with swirls and thorns, its corners decorated with matching shapes in wrought iron. Daemon pushed open one door and slipped inside without a word. Before Firal could identify more than one leaf carved into the door's thorny mural, the soldiers forced her inside.

The great hall was no brighter than the rest of the palace, but the light here was warmer and rose from small fires held in spiked iron braziers between fluted stone columns. Dismal tapestries lined the walls. Traces of a carved relief along the ceiling's edge caught and refracted flickers of the ruddy light. A threadbare red carpet ran the length of the room, and Firal's eyes followed it to a throne atop the high stone dais.

A fair-haired woman sat upon the throne, as frigid and beautiful as the cold lights in the corridors behind them, and Firal's breath caught in her throat when she met her icy blue eyes.

"Well, now." A strange smile played upon the woman's full lips as she brushed a curl back from her face. "It's not every day we have a guest. You've done well to retrieve her, my pet." Her words were tinted with amusement, her tone almost sultry as her eyes slid to Daemon.

He moved to stand beside the throne, the limp gone from his stride.

"I didn't mean to intrude," Firal started, twisting her arms in the grasp of the soldiers that stood with her. "I was just—"

"Lost?" The woman chuckled and shook her head. She wasn't beautiful; that had been a poor choice of words. She was glorious. Her skin was like fine porcelain and thick, dark eyelashes lined her too-blue eyes. Platinum blonde curls fell past her full breasts, and her fine red silk dress hugged her supple hourglass figure in a manner that was almost obscene.

Firal had to swallow before she could speak again. "You're the queen of the Underlings, aren't you?"

"Really, is it that terribly obvious?" Lumia laughed, a sardonic edge to her voice. "And here I was told the Eldani didn't believe in our kind."

"I know only what I have been taught, M...Majesty." Firal tried not to cringe at the bitter taste the title left in her mouth. She almost didn't catch the flick of the queen's hand, but the soldiers released her, bowed, and retreated to the doors. They'd held Firal for so long that the sudden absence of their hands left uncomfortable cool patches on her skin.

Lumia pulled back Daemon's hood and threaded her fingers through his dark hair as he crouched beside her throne. Her eyes never left Firal's face. "Tell me, girl. What is your name?"

"Firal, Majesty." She offered a curtsy, suddenly aware of how dirty and ragged she was in comparison to the woman before her. "I'm a student at the Kirban Temple."

"I recognize magelings when I see them." Lumia lifted her chin. "If not by appearances, then from feeling the magic within them."

Firal blinked at the Underling woman in surprise. Were all of their kind Gifted? She had sensed it in Daemon, but not in

Lumia. Come to think of it, she couldn't feel any energy in Lumia at all. As a healer, she should have at least sensed the queen's life force. A shiver stole down her spine.

The queen did not seem to notice. "Are you planning to tell me what you were doing in my ruins, little mageling? Last I knew, leaving the temple grounds without an escort was against the rules. Or has that changed in the last century?"

How could the woman know temple rules? Firal's brow furrowed, but she did not ask. She doubted Lumia would appreciate questions instead of answers. "I did not mean to trespass, Majesty. I beg your forgiveness. I was only curious."

"I assume, then, that you don't know the ruins are sacred." Lumia sniffed and drummed her unoccupied fingers on the arm of her throne. "Visitors are not welcome, and from what I understand, this was not your first venture into my territory."

"No, Majesty." Firal's heart pounded in her ears. Here she thought she'd escaped punishment by evading the attention of the temple Masters. "I went for a walk and I lost something precious to me. I hoped to find it again. But I didn't know the ruins belonged to anyone. I thought they were only forbidden because we could get lost, or—"

"Then none of you have been taught what this labyrinth once stood for! What a pitiful state the temple is in. Why, if I hadn't been sent off like a—" Lumia stopped herself short and swallowed the words before they could escape. Her shoulders bunched as they went down hard.

She drew a deep breath before she spoke again, her voice dangerously cool. "With that sort of attitude, it's no surprise we are rejected by your kind. My followers, they have done no wrong. Their only fault is that they were not born Eldani."

Firal shrank back as the queen went on.

"This is our home." Lumia curled her empty hand to a fist. "Every day, my people struggle just to keep living, hiding here, forced into caves and tunnels beneath our glorious island. Why should you be allowed to crawl into our home? Why should you be allowed to walk free, when the rightful rulers of the island hide to protect their very lives?"

"What does that have to do with me?" Firal cried. "I didn't know!"

The Underling queen's fine features hardened. "We bear the burdens our fathers leave behind, child. Remember that when the wars begin."

"Wars?" A thread of ice wormed its way into Firal's heart. Unconsciously, she rubbed her arms as if to ward off a chill.

"Selfish men rarely give up stolen things." Lumia shrugged. "I see no reason to expect your king will look upon us kindly when we seek a return to the surface. But we will address that in time, hmm? It shall be interesting to see which side your temple takes."

"The temple is loyal to King Kifelethelas," Firal said, strong and certain, for all that she felt a twinge of doubt.

"The Eldani king," Lumia murmured. There was something in her voice—not quite contempt, but still laden with venom. "One more grudge for me to hold against them." She stroked Daemon's hair one last time before she motioned him forward. "She is yours, darling, since you found her. Do with her as you wish, but see to it that you get rid of her."

Daemon rose, adjusting the plain mask that covered his face.

The dark heat that burned in his luminescent eyes made Firal's blood run cold. She took a step back, then darted for the doors.

He shot from the dais like an arrow. His talons shrieked against the cold stone floor. He was fast—too fast for her to have any hope of escape. Her panicked cry cut off as he caught her by the collar of her dress. It tightened around her throat, threatening to choke her as he hauled her back. She cried out and lashed against the monster as he reeled her in and wrapped an arm around her waist to drag her step by step across the room.

Lumia gave Daemon a nod of approval as he pulled Firal behind a tapestry and into a hidden hallway.

His grasp on her tightened and Firal gasped for breath. She kicked at his legs and stomped at his feet. Neither yielded results. Firm as his grasp was, he held her waist, not her arms. She clawed at his arm, the edges of his scales sharp beneath her digging fingernails. She wrenched those scales backwards. He did not react.

"Let me go! Please!" she wailed.

His glowing eyes turned crimson behind the slits of his mask and her stomach flopped. Finally, he released a low, hissing breath. "Over and over again, I spare you when any of my men would see you dead. To speak as you did before Lumia..." He shook his head in disgust. "Hold still. You try my patience."

She growled and kicked again. Her toes hit his shin hard enough to hurt and she bit back a yelp. He merely grunted as he hauled her around the corner. From the lackluster reaction, she assumed she got his good leg. Angry, she shoved against his shoulder and wriggled in effort to escape.

Daemon caught her by the biceps and gave her a shake. "If you don't stop, I'm going to tie your feet together and sling you over my shoulder."

She froze, her eyes wide. He wouldn't dare. Her jaw tightened and she stubbornly met his eye. "Where are you taking me?"

His hand slid down her arm until his clawed fingers could wrap around her wrist. "Be quiet," he commanded.

Sullen silence fell between them as he led the way, his grip firm, but not painful.

The twists and turns were innumerable. The hallway split so often that Firal grew dizzy trying to keep track. Eventually, she squeezed her eyes closed and concluded the passages underground were worse than the labyrinth overhead. At least in the ruins, one had the sky above them to help distinguish compass directions. The catacombs wound up and down, looping and twisting over each other until she suspected they would emerge on the other side of the world. Instead, they stopped at a spiral stairway illuminated with the same blue-glowing lights that lit the path to the throne room. Daemon pushed her forward and she was all too happy to move ahead, one hand on the wall for balance.

The stairs wound upward forever. Firal's legs burned with overuse by the time they reached a hallway that was long and straight and unlit, save a dim glow at the far end. It wasn't until they reached a short flight of squared steps at the end of it that she caught the stirring of wind and the scent of fresh air.

They emerged from a yawning cavern built into the wall of the ruin itself. The ground was trampled to a smooth dirt path, the corridor tidy and free of fallen stones. Stars winked in the sky overhead, the position of the moon declaring it well past midnight.

Daemon caught hold of her arm again and guided her wordlessly through the maze, never once stopping to check the walls for the guide marks he'd sworn were there.

Suddenly they were in the open space between the ruins and the temple, and Daemon shoved her forward.

"There. Get out." He dusted his hands against his shirt as if to brush away her existence.

Firal stumbled over her own feet. After the chase, the threats, the order to get rid of her, that was it? "But—"

"Hurry up. Before I change my mind."

She stared. "You're letting me go?"

Daemon gave her a hard look. "Don't come back. Lumia was generous to let you go this time. She has no love for mages. Don't expect she'll be willing to give you another chance."

Firal swallowed hard as a vision of the Underling queen's stern blue eyes flashed through her head. She regarded him in silence for a long moment before she picked up her skirts, turned toward the temple, and ran three paces before she skidded to a halt. "Wait, my journal! What about—" She spun back and stopped short.

Daemon was already gone.

10

STRANGERS

"WAKE UP!"

Firal squealed as Kytenia tore her blanket away. Gooseflesh rose on her exposed skin. "Hey!" She snatched the cover from Kytenia's hands and pulled it up to her chin. The room was dim, the shutters closed and the sound of rainfall drumming outside, but she could still see her friend's scowling face.

"Where have you been?" Kytenia planted her hands on her hips. "You left without a word, didn't come back when that bad storm rolled through, stayed out until nearly sunrise, then just sneaked back into your room without telling any of us you're all right?"

Firal bunched the blanket at her throat. The air in her room was thick with heat and humidity but she still felt cold, as if the chill of the underground had settled in her bones. "Well, I apologize for suffering a calamity!"

"Where were you?" Kytenia reached for the blanket again and frowned when Firal yanked it away.

"I was—" Firal stopped short, uncertain. Where had she been? A crypt, caverns, tunnels, a palace...she opted for the simplest explanation. "I was under the ruins."

"*Under* the ruins?" Kytenia pulled the chair from the desk

beneath the window and spun it to face the bed. She sat and crossed her arms, making it clear she had no intention of leaving without the full story. "What do you mean, *under* the ruins?"

"I fell." Firal hugged herself, the blanket wadded in her arms. Her brows drew together. "I tripped, I think, and the ground gave way. I thought the catacombs might stretch on forever."

Kytenia leaned back in her seat. Her face twisted with skepticism. "How did you get out, then?"

Firal didn't appreciate the doubt. She discarded the idea of making something up; the truth was absurd enough. "An Underling showed me the way."

"An Underling!" Kytenia laughed aloud. "Really? What was it like?" A sarcastic smirk twisted her lips. Firal saw the thoughts behind her friend's sparkling eyes. After that story Ran had made up—or that Firal thought Ran made up—it would seem like a convenient defense, and the girls would tease her mercilessly.

"*He* was awful." Firal shuddered. "I was hunting for my journal when he found me. He threatened me. I ran, but I didn't know where to go. I only got more lost. I don't know what happened after that, exactly." The bits and pieces she *did* remember didn't make sense. Daemon had grabbed her, but she could have sworn he'd done it knowing the ruin wall would fall on them. Protecting her? That made no sense at all. She pursed her lips. "I remember screaming when he grabbed me, then falling."

"And what did this Underling look like?" Though the question came out mocking, there was a hint of genuine curiosity in Kytenia's expression. Perhaps she believed someone had been out there, if not an Underling.

"I don't know," Firal said. All the feelings of fright churned up anew. She put her hands to her stomach as if to settle it. "He was wearing a mask. He stood like a man, but his hands, those feet...I've never seen anything like it, not even in books. Like a great lizard, I suppose. I thought Ran was the one who brought me back from the ruins before. I mean, he said as much, but Daemon's eyes..." She trailed off and stared into nothing, unsure what else to say.

Kytenia started to speak, then closed her mouth. Her brow furrowed and she seemed to puzzle over it for a time before she spoke again. "You really believe this happened, don't you?"

"He'd gotten hurt. I was going to just leave him, but he had my journal. The beast read from it." Firal shook her head, angry at herself for failing to get it back. "I tried to strike off on my own, but I couldn't find the way. I had to heal him. It was dark, the tunnels were so foul and wet and cold. I don't know why he brought me out, or why he let me go. I don't understand it, Kyt."

Kytenia sat back, her face unchanging, though Firal saw a gleam in her friend's eyes that indicated Kytenia thought her mad. She bristled.

"I know what I saw, Kytenia." The bruises spread across Firal's body and the blisters on her feet should have been proof enough that something strange had happened.

"So did you get your book back?" Kytenia asked, neatly sidestepping the issue.

"Not yet, but I will. Now that I know where to get it." Firal sniffed and pushed herself out of bed. Her thin shift twisted around her legs and she pulled at it in irritation. Kytenia's eyes followed her to the mirror, where she'd hung her dress the night before. Firal pulled the dress on over her head and sucked in her stomach to do the laces up the front of the bodice.

Kytenia sighed and turned toward the shuttered window. With as wet and gray as it was outside, little light shone through the cracks. "The carriages taking us to Ilmenhith for the solstice are due to arrive this evening. We're to depart tomorrow afternoon. Are you going to be ready to travel? Will you even be here? Every time you set foot in those ruins, you're gone a little longer." Something—not quite accusation—colored her tone. It was closer to concern, though Firal heard something else, too. It reminded her of Nondar's suggestion she was growing addled, and she didn't like it one bit.

"I'll be here, Kytenia." Firal tugged the laces a little harder before she tied them and tucked in the ends. Kytenia eyed her, and she sighed. "I mean it. You know what this chance represents for me. For now, I'm hungry. I'm going to get something to eat before the dinner hall gets crowded."

Kytenia waved a hand. "It's probably crowded anyway. There have hardly been any classes since the ball was announced. Everyone's been so busy getting ready. It's not like anyone will notice you sneaking out."

"I'm not missing the solstice ball, Kytenia. It's too important." Firal pulled her cloak around her shoulders. "One way or another, I'll be there."

Kytenia smiled at her as she left, though the expression didn't touch her eyes.

Once Firal was out of earshot, she allowed herself a wordless grumble. Let her friend think her mad. She wasn't—she'd struck a deal and Daemon hadn't held his end of the bargain. Agitation prickled hot beneath her skin as she made her way to the dinner hall. Kytenia was correct; the tables were packed with magelings and Masters. Firal stayed just long enough to snatch a few pastries. She had another stop to make before she could finish what she'd started the day before.

The library doors were closed against the rain, but unlocked this time. Firal inhaled the comforting scent of books as she ducked between the stacks. It didn't take long to find the dusty, worn collection of books she remembered, though she had to put down her food before she could carry all the tomes. Aside from a few blue-robed magelings and a single Master in white who served as chief librarian, the place was empty. It usually was. The mage-dried air that helped protect the books from the tropical climate tended to make one's nose bleed if they stayed too long.

Firal claimed a small table hidden between bookcases and

paged through one book after another as she ate. Food was not allowed in the library, but she was in a hurry. She suspected the librarians were too busy to notice, anyway, their usual volunteers absent. Distracted by travel preparations, Firal assumed. She stuffed half a pastry into her mouth and opened another book.

With all the stories about Underlings they'd heard as children, she couldn't fault Kytenia for her skepticism. But Firal had never lied to her friends. Not told the whole truth, perhaps, but never lied. It both stung and rankled that her dearest friend didn't believe her, but surely there was something in the library to set her straight. She had more information now. She'd met their queen. One book would be enough; one volume she could leave on Kytenia's desk before she returned to the ruins.

None of the books held any mention of a queen or a connection to mages, though, and it wasn't long before Firal turned her attention to history books instead. If the Underlings truly had been driven into the ruins, there had to be at least one historical record of the encounter.

There was Lumia's brief outburst, too, something about being sent off, but Firal wasn't sure how to search for that. Surely the woman hadn't meant to say she'd been sent away from the temple. Firal hadn't sensed so much as a stirring of a Gift in her. She hadn't mentioned Lumia in her short conversation with Kytenia, though the Underling queen's words put a weight on her heart as they ran back through her head.

War didn't seem like an empty threat, but what could Firal do about it? Kytenia already didn't believe her. Firal dreaded to think what Nondar would do if she tried to tell him. Kifel came to mind, but one lesson in swordplay hardly made her friends with the king. Even if he deigned to let her speak, he'd likely also think her mad for suggesting people from folklore planned to move against his country. Yet even if someone did believe her, sending word meant going to one of the Masters, and that meant revealing that she'd been in the ruins.

The racing thoughts gave her a headache; she needed to clear her mind. Firal shook her head and licked her fingers clean as she finished her food and closed the books. She considered taking them back to her room, but decided against it and left them on the table. There would be no time to read further until they returned from Ilmenhith, and it wasn't as if the library was going anywhere. She still needed her necklace. Drawing up the hood of her cloak, she ventured back into the rain.

Even through the heavy wool of her cloak, the fat raindrops stung. Thick clouds overhead indicated the storm wouldn't let up any time soon. For only a moment, Firal regretted having started toward the ruins in the rain.

The ground squished beneath her sandals and gritty moisture seeped around her toes. She should have asked Marreli to heal the blisters she'd earned in the underground. Aside from Kytenia, Marreli was best at tending injuries; odd, considering the girl's earth affinity. At least the sores were scabbed over now. The mud just served as an unpleasant reminder of their existence.

Firal wasn't sure where she was going, though the ruins seemed more stable here, which eliminated the fear of walls collapsing. Thick moss grew over stones of mixed grays. Between the stones, tangles of vines tried to choke out scraggly wildflowers that had only just begun to bud. As she rounded a corner in search of the stairway into the underground she now knew existed, she studied the stone. As she'd expected, there was nothing there. No marks. She snorted. Why had she believed a word Daemon said?

A crunch of stone made Firal pause. Staying as still as she could, she waited, and cringed when it crunched again. She wasn't alone, but she didn't think she was anywhere near the passage Daemon had used to get her out of the underground. What were the odds he would have heard her? Her stomach wrenched with anxiety, but she continued forward.

Whether or not she was afraid of the confrontation, she

intended to find Daemon. Underling or not, he had agreed to give her journal back, and she wasn't about to let him go back on their deal.

Her sandals squeaked on the wet weeds as she darted around the corner and collided with a steel breastplate. She shrieked, reflexively swinging her fist upward as she stumbled back.

"*OW!*" All but howling, her adversary jerked his hands to his face. "What was that for? What did I do?" His words were muffled, but the hateful look in his bright blue eyes couldn't have been clearer. "I think you just—"

"Blight it all, Lomithrandel, I swear I'll gut you alive!" Firal snapped.

"I think you just broke my nose," Ran finished angrily.

She huffed, though her heart still raced. Was she glad or disappointed that it hadn't been Daemon? "Oh, quit fussing. That probably hurt my hand more than your face. Brant's roots, but that felt like walking into a wall. What are you wearing?" She glared up at him and reached to take hold of his cloak.

"Stoppit!" He slapped her hands down and wiped a dark trickle from his chin.

Concern flitted across her face. "Did I get your mouth? Well, your nose is fine, then. I might have busted your lip, that had a good pop. Here, let me see." Firal grabbed for his jaw, undeterred by his efforts to shove her hands away. He missed her arm and her fingers landed on the dark, sticky bloodstain that marked his chin. She paused, surprised. "You have a beard."

"I do not," Ran fired back, pushing her away and rubbing the last of the blood from his face with the edge of his hood. "Stop touching me."

She eyed him strangely as he straightened his cloak. "I'm sorry."

"What for? Hitting me?" He waved a hand as if to dismiss it. "I exaggerated. A little. It doesn't hurt that bad, though that was a pretty angry swing for you."

"Better mind yourself, or the next time it'll hurt a lot more,"

Firal muttered. "Where have you been? I haven't seen you since that afternoon in the gardens. You've been gone for days. Even Nondar didn't seem to know where you went."

"I went home." He beckoned her as he turned. "Come on, we need to find a place to hide. It's about to storm."

She turned her face toward the driving rain. "It's already storming," she said, though she followed him. "Where are you going? The temple is in the other direction."

"Just come on, there's cover this way. It'll be safer to wait it out than to try to get back to the temple after it starts. And for your information, this is a drizzle. I could see the worst of the storm from the top of the wall I climbed over, just before you ran into me. Quite literally, might I add." A hint of teasing colored his words.

Smothering a heavy sigh, Firal drew her saturated cloak closer.

The path Ran picked was difficult for her to follow. He scaled walls and vanished to the corridors on other side before she could find a place to climb, then bounded through thick undergrowth as if it were nothing. Firal struggled to keep up. Even when they walked in a straight line, he moved at a pace that left her lagging behind. Now and then he'd pause and wait for her to close the gap between them.

"I thought you said there was shelter close?" Firal panted, leaning forward and bracing her hands against her knees.

"I said it was closer than the temple," he corrected.

She held back a complaint when he vanished over the top of another wall and left her to struggle over it on her own. Her fingers ached from clawing at the rock, her nails chipped and fingertips raw. It took some effort to find a foothold and it took more to hold her tongue when she scraped her knees on the way over. She slid into the next corridor behind Ran and sank to the ground with her back against the wall.

Just as she settled, the growl of thunder deepened overhead. Black clouds rolled in from the west, though the rain had tapered to almost nothing. She looked at the sky with a frown and twitched in surprise when Ran appeared in front of her. He offered a hand to help her up and she eyed it with suspicion.

"Hurry up, the weather's about to get ugly." His expression softened when she reluctantly took his hand. "Don't worry, we're there."

She perked up at the announcement and pulled herself to her feet with his help. She wasn't certain where *there* was, but they'd reached what, at first glance, looked like a dead end. A crumbling stone archway stood at the end of the corridor, to the left. Rust stained the eroding rock where hinges had been, the only remainder of the doors the archway must have held. Lush wildflowers climbed the stone, hanging across the broken arch like a curtain. Firal let go of Ran's hand and moved closer. Had he led her to an entrance? She swept the dangling flowers back from the stone and yelped.

Beneath the delicate vines, the stone was carved in the shape of a beast's yawning mouth. A nose and eyes were etched into the top of the broken half-arch, the features worn away by centuries of weather.

Ran brushed up beside her. "Come on." He caught her arm on his way through the arch and tugged her along. Jagged teeth lined the archway's jaws and he had to duck to keep those on the top from grazing his head. A handful of slick, grimy stairs led them downward. Firal shuddered. Though it seemed the entrance had once led to the underground, the passage at the back had long since collapsed. She studied the dark stone that blocked the way. From there, her gaze drifted upward. The ceiling was ribbed like the roof of a feline's mouth, and the dead end did little to make her feel less like she was being devoured.

"Well, this is pleasant." Firal wrapped her arms around herself to ward off another shudder. "I can't imagine a better place to suffer through a storm."

"Oh, hush." Ran steered her farther into the small cavern and gestured for her to sit. He sat across from her and leaned back against the wall. "Beggars can't be choosers."

She sank to her knees in the middle of the floor. Her skirt and cloak pooled around her. The sky opened up as soon as she settled, releasing heavy torrents of rain outside. Streams of water poured down the stairs but diverted at their foot, channeled away by a trough carved along the bottom of the wall behind her. She watched disinterestedly as the water disappeared into a crevice beneath the collapsed stone. Once upon a time, this passage would have taken her where she needed to go. She was only centuries too late to see how deep it led.

"It is a little frightening, isn't it." Ran stared at the fissure that swallowed the rainwater, his eyes glazed. "The Underlings seem to have a fascination with structures like this. They're all over the ruins."

Firal cocked her head. "You believe the folk tales?"

He raised a brow. "Don't you?"

"Maybe." Her cheeks reddened and she hugged her knees. "What do you remember from the stories the Masters used to tell?"

Ran shrugged. "A bit. Whole bunch of nasties that live in the ruins, said to be ruled by a monstrous queen. Plagued the people of the island, stole children. That's about all there is, I think."

"That was what started the war that drove them underground, wasn't it? When they kidnapped a child tied to the crown?" Firal barely recalled that part of the tale, buried in the recesses of memory.

"I think the war was before that, though I'm pretty sure that ended it," Ran said.

"Do you think that really happened?" she asked.

His eyes snapped to her, his gaze gone hard.

Firal resisted the urge to squirm. "Or did any of it? I always thought they were just stories."

Ran's expression softened and he glanced toward the rubble at the back of the tunnel. "I don't know for certain. But when I'm walking around in a place like this, it's hard to pretend they've never been here, building things most people on this forsaken island will never see."

She wiggled her feet in her sandals and peered at her toes as they peeked out from under her skirt. "So you've seen a lot of cavern openings like this one?" Perhaps not all was lost. If he knew the location of one of the other entrances, maybe she could still find Daemon before she had to return to the temple. She doubted the court mages would speak to her without some evidence of her heritage, but she couldn't ask them anything if she wasn't there.

Ran nodded. "Strange mechanical things, too. And some things that look almost like clockwork, though they're so rusted out now that they'd never work again. Have you ever seen a clock, Firal?" He paused only a moment, then continued in what sounded like disappointment. "No, I don't suppose you have. Being in the temple your entire life and all. You'll have to see one when you go to the capital for the solstice."

"Do they have them there?" Firal asked. Her cheeks colored the moment the question was out. "I'm sorry, of course they do. I'm sure the king has a dozen sitting around his palace. Although I don't see what's so spectacular about a handful of wheels and gears that can tell you what time of day it is."

"It's not about what it's made of," Ran said, "or what it can do. It's about who made it. About the fact that a person, any person like you or I, could sit down with that handful of wheels and gears, arrange and bend and rearrange them until all of a sudden, there's a device that could change the entire world." The glint in his eye made her suspect she'd stumbled on some passion she'd never known about. He motioned toward the storm—or maybe the feeble daylight—outside. "No more guessing, no more sundials. No more depending on a cloudless day to tell the hour. Don't you have any appreciation for that?"

"Of course I do." She smoothed her damp skirts out around

her and clasped her hands atop her knees. "Just not as much as you do, I suppose."

Ran seemed to be satisfied by the response, for he said nothing else. Firal watched him wordlessly, studied the way he gazed at the rain and the rivulets of water that cascaded down the stairs. Her eyes searched his face and halted on the fine stubble that adorned his chin. It was such a fair color that she would have missed it if he hadn't been silhouetted by the dim light that shone in from outside.

"Ran...are you a half-blood?"

He started at the question, canting his head to the side and giving her a quizzical look. "What makes you ask something like that?" He sounded patient, but there was a cold intensity in his gaze.

"It would make a lot of sense, that's all." Firal feigned indifference. "It would explain why the Masters would make exceptions for you. Why they don't expect as much from you. Why they would let you pass, even though your training is so erratic that you can't even focus well enough to light a candle. It would explain the way you look."

"What about the way I look?" A stormy look filled his eyes.

"I don't mean it like that," she said hastily. "I mean, it would explain why you're so broad through the shoulders. Why your features are harder and your ears aren't pointed. And why you've got that beard you're pretending you don't. You look—" She paused to gauge his reaction before she finished. "Well, you look human."

He sat silent for so long that she started to fear she'd offended him. Then he sighed and turned his blue eyes back to the water that filled the channel in the floor. "Sometimes I think life would be a lot easier if I knew what I was."

Firal's brow furrowed. "You mean you don't know your own heritage?"

"And what does it matter if I do or not?" He crossed his arms and slouched against the wall. "If the king can live without certainty of his own bloodline, then why can't I?"

"Ran!" she gasped. "How could you say that?" Whether or not he knew the king, a statement like that was sedition.

"It's a rumor that's been flying for ages. I'm surprised you haven't heard it." His expression softened, but his tone remained sullen. "The claim that the Eldani king isn't all Eldani has been around for longer than you or I have been alive."

"Well I've never heard anything of the sort." She moved farther away from him, as if she could physically distance herself from his words.

"Then you can color me surprised." He laughed dryly. "It's not a recent thing. They've been saying for years that the royal family is tainted with human blood. They say it's why Kif—I mean, the king—can't use magic."

Couldn't he? Firal tilted her head, trying to recall if she'd felt any hint of magic about the king during their brief encounter. Half-blood mages sometimes struggled with magecraft, but magic was still present within them—unlike humans, who had no Gift at all. The term *Giftless* most Eldani used for them was born of both condescension and pity. She didn't remember noticing Kifel's Gift, but she had been distracted.

"There's no way to prove it, really," Ran added, "but they can't disprove it, either. The problem comes from the royal family's history of marrying outside of proven pedigrees."

Firal tucked her chin into her chest. "And what about you? Do you know anything about your family?"

His shoulders slumped. "I don't know my real parents. I guess in some ways, my story is a lot like yours."

Likening the two of them threw her off. At the same time, the comparison made it painfully clear why Ran had never spoken of home or family. Firal had spent her entire life within the temple, fostered by teachers who pitied her. It wasn't uncommon for high-ranking mages to leave children in the temple or the chapter houses, but most of them at least kept contact with their offspring. She'd had no real upbringing, only a different woman each night to make sure her hair had been brushed and that she'd had something to eat before bed. She had lived with the hope that her parents, whom no one seemed to recall, would come back for her. But like with most things, time's passing had eventually washed that hope away.

Her fingertips brushed her neck, feeling for her missing necklace. She swallowed and forced her hand back down.

"Who raised you?" she asked finally.

Ran hesitated, staring out past the steps and teeth at the front of the cave, watching hailstones fall with the rain.

"Ran?" She leaned forward, trying to catch his eye.

He sighed. "I suppose it wouldn't surprise you at this point if I said I was raised in the palace. You want to know what makes me so special? There you have it. I have my own room in Ilmenhith's castle." Ran waved a hand with the admission and slumped against the stone. "I know I can never replace a blood child, but Kifel has always been a father to me. He's treated me like I was his own flesh and blood. Being welcome in his house is the only thing that's ever made me feel like I belong among the Eldani."

Firal cracked a smile. "That explains why you're so at ease swinging a sword at him, then. But why..." she trailed off, unsure how to ask.

"Why me?" He quirked a brow and managed a half-hearted grin, though it didn't stick. "I've asked myself that a hundred times."

The troubled look that came over his face was so out of character that it made Firal's heart ache. She twisted the hem of her skirt between her fingers. "Now I really know why the Masters give you special treatment."

Ran snorted. "Members of the royal family aren't supposed to be trained as mages, you know."

"But you aren't part of the royal family, are you?" she asked. "If you're a foundling, then—"

"Then it's a gray area, and that makes things more awkward for all of us. But the Masters thought I would be dangerous if I wasn't taught a little." He flexed his hand as if to soothe some sort of discomfort. Or maybe he was trying to conjure something to emphasize his point. Firal had not shared many classes with Ran—she didn't even know his affinity, now that she thought of it—but she had noticed his propensity for gesture in manipulating the flows. No magic sprang from his fingertips, though, and Firal squinted at him in thought. Matters regarding the royal lineage were considered taboo, but now that Ran was talking, she couldn't help digging.

"How is it Kifel has no children, anyway? Why didn't he ever take another wife?" She watched his face for signs of secrets, but he'd held these so long without slipping, she wasn't sure she'd recognize them.

"I don't know," Ran said. "He's never spoken much about..." He made a brushing motion with his fingers. Odd that he would be uncomfortable talking about the king's family now.

He cleared his throat. "There just aren't any children. At least, not any now. I think there was one, once, but something happened. From my understanding, that was when the queen abandoned her throne."

Firal tried not to cringe. That was one of the reasons the king's familial matters were not discussed in polite company. Everyone knew the tale, but the suggestion the queen had chosen to abandon her kingdom bordered on sedition, as well. Knowing the king had raised him, she supposed she could offer Ran some leniency, but she'd spent her whole life surrounded by Masters who shushed magelings who spoke of the ill-fated royal marriage. The king had been encouraged to remarry many times through the years. He never had.

Ran leaned forward until he was at eye level with her. "Why do you ask, anyway?"

"Well, just a thought," Firal said. "I find it unlikely a king would simply take in a child. But King Kifelethelas has been without a queen for as long as we've been alive. It's not impossible for there to be an illegitimate heir out there somewhere."

Ran stroked his unshaven chin. "I'm not sure what you're trying to hint at, but it sounds ridiculous. I'm pretty sure if I truly was his son, I'd have found out by now. And if there was a living heir to Kifel's throne, I'd have met them."

"Unless the Underlings carried them away," she teased. "Honestly, Ran, it's baffling how you can believe there's some credence to fairy tales, but you don't believe a king needs a good reason to foster a child."

"I don't think Underlings really carry children away," he muttered. "I think that part of the story is just a bedtime spook-tale for naughty children."

"Well, I'll take that with a grain of salt." she replied coolly.

Ran shrugged and turned back to the weather that raged just outside their shelter. "What are you doing out here, anyway? We're pretty far into the ruins. It doesn't look like you were trying to find someplace to sit and study."

"I ought to ask you the same thing," Firal said.

"Fastest way to the temple is going through the ruins, not around them."

Her brow wrinkled.

"Coming back from Ilmenhith," he clarified. "I'm a fosterling, not a prince. I'd be shamed for wasting the king's resources if I asked to travel by Gate. What about you?"

She debated how much she should tell him. He could point her in the right direction, perhaps get her close to the underground palace, where she was most likely to encounter Daemon. Then again, the last thing she wanted was for Ran to invite himself along. "I was looking for my journal. I lost it several days ago."

"Why don't you just get a new one? Seems like a lot of trouble to go through for a couple class notes."

"It's not the journal," she snapped, though almost

immediately, guilt pricked at her and she bridled her annoyance. Ran had been nothing but polite. One unwelcome question did not deserve her temper. "I mean, it is. But not for the notes. I can replace the notes and even the drawings, but my necklace broke, and I put it in the cover to keep it safe. I suppose it wasn't such a safe place to keep it, after all."

Ran tilted his head. "I didn't know you had anything you found that valuable."

"It's not that it's worth anything." Firal toyed with her skirt. The fabric had almost dried. "I was told it belonged to my mother. She left it for me, when she left me at the temple. It's all I've got from my parents. I don't want to lose it. This is my only chance to get it back before we leave for Ilmenhith tomorrow. I need it, so I can...well, I need it."

His brow furrowed with sympathy. "I understand. I have something sort of like that."

"Do you?"

He nodded and touched his throat, though she saw nothing there. "An amulet, actually. For protection. I've had it since I was an infant. It's a funny looking stone, sort of black and blue and iridescent inside."

"I'd like to see it sometime," Firal said.

The conversation fell into a lull and both of them were content to let it, though Firal grumbled to herself now and then about being trapped. Hail came in waves, rain never ceasing, though the sky darkened as the day crept on. The air grew cool and the stone was chill to sit on. Hours crawled by and her thoughts turned to the temple.

The carriages from Ilmenhith would be arriving about now. Her friends would be packing for their trip. Departure was planned for afternoon. She'd have to rush to gather her things, though she'd be fine as long as she made it back to the temple before dawn. Her chance for retrieving her necklace was gone. All she could do was hope the court mages would speak to her.

Without the evidence she so desperately needed to support her claims, she wasn't sure they would.

"I'm so tired," she groaned finally, pacing at the foot of the stairs. The last light of the sun cast sickly green-gold hues through the clouds. "How long have we been waiting?"

"Do you ever stop whining?" Ran raked his fingers through his tawny hair and frowned when she stiffened at his choice of words. "What?"

She forced herself to shake her head. He was right; complaints came easy to the tip of her tongue, particularly when she grew weary. She couldn't be upset with him for mirroring Daemon's observation about the frequency of her complaints, no matter the bad memories that came with the thought of the Underling. "Nothing. I'm just getting tired, that's all."

"It is getting late. I don't think the storm will be letting up any time soon." He removed his cloak, spread it on the floor, and stretched out on top of it. He wore a few pieces of armor underneath, but nothing remarkable. She wasn't sure why he hadn't wanted her to see it when she'd first walked into him. If he'd been raised by the king, it made sense for him to take such precautions when traveling. Particularly when traveling alone.

"You could sleep, you know," he said. "I won't hurt you."

"No, you won't. You'll just get up and leave me all alone in the ruins as soon as the rain lets up." Though it was probably better that she return to the temple alone. After her friends' teasing about rumors, emerging from the ruins alongside Ran was the last thing she wanted.

Ran stifled a laugh. "You know me too well."

Firal fanned her own cloak out across the stone in mimicry of what he'd done. It was a good idea; at least it would take the edge off the cold. "It's strange you think that," she said. "After everything we've talked about, I'm starting to feel like you're still a perfect stranger."

"Nobody is perfect," he muttered with a hint of bitterness.

She rolled over, wrapping herself in her cloak. "Don't touch me while I'm sleeping."

He said nothing more. Peace washed over her as she succumbed to fatigue and drifted to sleep despite the cold, uncomfortable floor.

11

PLANS AND PREPARATION

When the door banged open and Daemon stalked into the war room, only Tren looked surprised.

"Temper, temper," Lumia chided, lifting her gaze from the maps and papers strewn across the table to give Daemon a half smile. A handful of officers stood around the small room, but only Lumia and Tren leaned against the table. Whether they had been waiting for him or not, Daemon wasn't sure.

"Make it fast." He didn't mean to snap, but he wasn't apologetic for the way the words came out. He joined his queen and the former general at the table. "Why did you call me?"

"To go over plans, of course." Lumia's smile grew strained. "Though you'd be wise to mind your attitude. You were summoned, not requested." She turned a map for him to see. It was little more than a drawing, a rough diagram of the temple and its surrounding outposts.

He traced the lines with a clawed finger. "What is this?"

"Kirban's market. The next target for the raiding party." Tren grinned in a way that was more animal than man, savage and unforgiving. "It should prove more fruitful than the last excursion."

Daemon's eyes darted to Lumia, light flaring in their depths. "Attacking a village that close to the temple is suicide."

"Only when the temple is full of mages, my pet." Her eyes narrowed. "Were you not the one who told me the mages would be traveling for the solstice? Unless you've been feeding me false information, I have no reason to think a raid on an unprotected landmark will be a problem."

"Unprotected being the key word. The king has stationed men at almost every other outpost near the ruins, blight him." Tren leveled his gaze with Daemon. It was an unreadable expression and that made it unsettling. Surely the man didn't think the increased security was his fault. Not when Tren had been the one to blunder the raid on Charth.

Daemon stared back.

Lumia finger-combed her pale curls, thoughtful. "Once this is complete, we should have a few more advantages against the king and his mages for the upcoming revolt."

"I don't think overthrowing the Eldani king's rule is going to be that easy," Daemon said. "You don't just raid a few villages and then take a throne."

Tren snorted. "No one asked for your opinion."

"You'll just have to trust me on this one." Lumia offered a smile so sweet it raised his hackles. "Besides, you aren't even going to be there."

Daemon's brow furrowed. "Where am I going to be?"

Tren laughed humorlessly. "At the ball."

Daemon gave him a wary look.

"He's right." Lumia paced around the table with her arms folded over her chest. "The celebration is for all citizens of the kingdom. The ruins fall almost completely on Eldani lands. That means we're citizens as well, doesn't it?" Her eyes glittered. "We need you there in case word makes it out of the market. You'll be free to enjoy yourself, if you're not required to take action. I trust that if word of the siege does reach the capital, you will do what you can to cause a distraction. It's imperative to our plans that they continue to believe human raiders are at fault."

He grimaced behind his mask. Even disguised, sending him into a ballroom full of mages seemed rather like sending him into a pit of vipers and crossing fingers in hopes he'd escape. There were some mages he would never be able to fool.

But Lumia was his queen, and she gave him no room to refuse.

"I live to serve, my lady," Daemon conceded, bowing his head.

"Good of you to remember it." She did not sound amused.

"So Daemon keeps an eye on things in Ilmenhith, I watch the men, and you'll handle whatever guards the king may have posted?" Tren paused and looked to Lumia for verification.

The queen nodded and Daemon glanced at her, surprised. She never accompanied raids. Before he could ask why, Tren went on, rubbing his goatee and staring at the crude map. "Now that all of that is worked out, there's the problem of the mage-barrier to address."

"Mage-barrier?" Daemon's eyes narrowed behind his mask. "At the temple?"

"The temple has artifacts in its possession that would aid us greatly. I'm certain you know of their Gate-stones?" Lumia raised a brow, but did not wait for his response. "Being able to open a Gate directly into the underground will make it easier to transport goods. Since you'll be elsewhere, we won't have your Gift to rely on. A small sacrifice, but you'll surely enjoy visiting the palace we mean to put you in."

Daemon chose to ignore the latter part. He leaned against the table, studying the distance between the temple and market. "You should have said something sooner. It would have been easier for me to enter the temple and take one of the stones myself."

"Perhaps," Lumia agreed. "I admit I had not yet considered

how much we would benefit from obtaining one. I don't believe it will be impossible to claim one myself."

Ah, so that was why she was going on the raid. Daemon grunted softly. "The mage-barrier shouldn't be a problem. If as many Masters are leaving the temple as it sounds, there won't be enough of them present to hold the shield. It's not anchored, and even the Archmage can't support the barrier on her own."

"So they're taking all of their defenses and dropping the only thing that might keep us out?" Tren asked.

Lumia shrugged. "Considering they've spent years telling magelings that we're nothing more than fairy tales, I doubt there's any reason they would anticipate an attack within their territory. Now, Daemon, I trust your scouting has been thorough. Please tell us what you know of the temple's layout and possible defenses on the Gate-stones. Once all that is out of the way, you may go back to your patrol."

He gritted his teeth at the word. Generals did not patrol, but they also didn't argue with their queen. Especially when she gave orders. Daemon adjusted his mask and reached for one of the sticks of charcoal that lay at the edge of the map. "If my understanding is correct, there are storerooms of artifacts here and here. The Gate-stones, if there are any, may be in either. It's also possible they'll be stored somewhere in the Archmage's tower." Marking the map as he recounted what he knew, Daemon rolled the thought of the solstice ball over in his head. If it was a distraction they wanted, he had a feeling he'd provide it whether he wanted to or not.

"I DO BELIEVE WE'RE MISSING SOMEONE."

Marreli turned her head as Shymin peeked behind the door of the room the older girl shared with Kytenia. As crowded as the small dormitory rooms were when all five girls gathered there, it wasn't unreasonable to think someone would be stuck behind the door. Marreli didn't mind close quarters, but Firal's absence made the room feel unusually spacious. She twisted the end of a braid in both hands.

"You know, Firal didn't attend dinner, either." Concern colored Rikka's voice, but she kept her face carefully serene. "She hasn't seemed herself lately. I stopped by her room earlier to see if she was all right, but she wasn't even there."

Marreli patted the empty space on Shymin's bed beside her in invitation, then wiggled to the side to make more room when Shymin sat. She doubted their evening gatherings would be half as fun in the spacious dining hall. The room Kytenia and Shymin shared was always their first choice. With two occupants, there was guaranteed to be someone there when classes were not in session, which made it a perfect meeting place.

"Do you think she went wandering again?" Marreli asked. "Maybe she just lost track of time." Hope filled her words, but her spirits sank when Kytenia shook her head and said nothing.

Kytenia sat on her own bed across the room, working to finish the hem of her gown while Rikka sat on the floor by her feet to stitch tiny beads to the neckline.

"I can't believe you still aren't done with that thing." Shymin draped her arms around Marreli's shoulders. The smaller girl giggled and leaned into the hug. Shymin often seemed like the big sister she never had. With only elder brothers back home in Ilmenhith, Marreli was used to roughhousing. She appreciated the gentle affection.

"I'm nearly done." Kytenia knotted a thread and clipped it off before poking a new length through the eye of her needle. "As for Firal, I think we all know where she is. I don't understand it, myself. it's just a maze of rocks. I don't see where the appeal comes from."

Rikka brushed her fiery hair away from her face. A strand caught at the corner of her mouth, accentuating her sly smirk before she tugged the hair free. "Ran has been absent for a few days, too. Perhaps they've run off together this time."

Marreli's eyes widened. "Do you think so?"

"Doubtful. Firal can't stand him." Shymin sighed and leaned back on her bed. She tugged Marreli's hair before making herself comfortable. "Do you think Ran will be going to the ball? As often as he makes a spectacle of himself day-to-day, he always manages to avoid the big to-dos."

"I'm sure Kyt hopes he's going. After all, how else will she get a dance with him?" Rikka smirked and then squeaked when Kytenia kicked her. "Hey!"

"That's not funny," Kytenia growled. "I could get him to dance with me anywhere if I really wanted to."

Marreli bit her lip to stifle a laugh. Her fingers curled around the ends of both her braids and she tugged them in thought. "Shymin is probably right, I don't think he's too likely to go. But you never know, maybe he likes big royal galas." She sighed dreamily. Ran certainly fit her idea of a prince; he was tall and dignified, with a powerful presence and brilliant smile. She could almost picture a crown on his head. "Maybe he's a noble in disguise. I wonder what he'd be hiding from? Assassins out to get him so a relative can steal his fortune, or an evil witch trying to turn him into a frightful beast?"

Shymin rolled her eyes. "An arranged marriage would be more likely, if that were the case. Honestly, Marreli, do you still believe in witches?"

Marreli flushed and lowered her eyes. "Maybe just a little." It wasn't uncommon for the word to be flung around as a derogatory term for mages, though superstitions about them only existed among the Giftless humans. Still, watching the other girls, she understood why their Gifts might be mistaken for witchcraft. She was the youngest of the group and the weakest, as well. For all she understood of the complicated magics the other girls worked, they might as well have been witches.

Though the notion of magic changing people to monsters was absurd, it didn't keep her from wondering what would happen if it were possible. But magic didn't work like that, as the Masters had made clear from the very beginning.

"Either way," Kytenia broke in, "I'm sure Firal's just gone out for fresh air. She'll be here when we leave tomorrow. She promised." She didn't look as confident as she sounded. A small wrinkle creased her brow, and doubtful looks crossed Rikka and Shymin's faces.

The stillness in the room began to feel awkward and Marreli squirmed.

Kytenia cleared her throat before she spoke again. "Is everyone packed already? This blasted gown is the last thing I need, but it's got to be finished before I can pack it."

"I think the rest of us just need to pick up our dresses in the market along the way. There's not much to pack, otherwise. It's a long trip, but we'll only be in Ilmenhith for a few days," Marreli said, a tinge of regret in her voice.

No one echoed the sentiment, but she knew they shared it. Traveling to the capital city was an exceptional treat, considering how rarely magelings were afforded breaks long enough to travel. If they were fortunate, they'd have a chance to explore the city before the temple called them back.

"How long until sundown?" Kytenia asked.

Rikka jerked her head toward the shuttered windows. "A little late for that. It's been dark for nearly an hour."

Kytenia gasped and thrust her sewing aside. "Why didn't you tell me?"

"Was I supposed to? You looked busy." Rikka pointed at the dress as it slid off the bed beside her. She held fast to the neckline, tiny beads still pinched between her fingers.

Kytenia harrumphed and pushed herself to her feet. "I'm going to check Firal's room, and if she's not back yet, I'm going to go speak with Master Nondar."

"You shouldn't!" Shymin sat bolt upright.

"Why not?" The scowl on Kytenia's face said she wouldn't likely be deterred. "The last time she ran off, she came back saying she'd met a...a...well, you remember the nonsense she was spouting."

Marreli hoped it was nonsense, at least. The story had bothered her. A part of her hoped it was only a fevered dream, but she knew Firal wasn't a liar. But whether Firal's sudden streak of imagination was caused by injury or illness, the fact either could have befallen her in the ruins was enough to make a return trip concerning. Marreli swallowed against the sudden dryness of her mouth and joined Shymin's protest. "The Masters wouldn't take to it kindly. Especially if she's out there with Ran, like Rikka said."

Rikka nodded. "Marreli's right. You could get Firal into a world of trouble. She's fortunate enough she didn't get knocked down a rank after all the gossip about her sneaking out the last time." She winced when she pricked her finger and sucked at it sullenly.

"Well I would rather her be in trouble with the Masters, and perhaps lose a few privileges, than have her be in trouble out where we can't find her." Kytenia tucked her chin into her chest as she spoke. She picked loose bits of thread off her skirt and cast them to the floor, but Marreli caught the fearful tremble in her fingers.

"I think you're worrying too much," Shymin sighed.

Kytenia flipped her hair back with a toss of her head. "Then call me a worrier and be done with it. I'll still speak to Nondar."

Rikka opened her mouth as if to argue, but a stern look from Shymin kept her silent as Kytenia stomped out of the room and left the door wide open. Marreli winced and looked at her toes. They sat quiet for a long time.

"Well, hurry up, Rikka," Shymin said at last, reaching across the space between beds to nudge her friend with her foot. "I still have packing to do and I won't get much of it done with the two of you hanging about in my room."

Rikka yelped when the gentle prodding made her prick her finger again.

12

DEPARTURE

MASTER NONDAR SIGHED AND PUSHED A BOOK BACK INTO PLACE with a fingertip. Shelves lined his office, overflowing with books, papers, and scrolls, but he managed to keep it organized. Sometimes it was all he could do. He didn't like to think about age catching up with him, but his half-blood heritage worked ever more to his detriment.

He'd never quite understood what made him different. The magic that extended the Eldani's lifespans was used unconsciously, utilizing the energies of everything around them without the individual even being aware they were doing it. But not all Gifts could be trained or taught. While Nondar had outlived his human relatives by more decades than he could recall, he knew his time would soon be up.

Sometimes he regretted the choice to pursue his craft, to live at the temple. He was the only half-blood to wear the white in the history of Elenhiise's mages—which was surely something to be proud of—but he left behind no family, no children. Looking back, he wondered at the decision of parting ways with his last lover. He would have married her if he'd stopped to think how lonely the end would be.

Nondar rubbed the gnarled joints in his fingers, looking out

145

the open doorway and into the night. He couldn't see the ruins through the predawn fog, but that didn't keep him from absently gazing toward them.

He'd grown more aware of the discomfort of being alone in recent years. Perhaps that was why he'd always felt a fatherly inclination toward Firal. He knew he'd coddled her when he shouldn't have, spent too much time spinning tales of how great a mage her mother had been when the temple was founded. Perhaps if he'd not shared the knowledge of her mother's career, the girl might have pursued her own passions instead of chasing her mother's legacy.

Kytenia's news of Firal's disappearance had been troubling enough before she'd mentioned Ran. That boy had been a thorn in everyone's sides since the day he was brought into the world. Nondar couldn't say he genuinely disliked anyone, but he had no love for that bothersome child.

It was ironic, perhaps, that the two had always gravitated together. The daughter of the royal family's greatest court mage, and the king's adopted son. They were terribly mismatched and well-suited at the same time, two endings to the same sad story. And his involvement in those tales was yet another reason to regret becoming a founding mage of Kirban.

If nothing else, had he not pursued the white, his life would have been simpler.

As Master of the House of Healing, Firal's affinity fell within his jurisdiction, and that made the girl his responsibility. Nondar had a suspicion about where he would find her, but he had not yet decided how to manage the situation. He'd always been aware of Firal's fondness for the ruins just beyond the temple grounds, but she had never ventured far or seemed likely to get herself in trouble. No doubt she wouldn't have, if Ran were not with her.

With a measure of reluctance, Nondar pulled himself out of his reverie, took his cane from where it leaned against his desk, and leveraged himself from his chair. No matter how his joints protested, he was expected in the Archmage's tower. The summons had come some time ago, and he could not afford to wait and deliberate in his office any longer. As it was, his hesitance to respond could draw questions. The ache in his knees and back made up his mind. He could not retrieve the girl himself, but Firal would have to be disciplined when she returned.

The courtyard beyond Nondar's office was noisy, even at night. Horses stamped and whuffed as their handlers moved them through the courtyard. Stabling one or two animals was reasonable, but the teams for the dozens of carriages that had arrived? That was out of the question. Instead, the drivers unhitched their teams in the field between the temple and ruin. A few at a time, the horses passed through the courtyard to be brushed and watered by the well in the stable yard where the temple's few animals were kept.

None of the horsemen paid the old Master mind as he worked his way toward the tower. The few who paused to look at him hurried on their way when they saw his limping gait. *Brant forbid they help an old man,* Nondar thought, surprised at his own bitterness. In sullen silence, he ventured up.

When he finally reached the top of the stairs, the door to the Archmage's office was open in some semblance of welcome. He recognized the other Masters around the council's table, though he was none too happy about the company.

Melora, with her sharp features and sharper tongue, sat licking her lips as though she expected a feast. Of all his peers, he liked the Master of the House of Wind the least. He tried not to look at her and skimmed the other faces instead. Anaide, Master of Water, and Edagan, Master of Earth, sat sneering and whispering between themselves as they watched him, as though their finely pointed ears meant they were not just as withered with age as he. They had been old even before the temple's founding. And Alira, her hair only just beginning to bleach, wore an expression that made it clear she thought she held every bit as much weight in the temple's council as the Archmage herself, despite the fact she'd taken control of the House of Fire scant decades ago. There were few male Masters stationed within the temple, and Nondar was not surprised to see he was the only one who had been summoned.

"How good of you to finally join us," Envesi said, the twitch of her stern mouth betraying her impatience.

"My apologies for the delay," Nondar replied, though his voice held no apology at all. "Perhaps next time, if you wish me here faster, you could ask the page to help me along. I cannot walk as I used to."

The other Masters waited in uncomfortable silence as Nondar settled in one of the many empty seats. Once he leaned his cane against the table's edge, the Archmage spoke.

"I've already spoken with most of the others, so these meetings shall not have to run all through the night. I trust all of you are prepared to travel in the morning?" Envesi barely paused, not seeming to care whether or not they answered. "Much of the temple staff has already departed on leave, so you will not have their assistance in the morning. I have arranged for every carriage to contain at least one Master alongside the magelings, to be sure none of them get out of hand."

"A wise choice, my lady." Anaide dipped her head in reverence.

Melora shifted, irritable already. "With all due respect, Archmage, I did not expect the five of us would be called to discuss travel arrangements. If this is all there is to speak of, I request permission to leave."

Envesi's resolute expression did not waver. "I trust the matter of affinities does not escape your notice, Melora?"

If it had, there was no missing it now. Nondar glanced at the gathered faces a second time. He had noticed, but hoped his assumptions wrong. Affinities were divided into many specialties, but only five warranted the title of House. The rest were best described as subsections of each major affinity, falling within its ruling House's jurisdiction. Each of the four women—Alira, Edagan, Melora, and Anaide—represented a House of element, while he represented the House of Healing.

To have called a Master to speak for each of the five major affinities meant nothing good.

"Out with it, Archmage, we're not daft." Edagan gave Nondar a sidewise look as she spoke, as if to imply she did not include him in the statement. He raised one bushy white brow in return.

Envesi motioned for silence. "When the caravan returns from Ilmenhith, I expect each of you to choose a mage from your House to promote and send to the palace as a new court mage. I have already promoted Lomithrandel to Master. He is ready to be sent." There was no preamble to soften the blow, no tip-toeing around the subject. Only Alira did not seem surprised. Envesi took in the shocked expressions the rest of them wore with smug satisfaction.

"How could you do such a thing?" Anaide slapped her hands against the tabletop as she leaped from her chair. "He is a royal, blood or not! He has no place as a Master. It's a breach of honor to bestow such rank to someone who cannot rightfully bear it. The temple has supported and been sponsored by the royal family for...forever! For as long as the temple has stood. How dare you put our king in such a position?"

"And why should Kirban remain loyal to a crown that will soon be up for grabs?" Alira snapped. "Kifel has no heir, and no immediate relatives remaining. The royal line dies with him."

"*King* Kifel has no *named* heirs." Nondar kept his tone level, though he wished to reach across the table and throttle the girl. Alira was but a fraction of Anaide's age. Whether or not she wore Master white, seniority should have demanded respect.

"You believe he would name Lomithrandel his heir, were he not a Master?" Melora broke in, giving Nondar a skeptical glare. "The royal family has enough scandal behind it as it is, without the next ruler spending his time on the throne trying to—"

"That is enough!" Envesi barely raised her voice, but the razor edge to her words was more than enough to silence them.

Anaide sank back into her chair.

Suffocating silence fell over the room. Troubled, Nondar rubbed the aching joints in his gnarled hands. The soothing motion had become a worried habit. Quiet lingered for a time before the Archmage spoke once more.

"The five of you have been called only because the laws of the temple mandate that any decisions regarding high-ranking Masters must be heard by the five Houses." Envesi studied each of them in turn as the words sank in. "There have never been secrets among Masters and never should there be. I cannot take this action without the Houses knowing. But with each of you here to represent your affinities, the decision has been spoken, and it will not be undone. None of you are to speak of this matter until there are five mages to send, in addition to my own selection."

Edagan snorted a laugh. "Yes, I imagine you wouldn't want the king to know you've put him in a political tight spot."

"Do you really mean to continue this action without calling a full council?" Nondar shook his head in disapproval. Mages were meant to maintain neutrality, offering their services to both factions that ruled Elenhiise. It was no secret between Masters that they were to train the king's potential heir—unofficially, and only until the boy's formidable power was restrained, not controlled. Raising him through the mageling colors had been controversial enough. Naming the boy court mage granted him authority he had no right to bear.

Nondar's mouth tightened. As she'd said, raising a mageling to Master was an action she couldn't take without the Houses knowing. He knew the rule well. Her choice to act first and inform later was certainly a departure from the norm, twisting the wording of the rules to her advantage.

"Gathering the Masters from the chapter houses could take weeks," Melora murmured.

"And in that time, Kifel's wrath will likely come down on our heads. You can't imagine he will take kindly to what you've done." Alira lifted her chin. She looked far too haughty. Again, Nondar stifled the desire to throttle her.

"The matter will be discussed in full when the solstice is over," the Archmage said. Her icy blue eyes settled squarely on Nondar. "This decision, however, will not be unmade."

He stared back, unwilling to be intimidated. He was within his right to object, and he would not stand down.

Anaide pushed herself up again. "Then we shall discuss the matter in full at a later time. For now, you must excuse me. I have packing yet to do before the carriages depart." She offered a curtsy that was spry for her age and excused herself without the Archmage's permission. No one dared comment and not another word was shared.

One by one, the Masters rose and left. The Archmage herself departed before Nondar left the table.

The burden of politics and conflict weighed heavy on his mind. He was not certain of Envesi's motives, but in his head, he saw the Archmage taking the first step toward a war of her own design.

———

A GRAY SKY AND SURPRISINGLY COLD DRIZZLE USHERED IN THE NEW morning; not the sort of weather anyone wanted to see upon waking. The temple's grounds hummed with activity despite the dreary weather. Above the buzz, the teachers put forward a frenzied effort to keep some sort of order.

A long line of carriages had appeared on the horizon at dusk the night before. Like all the other magelings, Kytenia had stolen glimpses of the caravan that was to transport the entire temple to Ilmenhith. She had not dared look long, but the look she'd gotten led her to believe the king had hired every team of horses on the island for this event.

Kytenia checked the wrappings of her ball gown for the twelfth time before she tucked it into her bag. She had stayed awake half the night to finish her dress and thought she was prepared, though perhaps not as prepared as Rikka, who had been ready to leave before the sun rose.

"Here she comes," Shymin murmured as she hefted her bag over her shoulder. A whisper of footsteps halted outside their door and a flurry of knocks sounded.

"We're coming," Kytenia called. She spared one last look for her room, then hitched her bag under her arm and scuffled to the door.

Rikka bounced on her toes in the hallway. Marreli was with her, but the smaller girl rubbed her eyes as if she'd just been dragged out of bed.

"We all want to go, you know," Shymin grumbled. "You don't need to herd us."

"I know." Rikka grinned sheepishly. "They'll be coming for a group soon, though, and I want us to be first in line."

Kytenia blinked in surprise. "They what? I thought the carriages weren't leaving until past noon!"

"They were," Rikka said, "but the Masters say they anticipate storms and the drivers decided it would be better to get a head start."

Marreli hid a yawn behind her hand. "Which made her even more glad she decided to chase me out of bed at sunrise."

The girls filtered down the hall together, baggage in tow.

"Did you check to see if...?" Kytenia trailed off with a hopeful glance in Rikka's direction.

Rikka started to say something, then closed her mouth and shook her head.

Kytenia's shoulders slumped, but she nodded in understanding.

It felt wrong to leave without Firal. In the back of her head, she blamed herself for their friend's absence; she'd been the one to tell her the carriages wouldn't begin to leave until afternoon.

Would things be different if she had insisted Firal be present at sunrise? She wrung her hands, but she didn't know what else she could do. She'd already spoken to Nondar.

The Master mage had not been pleased by Kytenia's report, and his mood had worsened when she mentioned Ran's suspected involvement. He hadn't said much, other than that he would address the matter. Then he instructed her not to speak of it anymore. Kytenia wasn't sure if she was allowed to speak to the other girls, but she'd told them of the meeting anyway. She hadn't kept names from her explanation, and while he hadn't indicated it, she expected the rest of them would face discipline for keeping secrets once he dealt with Ran and Firal.

Shortly after they reached the front of the dormitory, a man in a driver's uniform presented himself in the entrance. Rikka was the first to follow him toward the carriages. Shymin and Marreli were close behind, while Kytenia lingered in the doorway. Uneasiness settled in the pit of her stomach as she crossed the threshold and trailed behind the others.

Their carriage waited at the gate and Master Nondar stood beside it. Kytenia almost groaned when she saw him. Of course he would be assigned to their group after she'd spilled Firal's secrets the night before.

The horses stamped impatiently as each of the girls clambered into the carriage with their luggage. The driver waited for them to settle before he helped Nondar up. The old Master seated himself just inside the door. It was more crowded than anticipated, and even once their luggage was stacked, there was little room to spare. Kytenia kept her head down and avoided Nondar's eye. The driver checked their belongings twice before he latched the door from the outside. The moment it closed, the sound of voices outside faded to white noise.

Long minutes passed before they heard the rattle of the driver climbing into his seat. When he snapped the reins, the horses leaped forward so eagerly the girls nearly fell atop one another.

"Well!" Rikka pulled back the curtain on the tiny window. "This is nicer than I expected. The windows are glass." She tapped the pane with a fingernail and listened to it click with silent appreciation. "From what I've heard, we should be arriving in Ilmenhith in just a few days."

"With fortune," Master Nondar agreed.

Kytenia was not the only one who winced. Amidst all the excitement, none of them had stopped to consider how long the trip from the temple to Ilmenhith might be. Now that they were settled in a cramped carriage, their excitement faded at the prospect of sitting mashed together for several days. Not that any of them would choose to stay behind.

The carriage swayed as its wheels found the narrow road. They could not see the conveyances in front of or behind them, but the way was familiar after their recent market visit. Kytenia gazed out through the drizzle beyond the carriage windows, and for a time, everything was quiet.

The convoy paused briefly in the market, and Shymin gathered all the receipts the seamstress had given them. She grew solemn when Kytenia gave her one, as well.

Kytenia smiled hopefully. She didn't know how much use it would be, but no one had opposed when she suggested retrieving it from Firal's room.

Silence fell after Shymin left to retrieve the dresses and the girls shifted uncomfortably for some time.

Rikka and Marreli chatted about the fashions they expected to see and which dances might be popular in the capital. Kytenia gazed out the window without seeing the people outside. Master Nondar produced a small book from his white robes and made himself comfortable to read. No one minded; it was unlikely their awkward small talk would have held his interest to begin with.

It took close to an hour for Shymin to make her way back to the carriage with packages wrapped in plain muslin in her arms. She passed them out before she returned to her seat.

Kytenia frowned when there wasn't one for her. "There are only three?"

Shymin spread her hands in a gesture of helplessness. "I asked about Firal's, but the seamstress said it was sent ahead. She said those were her directions from whoever paid for it."

Nondar turned a sharp blue eye toward the girls at mention of Firal. Kytenia said nothing else, her face grim as the driver set the carriage in motion again.

The convoy pushed on through the first night with few breaks, the rocking of the coach on the rutted path eventually lulling all of its passengers to sleep.

Travel stopped in the morning for a sparse meal distributed from a supply wagon. Kytenia did not know when the kitchen staff found time to prepare food for the voyage, but when they paused again at noon for lunch and the rain had grown too heavy for a cook fire, everyone was grateful for the cold vegetables and thin slices of meat.

They formed camp some time after dark. The carriages drew into a circle and the drivers pulled tents from the railing on the roofs of each transport.

Kytenia planned to sleep in the carriage when Shymin, Rikka and Marreli moved to a tent, but Nondar stayed behind as well, and Kytenia decided to join the other girls for propriety's sake. The four of them lay in a row, crammed into a low-roofed canvas tent pitched as close to one of the many campfires as they thought safe.

"Do you think she'll make it?" Marreli asked in a whisper that was barely audible over the drumming rain. Shymin glanced toward the carriages as if she thought Nondar might overhear.

"I think so," Kytenia whispered back. She hoped so, in any case. Hoping was all she could do.

"GOOD MORNING, SUNSHINE."

The words purred right beside her ear. Firal groaned and nestled her face into the warmth of the body beside her, inhaling his sweetly masculine scent with a sigh.

"I thought you weren't going to touch me?" she asked in a murmur. Her eyes didn't want to open.

"I never said that." A gentle hand stroked her back. "Do you always get so cuddly with strangers?"

Firal grumbled. She forced her eyelids apart and blinked dazedly at the figure she lay against. Her fingers curled in his shirt. Instead of the armor she remembered Ran wearing, she felt firm muscle underneath thick, rough-spun fabric. Her breath caught in her throat and she lifted her eyes.

Daemon tilted his head as he looked down at her, his eyes glowing dull violet behind his steel mask.

She shrieked and thrust herself away from him. "Keep your hands to yourself!"

His laugh was muted by his mask. "Me? I sat down and you climbed into my lap."

Firal glared, unable to keep from blushing. "What are you doing here?"

"I could ask you the same question." His voice dropped dangerously. "I was under the impression we had an agreement. I get you out, you stay out. Am I the only one who got that?"

"Any deal we had was off as soon as you didn't give back my property." Her eyes darted to the sky beyond the jagged stone teeth that lined the cavern's entry. A thin mist hung in the air. The sun was just cresting the horizon; the storm had passed.

"You came back just for that?" Daemon sounded more amused than anything. He inched back across the floor to recline against the wall with his arms crossed. "What in the world could be so precious about one little book?"

"It's not the book." Firal gave him a look so acidic that it made him pause.

"Then what is it?" he asked finally.

She picked her cloak up off the floor and wrapped it around her shoulders. "What do you want from me?"

"Nothing." He shrugged. "Nothing you'll give, anyway. I've already told you what I want. I want you to stay out of the ruins, but you seem to have difficulty with simple instructions."

"If you had given me my journal, I wouldn't have had a reason to come back," she protested.

"Stubborn girl. You've been quite troublesome, you know that? Interrupting important business with your constant invasions of our territory." Daemon reached behind his back. Firal hadn't noticed the small leather satchel he'd been leaning on until he shifted to get something out of it.

Her journal.

He turned the small book over in his scaly hands before he held it out to her. Firal's eyes widened and she snatched it out of his grasp.

"There. Happy now?" He settled against the wall again.

Glaring, Firal untied the book's strap and flipped it open. The pages were intact. Not a single hint of water damage. Had he had the blighted thing the whole time? She bit her lip and dipped her fingers into the pocket of the cover. The necklace was still there.

Closing her eyes and sighing with relief, she pulled the broken chain free and caught hold of the pendant. Her thumb brushed over the relief of the many-pointed star. "It's not the book that matters." She cast the leather journal to the floor between them. "Just this."

Daemon's eyes flickered behind his mask. "All that for a broken necklace?"

"My mother's." She tucked the pendant into her bodice. "Keep the book, for all I care. All I need is this."

He watched her tuck her pendant into the bodice of her dress, his gaze lingering at her throat for a long moment afterward. Then he blinked several times, as if to clear his vision, and turned away. "I'm sorry," he said, so soft she almost thought it sincere. "I didn't know its importance."

"I don't expect you to understand," she snapped. "You don't have to pretend you do. I don't want sympathy, especially not from you."

He stared at the journal by his feet for a time. Eventually, he picked it up and wrapped the strap around it to bind it closed again. "I've watched the temple for a long time, but sometimes it seems I know very little about how life inside it works."

Firal didn't reply. Beyond their shelter, the mists burned off as sunlight spilled across the ruins. It was going to be miserably humid.

Silence weighed heavily for a time before she mustered the will to speak again.

"So what happens now?" she asked. "Do you escort me out again, or do you mean to kill me for returning?"

"It does seem like you have a death wish, coming back after meeting Lumia. It would be better for both of us if I grant it, wouldn't it? Lumia is not a forgiving woman."

She grimaced, but the threat of death seemed hollow. Twice, he'd had the opportunity to hurt her; twice, he'd sent her back to the temple unscathed. She didn't understand why and couldn't imagine what stayed his hand—especially after their encounter with his queen—but all things considered, she didn't think it was luck that had kept her alive.

"Very well," Firal said finally. She returned to his side and knelt beside him, sat on her heels and clasped her hands in her lap. "Please make it fast." She squeezed her amber eyes closed.

She didn't have to see him to know he was surprised; the silence made it clear enough. But she felt the weight of his eyes on her, felt the proximity of his hand hovering at her throat. Then he brushed her hair back from her face and wound his claws in her ebony tresses.

Goosebumps crawled down her spine.

"Your hair feels like silk, but it doesn't snag when I touch it.

Perhaps I'll keep it." He chuckled when she shivered. "It's so pretty on your head, though. Perhaps I'll keep that, too."

"Do you intend to tell me all your plans to dismember me, or will you do me the courtesy of getting it over with quickly?" Firal opened her eyes to glare at him.

He regarded her thoughtfully for a time before he untangled his hand from her hair and stood. "Get up." He picked up his worn leather bag and tucked her abandoned journal inside it. "I've better things to do than kill you."

Relief washed over her in a wave. She was right, then. He didn't mean to harm her. But at the same time, she wasn't sure she liked the idea of those 'better things.' She got to her feet. "Like what? You sound like you have something in mind."

Daemon was already walking up the stairs that led into the ruins. Firal hurried to close the gap between them.

The sky overhead was not completely clear. Sunbeams fell past patchy clouds, but a thicker layer of cloud cover with a gray underside hovered to the south. It would rain again soon.

"I have a few things in mind," he said casually as he started down the corridor at a languid pace. "Of course, I hope you know you're indebted to me now, since I'm choosing to spare you. Mistress would hardly approve, but what she doesn't know won't hurt her."

"Mistress?" Firal pulled up the hood of her cloak in spite of the sun.

"Lumia, Queen of the Underground. I thought we'd already established the part where I serve her." He peered at her over his shoulder. Even with the mask he wore, she had the strange impression of a quizzical look on his face.

She huffed. "You ought to call her *my lady* or *Her Majesty*, not *mistress*. You can hardly expect me to understand the ways of you beasts after one meeting with your queen."

"Beasts?" He barked a laugh, harsh and humorless. "I think you have a terrible misconception of what we are. My men are no more beastly than I am."

159

Firal's nose crinkled and she glanced at his strange feet, with their elevated heel and three elongated, claw-tipped toes. Her lip curled with distaste. "Well, that isn't saying much, is it?"

Daemon rolled his eyes. "The people of the underground have a very stable civilization and a unique culture led by different factions. They even have their own written alphabet. They're hardly beasts. They're every bit as human as the people in Alwhen."

She paused mid-stride. Firal knew Alwhen was the capital of the Giftless lands, though she was not entirely sure where it was. Human settlements on the island seemed to be as short-lived as their people. "But there are unnatural things among your kind. The stories saying your queen is immortal, for example. And—" She bit her her tongue and stopped short.

"And me?" Daemon finished for her. "I know exactly how you feel about me. It's not like you try to hide the way you stare. There's no need to hold your tongue, mageling. You offend me more by feigning indifference."

"Who says I'm trying to avoid offending you?" Firal scoffed. She craned her neck, searching for the sun's position. She turned when she found it, starting toward the south and leaving him behind.

"Where are you going?" he called after her.

"Home," she yelled back. She heard Daemon following her and didn't care. It took effort to keep the sun to her left as she traversed the winding halls. It was fortunate the sun was still visible between clouds; the direction would have been impossible to discern otherwise.

As soon as the Archmage's tower became visible over the crumbling walls of the ruins, she broke into a run. Rounding the corner of the last wall, she burst into the open field between ruin and temple. The hedgerow at the edge of the garden was just ahead. She hastened toward it, but skidded to a halt when she saw the courtyard on the other side.

There wasn't a soul to be seen.

No students milling about, no Masters in their stark white crossing through the garden. Silence lay over the temple like a heavy cloak, driving her heart to the pit of her stomach.

"Is it always this quiet?" Daemon's voice at her heels made her jump.

She shot a glare over her shoulder and took a step closer to the hedges. Her eyes scoured the courtyard. There was no mistaking it. Everyone was gone. "They left without me!" she cried. How early had the trip started? How late had she slept?

"Ah, right." He chuckled and folded his arms over his chest. "The solstice. Poor little Firal, the odd mage out. Left behind while everyone goes to the palace."

Firal's eyes narrowed. "How do you know about that?"

He met her gaze levelly. "Considering the knowledge spread like wildfire across the kingdom, I'd be more surprised to find someone who didn't know."

"I told Kytenia I'd be back in time. They weren't supposed to leave until this afternoon. I told her...I'd..." Her shoulders bunched and she swallowed. Tears blurred her vision and her throat grew thick.

For the first time in her life, she'd had a chance to find answers. In her desperate attempt to recover her necklace and ensure it would happen, she'd robbed herself of the opportunity.

And then there was why she'd missed it, and where she'd been. There would be no avoiding the scrutiny of the Masters now. The idea of punishment made her queasy.

Her shoulders slumped and she sucked in a shuddering breath. "I have to catch up with the carriages." How she was going to do that, she wasn't sure. She wasn't even certain she could find the market on her own.

"Catch up? You don't even know which direction they went," Daemon snorted.

She grimaced at the reflection of her thoughts in his words. "What, and you do?"

"I am well acquainted with the way to Ilmenhith, yes."

She stared at him, her mouth working to form words.

He watched her lips in mild amusement. "Do you really want to go that badly?"

There was nothing she wanted more. Firal pressed a hand to her aching chest, above where she'd hidden her necklace within her bodice. "Yes," she whispered.

"Then let's make a deal." Daemon paced forward and circled her slowly. "I can take you to Ilmenhith. I'll even make sure you make it back to the temple safely."

Her heart leaped. "You can?"

"Hinging, of course, on the condition that you give me what I want in return."

Firal's excitement waned. "What do you want?"

"Knowledge." The smile was audible in his voice. He stopped beside her. "I want you to give me knowledge the temple would deny me. You already know I bear the Gift, but I can't control it without training. Agree to school me, and I'll see to it that you make it there in time."

As quickly as her spirits had surged at his offer, her stomach sank. She wasn't the strongest of magelings, nor was she authorized to use her magic for her own means. How was she supposed to teach someone else to wield a power she could barely contain, herself?

No, that was a lie; she was perfectly capable with magic and she knew it. She had assisted Ran several times, hiding in places the Masters wouldn't see them, trying to teach him what he'd missed in class. It wasn't lack of skill that made her balk. It was danger. "And if I don't?" she asked cautiously.

"Then it's not too late for me to change my mind about letting you leave the ruins in one piece." Daemon shrugged, so indifferent it made her stomach turn.

Swallowing, she turned toward the courtyard. "Just let me get—"

"No," he interrupted. "Decide now, move now. I'm not foolish enough to give you the chance to run away."

She started to protest, then remembered the mage-barrier. It would keep him from following her past the hedges and onto temple grounds. Since he hadn't suggested he accompany her, she suspected he knew. Firal hesitated, considering. She wasn't afraid of him, his threats ringing hollow against the memory of him turning her free. It was the Masters she was concerned about.

And losing her only chance to learn her mother's name.

Firal weighed the possibilities in her head, every muscle in her body tense. In her heart, she'd already made her decision. It was convincing her head it was the best choice that would be a problem.

She gestured for him to lead the way. "Tell me what you can already do."

Daemon grasped her elbow and turned her back toward the ruins. From the confident way he moved, she wondered if he'd predicted her answer from the beginning.

"I've done a few things before," he said, "but most of it is accidental, or it's so out of order that it's useless. For instance, when you healed me. I can mend a broken bone, but I don't know how to set it, and I can't even coax the tiniest of cuts to heal. I can call a bolt of lightning from a clear sky, but I can't light a candle without matches or flint. I want to learn practicality."

"Teaching you proper techniques could take months. I obviously can't stay hidden in the ruins for that long." Firal held her skirts just high enough that they wouldn't snag on prickly weeds. He moved ahead, across the clearing between temple and ruin, and she frowned at his back.

"Then you stay in the temple and come to the ruins to teach me every evening, beginning the first night after you return from Ilmenhith. You will be granted safe passage in the ruins whenever we meet for lessons. Agreed?" Daemon stopped in an entrance to the ruins and faced her. It took her a moment to realize he wanted an immediate answer.

She eyed him doubtfully. "So you promise safe passage to

Ilmenhith, a safe return to the temple, and risk-free access to the ruins in exchange for lessons in magic?"

Daemon nodded.

"Done," she said, presenting her hand.

He clasped her fingers in his clawed grasp. The amount of care that went into his touch surprised her; the sharp tips of his claws hardly brushed her skin. Then he spun away so fast it made his cloak flutter. Daemon brought his hands together, drew a line upward and then stretched his arms out overhead, tracing a squared shape in the air before him.

The hair on the back of Firal's neck prickled as the flows of magic in the air shifted. "What are you doing?"

Power crackled in the open space ahead of them, the trails he'd traced sizzling with white sparks of energy. Her heart skipped a beat as the power began to weave a spiderweb of lines, raw magic zigzagging across the open air. "Stop!"

He continued, slowly drawing the edges of the networking flows toward the ground.

"Stop!" she screeched, launching herself at his back. His hold on the energy flows snapped as she struck him. The crackling lines converged and then shot outward with a deafening boom as the two of them hit the ground.

"Get off me!" Daemon snarled, twisting out from underneath her weight.

Before he could escape, she slapped him so hard his mask rang with the blow.

"Don't do that! Don't you even dare! Do you have any idea what you could have done?" She cradled her hand to her chest and glared at the steel shield over his face. "A single mage should never open a Gate! They should never even try! You could have unmade yourself, trying something like that!" Her voice cracked and she fell back to sit on her heels.

He stared at her, dead silent, for so long it made her want to hit him again. What in the world had possessed him to try something like that? How had he even discovered the complex manipulation of energy required for a Gate?

Daemon pushed himself up and shook out his cloak. "The solstice ball happens in Ilmenhith a week from now," he said, somewhat shakily. Hadn't he known what could have happened? "We'll begin lessons immediately. I'll take you to Ilmenhith myself, by foot, and you'll teach me along the way. When you arrive back in the temple after the solstice, we'll begin nightly lessons in the ruins."

Firal gaped. "We can't walk to Ilmenhith from here!"

"You've seen the passages underground, and I know the ruins better than anyone." His voice grew steadier as he spoke, though he flexed his hands as if they still tingled with the power he'd tried to manipulate. "The carriages will have to loop around the outermost edges of the ruins and follow established roads. I can get us there just as fast, if not faster."

She got to her feet and brushed at her knees. "No Gates."

"No Gates," he agreed.

"Then it's a deal." Firal adjusted her dress and checked the necklace tucked into her bodice.

"Good. Let's go." He turned and started down the hallway at a brisk pace. "We've got a lot of distance to cover."

She sighed, picked up her skirts and started after him, both of them unsteady on their feet.

13

LESSON ONE

"I THINK IT'S GOING TO RAIN AGAIN," FIRAL CALLED AHEAD AS SHE fought her way through a thick patch of overgrowth. Progress had been steady when Daemon cut a path for her, but he'd climbed the leftmost wall some time ago. He walked along its top with no regard for her inability to keep up. She stumbled when she made it past the tangle of weeds, her skirts twisted about her ankles. It took her a moment to right herself and run after him. "Should we find someplace to take cover?"

Daemon paused. Smoky-white clouds had filled the sky, their underbellies heavy and gray. A darker, smoother shade of gray had already swallowed the horizon. "Nah," he replied, starting forward again.

"Well, you might be all right with getting wet, but I'm not." Firal scowled when he made an abrupt turn above her and she scrambled to follow. She'd almost missed the opening to the new path.

"It'll clear up," he said with a touch of amusement.

He'd barely spoken since they started off, but the farther they went, the more his mood seemed to improve. It was a sharp contrast to the growled orders and barbed comments she'd gotten from him before. His voice was rather pleasant when he

BETH ALVAREZ

wasn't in a foul mood, she realized with a blush. She shouldn't have found anything about the situation pleasant.

Firal turned her thoughts to her aching limbs. "How far do you think we've come?" It had been several hours since they'd stopped for a rest. The muscles in her legs burned with fatigue.

"Hard to say. The ruins double back on themselves so often, it's easy to lose track of distance." He spread his arms for balance and took a wide step over a hole in the top of the wall.

"Do you know what time it is?"

He looked skyward, paused, and turned atop the ruin wall until he located a brighter spot in the clouds. "A bit before noon."

Firal frowned. Her stomach grumbled; she hadn't brought any provisions into the ruins yesterday, only planning a short trip. If he'd let her gather her things from the temple, she would have fetched food from the dinner hall.

Her sullen silence didn't go unnoticed. The weight of Daemon's eyes made her skin crawl.

"We'll walk until dusk," he said, firm enough to still any debate before it happened. "Then we'll set up camp and stay put until morning."

She stifled a groan. Nothing but the sprawling hallways of the ruins lay ahead. She understood the need to hurry; with clouds veiling the sky, it would be impossible to keep a sense of direction and navigate the ruins after dark. But understanding didn't alleviate her desire to complain about the decision, and she bit her tongue to keep it still.

After so many hours, every hallway began to look the same. They passed dozens of identical corners and traced more halls than Firal could count. More than once, they slipped through rooms with wide-trunked and mushroom-topped trees, and they were all so alike she wondered if they'd traveled any distance at all.

Just when she thought her growling stomach wouldn't let her

168

go a step farther, Daemon stopped atop the wall beside her and tossed something her way. "Catch."

Firal barely snagged the dark-colored object from the air. She stopped in the middle of the corridor and looked down at her hands. The oval fruit fit into her palm. Its deep purple skin reminded her of a plum, though its surface was smooth and bore a waxy shine. "What is this?"

"Food." He held up one of his own before turning away to eat.

"Where did you get it?"

He snorted. "Didn't you see the trees?"

Doubtful, Firal took a tiny, experimental bite. Sharp, sour flavor filled her mouth and she squealed as the taste sent a violent shudder through her frame.

Ahead, Daemon laughed.

When dusk finally came, the moist air felt unusually cold. Lightning crawled across the undersides of the clouds and Firal counted the seconds before the rumble of thunder.

"It's still more than fifteen miles off." Daemon said, voicing her thoughts. He did that too often for comfort. "We should be able to cover a little more ground before the rain gets—" A plump raindrop pinged against his mask and cut him short. "Or maybe not," he murmured, chagrined.

Firal gave an angry wail and sank against the stone wall. "It's after dark, we're still walking, and before I even get a chance to rest, we're rained on!"

Rolling his eyes, Daemon slid down from the wall. He caught hold of her arm and hefted her back to her feet. "Oh, come on. Did I say we were stopping here? We'll keep going while the rain is light, and then—"

"We'll be soaked." She tried to wriggle out of his grasp. His hand tightened and she gritted her teeth. "Or your stupid mask will get us hit by lightning, or—" When she couldn't escape, she withered to ground like a ragdoll and glared up at him. She'd make them stop and rest, one way or another.

169

"Stop that!" Daemon dragged her back onto her feet and gave her a shake. "What is wrong with you?"

"Can't we stop? We've been walking all day. I don't think I can go any farther." Firal's voice cracked and she licked her dry lips. "I'm starting to feel weak."

"I'm not sure I'd say you were strong to begin with." He held her fast, as if he expected her to try to slither away again. "Come on, there's cover not far from here."

Reluctantly, she followed.

Despite his continued reassurances, they walked in the rain for at least another half hour. As her strength flagged, his arm slid around her shoulders to offer support. Words fell short of the relief she felt when they rounded a corner and met an entrance to the underground. There was no elaborate doorway here, no frightful gate or sculpted monsters. A pair of simple black stone pillars rose to frame the stairway, which vanished into a cavernous hallway.

The stairwell itself was well maintained, clean and clear of debris. Tiny channels carved into the stone diverted the flow of rain into deep trenches at the base of both black walls. The walls reminded Firal of those in the underground, swallowing every trace of light and leaving her unable to see. Unhindered, Daemon guided her steps without difficulty. Once the hallway leveled out, he settled her in the middle of the floor.

"We'll stay here for the night. It's safe." His voice echoed in the hallway, the sound so empty it sent a shiver down her spine. "You wait here, I'll go find something to eat. And some firewood, if we're lucky."

"You're leaving me here alone?" Firal rubbed her arms when he let her go. "But what if—"

"Wait here," he repeated firmly. "Unless you want to spend more time in the rain?"

She swallowed and turned away. The glow of his eyes in the dark would always be unnerving. "Fine." Firal crossed her arms tight across her cold chest, not caring that it made her look like an impudent child.

"Good." He patted her head and left her there, the claws on his feet clicking a soft rhythm against the smooth floor as he crept back out into the rain.

Firal glowered after him, rubbed her arms and drew her knees to her chest. As an afterthought, she took off her wet cloak and spread it on the floor to dry. She was too weary to snare the magic she'd need to dry it, or she might have used it for a blanket. If she was lucky, it would be dry by the time she went to sleep.

Without thinking about it, she tugged the broken chain of her necklace from between her breasts. She twisted the links between her fingers as the metal cooled. Having it back was a comfort, but she suspected that was the only comfort she'd get tonight. Idly, she rubbed the pendant with her thumb. She could do nothing else but wait.

"GET UP."

Firal didn't know she'd fallen asleep until a clawed foot nudged her side to rouse her. She blinked at the shadows and fought off disorientation. Wood clattered to the floor and she pushed herself upright. Her toes hit the wood pile and she grunted.

"How long was I asleep?" Her voice rasped in her throat. She grimaced and swallowed against the dry stickiness in her mouth. The dim purple glow of Daemon's eyes was bright enough to locate him in the dark, but she could see nothing else.

"Don't know, I wasn't here when you fell asleep." The wood scraped against the floor as he pushed it into a pile. "The firewood is wet."

"Excuse me?"

"The wood is wet. It has to be dried." He sounded irritated at having to repeat himself. "Even if it were dry, I don't have any flint. We'll have to start it another way."

"Just draw a flame, then."

He hesitated.

"You can't make a flame?" She felt bad the moment she spoke. Summoning a flame was an easy trick when you had a teacher, but it wasn't likely he'd ever get the knack on his own. She went on before he could reply. "Well, we'll have to dry it out, first." Uncertainty tried to creep into her words and she pushed back against it. A part of her had hoped he wouldn't expect a magic lesson so soon, but a deal was a deal, and she wouldn't go back on her word. At least the nap had refreshed her enough to do it.

Firal fumbled blindly in the dark and twitched when he put his hand in hers. The texture of his scales was glassy and smooth, unlike what she'd expected. She traced the shape of his fingers for a moment before she moved his hand over the wood. She knew where that was, at least, having bruised her toes against it. "All right, let's begin. All magic has a source."

"Yes, yes. I know that," Daemon growled. "And the source must be contacted before you can draw energy to focus into a physical form."

Firal shook her head. "Not quite. It's not so much an issue of contacting the source as recognizing it. It's always there, waiting for you to touch and guide it. The magic flows with or without us. All we have to do is shape it. You said you already know some healing, correct?"

"Some," he replied reluctantly. "It's performed by manipulating the energy flows of a person's body."

"Not entirely, but that is the basic idea." She let go of his hand and sat back on her heels. "I think we need to discuss the origins of magic before I can show you how to use it properly. I forgot you haven't even had the basic lectures."

Daemon rolled his eyes. The gesture was impossible to miss in the dark. "Fine."

She gave him a reprimanding look, but continued anyway. "Magic is, in essence, the manipulation of energy around you. Anyone who is capable of sensing the energy flows can manipulate them. Some, like the Eldani without a trainable Gift, are able to contact it, but only unconsciously. To extend their lives, for example, they absorb small amounts of power from everything around them. Every object, every being, has an energy source that can be tapped, redirected, or borrowed. But never taken."

"What's the difference?" He watched her too closely for her to be comfortable, even in the dark.

Firal drew a breath. This would have been easier if she'd had time to prepare. "Borrowing something's energy can weaken it, but only temporarily. Once it regains its energy, it recovers. If you take the energy from it, instead of borrowing, it may never regain that strength." She frowned. "Especially when borrowing energy from inanimate things. You could never take all the energy the wind has to offer, but you could take everything from a tree. It could die slowly, or worse, it..." she trailed off and swallowed hard.

"It could be unmade," Daemon finished for her, unperturbed by the weight of his words.

She suppressed a shiver and forced herself to go on. "You must be self-aware to wield the energy you're borrowing. It can be used to do almost anything, if you know how to bend it. All mages have a natural affinity, though. At the temple, affinities are divided and governed by the five Houses. Affinities are what you excel at, but they also limit the energies you can draw on. If you don't yet know yours, we'll need to determine it, first."

"How do you channel energy if there's nothing present for you to draw on?" Daemon asked, skeptical.

"In that situation, you rely first on your own energy. You can still manipulate things outside your affinity, as long as you have the strength to tie yourself to it first. It just takes more effort, and it can be more draining." She shrugged.

"I can't anchor myself to anything. I can't feel it."

"You could feel it if you knew what you were looking for." Firal pointed toward the wood. "For this, the starting point is water. So, see if you can feel the water there, first. Physically. To draw it out of the wood, you just have to find it, attach yourself to its energy, and pull it out." She took hold of his hand again and guided his claws to the surface of the wood.

Daemon's hand flexed in her grasp. He moved his fingers away from the firewood, then closer to it. He spread his fingers wide, folded them together, touched the wood, let his hand hover over it. Long moments passed. "I don't feel anything."

"Liar. You can feel that it's wet, can't you?"

"No, I can't," he replied, irritated. His voice echoed, sharp, in the confines of the narrow hall.

Firal opened her mouth to chide him, then stopped as she recalled his scales. Perhaps he wasn't as sensitive to touch as she was. Without that awareness, maybe he wouldn't feel when he had the thread of energies in his hand, wouldn't feel the gentle slide of the water's energy flow against his skin.

He pulled his hand from her grasp. "You do it. I don't know what I'm looking for. Maybe seeing you do it will help."

She bit her lip, but said nothing as she touched her fingertips to the damp tinder. Pressing down, she caught the minute sensation of the water on her skin. She snagged the water's presence and drew her hand downward. The water seeped out of the wood. Then she flicked her hand through the air to snare the feeling of warmth in her fingertips, like grasping a strip of heated silk. It slipped and she tightened her hold to draw it upward. A tiny flicker lit and golden flames licked the firewood.

Daemon flinched at the sudden spark. Firelight gleamed on the metal of his mask and his eyes squeezed shut.

"Sorry." Firal inched closer to the fire and held out her hands to take in the warmth. Her stomach's grumbling interrupted the stillness.

"Hungry?"

"That's a stupid question." She laid a hand on her stomach. "Did you bring any food?"

He nodded, fishing beneath his cloak and producing a leather pouch that looked full to brimming. "Yes, but you'd better be really hungry." He flipped back the lid of the pouch and spilled a portion of its contents to the floor. The black mass writhed and began to untangle itself, tails and claws waving as dozens of prickly legs kicked and crawled.

She shrieked and scrambled backwards, her amber eyes wide. "Scorpions? Bugs are not food!"

Daemon picked up one of the smaller sticks he'd slyly set aside from the rest of the kindling. It twirled between his nimble fingers. "Arachnids, actually. They have eight legs, so they're not bugs." He brought the sharp end of the stick down in the middle of a black carapace, spearing the vermin one by one.

"I'd be even less likely to eat a spider, thank you very much!" Firal forced her eyes closed as she fought the heave of her stomach.

"Oh, come now. They're a delicacy in the underground. I went through a lot of trouble to catch these. You have to at least try it." He plucked off their stingers with two claws, then swept them into the trench at the foot of the wall to let the water carry them away. "I've been told they taste a lot like lobster, or crayfish, which is why they're so good with lemon. I couldn't say, really. I don't think I've ever had either. They taste a bit like chicken to me." He held the makeshift skewer over the fire, seeming amused at the horrified look on her face.

Firal shuddered. "They say everything tastes like chicken. Nothing ever does."

Daemon shrugged and turned the skewer. Pops and hisses filled the air as scorpion shells split in the heat. "Do you want to try some?"

"No." She gave him a disdainful look, drew back farther, and settled at the edge of the trench beside the wall. "You help yourself, but I think I'd be better off hungry."

"GOOD MORNING, SUNSHINE."

Firal groaned at the cheerful words. She couldn't seem to straighten her legs or back. Her muscles protested every move. She'd curled up in her cloak after it dried, but the ground was hard and cold and she would surely suffer for it today. Dim light filtered in from the mouth of the passage and she thought she smelled rain.

The fire had long since gone out. Daemon swept the ashes into one of the trenches with his foot. "I brought you some food. I figured it'd be faster for me to try foraging alone." He touched his shirt and pockets as though he'd forgotten where he put it.

She scowled and gathered her cloak around her shoulders as she forced herself to sit up. "If more than four legs are involved in this particular meal, then you can keep it."

"No legs, don't worry." Daemon found the pouch in a pocket on the inside of his cloak. He tugged it open as he drew it from its hiding place. It was not the same pouch he'd put the scorpions in; she wondered if he still had them. He turned it over and gave it a shake. Huge blackberries spilled into his palm.

She hesitated as he crouched beside her. "Are they poisonous?"

"Poisonous? They're blackberries. Besides, why would I do such a thing to my teacher?" He took a berry between the claws of his forefinger and thumb and slipped it beneath his mask.

"I'm not sure I believe you ate that." Firal picked up a berry and leered at it distrustfully. It was plump and tantalizing after a long night without a meal.

"I'm really not sure why you're so convinced I'm going to hurt you. You didn't seem to believe I would before. Besides, we made an agreement. Doesn't that count for anything?" He lifted a green-scaled hand to his chest in a gesture of hurt that didn't seem sincere.

She frowned at him before she tried his offering. The fruit was still warm from the earth and air, soft from sunshine and rich with flavor. She chewed slowly, waiting to make sure there were no adverse effects before taking another. "Thank you, by the way."

"You're welcome."

"How much farther do we have to go?" she asked.

Daemon shook a few more berries into the palm of his hand before he tossed the rest of the pouch to her. "We should be at the border of the capital in a few nights, if we can keep the pace we held yesterday."

"Oh." Firal drew up her knees and hugged them with one arm as she ate. She wasn't looking forward to another day of aching muscles and blistered feet. "Have you been to Ilmenhith before?"

"Many times."

She picked up the pouch of blackberries. "What will you do when we get there?" As strongly as she hoped to find other magelings from the temple, she had no idea what their lodging arrangements would be, or where to look for them. She wasn't eager to roam the city on her own, but she would if she had to.

"I have my own business to attend to." Daemon brushed at his clothes as he stood. He double-checked the ground for belongings, then turned toward the open air.

Firal stumbled over her feet as she hurried after him.

"Now," he sighed, starting off at a brisk pace. "Let's begin the next lesson, shall we?"

Her shoulders slumped as they emerged into a dreary drizzle.

Daemon kept her distracted with a seemingly endless barrage of questions. His eagerness to hear about the temple's methods and teachings was surprising, his enthusiasm encouraging. She didn't know the answer for some questions, but at least stewing over them made travel less monotonous.

"So how many classes, on average, does a normal mageling

—" His face twisted as if the word left a foul taste in his mouth. "I mean, how many classes does a student usually have?"

"It depends on their affinities, really, but most have five or six a day. The magelings are divided by skill level, which is denoted by color and associated with strength, but they're usually divided by affinity as well." Firal paused to pick a burr out of her skirts. She examined its shape before she cast it to the ground. There were a number of useful plants in the ruins, and she tried to note where each of them grew. "There are a few classes everyone is required to take, though, regardless of affinity. Healing, for example. It's considered a vital skill, so they make all magelings study it."

"I'm not sure I understand the divisions the temple has set up." Daemon paused to let her catch up. He was a full head taller than her and his long-legged strides were difficult for her to match.

"Well, first, there are the colors," she said. "Gray marks the least skilled mages, followed by lavender. Yellow is about the middle, green a step higher, and blue comes just before Master. Masters wear white, but Masters of a House or the royal court also mark their eyes."

"Yes, yes, I know that," he snapped, waving a hand as if to dismiss the explanation. "I mean I don't understand the affinities, or why they would divide students because of them."

"Oh." Firal stopped to untangle a vine from her sandal before she replied. "Well, there are five recognized affinities. Those are the Houses. There's Fire, Wind, Water, Earth, and then Healing, though I suppose it should be called Life. One's affinity dictates the power sources they can draw from, I think I mentioned that before."

"Sort of," he said, "but go on."

"Affinities are a safeguard of magic, I suppose you could say." She tucked a curl behind her ear. "They keep one from drawing more power than they can handle. Those with a wind affinity, for example, can usually only harness the power of the wind to fuel their magic. Everyone can use their body's own energy, though, and use it to influence elements outside their affinity."

Daemon eyed her over his shoulder. "What's your affinity?"

"Healing." Pride swelled in her chest and escaped as a smile. "It's why you're walking on that leg so soon. Of course, healing has its own downfalls. I can't heal myself. No one has the ability to manipulate their own body with magic. And it's a dangerous affinity to have. It means I can only use the energy of living things. I'm always afraid I'll draw more than what's safe to borrow. It's one thing to unmake a rock, or a tree, but when you're using someone else's energies to heal them..." She shuddered.

"You must spend a lot of time studying." He changed the subject smoothly, pulling himself up onto a wall as they rounded a corner.

She was grateful for the change of topic. The risks of magic weren't pleasant to discuss. "I have nine hours of classes on normal days. Lately, though, the schedule has been a mess. There haven't been any regular classes held since the king visited."

"Nine hours a day." He shook his head. "And yet you still have enough free time to trespass where you aren't wanted."

Firal pursed her lips and did not reply.

Daemon glanced down at her. "I'm just teasing, you know." He walked with his arms outstretched to maintain his balance on the narrow wall. Now and then he faltered when loose stones slid out from underfoot.

Firal cringed, certain he would fall. "I don't find that sort of teasing very funny."

"I didn't figure you would." A hint of sarcasm colored his voice and he changed the topic abruptly again, though he spoke as if continuing a thought. "You know, I've seen mostly women at the temple. Why don't more men practice magecraft?"

"A good number of men aren't able to." She tried not to look as he stepped over cracks in the wall. "Really, I'm surprised that you have an active Gift. Most who follow a soldier's path can't be taught."

"Why not?" His tone reminded her of a curious child.

"Magic is tied closely to emotion. Connecting to energies also requires a strong connection to feelings, particularly in healing. Empathy is important. Without it, one would not be able to sense the energy flows. Most men throttle their feelings into oblivion. There are just as many Gifted men as women, but I think most men are taught that strong emotion is undesirable, maybe even unacceptable. They aren't considered masculine traits, you know? But when they shut out those feelings, they shut out the only tie to their Gift. It's almost impossible to open that pathway again." Firal frowned in thought. "I suppose that's part of why most mages are women, and male mages are sometimes viewed as sissies. Though that's just silly, I can't imagine anyone thinking that of Master Nondar."

"So do you think I'm a sissy?" Daemon asked.

She glanced up, taking in his mask, rough-spun clothing and worn leather armor, his scales and claws and the daggers sheathed at his belt. "Oh yes," she intoned sarcastically. "You're the worst I've ever met."

He laughed.

She felt uncomfortable every time she heard his laughter. It was so free and lighthearted that it seemed wrong, coming from a creature so frightful, and it carried a tonal familiarity that gave her chills.

"Really, though," she continued. "There's no difference between the strength of male mages and female mages. Female mages are just more common."

"Do mages still marry?"

The question caught her off guard. She looked at him strangely. "Some of them. There's nothing to say they can't, but most who marry end up wedded to knights or nobles. A life of magecraft is very prestigious, after all. Mages are a class unto themselves. Why do you ask?"

"Because I've never seen a mage as a parent."

Firal laughed aloud. "I wouldn't expect you've seen many mages at all."

"What makes you say that? I've seen plenty of mages at the temple."

"Watching from the ruins won't tell you anything about the mages at the temple."

"And what makes you think I watch from the ruins?" Daemon cocked his head. "I've visited the temple plenty of times. Especially after dark. I may not be an expert, but I know your mage-barrier only keeps out unwelcome visitors. I mean the temple and its people no harm, so it lets me cross freely."

She stumbled mid-stride. "But the barrier is supposed to keep everyone out!" Agitation swelled within her and she scowled. She could have fetched her things after all!

He spread his hands in indifference. "I grew up coming and going from the temple. Maybe that's why the barrier still lets me through."

Firal's irritation subsided. It was the first time he'd mentioned anything personal, and it wasn't what she'd expected to hear. If he'd visited the temple, why hadn't he learned to control his Gift? And why would the Masters have allowed him to come and go, if they knew what he was? Her gaze settled on his feet and gooseflesh crawled up her arms. "Tell me more," she said slowly.

"About the temple?" he asked, confused.

"No. About you." A flush rose in her cheeks, uncomfortably warm.

He almost fell off the wall. "There...there isn't much to tell."

"You just said you grew up around the temple. How is that?" She smiled up at him, knowing the expression would keep him off guard.

"I was born there. I visited frequently. The mages wanted to study me. They said I was the first of my kind." He looked at his clawed hand and flexed his fingers as he studied them. "I hope there are no more like me. I wouldn't wish this on anyone."

"How can you be the first of your kind?" Firal asked.

"They made me," he replied gruffly.

She hastened to close the distance that had grown between them. "What do you mean, made you? Who made you?"

"No more questions," Daemon snapped, so heatedly it brought her up short.

"But—" she faltered.

"No more questions," he repeated, softer.

She bit her lip. She hadn't meant to uncover old wounds, but his claim was ridiculous. She'd grown up in the temple. Wouldn't she have seen him before? She stumbled through another patch of growth and gave a small cry of surprise when a raindrop struck her face.

Daemon glanced upward before he leaped down from the wall. "Come on," he murmured, beckoning her with a hand. "I'll find us some cover."

Firal nodded and held in her questions.

It didn't take long for Daemon to find another yawning cavern that stretched above ground, its rocky formation integrated into the walls of the ruins. The cavern's natural mouth had been widened and lined with neat stone blocks, but its crude stairs still led into a darkened pit. Daemon descended without hesitation and disappeared from sight.

Firal lingered at the opening despite the heavy rain, wishing she had her lantern. When she didn't follow, Daemon reappeared at the mouth of the cave.

"Coming?" he asked, the set of his shoulders betraying his impatience.

She picked up her skirts and descended the stairs. The air smelled stale but not musty, in spite of the thick humidity.

Daemon pressed something into her hand as soon as she reached the bottom. "Here."

She glanced down at the square-shaped copper coin in her

palm. Dim as the light had grown, she could barely make it out. "What's this?"

"Make a light with it," he replied, starting down the corridor. He vanished into shadow after only a few strides. Firal blinked and hurried after him as a mage-light flared to life in her hand.

The rough stone of the entrance soon gave way to smooth walls, as different from the underground tunnels she'd seen before as night and day. Green veining marbled the cool white stone. Gray granite formed the floor, cut square and polished smooth, though it was covered in the grit and grime of countless centuries. Peaked arches and fluted columns stood at regular intervals, breaking the seemingly endless hallway into sections.

"Did your people build this?" Firal asked. Roots broke through the stone ceiling in places, allowing stringy tendrils to dangle through. Dim streaks of light poured in with the rain where stones had fallen and left bright holes in the tunnel's roof.

"No, we just added to them. These tunnels are as old as the labyrinth up there." Daemon shrugged. "The whole place was already a ruin when the first Eldani came, but even my people have little record of why all this is here. The tunnels, that is. We know why the ruins are here."

Firal perked up. "What do you know? The temple's library only has studies on the ruins, not histories, and—"

"There's a lot the temple doesn't have," he interrupted. "The temple exists to train tools, nothing more. I refuse to be one of them."

The mage-light she held reacted to her curiosity, brightening and casting a red-gold color onto the walls. "Is that why you left?"

He gave her a sidewise look and she silently cursed the expressionless mask he wore. "I left for a lot of reasons. But I'll never escape."

Questions swirled through her thoughts, but she pushed them out of her mind. There would be time to ask more later. She didn't want to push her luck.

"Teach me to make a light." Daemon stopped suddenly and turned to face her.

"Right now?" she asked, surprised.

"Yes, right now," he growled.

Firal frowned. "That lesson comes in steps. First you have to learn to sustain a light without thought. Lighting it is the more complicated part."

"How am I supposed to sustain it if I can't even make it to begin with?"

"Here." She stepped forward, grabbed his hand and dumped the coin into his palm. It went dark immediately and Daemon grunted in surprise.

"You have to catch it." She took the coin back. It flared to life again as she turned it between her fingers. "It's energy. Be open to it and expect it. Take it, then feed it with your own strength." She moved the light slowly this time, easing it back into his scaly palm. The light flickered, then steadied.

He turned the glowing coin over in his hand. "It feels warm."

"It should. It's good that you can feel it. That means you're supporting it with your own energy now." Firal smiled at him.

He met her eyes, startled. The mage-light reacted. It flared brighter, until the light hurt to look at, then flickered and suddenly went dark.

Dismayed, Firal blinked at the spots left in her vision. "What happened?"

"I can't do it," he said in a rush, thrusting the coin back into her hands. She re-lit it to see him walking away, fists clenched at his sides.

She almost scowled. "Don't get angry at me because you failed. Your emotions have an enormous impact on your abilities. If you let them break your control, you'll never get anywhere."

"Don't preach at me, girl," he growled.

She set her jaw and stomped after him. "You have a serious

attitude problem. Would you shut up and listen for half a minute? We'll do drills while we walk."

Daemon rolled his eyes as she launched into a lecture about control. The growl of thunder seemed dim and distant as they walked.

———

THEY DID NOT STOP OFTEN. THE OCCASIONAL HOLE IN THE CEILING spilled sunlight into the underground, the angle of the beams revealing how much time had passed. Time of day made little difference in the darkness of the tunnel, though a certain eeriness came over the passageways when night fell.

The tunnel stretched straight ahead for miles, interrupted by occasional junctions where other hallways met theirs at right angles. It didn't take long for the trip to become tedious, though it provided ample opportunity for Firal to explain the core principles of magecraft in better detail. Daemon didn't seem to understand it all—she didn't expect him to, not right away—but he accepted her explanations with a more open mind than she'd anticipated. She explained everything she could until her voice grew hoarse and the water skin Daemon carried ran dry. At last, his questions ceased.

"Can't we sit for a bit? I don't think I can walk another step." Firal leaned down to massage her calves with both hands. As much as they ached, her feet were worse, rubbed raw again by the straps of her sandals. "You may have to carry me the rest of the way."

"If you can't walk on your own, then I suppose you'll have to stay here." His words were humorless, though he did stop and ease himself to the floor.

"I'd rather not." She gave him a sarcastic smile in return. "I don't think I'd last too long down here."

"No, probably not." He held up the mage-light as if he expected it to illuminate farther than a few paces before them.

They had taken turns carrying it so he could practice passing the energy back and forth. How quickly he'd gotten the hang of it—and figured out how to relight it himself—made her wonder how truthful he'd been about his level of experience with magic, but she hadn't inquired. She suspected he wouldn't have answered, anyway.

"Speaking of lasting, I don't suppose there's anything to eat, is there?" Firal laid a hand over her stomach. The berries they'd found along the path above-ground hadn't held her over long and a dull ache gnawed in her middle. She'd refused to eat more of the sour fruits from the odd trees.

Daemon grunted, laying the mage-light on the floor between them. She was surprised when it didn't go out. They hadn't even begun to speak of how to set energies in a cycle to temporarily sustain themselves. She chewed her lower lip, watching as he pulled a pouch from his belt and tugged at the ties that held it closed.

"What's that?" Firal asked, unsure she wanted the answer.

"Dinner." He shook it a few times, as if to loosen its contents, before he held it out.

She gave him a distrustful look, but leaned forward to peer into it. "If that's full of bugs, I swear..."

Daemon snorted. "It's just jerky." He pulled a reddish sliver from the pouch with two claws. Her eyes narrowed, but she took it. He fished out a few more pieces to pass to her before he slipped one under his mask. "Beef. Don't worry, it's actually pretty good. Dry, but good."

She scowled. "If you had that, why did you try to feed me scorpions last night?"

"Because I wanted scorpions. I told you, they're a delicacy."

"I would have rather had the jerky." She slouched against the wall. "Though I've never had it before. I'm not used to things like soldier's rations." When she finally took a bite, her face twisted with the effort it required to chew. The flavor was enjoyable, at least.

He chuckled at her expression. "You get used to it."

"I'd rather not have to," Firal said. "But it isn't bad, even if it is a bit chewy."

"Not sure what else you'd expect from dried meat." Daemon leaned forward until he could grasp the ankles of his outstretched legs. "Would be better with a drink, though, I'll say that. We'll have to find somewhere to refill the water skin. The runoff is too muddy."

Firal smirked. "Oh, I can take care of that." She planted a hand flat on the floor. A silvery gleam formed under her fingers. She lifted her hand slowly and water collected under her palm in a rippling sphere. It rose from the floor, levitating, and she moved her hand underneath it to grasp it like a ball.

"What—" Daemon said, startled.

"I thought you'd seen a lot of mages and magic?" She lifted the sphere of crystalline water with a giggle and drew a sip off the top. The sphere rippled and shrank, but never lost its form. She held it out to him, wiping her mouth with the back of her unoccupied hand.

He reached to take it. The water ball wobbled as she passed it to him, but settled into his palm as he curled his claws around it. He pulled it closer, studying the ripples in the surface. "Incredible," he murmured, turning it in hand. He lifted it before his mask and the sphere burst. He shouted as the water poured down his front, his eyes flaring with angry crimson light. "You did that!"

Firal cackled.

Daemon shook water from his scaly hand and scrubbed his wet fingers against his leg. "That's enough," he growled. "No more magic for tonight."

She laughed harder, but wiped a tear from her eye and nodded in agreement. "Yes, that's enough for now. We can begin again in the morning."

He glowered but said nothing more. He folded his arms over his chest and settled against the wall to sulk.

14

ARRIVAL

A<small>FTER A TIME</small>, F<small>IRAL BEGAN TO WONDER IF THE CORRIDOR WOULD</small> ever end. She threw the mage-light down the hall and watched it bounce into the endless dark.

Unamused, Daemon gave her a sidewise glower. "Don't lose my coin."

"How could I lose it? It's not like it could go anywhere." She scuffed her toes against the floor and sighed, trudging toward the tiny glow some distance ahead.

He slipped past her and she watched his silhouette as he picked up the glowing coin. She expected him to keep walking, but instead, he cast a glance toward the ceiling and then sank to the floor.

"Are we stopping?" Firal asked.

"Stupid thing to ask, considering I just sat down." He turned the coin between his fingers, his claws casting eerie shadows on the walls. "We'll rest here for tonight. For a few hours, at least."

"How do you know it's nighttime?" She sat close by, relieved for a chance to rest, and plucked the mage-light from his hand. She put it back on the floor where it had landed. They had no firewood, and it wouldn't have been wise to light a fire where there was no ventilation anyway, but she wrapped herself in her cloak and pretended the light offered warmth.

"It feels like it, for one thing. For another, I know you can't read them, but there are distance markers at each of the intersections." He gestured down the corridor and slouched against the wall behind him. "Judging by the number of miles we've traveled, it has to be past sundown."

Firal searched the walls for signs of markers, but saw nothing. "Are you sure you don't know what these tunnels are for? You seem awfully familiar with them."

"I live here," he replied flatly.

"With the rest of your people, I know. I saw the palace." She rubbed her hands in an effort to restore warmth to her fingers. "There were tapestries. None of those document the history of the ruins or what's under them?"

He crossed his arms. "There are some stories," he conceded. "But as I said, the tunnels were here before us. If I had to guess, I'd say they were part of some kind of shrine or a temple. A place of worship built by the first inhabitants of the island."

Her nose crinkled. "How do you figure?"

Daemon shrugged. "They say this island was where Brant planted the seeds of life, before the soul-blight began and he withdrew his roots. The people who grew from those seeds were so ashamed of their corruption that they built the ruins to keep everyone away, protecting the place where life began, just in case Brant decided to return."

"Dramatic," she murmured.

"There's a bit of poetry in it, I suppose. The ruins are called Kirban. In the old language, the one written on these walls, it means Heaven." He snorted softly. "I guess in the end, it at least became a safe haven. Some still think the land is sacred."

"And what do you believe?" Firal asked, tilting her head.

He grunted, staring into the darkness. "That it doesn't matter what's here or why. Oak trees care nothing about the acorns they drop that sprout beneath their branches. The Lifetree—Brant—is no different. We were born and then abandoned. Left to all our atrocities and abuse of power."

"You sound soul-blighted, yourself."

"I am what they made me," he replied.

Firal studied his feet for a time, then allowed her eyes to travel to his mask. "And what are you?"

"A man." He flexed his hands in front of him, the light glinting off his sleek scales. "That's why I have to learn to use this power."

"So that you can abuse it, too? Like you accuse everyone else of doing?" She arched a brow and gathered her cloak a little closer.

"So I can control it," he growled, "and right what the mages have done to me."

An uncomfortable stillness fell in the wake of his words, as if the ruins themselves feared what he might mean.

Eventually, Daemon sighed. "Sleep, mageling. We'll continue in a few hours."

Firal said nothing else, and the silence in the corridor became oppressive.

The cold drove them closer together as bone-deep exhaustion pushed her toward drowsiness. She stifled her complaints in favor of sharing his warmth, and the fading glow of the mage-light lulled her to sleep.

———

FIRAL SHOWED DAEMON HOW TO DRAW WATER FROM THE EARTH before they began travel the next morning, demonstrating methods to spin it into a long thread to fill the water skin. It only took him a handful of tries to figure it out, though he certainly lacked the grace that she possessed.

The following day, he taught her to identify edible roots from those that broke through the stone and dangled overhead, and she showed him what she could of magic. They shifted earth and stone, moved plants, drew water from the earth and air. The lessons were rudimentary and brief, so they could preserve as much of their energy as possible for travel. When night fell, she roasted fat tubers with her Gift, a feat he couldn't seem to replicate.

Another sunset and sunrise came and went, visible through the gaps in the ceiling, and Firal counted the days on her fingers. Daemon assured her they were getting close, though the never-changing hallways did little to inspire confidence in the claim.

"We're not going to make it, are we?" she asked at last, crouching beside the mage-light he'd laid on the floor. They'd stopped before sunset, this time. Without proper food or rest, the fatigue of the days behind them had become overwhelming. The blisters on her feet had long since been replaced by thick scabs under the straps of her sandals. Firal had feared infection, but Daemon provided some sort of moss that stopped the bleeding and stained her skin, and inflammation had never set in.

Daemon hesitated. "We can still get there before the solstice."

"How?" Firal sighed and hugged her knees. "I don't feel like I can stand again, never mind walk any farther. I don't even know how much farther it is."

His mask shielded his expression, as always, though the look in his luminescent eyes spoke volumes. "There is one way."

She tried not to scowl. She already knew the answer, but she asked anyway. "And that is?"

Daemon said nothing more. He straightened, gazing down the open hallway. His posture indicated he was thinking, his clawed fingers twitching with a desire to draw the lines of power she'd forbidden.

She watched for some time before she spoke. "You really believe you can handle a Gate on your own, don't you?"

"I've done it before," he said.

"You've opened a Gate by yourself?" It took effort to keep

from laughing. The magelings had taken carriages to the capital for a reason. It took at least a half dozen Masters to open a Gate large enough for a single person to pass through, and even then, they couldn't hold it for more than a few moments. Moving hundreds of magelings through Gates would have taken an incredible amount of power—more than the temple staff possessed.

"I didn't know it was that dangerous. No one told me. I saw a group of mages open one a long time ago and I just..." He glanced over his shoulder and she thought she saw worry in his eyes. "I never knew how many mages were involved. I wasn't close enough to feel who was manipulating the flows."

Firal stared at him in disbelief. "And you worked out how to do it on your own? Just after seeing someone do it once? You couldn't even make a mage-light!"

"Well," Daemon said with a hint of chagrin, "opening a Gate did seem a lot more interesting than making a light. I must have done it a hundred times without knowing I shouldn't."

She bit her tongue in frustration. He could have had them out of the ruins in a moment if she'd given him free rein with his power. If he had doubts about his ability now, she only had herself to blame. She'd said no Gates and he'd kept the agreement. But whether or not he had opened them alone in the past, letting him do it again was foolish. Firal pushed herself to her feet. "Let me help."

Daemon blinked in surprise. "Have you ever opened a Gate before?"

"No, but I can help." Firal lifted her chin. "If nothing else, I can offer more energy to help you keep it stable."

He regarded her silently for a time. Eventually, he nodded.

She hadn't expected him to agree. She inched closer as he drew his hands together before him. Energy shifted in the air.

Firal reached for the moving flows, relaxing, pouring out her strength to where he could reach it.

He seized it without warning, before she was ready, making

her gasp as his energies merged with her own. Power surged through her body like an electric shock, roaring in her head and making all her hair stand on end. The raw might filled her until she thought she would burst. Every inch of her skin prickled with pins and needles. Every pulse of energy stole her breath, and stars flashed before her eyes until her vision filled with light.

"Firal!"

She gasped, jerking hard, her eyes flying open as he shook her. Trying to rouse her, she realized. Spots of light and shadow swam in her vision as her sight returned. Sunset lit the sky afire overhead and she lay on the ground, her head cradled in Daemon's hands. She blinked hard, suddenly aware she was panting for breath. "What was that?" she managed, her voice quivering.

He exhaled, his shoulders sagging with relief. "What do you mean, what was that? Didn't you feel any of that?"

"I don't know what I felt." Firal pushed his hands away. Her entire body trembled. "What happened?"

Daemon seemed reluctant to let her go, resting his hands on his thighs. He knelt beside her in a hollow of a grassy field. Hills swelled around them on every side, effectively hiding them from sight. "I took hold of you, like you said, opened the Gate, and...I don't know. I pulled you through the Gate when you didn't move, but as soon as we were through, you fell in convulsions." The unsteadiness of his voice surprised her. Was he concerned?

"There was so much energy, I thought it would burn me to cinders." She swallowed. "Was that...you?"

His eyes hardened, a guarded look replacing emotion.

She sat up, smoothing her skirt with shaking hands. "I've never felt anything like that. It felt like everything was out of control."

"Are you all right?" he asked.

"I'm not sure," she admitted.

He smoothed her dark hair back from her face, his claws lingering against her cheek.

Startled, she locked eyes with him. He was concerned. And a little frightened, she thought, though he tried to hide his fear. The power she'd felt in him had been enough to tear her apart. She took comfort in knowing he hadn't intended her harm.

Swallowing again and trying to ignore the sharp, metallic taste lingering in her mouth, Firal looked around. "Where are we?"

"Just outside of Ilmenhith." He stood and offered his hand.

She ignored it and struggled to her feet on her own, gazing out over the landscape between them and the Eldani capital.

A simple market stood on the other side of the wide, grassy field ahead. She teetered on her feet, almost unaware of Daemon's hand on her arm to steady her. After the unyielding stone floors of the tunnels, the soft turf underfoot was a comfort to walk on. Firal paused to remove her sandals and strode across the tickling grass barefoot.

With the arrival of dusk, thick cascades of netting had been drawn across the fronts of tents and market stalls to hold the coming night's insects at bay. Up and down the streets, lamps atop metal poles were illuminated with mage-lights rather than flames, keeping things almost as bright as they would have been during the day. Unlike the bazaar she had visited before, this one seemed less busy now that the sun was setting.

Past the market, stone cottages with thatched roofs stood among larger buildings that looked to be shops and inns. The odd mix of structures ran all the way to the wall encircling the inner city. Beyond them, the palace's spires stood as dark shadows against the softer backdrop of the night sky.

"Disgusting." Daemon snorted his disapproval, shaking his head.

"What?" She tried not to laugh. "The city is miles from the ruins, and who knows how far from the tunnels. It isn't as if they're encroaching on your territory."

"That depends on how big you think our territory is." He grasped her elbow and urged her forward. He had donned gloves to hide his hands and had drawn the hood of his cloak up as well, effectively shadowing his mask.

"There's no need to hurry. I still feel a little odd, but I'd actually like to take a moment to look around, just to see if—" She cut off with a squeak as he quickened his pace and nearly pulled her off her feet.

"You don't need to look. And in case you've forgotten, all your money is back in Kirban, so I'm fairly sure you have nothing to barter with but your body."

Firal gasped and dug in her heels. When he turned to protest, she struck, yelping when the slap landed on the metal mask she'd somehow forgotten. She cradled her injured hand and glowered.

"I wasn't insinuating you would, you know." He released her arm and adjusted his mask beneath his hood. "But if that's the way you'd like to be, then go ahead. Entertain yourself while I find a place for us to sleep. They post guards at the gates when the sun falls below the horizon. I won't be able to get past them, which means we'll be stuck outside the city proper until morning."

"Fine." She huffed and held her chin high as she crossed the dusky field to join the crowds at the edge of the market.

Once alone, it took a moment to gain her composure. She still felt odd, off-balance and unfocused. Her skin still prickled with the residue of energy. If that was the power that went into opening a Gate, it was a miracle Daemon had never unmade himself. She tried to shake the thought as she let herself be swallowed by the bustle of people. A number of merchants tried to coax her into looking closer, waving strands of gems and silver in the air. Now and then, she paused to inspect their wares.

The broken necklace she still carried in her dress hovered in the forefront of her mind. She imagined one of the jewelsmiths in the market could fix it, but the strange, lingering sensations of power muddled her head and kept her from looking at their work too closely. The women wandering the crowds with baskets of fruits and fresh bread, however, caught her attention. The smell made her stomach growl and she silently begrudged having nothing to trade for a loaf. She'd just started to wonder how she would find a meal when Daemon surfaced in the crowd beside her.

"That didn't take long," Firal said.

"If you're as tired as I am, I'm surprised you'd complain." He took hold of her arm once more. This time, she didn't resist.

They made their way closer to the walls of the inner city and stopped at a shabby-looking inn. Daemon took the innkeeper aside and spoke to him so quietly Firal couldn't hear a word, though she caught the gleam of gold when he pressed something into the innkeeper's hand.

The room they were given was small, but clean. Firal tried not to make a face when she saw only one bed. She settled on it and wrapped the blankets around her shoulders. After days traveling the underground tunnels, it was a comfort to have normal furnishings again.

"I was hoping I'd find a jeweler who could fix my necklace," she said, disheartened. "I doubt any of them could finish it before the solstice, though."

"It's just as well, since you can't pay them." Daemon lingered beside the door until a woman brought a tray of food and a pitcher of wine. He took both from her with a murmured thanks and locked the door after she'd gone. There was no table, so he put the tray in the middle of the floor and sat beside it.

Firal slid to the floor to join him, taking the blankets with her. She was glad to lay eyes on real food, even if it was only a slab of overcooked pork, a mass of something she supposed was yams, and a few pieces of buttered bread. She had just begun to eat when Daemon put out the lamp's flame and left them in the dark.

"No complaints," he ordered before she had a chance to speak. "I'm hungry too, and I can't use a fork with my mask on."

"That doesn't explain why you put out the light." She scraped a fingernail along the crust of her stale bread. The hall beyond their door was dark and the shutters over the window allowed only the thinnest sliver of moonlight to enter the room. Her plate was a faint white outline on the floor; she could make out nothing else.

"Just eat," he said.

Their hands collided over the tray now and then, and they took turns mumbling apologies until blind exploration of the plates proved they were empty. She caught the sound of scraping metal as Daemon retrieved his mask from the floor.

"Why do you wear that mask, anyway?" Firal shrugged the blankets higher on her shoulders and searched the floor for her cup.

"My flesh will scorch, melt off my face and turn to ash if it's exposed to the light."

She choked on her wine.

Daemon laughed. "No. Actually, I'm just ugly."

"Well, I want to see you." Firal reached toward him in the dark, guided by the faint light of his eyes. He caught her wrist and she twisted it in his grasp, wriggling her fingers. "We've spent what, nearly a week together? Day and night? And you're still a mystery."

"No." His hold on her tightened and he pushed against her arm, forcing her back. "Don't ask again." He didn't lift his voice, but the low threat in his tone sent a shiver down her spine.

She set her jaw and leaned closer. "At least let me touch you."

He paused, his crushing grip on her wrist easing a shade.

"All I know is the color of your eyes and that we're nothing alike. If I'm going to be spending more time with you in the future, I want to know who I'm with."

His mask clinked against the floor again and a warm stirring of air—breath—flowed over her hand. He closed his eyes and all traces of light disappeared. Slowly, he pulled her hand closer, but didn't let go. She flexed her fingers once before reaching out, toying with tangles as she slid her fingers into his hair. It was gritty with dust and damp with sweat at his temples. Moving closer still, she lifted her free hand to lay a palm against his cheek.

His face was smooth, skin soft beneath her touch. She wasn't sure why it surprised her, considering his mask sheltered his face from the sun. Her fingers and thumb found the barest hint of stubble along his jaw. He couldn't have grown a beard if his life depended on it. His eyes never opened and he didn't try to stop her.

Her thumbs traced his well-proportioned nose and angry brows, her fingertips sliding over the tops of his ears. Smooth and nicely rounded, the top of the left pierced with two rings, several more in either lobe. He bore no Eldani blood, then, no trace of a point to his ears. Another mystery, coupled with the magic might he possessed.

"So that's what you look like," she murmured, leaning closer. The musky-sweet scent of him tingled in her nostrils and she inhaled deeply. "I don't see why you need to wear a mask. You feel like—"

"That's enough," Daemon said.

Firal cringed and drew back. She'd overstepped her bounds.

He moved away and she heard his footsteps cross the room. He returned a moment later and placed something on the floor before her. She reached for it in the dark. A candle.

"What's this for?" she asked.

"Another lesson. I want you to show me how to make fire again." It was not a request.

She hesitated. Was she ready to touch magic again? The hair on the back of her neck still prickled, though the strange residue of energy seemed to be gone and her head was clear.

"All right," she agreed, letting her hand hover over the candlestick she couldn't see. "I suppose we can practice until it's time for bed. You remember what I told you before, correct?"

"Something about focusing on the source of the warmth, catching it and making it grow." He managed to sound impatient even when he was being compliant. Fabric rustled as he sat.

Firal groped in the dark for his hand and clasped it in both of hers when she found it. She traced a finger over his smooth scales. "You probably can't feel the shift in the air current that's caused by the warmth, can you? It's a very delicate shift. I apologize that I didn't think of it before. Instead of waiting to feel the sensation of the energy flowing through the air, you'll have to learn the timing between the focus of your energy and the shift of the flame's potential."

His hand flexed beneath her touch. "How am I supposed to do that?"

"I'll help you. It's much more complicated, but energy is just like anything else. When you push toward it, you make waves. It has to bounce back at some point. The harder you push, the harder it will return. I'll show you when to catch the flow of energy. Gestures aren't necessary, but they do help when you're learning. You may outgrow them later." She let her eyes slide closed as she waited to sense the flows surrounding the candle.

The moments seemed eternal. Firal she forced herself to be patient. She didn't realize she was holding her breath until she felt the delicate shift in energy beneath her hand.

"Now." She brushed her fingertips across Daemon's palm, emulating the sensation of magic crawling across her skin.

Daemon's clawed fingers closed on the warmth and drew it upward. The candle wick sparked, flickered, and a thin plume of smoke scented the air as it extinguished. He growled.

"Too fast." Firal positioned his hand over the candle again. "You mustn't rush it. Fire is difficult to start, but easy to manipulate. You have to feed it as you draw the energy to wherever you want it to be, or it'll starve. Try again, but don't pull so quickly."

He didn't reply, but she felt him adjust the position of his hand. Much sooner than before, the flow of magic rose against her hand. She touched him to signal it and he grasped the ribbon of energy running between his fingers. The candle sparked again and this time, Firal turned away as light flared and the flame took hold.

"Good!" She blinked hard to help her vision adjust. The candlelight glinted off his mask. Strangely, her stomach sank when she saw he wore it again. "Did you count out the time?"

"Yes." He pinched out the flame between one clawed finger and his thumb. "Show me again."

They repeated the exercise more times than she could count, each attempt coming to fruition faster. She felt him falling into the rhythm of it, pouring his energies into the candle, counting the seconds until the flow presented the opportunity to bring the flame to life. After a time she stopped guiding him, leaving him to rely on the timing he'd learned.

Firal drew back and clambered onto the wide bed. She sank into the down-filled pillows and the soft mattress, sighing in appreciation and letting her eyes slide closed in the first moment of contentment she'd felt for days.

The candle continued to flicker in and out for a long time in the silent room. Eventually, it went dark and did not light again. She'd almost fallen asleep when she heard movement at the side of the bed and the rustle of his leather armor being discarded. Daemon settled on the floor beside the bed.

Guilt stole through her heart. They'd traveled under the same circumstances. He had to be as exhausted as she was, yet he meant to sleep on the floor? She bit her lip. If he meant her ill, it would have already happened.

"Daemon?" she murmured.

He grew still.

"I'm cold."

Seconds crept by. Then he climbed onto the bed beside her. He sidled close and nestled his face in her hair, his body curved close against her back. Drowsiness stole over her again and she gave in to it, relaxing into his warmth as sleep took her.

———————

SHYMIN PICKED AT THE TWINE ON HER BALLGOWN'S WRAPPINGS. Arrival in Ilmenhith should have been a relief, but the city was so full of people, it was impossible to take in the sights. She had decided early on that it would have been foolish for any of them to get out of the carriage, lest they get separated. Though the other girls sulked, she at least tried to see something from the small glass windows. Bright banners and streamers decorated every street, even in the bustling marketplace at the city's outskirts. Shymin could only imagine how resplendent the palace would be.

At sunset, the carriage halted in front of the largest inn any of them had ever seen.

The inside of the inn was different from the other buildings Shymin had seen in Eldani cities, shunning the airy feeling many seemed to favor. Instead, the owner had chosen dark, heavy woods for the walls and furniture. The front room doubled as a dining hall, its tables and chairs neatly arranged and most seats already filled with visitors. A number of patrons were students from the temple, but just as many were strangers. A long, polished wood bar ran across the far wall with a half-door behind it that never seemed to stop swinging, barmaids sweeping endlessly in and out of the kitchen with platters and mugs in hand. Master Nondar stopped just inside the doorway and considered that bar, but the empty seats were few, and none together.

Rikka elbowed Shymin in the side and pointed toward a table as its occupants began to depart. The magelings hurried to claim it.

The evening meal was already being served, tempting scents heavy in the air. Their meal had been paid for, as well as their stay. By the time they all sat, a barmaid had already deposited a platter of food at each place. After the modest fare they'd had during travel, the meal seemed a feast. Slices of duck in a thick herb gravy, buttered lentils and grilled leeks, wedges of sharp yellow cheese and coarse bread with a nutty flavor decorated the table. Shymin's mouth watered. In the center of the table, the barmaid left a bowl of dates and a tray of sweet oat cakes dripped with melted butter and warm honey. The barmaid offered a pitcher of water and a jug of cider, and Master Nondar asked her to leave both.

"I can't believe we're finally here." Rikka admired her fork, even though it was plain tin. Compared to the temple's worn furnishings, everything seemed fine. "This has to be the nicest inn I've ever seen. The plates are actually porcelain, and the cups are molded glass!"

"Probably gets expensive when patrons get rowdy." Shymin frowned at the finery the meal was presented on, self-conscious. The temple rarely served food on anything but plain earthenware or wooden dishes, both easily replaced. She couldn't recall ever eating from porcelain.

"Maybe, but with how many people here aren't from the temple, I imagine they do brisk enough business to afford it." Rikka glanced over her shoulder before she stuffed a forkful of food into her mouth.

Kytenia shrugged. "With all of us here, and probably half the rest of Elenhiise to boot, there won't be an empty inn for miles. I imagine we're lucky to stay in one as nice as this."

"Do you think Firal is staying somewhere as nice?" Marreli asked, bringing the meal to abrupt halt. Shymin glared at her and Marreli shrank in her seat, a ruddy tinge to her cheeks.

Master Nondar cleared his throat. "Wherever she's staying, I'm sure she's made herself quite comfortable."

The girls relaxed at the quiet dismissal, though Marreli still gave them apologetic glances.

Shymin shrugged and returned her attention to her food, afraid to catch Nondar's eye. She reached for her fork and mustered the will to eat, her appetite suddenly gone. "I guess we can only hope."

The others nodded and turned back to their plates. Together, they fell into a morose silence in the midst of the tavern's noisy cheer.

15

ILMENHITH

RAN STRAIGHTENED HIS SLEEVE AND INSPECTED HIS REFLECTION. IT was strange to see himself in white, and stranger still to see the black ink that rimmed his eyes. It would take practice to paint his eyes evenly. He was still too heavy-handed, afraid of poking his eye with the thin ink brush another Master had given him. Others painted swirls, patterns, or shapes, sometimes related to their affinities and sometimes merely designs they liked. He'd opted for simplicity, a plain line along the edges of his eyelids, as if they'd been lined with kohl.

Though he looked the part, Ran still couldn't think of himself as a Master. He'd had the white robe made to his specifications, having grown used to the way his blue robes fell at knee length. There were plenty of robes that size in the temple's storerooms, though they would have needed alteration anyway; none of them bore the blue banding needed to mark him as a mage of Ilmenhith. Better to have one made. At least that way, the sleeves were the right length.

"Perfect," he said at last, turning toward the messenger who waited by the door. "No need for any other adjustments, thank you."

The messenger dipped into a bow. "And the other parcel, milord?"

"With luck, it'll be fine as it is." Ran spared a glance for the paper-wrapped package on his bed. "Too late to do anything if it's not, either way." He smoothed his robes one last time before he crossed to the bed.

The twine on the parcel came undone easily. Ran folded back the paper and brushed his fingers across the garment inside. The black and red silk snagged on his rough hands as he took it from its wrappings. It was perfect, just the way he'd envisioned. He shook out the dress and held it up for the messenger to see. "There, what do you think?"

"Ah...bit of an unusual color, milord," the boy said.

Ran snorted, looking it over again. "My father said the same thing. Said she'd look better in green, but she wears green every day at the temple. Seems like she'd want to wear something else, once in a while." He'd tried to explain as much to his father. Kifel hadn't liked the choice of color, but he'd still paid for it as soon as Ran explained who it was for.

With the gown draped over one arm, Ran fished a coin from his pocket. He flicked it to the messenger and grinned when the boy caught it. "Give the seamstress my thanks."

"Of course, milord. Thank you, milord." The messenger bowed again and scurried from the room with his payment clutched to his chest.

Tucking the dress back into its wrappings, Ran glanced toward the window. The sun peeked over the city walls. Just past breakfast time, he imagined. The rest of the court mages would be meeting with the Masters in the chapter house just outside the palace walls. He wasn't expected to join them with any sort of regularity until the solstice festivities ended, but if he was in the city with nothing else to do, there wasn't any reason not to. He couldn't say how his father would react when he learned of Ran's new position as a court mage, but it seemed like a good idea to learn his responsibilities before meeting with Kifel.

He peered into the hallway to ensure it was empty before he slipped out of his room. The door swung closed noiselessly behind him and Ran sprinted toward the small back staircase the serving staff used. If he hurried and he was careful, he might make it out without being seen.

———

FIRAL WOKE ALONE, A COOL HOLLOW IN THE BED BESIDE HER. Daemon's scent still clung to the sheets, all that remained to show he had ever been there. The tray and dishes from the night before were gone, the candle they'd practiced with back in its place on the bedside table.

The room seemed more modest by daylight, though the wash basin and mirror against the far wall were more than enough to make Firal happy. Her hair needed a good washing, but her curls were so thick, the small pitcher of water on the wash stand never would have been enough. Still, she was not displeased to settle for washing her face and neck. Refreshed, she smoothed her dark hair back with wet hands and patted her face dry with the towel beside the basin.

The innkeeper had a plate of breakfast ready for her when she reached the front room, the meal already paid for. Firal would have to remember to thank Daemon later. Breakfast was little more than ham, bread with butter, and eggs that had already gone cold, but after the sparse offerings Daemon had provided during their trip, it seemed fit for a queen.

She hadn't expected to see Daemon in the inn, but the morning crowd had already dispersed and it was strange to sit alone in an unfamiliar place. He had claimed to have business in the capital, she reminded herself, though she couldn't help but wonder what it might be.

By the time Firal set out from their lodgings, the market had begun to stir with life. The palace towered over the city's expanse, casting long shadows over its heart in the morning light. The longer she looked at it, the more her stomach fluttered. It seemed too soon to make her way there, but where else was there to go? She didn't know where to look for other mages, but they would reach the palace for the festivities eventually, regardless of where they stayed.

Firal expected the palace would turn her away. After all, one afternoon spent in the company of royalty hardly justified allowing her into the palace early. If she was fortunate, perhaps someone in the palace would take pity on her and give her a coin to pay for another room at the inn. Her sense of time had grown muddled in the ruins, but she was certain the solstice was still several days off.

Gentlefolk roamed the tidy cobblestone streets within the city walls. Most left her alone as she wound her way toward the palace, but some gave her looks that made her skin prickle. She wished she had worn her mageling's robes, anxious for the visible rank the clothes would give her. As it was, she was dirty and unkempt, looking more the part of a beggar than a prestigious mage. Embarrassed, she bowed her head as she walked.

The streets of Ilmenhith radiated from the palace like the spokes of a wagon wheel, starting at the wide avenue that ringed the palace walls and stretching to the city walls behind her. Banners of blue and silver rippled in the breeze, sending shadows rolling across the road. No guards patrolled the tops of the high stone walls that sheltered the palace gardens from common folk, though guardhouses stood at regular intervals along its curving length. North of the palace, the streets grew empty. No shops stood on this side of town, no signs for inns hanging in front of the large buildings. She assumed that meant they were houses, though some were as large as the temple's dinner hall.

The lack of guards stationed at the palace gate came as a surprise, though she should have expected it. Rikka and Marreli had both been born in Ilmenhith, and they'd often said the city was so peaceful that occasional patrols were enough to maintain safety.

Firal puzzled over what she was supposed to do at the gate, looking up the walls and over her shoulders, pursing her lips and inching closer to the large portcullis. She laid her hands on the sun-warmed metal with a frown. The courtyard on the other side was pristine, but what she could see of it was rather featureless. A plain, tree-lined path led to the stairs of the palace. Large as the arched doors at the front of the castle had to be, the gate was far enough away they looked as if they covered a mouse hole. She leaned forward, straining to see the empty yard, and startled when the portcullis rattled dully in the gateway.

"You shouldn't be here." The words that came from the other side of the wall were unmistakably angry.

Firal let go of the iron bars and stepped back in a hurry. Maybe visiting the palace had been a bad idea. She opened her mouth to speak when a figure in white swept into view on the other side of the portcullis. The words withered on her tongue.

Ran spat a curse the moment he saw her face, white robes swirling as he ducked back behind the wall.

"Lomithrandel!" Firal shrieked, banging her fists against the gate. "You get back here right this instant! You left me in the ruins! Do you have any idea what could have happened to me because of you?"

"You didn't see me!" he snapped, his back to the wall. Only the toes of his boots remained visible.

"What? Of course I saw you!" And what had she seen? Her mouth dried as she recalled the fleeting glimpse she'd just caught. White robes, trimmed with blue to mark him as a Master of Ilmenhith, his eyes rimmed with black ink. Her stomach sank. "You're a court mage?"

He groaned and pushed himself around the corner to glower at her. "What are you doing here alone? You should be with the rest of the mages."

Firal snorted. "I didn't have much choice in the matter.

Besides, I was coming to the palace for the solstice anyway, wasn't I?"

Ran eyed her a moment. His shoulders heaved with his sigh. "Hold on." He disappeared to the other side of the gate. A low clank overhead caught her attention, followed by a whir and a rattle. The heavy portcullis lifted at an agonizingly slow pace. Firal watched until it clanked to a halt at the top of the archway. Then Ran reappeared before her, caught hold of her arm and hauled her onto the stone walkway in the courtyard.

"Come on. I don't have time to stand and fuss over you all day," he growled. He hit a latch embedded in the wall with his palm before he started toward the palace doors.

Firal did not reply, letting him lead the way as the portcullis behind them rattled back down to the ground.

The castle was constructed of white marble veined with pale blue-gray. Ran dragged her inside and shut the door behind them. She slowed, gaping at the magnificence of the entry hall. A dozen marble pillars lined the center of the room and a rich, silver-trimmed blue carpet ran between them. At the far end, two large, peaked doors closed off what she assumed would be the throne room.

Banners hung upon the walls, each displaying the royal crest —the seven-pointed star with a ringed center she knew from her mother's pendant—again in blue and silver. Silk streamers decorated the marble columns and live trees in massive stone basins along the walls. Natural sunlight lit the room, filtered through glass skylights in the vaulted ceiling that soared three stories above. Each floor hosted an open walkway around the top of the great hall. Servants roved up there, some pausing to peer down at their visitors with curiosity. Ran caught her wrist and dragged her onward.

The throne room was decorated like the hall before, but the carpet here ended in a large circle before the throne's dais, the center emblazoned with the royal crest. High arched windows lined the walls and the skylights were fewer. Between the panes of glass overhead, the ceiling was painted deep blue, constellations depicted with faint lines to link the stars. Firal couldn't help the tingling sense of wonder as her eyes traced the map of the sky.

With no queen to rule alongside King Kifel, his throne stood on its own, elegant in its simplicity. The wide silver seat was modeled like twisted vines and a single large sapphire cut into countless facets was embedded just above the headrest, set off by the blue velvet upholstery. Somehow, Firal had expected Kifel would be there.

"Stop gawking and hurry up," Ran chastised. She had been so distracted by the sights that she hadn't realized he'd let her go. He stood at the foot of one of the two staircases that curved up into the corners of the room behind the throne, their tops converging in the center of the second floor.

She flushed and hurried to follow him upstairs. "Where are we going?" Her voice echoed in the vast room. She winced at the sound of her own cluelessness.

"To speak with Medreal. Kifel's steward, I suppose you could say. She'll know what to do with you."

"Will I, now?"

They both jumped. Firal turned to face the woman who had appeared at their backs without so much as a sound. Ran grimaced and did the same.

The woman was stocky and looked perfectly pleasant, her skin dusky and her white hair drawn into a messy bun at the back of her head. Her eyes were so dark they appeared black, and they glittered with some hint of amusement. Though she wore simple clothing, the air she carried held too much dignity to mistake her for a mere servant.

Ran scarcely opened his mouth to speak before Medreal held up her hand, keeping him silent. She smoothed her apron and stepped forward to give Firal an appraising look. "And what is it you've dragged into my palace this time, hmm?"

"*Your* palace?" Firal asked. She felt a spark of something in the woman, something strange, but muted. A Gift that had never come to fruition, she assumed. She gave Ran a sidewise glance.

"Kifelethelas may rule it, but I run it." Medreal grasped Firal's jaw and turned her head to look her over. "Hmm...looks as if she hasn't had a good night's sleep in days. I hope you're not keeping her awake, young man."

"It's nothing like that!" Ran choked out, his eyes so wide they looked ready to fall from his head.

The old woman gave him a skeptical look, but turned with a wave of her hand. "Well. Come along, then, and you can tell me what it *is* like. It's about time for a bite to eat, and you both look like you could benefit from it."

Firal didn't protest. With the sun reaching its zenith, the morning meal was farther behind her than she'd first realized. She wouldn't object to something to make up for the meals she'd missed. Ran seemed reluctant, but he nudged her forward, letting Medreal lead the two of them through the twists and turns of the hallways that sprawled out in every direction.

Even with an assortment of tables and vases, narrow benches, chairs, and obscure paintings to adorn the walls, it didn't take long for Firal to lose her bearings. It was astounding how she kept ending up in mazes of walls and doorways, never knowing which way she was meant to go. Trying to watch where they were going made her dizzy, so she settled for following with her eyes focused on Medreal's back.

They turned abruptly and moved down a narrow flight of stairs. At the bottom, a door stood ajar. The smell of warm food was almost overpowering. The rattle of pots and pans indicated someone at work on the other side.

"We'll be eating in the kitchens, then?" Ran asked, displeased.

"Unless you plan on cleaning the banquet hall yourself, after the meal." Medreal gave him a dark look. If his place as the king's surrogate son had given him any rank, he clearly held none with her.

The kitchen lacked the vaulted ceiling the rest of the palace boasted, though it seemed airy and well-lit. Wooden beams stretched overhead with nails driven into them, from which hung pots and herbs, smoked meats, strings of vegetables, and countless other things Firal didn't recognize. Men and women dressed in the plain garb of servants circled about like busy ants. A small table with several chairs around it stood far to one side and no one paid them mind as Medreal led them to it. Scarcely a moment after they sat, a pair of kitchen maids brought trays of food and a kettle of tea.

"You'll have to excuse me if I seemed discourteous upstairs." Medreal smiled warmly and smoothed her hair as she made herself comfortable. "Allow me to introduce myself more properly. I am Medreal, friend and adviser to King Kifelethelas, stewardess of his household and one-time nursemaid to his children." She paused there, giving Ran a look.

Firal hid a smile behind her fingers. It was no wonder he held no authority with her, then, if she'd been the one to see to his diapering. "A pleasure to meet you, lady Medreal." She couldn't give a proper curtsy at the table, but she still bowed her head respectfully.

The glitter in the older woman's eyes brightened, then disappeared as she reached for the teapot. "So, tell me, Lomithrandel. Why are you sneaking young women into the palace?" Medreal asked, her tone dangerously neutral as she poured tea for the three of them.

Ran hesitated to answer. "I found her at the gates. I don't think she has anywhere else to go."

"And are we in a practice of taking in every needy person, now?"

Firal tried not to squirm at the needling in the older woman's tone, though a surge of indignation rose along with the flutter in her stomach.

"She's a mageling from Kirban," he replied, leveling his gaze with Medreal's without flinching. "As someone who will eventually serve the king as a full-fledged mage, she has every right to be here."

Medreal's smile seemed to catch him off guard. "That doesn't make her any less needy." Her tone was gentle, but there was an intensity in her eyes when she glanced at Firal. It was a piercing look, one that sent a shiver through her from head to toe. The response didn't go unnoticed. "Are you quite all right, dear?"

"Fine," Firal lied, though the old woman's penetrating gaze made her heart beat faster.

"You'll have to excuse me if I missed your name," Medreal said, adding honey to her teacup and gesturing for the two of them to help themselves as she stirred.

"Firal, my lady." She tried not to flush at the courteous reminder that she hadn't even introduced herself.

The elder woman's mouth tightened. "And your surname?" she urged gently.

Firal bit her lower lip and ducked her eyes. "It's only Firal, my lady. My mother saw fit to leave me with the mages, but she didn't see fit to leave a family name."

"I see." Medreal pushed back her chair and rose with her teacup in hand. "Very well then, Firal of Kirban. I will have to make sure there is a room to accommodate you. We have a large number of guests coming who will expect to stay in the palace. Please stay here and enjoy some tea. Both of you." She gave Ran a glance that indicated she expected him to be there when she came back. When he merely averted his eyes instead of arguing, she excused herself without another word.

Firal let her attention settle on Ran. Her jaw clenched as he pushed the jar of honey toward her. "Well, it's nice to see you've finally remembered some manners."

"It's good to see you too," he murmured.

She snorted. "Is that it?"

"I have nothing to say to you," he replied, never looking up, swirling his spoon in his teacup.

"Really?" Firal asked, her tone biting with sarcasm. "I'd think you'd have plenty. You could apologize, for example, for abandoning me so far in the ruins that an Underling had to show me the way out. Or," she plunked a spoon filled with honey into her cup to punctuate the word, "you could have told me you'd been made court mage. Imagine that, prince of Elenhiise and a Master mage both."

Ran slowly lifted his eyes to her face.

"What, were you thinking no one would ever find out?" she snapped.

"I'm not a prince." He set his spoon aside. "I thought I made that clear enough before."

"Don't lie to my face!" She flipped hair back over her shoulder, uncaring that the kitchen staff turned toward them at her outburst. "I saw the way she looked at you when she said she raised the king's children."

Ran's eyes darkened with anger. "I didn't lie to you. I told you everything I could, and I was honest. Kifel is not my father."

"And how does a foundling like yourself become a king's adopted child?" The words escaped before she knew what she was saying. The two of them had more in common than she'd ever realized. Both without real families, both struggling to fit in at the temple. She continued before he had a chance to answer and open old wounds that had never quite healed. "You could have told me about this ages ago, you know."

Ran sighed. "And what? Have the whole temple coddle me because I may end up being the only option for an heir? Have everyone falling at my feet and seeing me as a noble, have every girl chasing me because she wants to be a princess?" He shook his head. "Would you have treated me the same if you had known? Through all the pranks, the jokes, the teasing?"

Firal squirmed, taken aback. "But I've never been kind to you."

"Exactly."

Her brow furrowed.

He went on. "Everything you've ever said or done has been

your reaction to me." He pressed a hand to his chest. "Not to the king's son, not a possible heir, not an uncrowned and untitled prince. Just me. I can't even begin to tell you what that means to me."

She chewed her lip. She hadn't expected a response at all, much less one so earnest. Now she couldn't think of anything to say, her temper defused. "Well," she huffed finally. "You're still just you. And your actions are just as unforgivable as ever."

Ran gave her a weak smile and turned his gaze back to his tea.

A servant appeared beside them as if from nowhere. "My lady," the girl murmured, sinking into a bow. "I am to lead you to your room."

Glad for the interruption, Firal pushed herself up. She brushed off her skirts as she stepped away from the table.

"Firal," Ran called as they reached the foot of the stairs. She turned her head to look at him. "Thank you."

The coals of anger still smoldered in the back of her mind, but she offered a single nod before she lifted her skirts about her ankles and turned to follow the servant girl.

THE GIRL LED FIRAL BACK TO THE OPEN WALKWAY ABOVE THE throne room, into a wide corridor beyond it, and up a small spiral staircase nestled in the curve of a turret. Two hallways joined against the small landing at the top of the stairs, both identical to Firal's eye.

The size of the palace made her uncomfortable. The temple was not small, but she suspected its grounds would fit within the palace several times over. The servant took her down the hallway to the right, where large paintings stood between closed doors, depicting each of the former rulers of the kingdom with their families. Plaques beneath the paintings declared names and the dates they had ruled. Then they rounded a corner, and there were no more paintings.

"Is there no portrait of King Kifelethelas?" Firal asked in attempt to break the uncomfortable silence.

"His Majesty had his portraits moved. He does not feel they should be displayed in a hall of remembrance until he has to be remembered." The servant offered her a smile, but it did nothing to ease her nerves.

The hall before them now was narrow, lined with smaller doors. Private bedchambers, Firal assumed. Halfway to the end of the hallway, the servant stopped to open a door that appeared no different than the rest.

"You'll be staying here, my lady. If you need anything at all, pull the bell-string beside the door and a servant will attend you. Once you are settled, I shall send a maid to draw your bath." The young woman dipped in a curtsy and took her leave so promptly that Firal hardly knew what to do with herself. She peered into the room open before her, wringing her hands.

The room that awaited was elegant, hosting furniture of dark wood with carved vines trailing up the sides and across the tops. The curtains, bedding, and even the oval rug on the floor were a deep green trimmed with silver; oddly earthy, compared to the airy feeling of the rest of the palace.

She stepped forward slowly, half expecting more servants would spring from the woodwork. Wide arched windows kept the room bright and a narrow door in the far corner opened into a private bath chamber that was almost as large as her room back at the temple. The tub looked like bronze, worked with the same vines as the furniture. Shelves rimmed the tops of the walls, packed with jars and bottles, scented soaps and candles.

Firal had scarcely set foot in the room before a girl appeared behind her with a large kettle of steaming water. More girls filed in behind her with kettles for the tub. Firal stepped aside to let them in. None of the girls said a word to her until the great bronze tub was halfway filled. Considering it was so deep that it stood almost to her thigh, that was plenty. She had to insist on stripping off her grungy dress on her own, shooing the maids out of the bath chamber, though they wouldn't leave until she promised to pass her dress out to be washed and checked for size. It was awkward enough to be bathing in a strange place. She might have died of embarrassment if she'd had to let strange girls bathe her, too.

She climbed into the bath and welcomed the heat of the water, sinking until it covered her shoulders, letting the weariness seep out of her bones. Bottles of oils and bars of soap sat on a ledge behind the tub. She smelled some and sampled others, puzzling at how some of them fizzed in the water. The bubbles tingled against her skin. Raking wet fingers through her hair left streaks of dirt on her hands. Wrinkling her nose, she sucked in a breath and dipped beneath the surface. A scented soap worked well enough for scrubbing her hair, and she washed it three times over before the water came away clear. She reheated the water with a touch of magic more than once, not caring that it would have gotten her in trouble back in the temple. All her fingers and toes were shriveled by the time she dragged herself out of the tub and wrapped herself in a thick towel the maids had left for her use.

When Firal emerged from her bath, a pale ivory dress and matching slippers waited on the bed. It was a better fit than most of the hand-me-down clothing she owned, but she figured there was no shortage of colors or sizes of clothing for visitors to the palace.

A bit of searching produced a comb and Firal seated herself in a chair beside the windows to work the knots from her hair while gazing outside.

There was a lot to see beyond the palace gardens. Sun-bleached wooden buildings stood at the edges of the city, mingled with the pale canvas tents and low cottages that belonged to merchants. Closer to the palace, thatched roofs were a cheerful splash of gold against the drab backdrop of pale stone houses and busy roadways. From where she sat, the countless people on the roads looked no bigger than mice.

From her new vantage point, she also noticed most of the streets led toward two buildings: the palace she rested within, and a tall, white building with a verdigris roof, halfway across the city. Firal hadn't noticed it on her way to the palace. A belfry rose from the front of the structure, enclosed with stained glass windows and hosting a large, round plate of milk-white glass on the front. Regular marks encircled the plate's outer edge, two verdigris arms reaching in seemingly random directions from its middle. It wasn't until she looked again that she realized the longer of the arms had changed position since she'd first looked. Firal had heard of clocks, of course, but seeing one was a sharp reminder of how far from the temple she really was.

"Brant's chapel is beautiful, isn't it, my lady?"

Firal jumped and squeaked.

"Begging your pardon, my lady." The maid bowed politely. "You did not answer when I knocked, so I thought you were still in the bath. I was sent to fetch you for supper, if you don't protest."

Firal hadn't even heard a knock. "No, of course not. I would be more than happy to attend." She set aside her comb, the worst of the snarls already removed from her damp hair. She hadn't noticed the grumbling of her stomach until the maid's mention of food. Tea with Medreal and Ran had been pleasant, but a proper meal sounded delightful. If she'd been glad to see what the inn had to offer, she was certain she'd enjoy the hospitality the king had to share.

16

KIN AND KINDRED SPIRITS

"CHECK." THE AIR IN THE ROOM GREW HEAVY WITH THE announcement.

Kifel studied every piece on the board, considering his options with a growing frown. "Every move you make seems to be an act of desperation." He traced back through the game in his mind. His hand hovered above the carved pieces for a long time before he moved one to defend his king.

"Perhaps it is." Ran made his next move without an ounce of hesitation. "Have you decided yet?"

"Not yet," Kifel replied, removing a piece from the board as he countered.

"It isn't as if you have any other choices." Ran didn't manage to keep the irritation out of his voice, though even if he had, his eyes would have betrayed the emotion. Watching him was almost as interesting as watching the chessboard. Kifel did a much better job of keeping his thoughts in check, his expression serene.

Ran's mouth tightened when he did not respond. He made his move. "Check."

Kifel plucked the threatening piece off the board. "It takes courage to play chess in such a reckless manner. Aren't you afraid of losing?"

"You're skirting the issue," Ran growled.

"It's an issue I'd rather not discuss now. To be honest, I don't think you're ready." If their casual game made Ran forget who he was playing against, Kifel's stony expression and hard tone should remind him. "I don't think you'll be ready for a long time."

"And someone else is better prepared? I've been here, Father! How many years has it been? How long are you going to keep looking? You have me!"

Kifel sat in silence. His outward composure never faltered, no matter how the words dug beneath his skin. When he found his voice, his tone softened. "It seems that every time we meet, now, we're locked in some sort of duel. We've crossed swords, met fists, now this."

Ran slammed a fist against the table, jarring pieces out of place. "Stop putting this off! Will you crown me or not? Will you ever recognize me, or are you just planning on leaving me to rot?"

"It's your move," the king replied patiently.

"No," Ran snapped. He dashed discarded pieces off the table as he rose from his seat and planted his hands where they'd been. "It's yours. I've waited for too long. What is it you're afraid of? You know exactly what will happen to your kingdom if you sit for too long with no heir. And yet you're still waiting? Explain this to me! What are you waiting for? What better option do you think you have? Blood or not, I am your son!" His voice cracked, though only anger shone in his eyes. "Yet you refuse to recognize me. After everything I've done, after everything you've taught me, am I still not enough?"

"You're young. You're reckless." Kifel kept his voice level, though it was a greater challenge than he expected. The emotion he reined in planted itself in his throat and made it hard to speak. "Power is a dangerous thing. I've taught you everything I can, but you won't learn to keep yourself in check. It doesn't matter what your heart wants when you're in a position like this. Until you can learn to rule your heart with your head, there is nothing more I can offer you."

Ran stared at him for a long time. His jaw tightened, his eyes never leaving Kifel's face. He lifted a piece and thudded it down on the board. "Check mate," he said through clenched teeth before he thrust himself away from the table and stalked from the room.

Kifel clasped his hands together and rested his chin against them as he stared down at his defeated ivory king. The sight of the obsidian knight that had backed him into a corner sent a chill down his spine.

His own days of reckless youth seemed a shadowed, distant memory. He wished it were as simple as naming Ran as his heir, but it wasn't. The black eye-ink of a court Master the boy now wore only complicated things further.

Mages were granted power and authority across the island, in both his kingdom and the human kingdom alike. A part of Kifel wanted to be proud that Ran had achieved such strength in so little time. Some mages studied for the better part of a century before they were granted the eye-marks that distinguished them as leaders in power. But as he'd told Envesi, Ran was his son, blood or otherwise. That the Archmage granted him such a rank created a conflict of interest.

There had never been true peace between he and King Relythes of the Giftless lands, but Kifel took some pride in that they had sat for years without war. There were occasional disputes, but both sides seemed content to remain silent and aloof, the distance separating them serving as a shield. They were both given to arrogance, he admitted. Neither half had named their kingdom, referring to the land only by the island's name—Elenhiise. As if ruling half somehow gave them the sole authority to use the name.

The recent increase in skirmishes and raids along the border had been concerning enough, but for Kifel's only viable heir to be promoted to a rank that would give him access to and power in Relythes's kingdom could only spell trouble. Whether Relythes would see it as an attempt to spy or part of some more sinister plot, Kifel didn't know.

"Majesty?" Medreal called from the doorway, interrupting his thoughts.

Kifel sighed. "Yes."

She inched farther inside. "I apologize that I was not at the door when you arrived. I came as soon as I heard you'd returned from your errands."

"Forgiven," Kifel said, rubbing his eyes. "I should have sent word that I'd be returning early. Are things in order for the ball?"

"The banquet hall and ballroom have both been decorated, food has been gathered and stowed in the pantries, and so far everything is proceeding as planned."

"What would I do without you?" Kifel pushed himself up as if the movement pained him.

"You would try to manage everything yourself and the turrets would fall down around your ears," she teased, though her eyes were full of pity. "The first of our guests arrived with Lomithrandel yesterday. He insisted that we put her up. I figured it best to let you speak to her. We have treated her as best we could without you here, my liege. She has been informed of your arrival and is waiting for you in your office."

He grimaced. "Dragging peasant girls into the castle and then expecting me to crown him during the solstice. He'll be the end of me, Medreal, I'm sure of it."

The elderly woman shooed him off with one hand and turned to resume her day's work. He did not doubt that the turrets really would fall down around his ears without her assistance.

Kifel made his way through the hallways on his own, pausing at the intricately carved wooden doors of his office. He was more practical than his ancestors, finding the large doors unnecessary for a private office, but all he could do was ignore them. He slipped inside and scanned the too-large room twice before he saw her. She was easy to miss, standing in the far corner beside one of the many high windows that lined the wall. Kifel's brow furrowed. The mageling was the last person he'd expected.

Firal had not dressed in finery for their meeting, something he found rather refreshing. Her ebony hair hung loose about her shoulders and her ivory gown only emphasized how dark her curls were. It was a charming image, one that stirred burdened memories and an ache in his heart. He couldn't help but sigh. "I suppose I ought to apologize that he pulled you into this."

Firal wheeled to face him, a crimson flush in her cheeks. She dropped into a bow before he could stop her.

"There's no need for that," he reassured her as he crossed the room to sit at his desk. "Actually, I'd prefer if you didn't. Please, come sit. I have to say I'm not surprised it's you that he's brought along."

"I beg your pardon?" Firal gathered her skirts and made her way to sit as he'd directed.

"Ran has always been...particular about who he is seen with, due to his circumstances. I suppose after our little bout of swordplay, he's comfortable having you in the palace." Kifel leaned back in his chair, grateful for the thick cushions. The weight of his troubles had begun to make him feel old.

She blushed again. "I suppose you are right, Majesty."

"Please, don't worry about the formalities while we're in private. If you are a friend of his, then you are a friend of mine." He smoothed back his tawny hair and frowned when she didn't relax. "I suppose by now you've been fitted for the dress I've bought you?"

Firal's amber eyes grew wide. "So it was you."

"A gift," he said. She opened her mouth to protest and he lifted a hand to stop her. "Please, don't misunderstand my intentions." Kifel had not even considered the gift he'd purchased on Ran's behalf might be misconstrued until Medreal prompted him. He was older than Firal by decades—perhaps centuries, considering the way the Eldani aged. But he was still well within the prime of life, and he was without a queen. It would have been easier to explain had Ran not asked that his name not be attached to the gift. An odd request, but Kifel assumed it had something to do with the embarrassment of asking for it.

"Actually," she said, "I feel a bit better knowing it came from you. The seamstress didn't show me what the style was to be and she wouldn't let me change it. I was afraid it was some prank Ran was trying to pull. I'm sure he'd dress me in something positively indecent."

Kifel laughed. "I wouldn't put it past him," he admitted. Now he understood why Ran hadn't wanted her to know who the gown was from. Perhaps he'd been mistaken in assuming Ran meant to court her. "But I don't imagine he'll bother you during the solstice. He and I seem to be of differing opinions on certain...political matters, as of late. I would be surprised if he still made an appearance."

"I don't see why he wouldn't," she said. "I'd think he might enjoy an event somewhere he doesn't have to hide who he is."

Kifel raised a brow. "I'm surprised he spoke of his position within my household with you."

"I suppose he had no choice, really, having to explain why he was sparring with the King of Elenhiise." Firal smiled wryly and lifted her chin. She was pretty, he decided; not the sort of woman he personally preferred, but her soft features bore a sweetness about them, and her pale, dewy skin was unusual for an islander. She was different. Kifel understood why Ran might be charmed.

"Indeed," he murmured. "In any event, since my son has welcomed you into my palace, you are free to roam as you will. Once the solstice is past, I will have you and the rest of the temple's guests escorted back to Kirban."

Firal squirmed in her seat. He tried not to let it bother him. It would be foolish to expect her to be comfortable in his presence, regardless of her apparent comfort with Ran.

"I beg your pardon, Majesty," she began, averting her eyes, "but I don't see why you would spare so much effort for magelings. The temple treats us like children. I expected the same treatment here."

Kifel gave a low chuckle. A number of rumors had swirled around the event, the most popular of which claiming that he had organized the ball with the intent to select a new bride. It was not that far from the truth—it merely focused on the wrong bachelor. "Crowned or not, Lomithrandel is of marriageable age. I would prefer to keep his options open."

"I don't...you mean, all this is a ploy to have him around women?" Firal gaped.

"Regardless of whether or not he is my blood, I would like to have grandchildren before my time ruling comes to an end." He tried to smile, though the expression was halfhearted at best. "Would that my wife had given me more children before I lost her, too."

Firal sat straighter. "You did lose a child of your own," she said, too thoughtful for his liking.

Kifel pursed his lips. He'd tried too hard to bury that memory to let it resurface now. "I think that's enough discussion for now. I enjoyed our visit. As I said, please make yourself comfortable in my palace. I doubt our paths will cross again before the solstice." He gestured toward the doors with one hand, wordlessly dismissing her.

She opened her mouth, but a sharper gesture cut her off. Apparently thinking better of speaking, Firal rose from her seat and dipped into a deep curtsy before she removed herself from the king's office.

LEFT TO WANDER ON HER OWN, IT DIDN'T TAKE LONG FOR FIRAL TO become lost in the sprawling expanse of hallways. She felt a little more at ease knowing she was welcome to explore, but she couldn't help the color that rose into her cheeks every time a maid or servant crossed her path. They scattered like dry leaves as soon as they caught sight of her, which made them seem less like people and more like ghosts.

When one girl brushed past her with an armful of linens, she murmured more profuse apologies than Firal had ever heard. Being treated with such deference was oddly unnerving. In the temple, magelings were treated as if they were always underfoot and needing to be looked after. But the servants here didn't know her rank, and even if they had, their behavior likely wouldn't have been much different. To the Giftless, a mage was a mage, all of them worthy of respect.

Firal paused when she stepped into a hallway lined with paintings on one side and windows overlooking the royal gardens on the other. The windows reached nearly from floor to ceiling. An uneasy feeling brewed in her stomach when she tried to peer out them, so she turned her attention to the paintings, instead.

There were paintings of generals, paintings of ships, portraits of the prior king and queen. She saw one or two family portraits showing King Kifelethelas as a child. Then there was a portrait of Kifel and a woman, her hair dark and her features lovely, but her eyes an eerily familiar shade of icy blue. Firal paused before the image and looked closer. Mage blue, she decided. There was quite a difference between eyes that were naturally blue and those that were the cold, eerie shade earned with magic. She forced herself to move on. A few more images of King Kifel with his parents, then one that stopped her dead in her tracks.

It was the eyes of the child that caught her gaze first, a stare so sharp that, even though it was only a painting, she felt as if the dark-headed boy's eyes bored into her. Kifel and the woman with the mage-blue eyes sat with him, looks of contentment and peace on their faces—even the child's, despite his eyes.

There was a child, but something happened, she thought. Recollection of Ran's words put a knot in her throat. *The child he'll never replace.*

"You look lost."

Firal yelped and wheeled to face the young man who had crept up behind her. He wasn't much older than she was, if her guess was any good. He had the smooth olive complexion and fair hair that was common in Ilmenhith, the bright blue of his eyes refreshingly natural and a stark difference from the sharp, icy gaze of the woman in the painting beside her.

"I'm sorry," she blurted. "Am I not supposed to be here? I didn't know."

"Sorry?" He raised a brow and stifled a laugh. "Sorry for what? The palace is easy to get lost in. I barely know my own way around."

On second glance, he was just as out of place as she was, dressed in homespun clothing instead of the bright livery of a page. For that matter, all the servants she'd seen had been women or elderly men.

Unsure how to address him, she mustered a polite smile. "I was just trying to get back to my room. Ran dumped me off on Medreal yesterday and she took me to speak to Kifel today, and now I haven't any idea where I'm going."

"Ah. One of Ran's girls." He grinned at her. "He just sneak you in? Come on, I'll take you back to the guest quarters." He jerked his head toward a side passage she'd missed, having been too distracted by the paintings, and turned to lead the way.

"I am *not* one of Ran's girls," Firal muttered, a prickle of irritation coursing through her. *One* of Ran's girls? How many girls did he have?

She fell in step beside the young man, casting a sidewise glance in his direction. The point of his ears was not as defined as she was used to seeing, though sharper than that of half-bloods, telling of a diluted bloodline. "Are you a friend of Lomithrandel's, then?"

"You could say that, though admitting it could be dangerous in these parts. You'll learn that soon enough." He smirked, a playful spark in his eyes. "I don't think I've seen you around before. Are you new to Ilmenhith?"

"I'm a mageling from Kirban. I came for the solstice, but I suppose I arrived a bit early." She tried not to look at him again, though a part of her wanted to. His smile was lovely.

"Ah," he sighed, sympathetic. "So you have the joy of waiting. I understand, I'm stuck doing the same thing."

"Are you here for the festivities?"

"No, just here on duty, I suppose you could say." The corner of his mouth twitched, but he caught himself before it became a frown. "I joined the army hoping to take my father's position as Captain of the Guard when I'm older, or maybe become one of the king's knights someday. But I didn't realize that becoming a soldier meant spending so much time as a message boy. It's all go here, deliver this, wait for that."

"Sounds like the temple," Firal laughed. "People come expecting the immediate glory that comes with magecraft, only to find that first year students spend more time doing chores than anything else."

The young man grunted his displeasure at the comparison. "I've been in this position for over a year. My lieutenant promises I'll be given a real post soon, but I won't hold my breath."

She did not reply, so they walked on in silence for some time before he spoke again.

"By the way," he drawled, "I don't believe I caught your name."

"I don't believe I gave it." She smirked at him. He grinned back and she felt a strange tightening in her chest. He was flirting with her! And shamelessly, at that. The experience was new and quite odd.

"Well in that case, let me introduce myself. I'm Vahn. Well, Vahnil, actually, but only my mother calls me that."

"I'm Firal," she replied, grinning sheepishly. "And just that."

"Lady Firal!" Vahn paused to offer a sweeping bow. "It is truly a pleasure to be gifted with your company."

She snorted a laugh. "Just Firal. My name alone will do fine, thank you."

It didn't take long for them to reach the open walkway that ringed the great hall of the palace. She vaguely recalled passing it the day before, on the way to her rooms after the evening meal. It was easier to travel when she knew where she was going, and her pace relaxed considerably.

"The guests for the solstice started arriving in the city yesterday, so at least you haven't arrived too far ahead." Vahn glanced down into the throne room below. The throne remained empty, but the room was full of people rushing about. He shook his head. "At best it's given you an extra day to prepare, since the ball is tomorrow. What color mask did you decide on? I hear green and gold are to be most popular this year, if only because everyone is tired of sporting the kingdom's colors."

Her step faltered. "Mask?"

"The solstice ball is a masquerade by tradition. Didn't they tell you when you were invited?"

"Oh, no. I completely forgot!" Firal groaned.

"Well, what color is your dress? Perhaps I can still find you one, out at market. I've errands to run that direction, either way." Vahn's smile seemed a little too warm. She tried not to squirm beneath the weight of his attention.

"It will be red and black, apparently," she grumbled, casting him an apologetic glance when he seemed confused. "I didn't choose the color, it was a gift."

He nodded and gestured for her to lead up the spiraling stairway. She was certain she knew the way now and didn't hesitate to move ahead.

Vahn followed a few steps behind. "Well, I'll do my best to

find you something to match. I'll have it sent to your room if I find it. Otherwise, don't worry. I'm sure you won't be the only one coming from Kirban without a mask for the masquerade."

"Thank you, Vahnil." Firal stopped outside her room, uncertain whether it was proper to invite him in or simply bid him farewell. He didn't let her wonder for long, sweeping into another bow and stepping back before she could say anything else.

"Just Vahn, please." He grimaced, though the expression morphed into a grin as he straightened. "Ran and I only hear our full names if Medreal's after our heads. I'd rather not hear it from a pretty lady as well."

Her amber eyes widened at the compliment. She retreated into her room and slammed the door closed.

On the other side, Vahn laughed.

17

SOLSTICE

CARRIAGES BEGAN TO ARRIVE AT THE PALACE EARLY THE NEXT DAY, the long line taking hours to work its way past the castle gates. The city boiled in chaos, merchants striving to make one last sale, innkeepers moving guests to make room for those who might have more coin, and all of the madness visible from the hundreds of windows set in the palace's uppermost floors.

Firal watched the arrivals with a lump in her throat. She was certain her friends would be among them. She couldn't imagine them giving up the opportunity to attend the event, but she wasn't sure what she could do to find them, or what to say if she did. How could she explain her presence, or that she'd arrived days early? How could she explain her place in the palace without betraying the trust Ran had shown in revealing his secrets to her?

Troubled, she forced herself away from the window.

Her dress had been delivered to her room that morning. Firal assumed Kifel sent for it; she certainly hadn't thought to have it delivered to the palace.

Her mask had been another surprise. It arrived not long after the dress, bundled in linen and accompanied by a note. She'd expected a teasing message from Vahn. Instead, it was a single line of flowing script.

Don't forget our bargain. -D

She supposed she should have been grateful. She didn't know where Daemon had gone or how he'd gotten the parcel to the palace, but it was the second problem he'd solved for her. That he thought she would forget her half of their agreement rankled.

Firal double-checked the latch on the door before she stripped out of her nightclothes to dress. With her gown, mask, and all her meals delivered to her room, locking the door meant respite. She had grown tired of batting away maids, irritated by their insistence that she needed help to bathe and dress and put up her hair, all things she could do by herself.

Though she had requested a chance to speak to the court mages before the event, they'd not had a moment to spare for a mageling girl come to visit from the temple. Firal had expected that. During the ball, they wouldn't be able to escape her. But the ball would be her last chance to speak to them, too. What if they tried to evade her questions? What if her necklace wasn't enough? Fear wriggled itself into her belly as she slid into her dress.

To the credit of the seamstress Kifel had chosen, the gown fit better than anything Firal had ever worn. After spending most of her life relegated to old clothing either too big or too small, it felt odd to wear something made just for her. She turned her back to the mirror and craned her neck to see the fastenings and, after attempting to do them on her own, almost called to the maidservants she'd locked out.

She couldn't say she cared for the style, but it wouldn't do to insult the king by refusing to wear his gift. It was elegantly made, the fine black and red silks worked with an expert hand. The bodice fit snug against her slightly too-ample curves and left her pale shoulders bare, a fashion popular in Ilmenhith that seemed positively scandalous to her. There was a thin silver-gray shawl to go with it, but even with the shawl wrapped around her shoulders, she felt naked.

The red silk created a wide, ruched panel down the front of the bodice, flaring at the waist to add a broad swath of red down the skirt's front. Matching red gores flashed in the full skirt when she moved. Considering the airy colors of the king's office and the pale blues and greens he always wore, the colors of her gown seemed unlike something Kifel would have chosen. She wondered again how much Ran might have been involved.

There was the small matter of jewelry, as well. A maid had brought a close-fitting collar of white gems to her room and said the king wished for her to wear it. It stood tall against her throat and cascaded over her collarbones, drawing too much attention to her exposed shoulders. Firal doubted any but the wealthiest women would have jewels to compare. Why did he wish her to stand out? Especially at an event orchestrated for the sole purpose of exposing his son to potential brides! She shook her head in disgust, though the thought gave her goosebumps. She rubbed them away and frowned.

One could do worse for a husband than Ran, she supposed. For all that she found him infuriating, he was handsome, charming, and wealthy, despite his lack of a crown. But courtship was not why she had come to the capital. She twisted her thick ebony hair into a bun and pinned it in place. Had she gotten the chain of her mother's necklace repaired, she would have worn it instead of the king's jewels. Instead, her precious pendant would have to be tucked inside the bodice of her dress.

The ways of nobility were strange, but at least she'd be free of them soon. Despite her desperation to see the court mages and secure the answers about her parents she sought, Firal was more than ready to return to the comfortable shelter of mundane life at the temple. And eager to resume her not-quite-so-mundane lessons with Daemon, though she was quick to shake that thought from her head. She added one last pin to her hair and reached for her mask.

Now that she'd seen the cut of her dress, she was grateful for the anonymity the masquerade provided. And though the mask was pretty, it was not what she would have chosen for herself. Cut in filigree swirls that looked like fire, it was painted in mottled shades of red and orange. A narrow piece resembling a bird's beak came to a point on her nose. Long ribbons of red and gold fastened to its edges, half of them to tie on the mask with and half as decorative streamers. She traced the mask's edge with a fingertip and considered putting it on, but thought better of it. With magelings filling the palace's sitting rooms, there was a good chance she'd see someone she knew downstairs. As embarrassing as her exposed shoulders were, she didn't want to hinder any chance of her friends finding her before they were swept into the crowds of nobles and strangers.

Smoothing her skirts, Firal took a final look around the room before she pulled on her black silk slippers. Fine shoes were perhaps the only luxury she would miss. She pressed a hand to her stomach to quell its nervous fluttering and slipped into the hallway. With any luck, she wouldn't be looking for familiar faces for long. And maybe, with her friends at her side, tonight would offer the answers she'd longed for her entire life.

KYTENIA DIDN'T LOOK UP WHEN THE DOOR CREAKED OPEN AGAIN. A dozen or more magelings filtered through the room every few minutes, eager for their turn to primp in front of the mirrors. After the third group had come and gone, she no longer bothered to look up.

They hadn't been afforded time to gape at the palace before they were rushed inside and sent to a sitting room, now packed with magelings abuzz with final preparations. Kytenia was glad for the opportunity to preen, since she hadn't considered that a jostling ride in the cramped carriage would rumple their skirts or hair. She tried to fix her upswept brown curls, turning her head to survey her work as she put the last few pins in place.

"How is this supposed to go, again?" Rikka held the bustle of her skirt in both hands. She was a mess of half-tied ribbons and unpinned hair. Exasperation and defeat weighted her expression. Kytenia wasn't entirely sure she'd finished dressing before their carriage came to collect them and they were forced to depart.

"Didn't we show you twice already?" Kytenia struggled to sound patient. "Let me finish and I'll tie it up for you."

"It's all right, Kyt. I'll get it for her," said a voice from the entrance, just as the door clicked shut.

"Oh, would you?" Rikka twisted around. "I've spent at least twenty minutes trying to find where those blighted—" She cut herself short with a shriek when she saw Firal's smiling face.

"Firal!" Marreli cried, bounding from her seat and tripping over her skirt in her hurry to cross the room.

Kytenia dropped her last hairpin and left it forgotten on the floor. She flew across the room, only a step behind Rikka. Firal laughed as they all tried to embrace her at once.

"I get the feeling I was missed." Firal squirmed to loosen the arms around her.

"Missed? We thought we were never going to see you again!" Kytenia said. Her heart thundered in her chest, making the bodice of her dress feel too tight. She sucked in a deep breath and tried to rein in her excitement.

"Why wouldn't you?" Firal's brow furrowed.

Rikka gaped at her. "You're joking, right? You vanished! We were certain something horrible happened to you in those ruins!"

A shadow of something flitted through Firal's expression, though she dashed it away with a shake of her head before Kytenia could ask.

"Something horrible did happen," Firal said. "I stumbled into Ran. But I was able to find an escort at the last minute when I made it back to the temple. I'll tell you all about it tomorrow, on the way home."

Kytenia pursed her lips. There was something about Firal's words that suggested they weren't entirely true, and the other girls exchanged worried looks before Marreli attached herself to Firal's arm. "I'm just glad you're all right." She hugged Firal's arm tight, her eyes lighting with a sweet smile when Firal patted her head.

Kytenia stepped back and gave Firal a good look-over. It was hard to let her gaze slide any lower than the jewels at her friend's throat, but seeing her in a dress that was the height of fashion among nobles was equally strange. "It seems you've done well for yourself," she said, raising a brow. "Care to explain that, too?"

Firal motioned her friends to one side of the door as another group of magelings came in. "I've been in the palace for several days. I've spoken with King Kifelethelas and the woman in charge of running the palace. It seems they wanted me to look my best, since I arrived with Ran, and..." Firal trailed off, her words burdened.

There was something else she wasn't saying, Kytenia thought, though the fact Firal and Ran were in the palace together was enough to make anyone suspicious. But Firal's expression brightened, and she went on. "Well, a mage's reception was better than I expected, I suppose I should say. I hope the rest of you have been treated as well as I have."

"You've been here longer than I would have guessed." Rikka eyed the dress and jewels with a suspicion that rivaled Kytenia's. "Did you have a chance to...you know..."

"Not yet," Firal said. "But I'm going to speak to one of the court mages during the ball. I'm determined to."

"We'll do everything we can to make sure you have the chance." Rikka hugged her once more. "Oh, I just can't believe you're here! Isn't Shymin back yet? Oh, Firal is back with us and of course Shymin is nowhere to be seen!"

Kytenia laughed and raised a hand to forestall the question she saw in Firal's eyes. "She said she didn't have enough pins for her hair, and that she needed a longer tie for her mask. Heaven forbid she ask to borrow some pins instead. Why, there are so many vain people gathered for the solstice I'd be surprised if there was a single hairpin left for sale in the entire city."

"I wish we'd spent as much time discussing masks as we did dresses," Firal groaned. "I'd forgotten it was a masquerade."

"We were able to find masks in the market here when we arrived." Marreli smoothed her hair and righted the braids coiled around her head. "I think you'll be all right if you don't have a mask, though. Plenty of the other magelings left the market empty-handed. None of the Masters are wearing masks, either."

"Oh, I have one, I'll just need help putting it on." Firal raised her mask for the group to see. The fiery swirls didn't look like something she would have chosen for herself. "The Masters won't be masked, you said? Is that tradition?"

"From what I gathered," Kytenia said. "My guess is the court mages will be unmasked, too. Though all the Masters intend to wear white, so they'll stand out among the crowd. We'll help keep watch."

"It's not just the court mages I'd like to talk to. There's one other Master in particular I'd like to see. After speaking with the king yesterday, I believe I ought to make my opinion of this whole affair clear." Firal lifted her chin and settled her birdlike, flame-colored mask over her face. Marreli helped her tie it, careful not to snag her hair.

Kytenia frowned, but there wasn't time to press for information. For now, she merely stepped forward to wrap her arms around her dear friend again, all of them smiling as Marreli and Rikka joined in.

A few peaceful moments with her friends were likely all she would get.

THE EVENT STARTED WITH A BANQUET, GUESTS AND SERVANTS flowing between the dozens of tables that filled the banquet hall. The roar of the crowd forced the girls to raise their voices just to be heard by those across the table from them.

Firal had never liked crowds. They made her feel confined and breathless, and the noise set her on edge. She stared at her plate instead of socializing, awkward and without an appetite, while the other girls dug into their meals. It was not for lack of appealing food; her mouth watered at the sight of the lavish meal the servants placed upon the tables. It truly was a feast, boasting meats and vegetables likely imported from the mainland. Roast beef and plates of chicken halves and broiled fish decorated the table. A suckling pig surrounded by greens crowned the offering. Buttered and fried squash sat only inches from her plate, and though the look and smell were tantalizing, her stomach did not respond. Trays of various cheeses and breads were added to the selection as she looked, decanters of wine replaced almost as soon as they were emptied. Firal spooned small portions of things onto her plate, though all she found appealing was the goblet of red wine she cradled in both hands. Even the wine seemed to stir butterflies in her stomach. She tried to drink it slowly.

Countless lords and ladies surrounded them; there had been no reserved tables or assigned seating. Firal and Kytenia had managed to find two seats together on one side of a table. Shymin and Marreli sat somewhere on the other side, and none of them were sure where Rikka had gone. Firal did not recognize any other magelings, though with so many wearing masks, it was no wonder. Those with full-face masks removed them for the meal; some with half-masks still wore them. Kytenia's leaf-shaped mask lay on the table beside her plate. Firal had not removed hers, grateful for the way the bold color drew attention away from her bare shoulders.

Little conversation was directed their way, though Firal didn't mind. The incessant laughter of the woman to her left grated on her nerves, though she exchanged comedic looks with Kytenia whenever the woman's shrill laughter pervaded the air. No one said anything particularly humorous and though some at the table giggled along, Firal took the notion they were laughing at the unpleasant giddiness of their company.

"Aren't you going to eat anything?" Kytenia whispered by her ear, glancing at the untouched food on her plate.

"Too nervous," Firal replied. "It would taste like sawdust in my mouth."

A new voice rose behind her. "Perhaps you'd like to dance first, then?"

Firal started and clapped a hand to her chest. "Oh, Vahnil!" She breathed in relief. "Where is your mask?"

Vahn grimaced. "Just Vahn, please. Really. Unfortunately, the masks were all gone by the time I made it to market. I see that didn't stop you, though. You'll have to tell me how you managed the feat." A hint of a smile twisted the corners of his mouth. He offered a gloved hand to help her from her seat, his eyes flicking toward Kytenia. His gaze lingered. "Is this one of your friends from the temple?"

"Yes, this is Kytenia." Firal touched her fingertips to his hand as she stood. "The others are sort of scattered, so I'm afraid you'll have to meet them later." She started to ask Kytenia to watch her place, but stopped when she saw her companion's expectant expression. A flush colored her cheeks at her own lack of manners and she added, "Kytenia, this is Vahn. He's been kind enough to help me find my way around the palace."

"A pleasure," Kytenia said, though she gave Firal a shadowed, curious look.

"Indeed it is." Vahn offered his arm to Firal. "Now, shall we? I'm certain it will help your appetite."

"Please." She tried to laugh, but the sound wouldn't leave her throat. She coughed softly instead. "If you would lead the way?"

"I believe the gentleman always leads." Vahn gave Kytenia a courteous nod before he swept Firal away. He led her between the large columns that supported the vaulted ceiling and guided her through the pair of great doors that stood open to welcome guests into the ballroom. The gleaming white marble dance floor was nearly empty, most of the guests still focused on the feast in the room behind them.

"You'll have to dance with one of my friends next," Firal said as Vahn took up her other hand to lead her into a waltz. She gave him a quick look-over as they moved into the first few steps. His clothing was not as fine as many of the guests, just a plain ivory shirt with a simple blue coat over the top. Silver embroidery decorated his lapels and coattails, while his blue trousers were unembellished. She mustered a smile as he twirled her about, though she felt clumsy on her feet. "If you don't, they'll kill me with gossip on the way home."

"I'm sure I can do that. Wouldn't want your dance partner to be the reason one gossips about you, after all." He gave the jewels she wore a meaningful look. She turned red.

"Now listen here," she protested. "I'm just trying to be a gracious guest. It's not my fault the king decided to drape me in jewels. He has some mistaken impression of something between me and Ran."

"And what is there between you and Ran?" The interest in his tone caught her off guard.

"Nothing," she replied, a little too quickly. Her toe caught against the floor and she stumbled a step. "I mean, he's a friend. Nothing more."

Vahn grinned. "Well. That's his loss, since you look as brilliant as a star in the sky."

Firal crinkled her nose, swatted his chest and stepped back. "Go dance with someone else," she laughed. As if on cue, another figure slipped past the others on the dance floor to join them.

"I hope you won't mind if I borrow this lad for a dance or

two." Medreal's weathered face creased with a warm smile she offered first to Vahn, then Firal. She wore no mask, but her elegant ivory dress was beautifully embroidered.

"Not at all, my lady." Firal moved back.

Vahn gave her a sheepish grin and offered his arm. "I would be honored."

"Flattery is a good thing to learn at such a young age." Medreal chuckled as she laid her hand on Vahn's arm, letting him lead her into the growing crowd.

Firal breathed in relief as her escort disappeared among the other dancers. She turned to start back for the banquet when gloved hands folded over her eyes from behind.

"Guess who," a familiar voice whispered at her ear.

She touched the soft leather gloves and resisted the smile that tugged at her lips. "Ran?"

He chuckled. "Not quite." He caught hold of one of her hands and turned her around.

Her smile faded. "Daemon."

He was dressed in finery to match any lord, his high-collared black coat and long black pants both worked with gold trim and embroidery. His new mask matched well and suited him perfectly, resembling the head of a black snake, the edge of each embossed scale painted with a hair-thin line of gold. His dark hair was neatly combed and tied in a short tail at the nape of his neck. Were it not for his snake-slit eyes, gleaming violet behind his mask, she doubted she would have recognized him.

"A pleasure to see you too," he murmured, pulling her close.

She blinked in confusion as he led her into a dance, looking down as he guided her steps. His pants were just long enough to brush the floor, but the wide-cut legs were not enough to hide his clawed toes.

"Not a very effective disguise," she said, trying not to frown. "You dance?"

He stifled a laugh. "Uncivilized as your stories portray my people, having rank among them does bring courtly demands."

Firal's eyes narrowed. "What are you doing here?"

"At the moment, I'm enjoying myself." Daemon was more graceful than she expected, a much better dance partner than Vahn, though she was too aware of his hand on her hip to follow his steps well.

"You shouldn't be here," she hissed in a whisper.

"I have just as much right to be here as you," he replied, tone surprisingly venomous.

She snorted. "If you knew the reason this event was public, I doubt you'd be so quick to claim that. If you're here because you think I won't hold my end of our agreement, you don't need to worry."

"Full of ourselves, aren't we?" He twirled her underneath his arm and reeled her in to hold her back against his chest. He squeezed her tight and bowed his head beside her ear. "I'm not here to see you."

Her cheeks colored as he released her, though with anger or embarrassment, she wasn't sure. "Then what are you—" She turned and stopped short. A glimpse of black between the couples on the floor was all that proved he'd been there, and then that, too, was gone.

KIFEL SIGHED AS HE WATCHED THE PEOPLE DANCE. HIS POSITION ON the balcony above made it easy to watch and easier for lords and ladies to find him, but some small part of him missed the days when he'd been young enough to be out there. His Eldani blood kept his age from showing, but year after year a weariness washed over him, settling a little deeper in his bones.

He'd taken the crown young, though he'd never wanted to rule. Had fate been kinder, he wouldn't have been an only child.

Of course, had fate been kinder, perhaps the celebration would have been for a different reason. A wedding, an engagement. Perhaps even the birth of a grandchild. He smiled ruefully at the thought, watching as another young man stepped in to dance with Firal.

"Are you still upset about our last visit?" The question was little more than a murmur beside Kifel's ear. It made the hair on the back of his neck stand, but he didn't move, waiting instead for the man in black and gold to step beside him.

Daemon leaned against the rail, his eyes following Firal across the ballroom, clearly having caught the way Kifel watched her.

"If you came to start a fight, you should have brought a weapon." Kifel kept his voice low.

Daemon laughed mirthlessly. "If I wanted to hurt you, it would have happened before now. Shall I take that as a yes?"

Kifel ignored the question and tore his eyes away from the people below. "It's either brave or foolhardy to come here as you are. With you, it's hard to tell which."

"I'm not afraid to show myself for what I am." Daemon kept his gloved hands clasped and his elbows on the railing, the violet glow of his eyes eerily intense when he turned to meet Kifel's eye. "Are you?"

Kifel frowned. "What do you want?"

Daemon looked back to the dancers beneath the balcony. "Right to the chase, then. All right." He shifted his mask with a thumb. "You might still be angry, but I'm not. I've been thinking. I've decided there are some things you need to know."

"And you think you can offer knowledge my eyes and ears can't?"

"I can offer knowledge your eyes and ears won't," Daemon replied. "There are strange things happening in Kirban. The Archmage raises Masters without consultation from the Houses. In the small hours of the night, she calls for meetings with Masters from every major city on the island. The Masters of the Houses don't know what these meetings are about. Your court mages don't even know they're happening. If she doesn't tell her own Masters what's going on, what isn't she telling you?"

The king gritted his teeth at the casual way Daemon spoke, as if watching the temple was anything to be casual about. He couldn't bring himself to look at the masked creature. The brazen way Daemon presented himself made him uneasy. "My dealings with the Archmage are no concern of yours."

"Yes they are. You've ordered her to watch the ruins, so she watches me. And so I watch her, too. You think she's missed the raids along the border?" Daemon cocked his head. "Relythes shouldn't have your full attention. There's a woman in the ruins. Someone I met while hiding from the mages."

Kifel's heart skipped a beat.

Daemon laced his fingers together and shifted his elbows on the rail, his shoulders bunching as he continued. "Something is about to happen in your temple. I don't know what it is yet, but Envesi is planning something. The Underling queen plans something, too. She intends to steal a Gate-stone from the temple, though I'm not sure why. She says it will make things easier. But a Gate-stone doesn't do anything I can't."

Kifel's jaw tightened. Ignoring the Underlings had seemed the kindest thing he could do. Incredible how only a few words could change his mind. "Why are you telling me this? Why now?"

Daemon hesitated, looking at the people below. Kifel followed his gaze, noted how his eyes tracked Firal through the crowd. The uncertainty in the way he watched her said more than words ever could.

"There are good people in the temple," Daemon said at last. "I don't want to see any mages hurt, despite all they've done."

Kifel bristled. "I am not at fault for the mages who have wronged you."

"I never said you were." Daemon spread his hands in a gesture of feigned helplessness, or maybe surrender. "Or perhaps I've misplaced the blame. Perhaps the only one at fault is you. You, supporting the temple so thoughtlessly, never considering what atrocities could come of it. What effect your selfish motives could have. What it could do to the people you loved."

Silence hung heavy between them, an ache growing in Kifel's chest. Not for the first time, he regretted the freedom he'd given the Archmage over how she used her magic. His eyes settled on the younger man's gloved hands as he laced his fingers together again. The glance didn't go unnoticed.

"Is it so wrong to want to walk in my own skin?" Daemon asked in a murmur.

"Do you really think anyone will give that to you? That the Underlings will?" The name left a sour taste in his mouth and the king frowned. "Is it worth clinging to that feeble hope, even knowing their queen will pit you against me?"

"She means to see me on your throne." Daemon pushed himself away from the railing.

"And do you want her to succeed?" The question came weighted with challenge, and it was met with silence. Kifel snorted and moved toward the curved stairway. "She'll be waiting a long time to see that, then."

"Kifel," Daemon called. The king paused. "Watch the temple. Please. Don't risk what you can't afford to lose."

Kifel looked Daemon over again, his gaze lingering on the clawed toes that peeked from the hems of his pant legs. "I've already lost it."

He descended the stairs.

FIRAL CHANGED DANCE PARTNERS SO OFTEN, SHE WONDERED WHAT likelihood there was that Ran would have spent more than a moment with a girl who caught his interest. She caught fleeting glimpses of her friends and paused to exchange partners with them when their twirling steps carried them close. True to his word, Vahn danced with the others. The way he flirted so shamelessly with them put Firal oddly at ease. She'd seen him dance with Kytenia more than once and she was glad someone else was the focus of his attention. So long as he didn't come back, expecting to monopolize her attention, Firal would be free to speak to the mages as soon as the meal ended.

"Do you mind if I cut in?" a voice asked from behind Firal. Her partner froze.

"Oh, Majesty, of course," the young man said, bowing as he backed away.

Firal's eyes locked with Kifel's as he offered his arm. She regarded him suspiciously, taking a half step back.

"Please, allow me a dance. I'll admit our last meeting ended poorly. I don't mean for there to be hard feelings between us. Lomithrandel has few enough friends, I don't intend to scare them off." He gestured with his offered arm, his tone patient. "He's capable of doing that on his own."

Firal didn't want to dance with the king, but she didn't know how to refuse. Her eyes skimmed the crowd on the dance floor. Unable to find anything to use as an excuse to escape, she placed a hand atop his arm and let him pull her into a dance. "He really doesn't need a ball, you know. I'm sure he could have any girl he wanted from the temple or anywhere else. Goodness knows Kytenia fawns over him enough. All you'd have to do is acknowledge his position in your household and he'd have to beat them off." She paused and moistened her lips with her tongue. "Although I have to say, I don't understand the secrecy. It's not as if you can hide his identity forever."

"I don't try to hide it," Kifel replied with sudden heat. "He was raised in my palace and he is my son. He may not be of my blood, but he is mine, crown or not. I have never tried to hide that. Hiding was his choice."

She brushed a stray wisp of hair behind her pointed ear and mulled over a response. "I'm not sure I understand your relationship with him," she admitted. "When I first met you at the temple, the two of you seemed like dear friends. Not really like a father and son."

"Unless he is crowned, he can't call himself a prince, so he will not acknowledge our relationship. Adoption is unheard of in noble families, too much concern over rightful succession. That's why, until I give him a formal title, he won't speak of it." He paused, shaking his head before adding, "But I can't do that. It isn't as simple as he thinks."

Firal bit her lower lip, feeling the hot prickle of eyes on them as the king spun her across the marble floor. "Then why would he want the secrecy? Wouldn't it be easier for him if he didn't have to play at the sort of double life he's trying to lead?"

The troubled look that crossed Kifel's face made her regret her choice of words, but the shadow was fast and fleeting. "His way of life is his own choice. But it does allow him to avoid controversy, which has always been a problem in the palace."

Firal pursed her lips. "Because he's your son, but not your heir." Ran's would-be rank explained why he was so often absent from classes, why he was excused for it, and why his feeble half-truths about his absences were acceptable in the eyes of Masters. "I always assumed they made exceptions for him in the temple because he might be of a weakened mage bloodline. I suppose it isn't because he's not full-blooded Eldani, after all."

"Well, my dear," Kifel said, a wan smile pulling at the corners of his mouth, "I am not full-blooded Eldani, either. But you didn't hear that from me."

She turned crimson as she realized her murmured musing was likely out of line. Then his words sank in. "You're not?" She looked at him as if seeing him for the first time. He was handsome, but more like a hero from a storybook instead of the delicate nobles she'd come to associate with Ilmenhith. His jaw was strong, his brow proud. If she hadn't known better, she might have thought he *was* Ran's father; they bore the same appearance of strength.

Kifel shook his head and his gaze drifted across the ballroom. The feast seemed to be over now, the floor more crowded than before. He spoke in a low voice, mindful of the ears around them. "Several generations ago, one of my ancestors took a Giftless woman as his bride. At the time, there were wars between our respective rulers, so their marriage was met with public outcry. They were accused of having wed only to calm the war. Unexpectedly, of course, the royal court later discovered her letters patent declared she was a half-blood." He smirked. "Forged, of course, but people settled after that. She lived an unusually long life for a Giftless woman, and over the years, all the fuss was forgotten. My great-grandmother was born to them. Then came my grandmother, and my mother. I was the first male child born into the royal family in generations. Of course, when I looked more the part of a seasoned warrior in adolescence than my father did at the height of my parents' rule, the old rumors stirred up again."

Firal bowed her head. "I suppose after seeing that all his life, Ran would want to spare you from unwanted scrutiny as much as he spared himself."

"One could suppose," he agreed, and left it at that. The rest of their dance was wordless.

As if from nowhere, Medreal appeared beside them and touched their arms to halt their dance. "Majesty, a moment?"

Kifel released Firal with an apologetic smile. The forced cheer faded the moment he turned to his stewardess. "What is it?" he asked, a note of anxiety in his voice. "Is it—"

"No, it isn't him." Medreal pulled Kifel aside.

Firal tried not to listen in, her brow furrowed with effort, but she couldn't have made out the urgent whispers that passed between them if she'd wanted.

After a moment, Kifel returned, smoothing his coat with both hands. "You'll have to excuse me," he said. That uneasy note returned to his words. "I'm afraid something urgent has come up. Please try to enjoy the rest of your evening." With a jerk of his head that beckoned Medreal to follow, he stepped away and disappeared before she had a chance to say a word.

"What was that all about?" Kytenia asked from the crowd beside her.

Firal clapped a hand to her chest and exhaled hard. "Why must everyone sneak up on me like that?"

"Sorry." Kytenia's voice dropped. She waved away her dance partner. Firal wasn't surprised to see it was Vahn. He flashed them a grin before a woman caught his arm and dragged him back into the crowd.

"Now," Kytenia said as she inched closer and lowered her voice. "What was all that?"

"I don't know." Firal struggled to smile and knew her attempt fell short. "I think I'm ready to finish this expedition, though. I'm not sure I'm ready for this sort of life. I know this is an exciting event for everyone else, but it's been strange for me. It's not quite what I expected."

Kytenia hugged her arms to herself. "I can't say I blame you. For all the excitement there was over it, the ball hasn't been all that spectacular. It seems like something is missing. Surely they didn't call us all here just because of the time of year."

Firal gave a sharp, humorless laugh.

Kytenia arched a brow. "Do you know something I don't?"

"Nothing I think I'm supposed to repeat," Firal said. "I'll tell you later. You go ahead. None of the Masters have come to dance, so I'm going to go find a court mage and...well, you know. Dance with someone tall, dark and handsome for me, would you?" She gave Kytenia's arm a pat and retreated before her friend had time to protest.

The banquet hall was mostly empty now, people crowded around the wide doors to the ballroom while they waited for an opportunity to join the dance. Firal's footsteps faltered when she reached the end of the crowd and emerged between the banquet tables.

Most of the Master mages still lingered beside the tables, separating themselves from what she was sure they considered childish frivolities. Firal skimmed their faces, lingering on those who were unfamiliar, searching for the blue bands on white robes that would signify a court Master. She'd expected them to cluster together, as the temple's Masters did, but when she found one, the woman sat alone.

Steeling her resolve, Firal clenched her hands in her skirts and crept closer. "Excuse me, Master, may...may I speak to you for a moment?"

The Master mage turned her head to face Firal, as disinterested as if an obnoxious child were tugging at her sleeve.

Firal fought back the queasy feeling in her stomach. "While I was here, I was hoping someone could tell me about my mother. I was told she was a court mage, but no one in the temple seems to know anything about her." She fished her broken necklace out of her dress and held it out.

The woman straightened when she saw the seven-pointed star on the pendant, intrigue creeping over her face. She stood and smoothed her skirts. "You'll need to speak with Temar. Come with me."

Firal's heart climbed into her throat as she followed the woman through the vast banquet hall. They wove between tables, crossing to the edge of the room where a small cluster of nobles and white-robed mages stood conversing.

The Master crept around the group and leaned close to whisper something to another woman in white. Then they both turned, the second woman murmuring a pardon before slipping away from the crowd.

Unlike the first Master, this woman greeted Firal with a warm smile. "Well met, child. I am Temar, head of Ilmenhith's court mages. I hear you have need of me?"

Swallowing hard against the lump in her throat, Firal nodded. "Yes, I...I hoped you could tell me about my mother."

"Ah," Temar chuckled softly and waved the other Master away. "You must be the girl Ran mentioned. I apologize that we didn't get to speak sooner. He approached me yesterday to ask I meet with you, but the solstice has kept everyone busy. What is your name?"

"Firal, Master." She curtsied, not sure how she was supposed to address such a high-ranking mage. The only Master above Temar was the Archmage herself. Flustered, she presented her pendant on one outstretched palm. "This was my mother's necklace. It was the only thing she left for me. I'm afraid I don't even know her name."

Temar made a small, thoughtful sound in her throat as she took the pendant from Firal's hand. She turned it between her fingers. "Yes, this is certainly one of ours."

Firal's heart leaped. "Please, Master, I just want to know who she is and where she's gone. I've been alone in the temple my whole life. If I could just find her, or at least learn her name—" The words caught in her throat and she could not finish.

Slowly, the court Master lowered the necklace back to Firal's hand. "I'm afraid I can't identify her by a necklace alone, and your name is not familiar to me. I only rose to this position five pents ago. She may have served before me. But I am certain our records can tell you what you need to know."

"Really? Can you show me? Could you take me there now?" Firal clutched her pendant with both hands to keep them from shaking.

"I'm afraid not." Temar raised a hand before Firal's heart could plummet. "Some time ago, the Archmage elected to move our records from Ilmenhith to the temple. It's easier to maintain archives where many Masters can control the climate. Only the most recent volume is kept here. What is your affinity? I will pass instructions to the head of your House to allow you full access to our records."

Firal's knees went weak beneath her. The temple. The answer she'd longed for had been practically at her fingertips, all that time. Tears of mingled relief and excitement pricked her eyes. "Healing, Master," she managed, dipping in a curtsy again. "Thank you, Master. I don't know what to say."

The court Master waved a hand. "No need to say anything, child. I shall pen a formal letter to Nondar first thing in the morning. But if you'll excuse me, I must return to our other guests. I hope you find what you are looking for. Do enjoy your time while you are here."

"Of course, Master. Thank you again." Firal swept the tears from her eyes before they could fall and stepped aside to let Temar pass. Joy bubbled in her chest and relief made her legs tremble beneath her. She considered slipping into the ballroom to tell Kytenia what had happened, but the crowd changed her mind. Instead, heart pounding and hands trembling, she put her necklace away and paced back toward the tables with a hand over her heart.

"It's a little early to be retreating from the festivities, isn't it, child?" The question caught her off guard, but she smiled when she spotted Nondar. He sat at the corner of a table, apart from another handful of Masters.

"I'm not very good at dancing." Firal joined him, pleased the old Master had come. She thought his age might make travel too uncomfortable. For a moment, she considered telling him what Temar had just said, but decided against it. Tonight's was a private victory, one she would savor by herself. There would be time to tell others during the trip home.

"Neither am I, anymore." Nondar shifted his gnarled hands atop his wooden cane and chuckled to himself. The levity was short-lived and his expression grew solemn. "You caused quite a stir with your decision to travel without us, you know."

She flushed and tried not to meet his expectant gaze as she settled on the bench beside him. That wasn't the happy sort of conversation she'd hoped for, but she owed the Masters an explanation. "I'm sorry, Master. I didn't mean to worry anyone." She removed her mask and toyed with its ribbons. "I was fortunate to find an escort and end up here, instead of dying somewhere in the ruins."

"Is that so?" Nondar murmured. "Then perhaps you

understand, now, why you aren't supposed to pass the mage-barrier without an escort. But that's a matter we'll discuss once we're home."

Firal cringed at the reprimand. She'd expected something harsher, though the threat of punishment put a knot in her stomach. He wouldn't dare deny her access to the records, would he? No; she chased that worry from her thoughts as soon as it landed. As the head of Kifel's court mages, Temar held great authority. Even over Nondar.

"Do you mind if I sit here for a while?" she asked, changing the subject.

"I don't mind at all, child," the old master replied blandly, watching the dancers in the next room.

"Thank you, Master." Firal put the worry out of her mind and followed the old mage's gaze. Nondar was a hard teacher, but a kind man, and she enjoyed his company. If not for his arthritis, she might have asked him to be her last dance. She supposed she could settle for her last dance being with the king, though he wasn't the most graceful partner she'd had.

For a moment, she thought it might be nice to dance with Daemon one more time.

FIRE AND FROST

FROM THE MOMENT THEY SET FOOT IN THE MARKETPLACE, TREN WAS unsettled.

The market village outside of Kirban was eerily quiet. That wasn't odd by itself, given the solstice festivities, but the houses looked as empty as the streets, windows lightless and streetlamps unlit. Market stalls stood with their sides rolled down and fastened against the drizzly weather, but peering beneath any of the covers showed every bit of merchandise—food, cloth, and otherwise—was still present. Didn't they fear thieves? Weren't they concerned about leaving their livelihoods unattended where anyone could have whisked them away?

He didn't think anything amiss, exactly—they'd planned this raid because it would be easy. A large number of people would have joined the caravan destined for Ilmenhith, as the chance to hawk wares in the capital was an unrivaled opportunity for most vendors. But nonetheless, he'd expected a fight.

As it stood, it was less a raid and more a burglary. Tren's men slipped into the market and collected foodstuffs and wares with ease. There was no need for caution; not a soul stepped from the houses, their windows shuttered and dark. Either there was no one left to protest, or those remaining didn't dare confront his small army. The thought sent a thrill down Tren's spine.

Lumia led the thievery, draping herself with jewels and silks, twirling and humming to herself as the raid progressed. Though a number of men cast frowns in her direction, Tren knew better than to think her addled. Lumia was odd, no doubt. But there was a shrewdness about her that glittered in her crystalline eyes, betraying deeper capability than he suspected others knew she possessed.

They had brought no carts. Once the men had filled their sacks with supplies, they turned south, skirting the edges of the ruins instead of trying to wind their way through the maze. Lumia called orders as they progressed, her lips twitching with a mysterious smile all the while.

Tren didn't respect the woman, not anymore; she'd proven herself too fickle and volatile for that. But he still served her unerringly. For the time being, she was useful. She spoke often of her plans to remove their people from the underground and her desire for Daemon to supplant the Eldani king, if only for the power it would grant her. He could have done as well or better on his own, perhaps, but riding the coattails of her success would be easier. If she failed, all he lost was time.

When they came within sight of the temple, Lumia ordered the men into two groups. Most split off with the provisions they'd gathered and headed toward the tunnels hidden in the maze that would lead them back to the safety of the underground. Tren and another two dozen men stayed with their queen. Together, they slipped into the outermost hallways of the ruins.

He'd expected the attack on the temple would be immediate, but their getaway hadn't exactly been clean. The ground was muddy and they'd left clear tracks behind, all leading directly to the ruins. Tren assumed Lumia meant for them to stand watch until the rest reached safety. But knowing why they stood watch and being glad to do it were different things, and he grumbled as they waited for her next command.

The moon crept behind rainclouds overhead and its feeble glow disappeared. The rain was not heavy, but it soon saturated his cloak. Tren adjusted it with irritation.

Lumia did not seem to notice the drizzle. She scaled a wall to perch on its top and peer toward the temple.

What was she waiting for? He knew better than to question her, but a heavy sense of uneasiness weighed on his shoulders. Sending only a handful of men to the temple was a deviation from the original plan. He didn't like that, either. Why send the rest away? Scouring the temple's expanse to find the Gate-stones would have been a challenge with fifty men, even with the information Daemon provided. Two dozen might be less noticeable, but with the mages gone, notice was hardly their concern. The market had been proof enough of that.

"What a smart woman," Lumia said, watching something in the distance. "Driving out the prying eyes before tending to dirty business. At least a half dozen messengers wearing the colors of Alwhen have left her tower in the past hour." Despite the rain and wind, not a single golden hair was out of place beneath the hood of her cloak. If he hadn't known better, he might have thought it magic.

"What do Giftless messengers matter?" Tren squinted at the sky overhead, unable to see anything else from his place on the ground. He figured it close to midnight, though he could no longer see the position of the moon or stars.

"I think you'll find they matter quite a bit. If she entertains messengers sent by King Relythes, then we've already made waves with our actions. That leaves one small problem to take care of before we can pursue what is rightfully ours." Her head turned and her eyes followed the lane that ran to the east. Watching another messenger, perhaps.

"What problem?" Tren asked, his prickling doubt shifting to a rolling wave of concern.

A laugh welled in Lumia's throat. "We move now. Come, men! Forward!" She leaped from the wall and left Tren and his men behind.

The men took to their feet and assembled behind Tren to surge through the broken halls. They emerged from the ruins just as Lumia snapped an arm toward the temple.

A tree in the temple's gardens ignited with a boom. She cackled and twirled in the muddy path between the temple and ruin, her head thrown back and arms spread wide.

"Take it apart and tear it down! Burn their temple to the ground!" she sang as the soldiers rushed to scout their assigned locations. She all but danced into the temple's courtyard, sweeping a gesture from the burning tree, giving her arm a sharp twist as if to fling it away. Flame streaked from the branches, leaping upward to the boughs of the tree beside it. Leaves sizzled and the whole of the gardens erupted in flames with another deafening blast.

"Isn't it glorious!" Lumia cried, wheeling to face Tren with a brilliant grin, her hands outstretched in invitation. Thick plumes of smoke rose overhead, painting the night sky with a ruddy glow. Burning leaves sloughed off onto the temple's roofed buildings, wooden beams crackling and groaning as they caught fire.

Tren stood at the gate as if rooted to the ground. *She's no mage. She can't be!* The thoughts roared in his head, though with the undeniable flames blinding him and smoke filling his lungs, he didn't know what else it could be but magic. If not a mage, what was she?

"Come to me!" She beckoned him with both hands.

"You're mad!" he shouted, the heat and smoke searing his throat.

"And beautifully so!" Lumia laughed as she closed the distance between them. She took hold of his arms and twirled with him, squealing in delight. Angry, Tren tore himself from her grasp.

A breath of icy air burst from the Archmage's tower and whirled across the courtyard, threatening the flames that engulfed the garden.

Lumia spun to face the white-robed figure that appeared in the doorway. Snow-white curls fell about the mage's shoulders and her mouth was set firm, a frigid fire burning in her ice-blue eyes.

"My, my, my." Lumia swept into a graceful curtsy and spread her black cloak to either side in mockery. "The Archmage herself. What a wonderful surprise."

"Don't offend me with your false bravado." The Archmage's voice was cold, her expression unshaken and serene. One slow step after another carried her into the courtyard.

Lumia brushed her skirts into order, her eyes never leaving the white-clad woman. "Oh, but Archmage, it's such a pleasure to be in your presence once more. And to imagine, raiding your beloved temple at the same time." A dark laugh escaped her throat, a glint in her eyes.

"Leave her be, Lumia." A cold sense of dread hit Tren's stomach like a dropping stone. "She's not our target. She's alone. One mage won't stop us."

"Alone, yes," Envesi acknowledged with a slight nod. "But no one ever said I was defenseless." Frigid wind howled through the temple grounds, a flash and glimmer too fast to be followed with the naked eye. A handful of Underling soldiers stepped from the storehouses and collapsed with muted cries as jagged spears of ice burst from their throats.

"Impressive," Lumia giggled, voice filled with admiration. The bodies of the fallen exploded in flame, their spilled blood catching fire as if it were oil. Fire streamed between the cobblestones. A darting gesture from the Underling queen's hand sent it racing toward the Archmage, igniting everything in its path.

Tren recoiled in horror as his soldiers around him stopped, frozen solid. Lumia's flames licked around them, their bodies crackling as heat warped the ice. Limbs broke and fell into the fire, leaving grotesque mannequins behind. As quickly as the fire thawed the dead, their dripping blood erupted into new streams of flame that threaded across the temple grounds like serpents.

His stomach turned. "Lumia, stop!"

"What are you aiming to do?" Envesi flicked her fingers. The gesture halted Underling men in their tracks. Lances of ice burst from between the plates of their armor.

"What I was always meant to do!" Lumia screamed. A ring of fire wound itself around her feet, its ruddy light casting misshapen, monstrous shadows across her face. "Destroy everything you have, everything you've forged, everything you hold dear!" Her words were emphasized by a heavy crunch and rumbling groan as a building behind her collapsed in ruin.

"You've already taken what mattered to me." Envesi directed veins of frost across the ground with a whirl of her hands. They darted up the walls of buildings and billowing clouds of steam joined the smoke in the air as a heavy layer of ice met each blaze.

"The child meant nothing to you!" Lumia screeched. Twin balls of fire ignited in the palms of her hands. She flung them one after another, shrieking in rage when they impacted an invisible barrier surrounding her opponent. Flames curled outward from the ward and dissipated harmlessly.

Tren spat a curse and darted for the open doorway of the Archmage's tower. He hadn't seen where all his men had gone, but the tower seemed the safest bet. Only a handful of soldiers stood inside. He cursed again. Even here, flames licked upwards, crawling over the spines of a thousand books. "Get out, now! Abort the mission!"

The soldiers abandoned their stolen goods and fled toward the ruins. Tren turned back to the courtyard and the women outside, powerless to stop the flames, unwilling to leave until he recovered his soldiers.

The Archmage's expression darkened as she moved forward,

jagged patterns of frost radiating from each footstep. "I will not be trifled with, Lumia of the Underlings."

Lumia's jaw tightened. With a slow, fluid motion, she drew a pair of long knives from beneath her cloak.

Envesi lifted her chin, her lips pressing to a thin line. "So be it." She stretched her arms to either side and curled her fingers into her palms. Dark, crackling scimitars of ice formed in her hands. Wind and snow spiraled against them as if to hone their edges.

The women moved almost faster than Tren could see. Cloaks and skirts and sinuous bodies crashed together and whirled apart with blinding speed. Clashing blades sent showers of shaven ice through the air. Slivers and icicles sprinkled the ground beneath the women's feet. Misting rain mingled with melting ice and billowing steam. Pools of water on the stone reflected the blaze so the ground, too, seemed afire. Tren bounded across the puddles in his search, but the only men who remained were dead.

So much for the rumors that the Archmage was aged and frail. Envesi darted closer, her scimitar meeting Lumia's blade only inches from the Underling's face. Each time Envesi's fragile weapons shattered, they reformed in her grasp without so much as a gesture to command it. Her footing was precise, her expression serene.

Lumia clenched her teeth, her lips curled in a grimace. She neither gained nor lost ground in their elaborate dance, no matter how wild her strikes became. Heavy smoke settled close to the ground, though neither combatant showed signs of withdrawal. A clumsy block left a stinging gash across Lumia's cheek; the Archmage took a hair-thin slice across her bicep. Envesi made no sound, her step light, her arm strong.

Faster, now, slices and swipes connected with flesh. Crimson trails stained Envesi's white robes and Lumia's porcelain skin. A sudden jab shattered Envesi's scimitars and the Archmage stumbled back. Lumia lunged into the opening and shrieked when Envesi caught and wrenched her wrists, forcing her to drop her blades. She twisted her arms in the Archmage's grasp and clawed at the woman's face in desperation. Envesi jerked an elbow into the Underling queen's stomach. The proximity allowed nails to rake across her cheek and the white-haired mage stifled a cry.

"That's enough!" Tren lunged forward and grabbed the corner of Lumia's cloak. He hauled her off the Archmage, surprised at how much strength it took to separate them.

"Let me go!" Lumia strained against his arms, glowering at the white-haired woman before her. Envesi glared back and spat blood.

"We've overstayed. I don't know what you're trying to do, but you won't achieve it tonight. You've done enough!" Tren forced her head up, forced her to look at the burning temple and the bodies of their fallen men around them.

Lumia screamed. She screamed as though beaten as he dragged her from the temple grounds, screamed like a child after candy. "It's never enough!" she shrieked, fighting harder as she watched the Archmage push herself to her feet, alone in the middle of the temple's ruins.

Unrelenting, Tren continued toward the ruins, though smoke burned his throat and eyes.

"It's never enough," Lumia groaned, and her head dropped in defeat.

A GNARLED HAND CLAMPED SHUT ON FIRAL'S SHOULDER AND jostled her awake. She squinted against the light of the banquet hall and the adjoined ballroom. The faces she saw were grim; even Nondar's mouth had a hard set to it. The couples on the dance floor stood deathly still. No one said a word. Firal's eyes felt gritty and she rubbed them with the side of her hand. She'd only meant to rest her eyes a moment; she hadn't expected to fall asleep.

Rikka and Marreli sat at the other side of the table. Both had removed their masks and their faces were pale. Shymin and Kytenia stood a few paces away, but their backs were turned to where Firal sat.

"Master?" Firal grimaced at the rasp in her voice. "What's going on?" She reached for the cup she'd left on the table and frowned when she saw it was empty.

"Get up, child. We're returning to the temple. Now." Nondar's tone hardened as he rose to his full height, as if the stiffness in his joints no longer pained him. She'd never realized how tall he was.

"What? Why? What's happened?" And why had she slept through it? Firal scanned the faces of the other girls again before she looked toward the ballroom. Kifel stood atop the balcony overlooking the dance floor. His voice echoed in the stillness as he gave orders to armored men. Her stomach twisted.

"The temple's been burned, Firal," Rikka said in a hushed tone. "The king just announced it. He said..." She swallowed, her voice both conflicted and confused as she went on. "He said men came from the ruins, but not men from Alwhen."

"*What?*" Firal squeaked and stood so fast it made her dizzy. "But Daemon is—" She bit down on her tongue the moment she realized what she'd said. Kytenia wheeled to face her.

Gulping, Firal shook her head and sank back to her seat. "Nevermind," she croaked. "I must have been dreaming."

Kytenia's expression grew dark.

Nondar watched with what might have been neutrality, if not for the steely glint in his mage-blue eyes. "The magelings are being gathered. King Kifelethelas has called together an army that will accompany us." The old Master gripped his cane as if he feared it would abandon him, his jaw set.

"But the temple is days away from here," Shymin said, glancing between the Master mage and her friends.

Nondar grunted. "There are enough Masters present to eliminate that problem. We only rode to Ilmenhith because the king could not spare his court mages. Now it seems he must."

He had no more than spoken when a woman in white joined them. Firal recognized her as Anaide, Master of the House of Water.

"Do you suppose—" Anaide began, blinking in surprise when Nondar raised a hand to silence her.

"Yes, I do. But we have company," he said, his head tilted toward the girls.

A sharp crackle sounded from the other end of the room and a hot gust of air poured through the palace. People retreated from the ballroom and Firal's eyes widened when she saw the source of the noise. Dozens of mages in Master white stood in a half-circle before a wide portal. Through it, she saw the gates of the temple. Everything beyond was too dark to see. Thick, acrid smoke flowed through the portal and into the palace.

"A Gate!" Marreli cried, her expression a mix of fright and awe. Gates of that size were rarely used, and for good reason. A Gate—even a small one—required a devastating amount of power. To call Gates dangerous was an understatement. To think of how carelessly Daemon had called one forth made Firal shudder.

Men in armor, weapons sheathed at their sides or strapped to their backs, marched across the ballroom beneath the blue and silver banner of the king. It was hard to see them past the bodies of the mages clustered around the Gate, but Firal thought she recognized several faces from the dance floor.

Nondar had already started toward the Gate, not to pass through it, but to join the half-circle of Masters that held it open.

"Come along, then. All of you." Anaide gestured for the magelings to follow.

Firal inched after the Master, though she cast a worried look over her shoulder. Behind her, Rikka took Marreli's hand and offered comfort as the smaller girl wiped tears from her eyes.

Kytenia and Shymin fell in beside them to form a bubble of protection.

The crowd slowed them down, murmured apologies and complaints everywhere as they pressed together in a mass of thick skirts and clumsy feet. Firal held her own skirts clear of being trampled as the Gate loomed before them. Anaide did not give them time to gawk.

A tingle shot through Firal like a bolt of electricity as she passed through the Gate's energies. All around her, magelings gasped. The sensation was wholly unpleasant, yet it was nowhere near the searing might Daemon had exposed her to before.

Smoke and shadow enveloped them the moment they were through, the light of the palace ballroom gone. Stifling heat threatened to steal the breath from Firal's lungs. She glanced over her shoulder and gaped in amazement. From the opposite side, the Gate was invisible. Magelings and Masters seemed to step from the air itself, flanked on either side by the soldiers Kifel sent with them. Was that what happened when there was no anchor on the other side?

"Don't dilly-dally!" Anaide herded them forward with a wave of her arms. They hurried onward, into the temple's courtyard, where a handful of Masters lit mage-lights in their hands. Firal squinted against the brightness. When her vision adjusted, her stomach lurched.

The fires had been extinguished, but thick piles of ash and charcoal still smoldered. Some of the temple's buildings were little more than empty husks, their stone exteriors blackened from smoke. The dormitory—Firal's room—was destroyed. The gardens were gone, save the scorched remains of the trees that had been in full bloom only a week or two before. In the middle of everything, a woman in white stood alone.

"Who is that?" Rikka whispered beside Firal's ear.

"I think it's the Archmage," Firal replied, reverent. The other girls were silent, though their faces showed an equal amount of awe.

The Archmage never left her tower, and magelings were not allowed in the upper floors where the woman lived and worked. None of them had known what to expect. While the Archmage looked a great deal younger than Firal had imagined, it was clear she could be no one else. Though small of stature, the woman bore an air of authority, and even from a distance, the presence of the Archmage's Gift weighed on Firal's senses so heavily she thought she would crumple.

Anaide gestured for the girls again. The magelings followed and the Master led them to the Archmage, who appraised them with a quick, cold glance.

The ice in her silvery-blue eyes made Firal shudder. She'd heard rumors about the Archmage, about eyes that chilled to the bone and a healing Gift that bit like winter, but she had never expected them to be accurate. Something in the woman's eyes unsettled her and, though Firal couldn't imagine where, she was positive she'd seen that piercing look somewhere before.

All but forgetting her manners, Firal belatedly swept into a curtsy and spread her skirts wide. The others followed suit as more magelings clustered around them.

It was not until the last soldier took his place in formation behind the mages that the Archmage moved. Her black-rimmed eyes narrowed as her gaze swept across the gathering of Masters and magelings. She lifted her chin and gestured behind her with a broad sweep of her arms. Two Masters stepped forward and drew the great doors of her tower open wide.

Firal gasped, tears springing to her eyes.

Beyond the doors, the library had burned.

Her throat tightened and she blinked hard as she stared into the soot-filled darkness beyond the doors. The temple's records had been kept in the library. If Ilmenhith's records had been there, too...Her knees threatened to give way beneath her.

"All mages are to come inside," the Archmage announced,

her voice pure and clear, as strong as Firal expected and yet somehow more feminine. "We must prepare arrangements for our guests. With all accommodations burned, the tower must be rearranged to hold everyone. Collect every remaining artifact, weapon, book, and scroll and take them to the top three floors. Stack everything neatly. Pack trinkets and loose papers into boxes. Play with no artifacts. Open no remaining books. Within this tower are many objects of yet untold knowledge. This knowledge is not to be shared with anyone outside the temple. I will be waiting on the third floor from the top to direct organization." Abruptly, the Archmage turned on her heel and glided into the tower.

Too numb to act on her own, Firal let the movement of the crowd carry her into the library. The smell of smoke was thick in the air, the ash of countless books like snow beneath her feet. It was all she could do not to sob.

"It'll be all right," Rikka murmured, patting her arm.

"You don't understand," Firal choked, tears tracking down her face. "It may not."

In only a few hours, she had gained hope, counted her blessings, then lost it all again.

The walls were as charred and black as the rest of the library. From the looks on the faces of the magelings ahead of them, the second floor was no better.

"Sweep up all of this rubbish and throw it outside," Anaide ordered. She whisked past the magelings and raised her voice. "All Masters are to report to the Archmage's office. Immediately!"

Mages in white slipped past them and crowded their way up the stairs.

Firal made it to the center of the room and then sank to the floor, hot tears tracing down her cheeks. "They just have to be somewhere else," she gasped softly, unable to fight the dread in the pit of her stomach. "Oh, please, let them be somewhere else!"

19

CHANGES

"WHAT HAVE YOU DONE?" DAEMON SLAMMED THE DOOR BEHIND him, rattling it on its hinges. His eyes glowed an angry red, their light reflected on the inside of his plain steel mask.

Lumia turned in her chair and batted her eyelashes at him with a coy smile. "Where have you been, my pet? I expected you back sooner."

"I don't need to report my every action to you." He raked clawed fingers through his hair, pacing before the closed door. He tried to calm himself, willing his feet to be still as he shifted his mask. It felt too warm but he didn't dare remove it, unsure he could keep anxiety from showing on his face. "After everything I've done, every inch of progress I've made in establishing contacts in the temple that could help me, you raze it! Are you mad?"

The queen's smile faded. "I would mind how you speak to me, pet." Her tone dropped dangerously. "Whatever illusion of freedom you have is simply because I allow you a very long leash."

He bristled. "I am on no one's leash! I'm no animal for you to cage," he spat. "No more than I was for the mages."

Her chair screeched against the stone floor as she shoved it back and leaped to her feet. "Impudent child, I own you!"

"But you don't control me," Daemon retorted, his eyes blazing.

Her eyes widened and for a moment, she was silent.

He rubbed the back of his neck as if to smooth his hackles. Rage wouldn't undo anything, he reminded himself. Still, he struggled to keep his composure. "I serve you so I can serve our people. I serve them so they can do more than simply exist, simply scrape to make ends meet in some hole in the ground. Why would you undermine that?"

She exhaled and waved a hand, gliding toward him with a seductive swing in her hips. "I fail to see why you would still want any connections in the temple, especially after disposing of that mageling you found wandering here."

The mention of Firal caught him off guard. What did she have to do with anything? He clenched his scaled hands to fists at his sides and tried to think of an explanation for what had happened to the mageling girl.

Lumia's eyes narrowed. She leaned close, a mirthless smile on her lips. "Oh, but you didn't dispose of her, did you? Did you think you could keep secrets from me? Don't forget, my pet, you're sworn to me." She trailed a claw-like fingernail down his mask. "But she is not my only problem with the temple."

His throat tightened. She knew? His mind raced back over their past conversations in search of where he might have slipped. A new thought sprang into his head and he frowned instead. She was trying to throw him off, shake his confidence and put a damper on his anger. There was no reason she should care whether or not he'd dispatched a single mageling. He put Firal out of his head and refocused on Lumia as she continued.

"The mages are funded by the very family that drove our people into hiding in the first place. You know that better than anyone. As soon as your ties to us became evident, any mage would turn against you. Or worse, try to use you to get to our little tribe and destroy what we have left. These people deserve better than that, my pet. They deserve glory. They deserve to have the cities built by the Eldani. And the temple deserved to burn." Her voice took a frosty edge. "After everything the mages have done to you, I thought you would agree."

His claws dug into his palms. "This isn't about what they've done to me."

"Your false selflessness is charming," Lumia chuckled. "Come, pet. Let me take these serious thoughts off your mind." She reached for his mask.

Daemon caught her wrists and thrust her hands away. "I think the time for that is past."

A flicker of anger lit her eyes before she caught it, but her expression melted into a pout. She rubbed her wrist as if injured, though he knew he'd barely touched her.

"I have plans for my own supply run." He ignored her sulking and pulled the ties on his mask a little tighter. "You are not to interfere and neither is Tren. It's my understanding you made quite the spectacle of yourself in the temple. If Tren hadn't dragged you away, the gossip in the underground would be worse than rumors of our queen making a fool of herself. That said, he should have stopped you sooner."

"How dare you!" she snarled, whipping up her hand to strike him. She stopped just before she hit his steel mask and bared her teeth. "I am your queen! Tren is not my keeper and neither are you! Who do you think you are, giving me orders?"

"The man who would give glory to your people," Daemon replied coolly, turning for the door. "The man you would put on the throne. Now I must repair the damage you've done. Don't follow me and don't send any of your spies, or you'll find your war that much harder to fight."

Lumia's fists tightened until they quivered at her sides.

He slipped out before she could reply, slamming the door again.

EVEN BEFORE HE SET FOOT IN THE ARCHMAGE'S OFFICE, A BURDENED sense of dread settled over Nondar's shoulders.

He hadn't liked that she'd scaled the tower and called for the Masters while the temple smoldered and magelings—some of them little more than children—mourned the loss of their home. It was not unreasonable to expect the Archmage to tend to her people. But she hadn't, and Nondar put himself into Envesi's disfavor by being late to the meeting she'd called.

If he'd felt any remorse for inconveniencing the Archmage, it had dissipated when he'd tucked one of the youngest magelings —a girl no more than twelve pents old—into a makeshift bed for the night. The Archmage herself was the greatest healer on the island, but as Master of the House of Healing, Nondar held a greater understanding of the nuances of health. He expected in the coming days, he would tend many things magic could not heal.

The Archmage did not acknowledge him as he settled into his chair some distance from her place at the head of the table. There was a bitterness in the air that he couldn't attribute to her demeanor. He needed distance to be comfortable. The solemn faces of the other Masters made him wonder if they'd started without him.

More than just the Masters of the Houses were gathered. The chairs around the long table were reserved for those who held high rank, but the Archmage's office was filled almost wall to wall with mages in white. Nondar saw bands of color on the sleeves of some, which indicated they'd been retrieved from their posts at the island's numerous chapter houses. His mouth tightened when he noted there were none present from Ilmenhith.

"As I was saying," Envesi began as he settled, confirming his suspicion they'd begun without all five Houses in attendance, "we will not continue to endure the neglect that caused tonight's misfortune. We will not allow a corrupt king to expect full use of the temple's strength without so much as a whisper of protection offered in return. He doesn't even care to protect us when his son is among our numbers."

"Ridiculous!" Edagan shouted.

Nondar turned his eyes toward the Master of the House of Earth, surprised to hear her give voice to his own mental objection.

Edagan's weathered face crumpled with a scowl as she continued. "Kifelethelas has never placed the temple under guard because it never needed to be guarded. Our mages are respected and valued across the entire island. You, Archmage, were the one who said there was no reason for anyone but yourself to remain in the temple!"

Anger flared in Envesi's eyes, but Melora half-rose from her chair before the Archmage could speak.

"No man serving Relythes or Kifelethelas would dare lift a finger against the temple," Melora said. "If we fell under siege, there's only one faction on Elenhiise to blame. And whose fault is that?"

"Enough!" the Archmage snapped, traces of magic amplifying both the volume of and the anger in her voice. "I am Archmage of Kirban Temple. My word is law! You are here to take orders, and if you fail to obey, your station is easily filled."

Melora's jaw clenched, but she sank back into her seat.

An uneasy silence fell over the room.

Satisfied, Envesi rested her hands against the edge of the table with her fingers intertwined. "I understand your reservations, but I do not act without consideration. The preservation of magic demands we move. We've come far and accomplished much. We cannot risk losing what we have managed to rebuild. Action to secede from Kifel's rule will begin immediately. Alira, you are to leave for Alwhen tonight. You will take two magelings to act as handservants. We don't know the city well enough to safely open a Gate, so you must ride."

The young Master opened her mouth as if to protest, clearly displeased at having been reduced to a messenger. But she cast a glance toward Melora, then seemed to think better of it. "As you say, Archmage."

"Foolishness!" Edagan scoffed, shaking her head in disgust. "You think to seek refuge from a king you dislike by entering the service of another king you dislike?"

"Dislike or otherwise, our chapter houses have never received anything but positive support from Relythes," Melora argued. "His lands are smaller, but his forces are greater. He has always feared Kifelethelas would seek to use us against him. If it comes to a simple matter of protection, it makes no difference which king we're under, as long as his armies are large enough."

"And why should the mages of Kirban Temple require protection?" Nondar asked, mindful to keep his words calm. "Aside from one terrible oversight, for what reason do we, the talented mages of Elenhiise, need the protection of the Giftless?"

The rest of the room remained far too quiet. Aside from the leaders of the five Houses of affinity, no one else had spoken. *Four Houses,* he corrected himself, glancing toward Anaide. The woman hadn't yet spoken a word, her head bowed.

"As Archmage, it is my responsibility to see that all of us are safe," Envesi said. "Not only the mages, but those in our employ. We have stewards. Cooks. Stockmen. More scullery and cleaning maids than I can count. We cannot be expected to protect the entire temple by ourselves."

"As evidenced by your inability to do so," Edagan muttered.

The Archmage cast her a withering look. The lesser-ranking Masters shifted on their feet, uneasy. But when the Archmage spoke again, she was calm.

"Nevertheless," Envesi said, "My word is beyond contestation. Alira, you are to leave immediately. We will shed these men Kifel has so belatedly posted here, leave this temple, and establish a new residence in Alwhen once Relythes accepts us."

Safely away from the reach of your mistakes, Nondar thought bitterly.

Alira rose from her place at the table and dipped in a graceful bow. "Yes, Archmage. As you command." Hers was the only voice of cooperation. Nondar suspected she merely wished to escape.

"Excellent." The Archmage rose and made a sweeping gesture toward the door. "Confidence of temple business shall seal your lips against sharing what has transpired here. With that said, you are all dismissed."

A great shuffling stirred around the table as white-robed mages followed Alira from the room. Envesi didn't wait for them to leave before she moved from the head of the table to her desk, spread a number of blank papers across its surface and reached for her pen.

The Masters seated around the table stood almost in unison. Edagan and Melora swept ahead in a hurry and disappeared among the crowd at the doors. Nondar rose more slowly. He didn't notice Anaide by his side until she spoke.

"So," she murmured, staring ahead, her eyes glazed. "This is how the end begins."

Nondar said nothing, but as he walked, he found he needed a great deal of support from his cane.

———

FIRAL'S ARMS TREMBLED BENEATH THE WEIGHT OF SOOT-BLACKENED books. She struggled to heave them an inch higher. Even standing on tip-toe, she couldn't reach the top of the stack. Among the charred remains of the library, a few volumes had survived. Though damaged, they might be able to repair some of them. Those that had not burned completely now crowded the uppermost floor of the tower, outside the Archmage's office. Combined with crates of goods that might be salvaged, most stacks reached nearly to the ceiling.

Little more than a narrow path remained between the towers of artifacts and books. At the end of the winding path, the doors to the Archmage's office were locked, though muffled voices spilled from within. The Masters were unlikely to leave the office any time soon, but the magelings took care to ensure few people worked in the narrow path at any given time, just in case the meeting adjourned.

Firal gritted her teeth and braced her shaking arms. If she could reach even an inch higher, she could slide her books into place. Though she'd been one of the first magelings to begin gathering books, she had not seen any of Ilmenhith's records among those that escaped the blaze. She prayed they were not among those reduced to crumbling, ashen husks.

To her surprise, another pair of hands lifted the books from her grasp and pushed them onto the stack overhead.

"Careful." Vahn flashed her a weary smile. He wasn't the only one who was tired; the sky grew rosy with the new dawn and none but the youngest magelings had slept.

"What are you doing here?" Firal smoothed her skirts and pushed her hair into some semblance of order. After so many trips up and down the stairs, it had come loose from its pinnings and framed her face in curls. She still wore her ballgown, the silk stained with ash. They hadn't been afforded a chance to change, though she suspected all their clothing had burned. She hadn't dared visit the dormitories.

Vahn sighed. "I got what I asked for, I suppose. I am part of the king's army, you know. All the soldiers in the ballroom were handy enough to be sent this way." He cast a glum look toward the blackened spines of books. "My first duty station and the place is half destroyed."

She bit her lower lip and brushed past him to move down the wide staircase. She kept to one side, leaving room for the long line of magelings scaling the stairs with their arms full. "Well, I didn't think the king's men were meant to help. I don't imagine the Archmage will want you touching things."

"She never actually said that. Besides, I think we're all ready for a little shut-eye." He tried to chuckle, but it sounded halfhearted. "The sooner we get everything moved, the sooner we can lie down. I just thank Brant I wasn't chosen for first watch."

Firal made a soft, thoughtful sound as she recalled the chapel and its milky-white clock face with a tinge of regret. Unless she managed to become a court master, she doubted she would ever see Ilmenhith again.

A pair of magelings slipped past her with an armful of books, murmuring gossip. Firal paused to glance at the titles, though she tried to shut her ears. She'd heard more than enough rumors about how the fires had started. The magelings carried no records, as far as she could tell. She didn't know whether to worry or feel relieved. "Have you seen much of the damage around the temple?"

"Most of the temple is ash. I don't know how it caught fire, but it looks like it burned fast." Vahn clasped his hands behind his back as he followed her, delivering his information as if giving an officer his report. "The stables are intact, and the dinner hall is half standing. Fortunately, none of the food stores were damaged, but I've heard the king already has wagons of additional rations heading this way."

As bad as the situation was, it was a wonder the damage hadn't been worse. Firal still sensed the faint residue of energy that indicated powerful magic had been used in the attack. Rogue mages were not unheard of, but they had no reason to attack the temple. There was only one other mage she could think of who might bear such strength. The knowledge weighed heavily on her shoulders and she tried to put it from her mind. "Did Ran come with you from Ilmenhith?" she asked as she wound her way back through the stacks of the burned library. Most shelves had already been stripped, the good books piled on the floor.

"Actually, that's why I was looking for you." Vahn inched

closer to her, making room for a mageling to pass. The second floor of the tower was crowded. He looked uncomfortable, though Firal didn't know why. The soldiers were the only ones given a chance to don their uniforms. His blue-trimmed coat had to be more comfortable than the finery all the mages wore.

When Vahn spoke again, he lowered his voice. "Several people mentioned seeing him in the temple, but I can't find him. I'll need to speak with him if I'm going to be stationed here."

Firal scooped an armful of salvaged books from the top of a pile. "All the Masters were called together for a meeting. I'm sure he's there with them."

He frowned. "Why would he be with them?"

"Oh, so he didn't tell you either?" She raised a brow. "Perhaps you can ask him about that when you find him. If it's important, go wait for the Masters to finish their meeting upstairs."

"I will, thank you." He offered a graceful half-bow and started up the stairs again.

She eased the books back onto the stack and wiped her brow. Lifting them had taken everything she had left in her. Carrying another armful of books upstairs seemed impossible. Wearied, Firal cast a glance back to the stairs Vahn had just climbed.

Magelings sat in clusters on the empty floor, none looking eager to resume work. Among them sat her friends. Firal hadn't crossed paths with them often, but if they'd given up moving things, she supposed there was no harm in resting a little, herself. She left the damaged books in their pile and made her way to join them.

"I'm exhausted," Shymin groaned. She sank to lay flat on the floor and heaved a sigh. Her skirts pooled around her in a mass of soot-stained silk.

"I think we all are." Marreli leaned against Kytenia's shoulder, her eyes heavy and glassy. Firal reached to smooth the younger girl's braids as she joined them.

"Can you believe how many men the king sent?" Rikka

asked, untangling her red hair with her fingers. "I don't know how all of us are supposed to stay in the tower."

"The Masters will just make the soldiers sleep outside if we don't fit." Kytenia fidgeted with the hem of her skirts. Her face was streaked with dust and soot and her hair had come out of its bun some time ago, though pins kept it off her shoulders. "Firal, was that Vahn?" A hint of color bloomed in her cheeks, not hidden by the dirt.

Firal understood Shymin's sigh; nothing had ever felt as good as sinking to the floor to rest. "It was. He was looking for Ran, so I sent him off to the Masters."

"Why would Ran be with the Masters?" Marreli asked.

Firal pursed her lips, sure it made her look as if she had a wedge of lemon—or perhaps one of those sour fruits from the ruins—in her mouth. Even an expression that sour wasn't strong enough for how she felt. "He wears the white now. With court mage colors."

"Ran does?" Kytenia exclaimed. "But he's not even—"

"All of you, on your feet!" Alira's roar from the stairs made all of them flinch and everyone scrambled to do as they were told. The Master's gaze weighed on their group longer than it did the rest of the magelings. "You and you." She pointed to Rikka and Kytenia, the two closest to where she stood. "Come with me. The rest of you are to take shifts working and sleeping until everything is moved."

Rikka straightened. "Where are we going, Master Alira?"

"We are to seek assistance in restoring the temple. I have orders from the Archmage to take two magelings with me. The men sent with us are useful as guards, but little else." Alira gestured for them to move. Neither looked pleased, but they obeyed.

Kytenia touched Firal's arm. "You're going to have to explain everything later."

Alira swept down the stairs, her white robes swirling about her ankles. She must have found a stash of robes that hadn't been damaged, or else used magic to clean hers, for the skirts of her robes bore not a smudge of dirt. Rikka and Kytenia hurried to follow her, though they looked weary enough to sleep on their feet.

As soon as Alira was out of sight, everyone sat again.

"Restoring the temple?" Marreli asked. "Where are they going to find carpenters and stonemasons at this time of night?"

"The sun will be up by the time they reach the market, you goose," Shymin said. "They may be headed to Wethertree, besides. I don't know where else you'd find carpenters and masons." She righted her skirts and tried to settle again. "I just hope Alira doesn't push too hard. I'd be surprised if Rikka and Kyt didn't fall asleep in the saddle."

"I'm sure they'll be all right," Firal said. "Nondar would throttle Alira if she did anything to hurt the health of one of his students."

"It's probably best for Rikka to go, in any case. I'm not sure she'd be able to sit still with this many eligible men about." A sarcastic smirk twisted Shymin's features. "She wouldn't rest until she'd found a husband. Lifetree forbid she find a man who's interested. She'd leave the temple in a heartbeat if she found someone to marry her."

"Do you think so?" Marreli tilted her head, stifling a yawn. Firal patted the floor beside her and Marreli laid down. The floor wasn't comfortable, but it had been scrubbed clean. Firal stroked the younger girl's braids.

"Oh, I know so." Shymin picked at the grit under her fingernails. "She told me as much. I guess her parents were the ones who decided she ought to attend the temple for training. The only way out of it is for her to settle down somewhere."

Marreli tucked her legs close. "I think it'd be nice to settle and have a family somewhere. I don't think I want to stay in the temple forever." She yawned again. Her eyes looked heavier by the moment.

Shymin shrugged. "I'd be lying if I said I hadn't thought

about marriage before. But Kytenia is more likely to jump at the chance than I am. I'm not sure it's for me. Regardless, I'd like to finish my studies before going home."

Home. The thought stirred an ache in Firal's chest. She'd always thought of the temple as home, having nowhere else, but now the word reminded her of how close she'd come to finding her family. "You're lucky to have somewhere to go."

Shymin grinned. "You could always go home with me and Kytenia, live with our family. They'd be happy to have another girl about."

Firal couldn't recall hearing either one of them speak of their family, though their shared blood was obvious. "Where is your home? Your family? I don't think Kytenia's said much about them before."

"Oh." Shymin laughed weakly and lowered her eyes. Marreli had already fallen asleep. "We're really only half-sisters. My mother passed away during childbirth. My—our—father remarried right away because he couldn't care for all us children on his own. I was so happy when Kytenia was born. I'd only had brothers until then. Five of them."

Firal drew up her knees and wrapped her arms around them. "Did the youngest make it? The one your mother passed with?" she asked cautiously, afraid she might strike a nerve.

"Yes, he did, but his health has never been good. That's why I came to the temple, actually. At first, Kytenia only came because she didn't want to be the only girl at home, but it helped her discover her own goals. I don't know if we've learned enough yet, but I've always hoped that between the two of us, we'd gain enough skill with healing to help our family. Especially my youngest full brother. He suffers so much."

"I'm sorry to hear that," Firal murmured.

"Everyone is dealt a hand in life, I suppose." Shymin shrugged. "But what about you? You said you haven't got anywhere else to go. Surely you have relatives somewhere."

Firal squirmed. Just the topic she wanted to avoid. "I suppose so. I mean, perhaps. I was told my mother was a court mage back when the temple was founded. I think I've told you that before. I don't know what happened to her, but she left me here. I don't remember her at all. So I...I had hoped the mages in Ilmenhith could tell me more."

A hint of surprise tugged Shymin's brows upward. "Did they?"

"Their leader said she would grant me permission to read the records to find my mother's name when I returned to the temple, but now..." Tears welled in Firal's eyes and she covered her mouth.

"Oh...Oh, Firal." Shymin leaned forward and rested a hand on Firal's knee. "We haven't combed the whole tower yet. The records might be upstairs. And even if they're not, it doesn't mean you don't still have a family. It doesn't mean anything. Perhaps your mother was one of the mage emissaries they sent to connect with the colleges on the mainland. She wouldn't have been able to take a child with her, traveling that far."

Firal scrubbed the tears from her eyes with the back of her hand. "I'd like to think someone would have told me, if that was the case." It seemed unlikely both her parents would have just disappeared from her life. She knew nothing of her father, but the children of mages weren't just abandoned, especially not those with a spark of the Gift perceptible within them. Left for training, certainly, but not abandoned.

She swallowed hard and tried to change the subject. "You know, I heard some of the older magelings talking. Some of them said that this isn't the first time the temple has burned, though it is the worst."

Shymin frowned. "I still want to know who burned it."

Firal hesitated. Perhaps that hadn't been the best thing to talk about, either. She'd seen Daemon at the palace, but where had he been until they danced? Knowing he could open a Gate alone made her nervous. The memory of teaching him to light a flame made her shudder.

"What's wrong?" Shymin asked.

"I think...I think I know who did it." Firal lowered her voice so no one else would hear. "But you'll think I'm crazy if I tell you."

Shymin snorted. "A week ago, if you'd told me someone might try to burn Kirban Temple, I'd have thought you crazy. Now, I might consider anything."

Still, Firal was reluctant to speak. Her mouth worked wordlessly a moment before she found her voice. "I think it was...well, in the ruins..."

Shymin shrank back. "Was it...*him*?" Firal gave her a startled look and she went on quickly. "Kytenia told us. I thought it was ridiculous at first. I thought you were just embellishing on those silly rumors that got started that first night you went out and Ran carried you back. But then you disappeared again, and now this."

Firal twitched at the reminder of Ran's confession. Had all of them known? "I don't know," she admitted. "I don't *want* it to be him. But I don't know if any of the others would be capable of doing this. I haven't met many." But it couldn't have been, could it? She'd only just agreed to teach him. He'd learned a lot in the days they traveled together, but that didn't even brush the surface of what she could help him learn. Why, then, would he risk their agreement by burning the temple to the ground?

"Why would you go back into the ruins after meeting him?" Shymin's question was free of accusation, though she wore a skeptical frown. "Weren't you afraid to run into him again?"

"Of course I was. But I lost my journal, that was the only reason I went back. I had to—Oh!" Firal cried, curling her hands to fists. "He still has my journal!"

"Be glad that's all you're missing. Everyone who was in Ilmenhith left belongings in the capital. I'm sure they'll be collected and sent with supplies for the king's men, but who knows how long that will take. We're stuck sharing everything until then." Shymin sounded frustrated, though Firal couldn't blame her. No one was pleased about being crammed into the Archmage's tower, much less having to share the space with soldiers. It was a small consolation that the soldiers would be confined to the lowest floors.

Shymin sighed before going on. "But Firal, about the Underlings—"

Firal hushed her. "I don't think this is the time or place to talk about that," she said, glancing around the crowded room. "You stay here with Marreli while she sleeps. I'm going to keep moving things for a while. With any luck, the soldiers won't be here long."

"With any luck, none of this would have happened to begin with." Shymin made herself as comfortable on the floor as she could manage.

Firal said nothing more, slipping off to return to the books.

Though she didn't want to think about it, Shymin was right. About several things. The fear the records had been destroyed threatened her hope, but she had one advantage the other magelings didn't.

Her most precious belongings hadn't been in the temple when it burned.

She still had her mother's pendant, tucked into the bodice of her ballgown, and there was still hope she might retrieve her journal. But that thought brought uncomfortable feelings, as well. Daemon's power had developed by leaps and bounds during their brief travel together, but he had never volunteered to give back her journal. She supposed it was her fault. She'd had a chance to reclaim it and pretended it didn't matter, but after her necklace, it was the only thing she owned that did. Since he'd taken it, she suspected he knew.

Unable to focus, Firal finished moving the stack of damaged books she'd picked up and then found somewhere between the scorched shelves to sit.

She'd never had reason to trust him, but in spite of everything, she wanted to believe they'd developed some small spark of a connection during their travels; maybe even a friendship. He'd even sought her out to dance with her.

But then he'd disappeared. Perhaps he'd done that on purpose, meaning to throw her off, intending to make her believe he'd been in Ilmenhith the whole time. He could have traveled to the temple before or after that point; she hadn't seen him again, and he certainly hadn't been there when the Masters opened the massive Gate that took them back to the temple's ruins. And if he'd had anything to do with the temple's destruction, she only had herself to blame.

That realization rang with crystal clarity in her head. She'd been foolish, letting her heart's desires cloud her judgment. Daemon had used her skill and her desperation to his advantage, and she'd sacrificed everything—maybe even her dreams—in a moment of selfish weakness.

Nodding to herself, she made her decision.

She would not risk it again.

No matter what she'd promised, their bargain had to end.

———

A GROOM WITH SADDLED HORSES WAITED AT THE STABLE DOOR WHEN Alira and the magelings arrived. It was a small blessing that the temple's few animals had been spared, but it was no wonder. The stable was in the farthest corner from the main gates. While it was hard to be certain where the fires started, the residual energy of magic at the temple's entrance had borne the oldest signature.

Master Alira's attention turned to Kytenia first. "Hold still," the Master ordered. She touched Kytenia's face with both hands.

Kytenia gasped as the jolt of energy poured through her. A shudder rolled through her body despite the warmth of the air. The sharing of energy wasn't unheard of, but outside of healing, the practice wasn't common. It poured into her with a hot, prickling sensation and made her skin crawl. But when the energy flow halted, she felt as refreshed as if she'd slept a full night. Rikka squeaked when Alira repeated the process with her, but neither girl dared protest. As strange as the sensation was, it would be better to suffer briefly than to make the ride while exhausted.

"Mount up and follow me." Alira climbed into the saddle and kicked her horse into a quick trot without stopping to see if they followed.

The groom boosted both magelings to their saddles. Kytenia turned her horse and twitched her heels against its sides. The beast needed little urging to follow Alira's mount.

At first, Kytenia thought herself disoriented from lack of rest. But as the temple shrank behind them and the road narrowed, she exchanged worried glances with Rikka. They were not headed in the direction of the market. Instead, Alira led them east, along a curving road no wider than a single horse. They fell in line behind the Master mage and Kytenia bit her tongue as she took up the rear.

"Master?" Rikka called, not sharing the same inhibition. "Where are we going?"

"The help we need can't be found in the markets here or in Wethertree," Alira said.

"But there's nothing to the east," Rikka said.

"I am not on this trip to give lessons in geography." Alira clicked at her horse and spurred it into a canter.

Rikka grimaced at the speed, but followed suit. Kytenia felt sorry for her. She and Alira might have been comfortable on horseback, but Rikka was not. She bounced hard in the saddle, wincing each time she came down.

Alira said no more.

"The only thing east from the temple is Alwhen, out in the human territories, isn't it?" Rikka asked quietly, mindful that the Master wouldn't hear.

Kytenia set her jaw. There was no reason for them to seek human carpenters when there would be Eldani craftsmen in

Wethertree to do the job. Alwhen was at least several days away, even by horseback.

The ruins and temple fell away behind them as the sun climbed into the gray sky. Thick humidity and an unpleasant drizzle turned Kytenia's hair to a frizz against her neck. The curls crawled against her skin and made her itch, but as they ventured farther eastward through the day, the rain began to subside.

For a time, Kytenia was grateful she would not have to assist with the day's cleanup efforts in the temple. But Alira did not let them stop often for rest and by the time sunset came, Kytenia wished bitterly that they hadn't chosen to sit so close to the stairs.

A STRANGE HAZE HUNG BEFORE THE MOON; REMNANTS OF SMOKE from the night before. Soldiers and magelings had spent all afternoon clearing debris, but once the setting sun painted the sky crimson, things grew still. There was little more that could be accomplished after dark. Daemon tried not to look at the murky sky as he picked another leaf off the weed he twirled between his claws.

Where was she? He checked the position of the rising moon again. They would have finished the evening meal some time ago. The soldiers would have quieted down, leaving the mages to settle in their tower. He'd ventured close enough to see the courtyard before sitting down to wait. A few had stayed up, men walking the gardens in some mockery of patrol and mages trying to find possessions left unburned among the ashes, but they were scattered enough that they shouldn't hinder her ability to sneak out.

He plucked another leaf and mulled over the wording of their agreement once more. It was the first night after Firal had returned to the temple. Perhaps she thought he hadn't made it back yet? He'd seen her come through the massive Gate not long after he slipped through, but it made sense that she wouldn't have spotted him, what with all the mages and men in armor pushing their way into the temple's courtyard. Perhaps she thought it unlikely he would have recovered enough to open a Gate on his own again so soon. But they *had* agreed on the first night after she returned to the temple.

A handful of mages had ridden off to the east the night before, but she hadn't been one of them. He'd recognized the magelings behind the white-robed Master as friends of hers, but she was still in the temple. Surely he wasn't remembering the bargain wrong.

Daemon stood, casting one final look to the stars overhead. His jaw tightened behind his mask as he flicked the leafless weed to the ground. The moon indicated it was near dawn. Clawed hands clenched to fists at his sides as he traced a path back to the edge of the ruins.

The temple sprawled before him, just across the grassy field. Where trees and shrubs had sheltered the temple before, it stood bare, naked, and everything within it was exposed. He watched, knowing his luminescent eyes might draw attention, no longer caring if they did. What could the king's men do to him?

A shadow moved across the courtyard in the wake of a soldier's patrol. Daemon straightened.

She moved like a specter in the moonlight, her red-slashed skirt swirling around her with every step. She stopped at the edge of the temple's grounds, pensive. He willed her to see him, a dark-cloaked figure in the night, revealed only by the soft light of his eyes.

Firal stared back. Then, slowly, her chin lifted and she turned back the way she'd come, leaving him and the crumbling outer rings of the ruins behind.

Anger swelled in his chest, followed by a crushing sense of defeat.

They had an agreement, and she didn't come.

2 0

NEGOTIATIONS

THE CRISP MORNING AIR WAS REFRESHING AFTER HOURS IN THE underground. Daemon would have preferred to stay in the caverns, sulking in the dark while he stewed over Firal's failure to fulfill her end of their agreement, but life went on. Regardless of whether or not she'd come to their promised meeting, he was still a leader to his people, and he meant to make the most of it. He studied the site of his first raid with a shrewd eye.

The village seemed lively, children playing in the streets while their mothers hung clean laundry in the sunshine. There were few men at work, the fields left fallow after the raid. Most who remained were injured, and the produce gardens between houses overflowed with weeds. A shame, as the weather threatened the harvests already.

Daemon tried to suppress the twinges of guilt that stirred in the pit of his stomach. Lumia cared little for the villages they raided; procuring supplies was her only concern.

He, on the other hand, couldn't help the pity he felt for the village men, strangers who had suffered at the hands of the party he'd led. That hadn't been his plan. It had never been his intention. The memory of the deaths he'd caused made his stomach lurch. He swallowed hard and willed it to settle.

Whether or not he was the general, there was nothing he could do about the casualties now.

It was strange to revisit the village after the raid. Daemon had circled Charth's border before sunrise to avoid notice. Now he made his way down the hill from the northern side, knowing he wouldn't escape notice as he entered the town. The eyes of the village folk weighed on him as he passed. He'd taken care to wear a travel cloak in a style popular in Ilmenhith, but save bowing his head, he could do nothing to hide his mask. It took effort to avoid meeting their distrustful stares. Instead, he put as much purpose into his step as he could. No matter what had transpired, he had to believe returning was the best choice.

All the buildings looked the same and he almost missed the girl who darted around the corner of the house he'd been looking for. Her mother struggled with a basket of laundry on the porch stairs. He stepped forward and put a gloved hand beneath the basket to steady it in her arms. "Careful."

"Thank you, sir. I—" The woman stopped short at sight of his mask.

Daemon's eyes narrowed, slit pupils thinning. This was it. One last chance to bring his plans to fruition. "Is your husband about? There's business I'd like to discuss with him."

"What manner of business?" she asked, voice gruff. If she felt more than uncertainty, she hid it well. A hint of suspicion lurked in her stare, but she stood her ground.

"Nothing you need be concerned about," he assured her. "Simply a proposal."

Little feet pattered around the corner of the house. He glanced down and the little girl squealed when she saw his mask. "You're back!"

"Hello, Lea." Daemon managed to sound cheerful. "Are those boys being nice to you and Cara now?"

Lea hugged her rag doll and grinned up at him. "Cara says she missed you."

"Lea," her mother prompted. "Rouse your father from his

nap, would you? Let him know we have a guest." She frowned, but slipped inside after her daughter and motioned for Daemon to follow.

He stepped in after her and closed the door. The front room was larger than he had expected and he silently envied the ability surface villages had to sprawl.

"Now, what's this about? Kena, who's here?" The farmer appeared in a doorway and froze. The man's leg was splinted and bandaged, marking his involvement in the skirmish before. His gaze lingered on Daemon's mask and his expression darkened. "He's not a leper, is he?"

Daemon snorted a laugh. "I assure you I'm not."

"He said he had business with you," the woman said.

"A beggar, then," the man concluded crossly. He leaned against the doorframe for support. "I've no business with beggars. What do you want? In case you haven't noticed, this is a poor village in a poor state."

"On the contrary," Daemon replied with cool patience as he unfastened the ties that held his cloak closed. "This area has plenty to offer, and I'm certainly no beggar. I'm interested in trade."

"Who are you, then? Hurry up and speak your case! My wife and I have plenty to do today!"

"Rolan," his wife reprimanded as she lowered the laundry basket to the floor. "If it's trade he's after, you owe it to everyone to speak with him. You know how much we need."

The farmer's scowl deepened, but he crept toward the low couches that formed a sitting area in the middle of the room.

"Don't mind him, please." The woman shot Daemon an apologetic glance and gestured for him to sit. "This is Rolan, my husband. I'm Kena. It seems you already know our daughter. I'll fetch some tea. Please, sit down, ah..."

"Daemon," he supplied. He eased back his hood and shed his cloak. The elaborate black-and-gold armor underneath was a vision he imagined haunted their dreams. "But I believe we've met before, haven't we?"

Rolan's jaw went slack, his eyes widening with memory and fear. Then his rage bubbled over. "You soul-blighted snag!" He whipped his belt knife from its sheath as he lunged forward.

Daemon's movements were so fluid that it took a moment for Rolan to realize his arm had been caught and redirected. His blade hovered just beside the gorget that shielded Daemon's throat.

"Most likely correct," Daemon replied, plucking the knife from his hand, "but that's hardly what I came to discuss. If you would please sit down, and refrain from shouting further profanities at me, I have a proposition you might be interested in hearing."

"You were the one who burned our houses! Killed our friends and family, good men I've known my entire life!" Rolan flexed his fingers helplessly, though his face contorted with fury. Daemon didn't let go of his arm. "Give me one good reason I shouldn't kill you here and now!"

"Would you really do such a thing in front of your daughter?" Daemon nodded the direction the farmer had come from. Lea clutched the doorframe, watching them with wide, frightened eyes.

Slowly, Rolan's arm went slack. Daemon released him and they sank into opposite couches, almost simultaneously. Neither said a word. Kena brought a tea tray from the other room. Shaking, she sank to her knees and put it on the floor between them. It seemed all she could do to hold the teapot steady as she filled two cups.

Daemon murmured a thank-you when she offered one to him. He took the cup from her trembling hands and stared at it for a time. Eventually, he settled the cup in his palm and awkwardly adjusted his mask. "Well. I'm not one for pleasantries, so let's get right to it, shall we?"

"Let's," Rolan agreed in a grumble.

"Very well." Daemon cleared his throat. "Simply put, our last visit ended poorly. Rather than face an unnecessary repeat of that event, I present you with these options." He paused just long enough to allow his words to sink in, idly rotating his teacup. "One, we arrive at the edge of your town in three days and are met with good will. We exchange our gold for your goods, paying more than fairly. No one gets hurt. Option two, you notify the king of our intended visit, see if you have time for his forces to arrive, and have your town host the battle between us. Obviously, if we win, we'd be raiding your village for supplies afterward." He paused again. "Third, you do nothing and wait for the same bloodbath to happen all over again."

Rolan and his wife exchanged looks and the farmer's expression dissolved into a scowl. "I've no reason to believe you'd give us anything but a knife in the back. Who's to say we don't prepare for a peaceful trade, only to be slaughtered when we're caught off guard?"

"I'm to say," Daemon replied, a gleam in his eye. "I protected this house during the last raid. For that, you owe me your trust, if not your lives."

The farmer leaned back. "I beg your pardon?"

"Come now, did you think it was luck that your house was not targeted? Please." Daemon scoffed. "I saw your child in the streets before the raid. She was kind to me. I placed this house under my protection for her sake. If you doubt me, you're welcome to ask her about the crest the Eldani king's men found on your door."

Rolan looked at Kena once more, both at a loss for words. Daemon cleared his throat again and leaned forward to leave his teacup on the floor. "In any event, you have three days to think on it. You will have no way to contact us, so don't try. My men will arrive armed, but hopefully our weapons won't be needed." He pushed himself up and settled his discarded cloak over his armor once more.

"How am I to make this decision?" Rolan asked, his voice cracking with dismay.

"Speak to the other village folk about it. Then prepare yourselves." Daemon shrugged. "Good day, and please tell Lea goodbye for me."

His cape fluttered as he turned to exit, and he stepped into the sun with a renewed vigor. In the blink of an eye, everything had changed. Whether it was for better or worse, he didn't know, but for a moment, Daemon felt a renewed glimmer of hope.

THE SUN CLIMBED INTO A STRANGELY CLOUDLESS SKY AS THE ROAD spilled into a wide, rocky plain. Kytenia squinted against the light. Gradually, the path became wider, though the mages still rode single-file. Deep ruts left by wagon wheels marred the road and led the way to settlements on the island's eastern half. The first time a horse stumbled over the furrows, Alira moved them to the side of the road.

They had ridden without cease, Alira refreshing horse and rider alike as needed. At first Kytenia thought it the simple sharing of energy between mages, but when she paid closer attention, she realized Alira was replenishing their strength with power drawn from other sources. Kytenia didn't like the idea of magic being used in such a fashion and suspected Rikka did not either, but they had no right to argue with a Master.

Farms and tiny villages stood along the road, markers posted at intersections to offer directions down each narrow lane that branched from the main road. The city of Alwhen loomed on the horizon and as they traveled near, the city's long shadow made Kytenia feel small.

Alwhen was worlds different from Ilmenhith. Save for the castle, the city was squared and low, lacking the soaring heights that Ilmenhith boasted. The castle rose above the city in a grand display, though it was blocky and squat compared to the steep spires of the palace they'd just visited for the solstice. And while Ilmenhith's palace was all sleek white stone and curves, Alwhen's castle bore dark, boxy parapets and shallow peaked roofs of deep gray slate.

It was solid; Kytenia admitted most of the construction in the Giftless lands was. Her own home village in the southern reaches of Elenhiise was not that different. The solid architecture offered protection from the savage storms that sometimes swept the island. Ilmenhith didn't need such protection, relying on the mages to protect the city. Mages were welcome among the Giftless and many Masters roamed the eastern side of the island to offer healing and aid, but Alwhen had no court mages of its own.

The city grew in clusters around the castle walls, some of the ramshackle structures built against those walls for support. Kytenia cringed to think how easily it could blow over.

No one said anything as the Master led them past buildings that could have been houses, if not for the painted shop signs that hung outside. Kytenia hadn't really believed Alira meant to hire craftsmen from Alwhen, but seeing her suspicions were correct still made her frown.

People stopped to watch them pass, some of them slack-jawed. They had to be a spectacle, Alira with her eye-marks and her Master's white to mark her as a mage of great importance, two magelings trailing along behind her in ball gowns. Though covered in dust from the journey and ash from the temple, Kytenia still thought those gowns remarkable.

The eyes that weighed on them made Kytenia self-conscious. She rearranged her hair as they rode, settling curls around her ears to hide their point. As mages, it was unlikely they would be bothered. No one disrespected a mage. But they were not wearing their robes, and not all Giftless folk looked kindly upon Eldani. She knew from experience how the Eldani behaved as if they were better or more important than Giftless humans. It didn't matter that Kytenia's face and figure showed her heritage as a half-blood; her ears were still peaked. Though no one had treated her family poorly, she suspected it was because her Eldani father lacked the Gift. That the Gift had risen again in some of his children had been regarded as a miracle.

Rikka's head turned when they passed what must have been a carpenter's shop, unfinished furniture and wood stacked around the outside of the building. When Alira didn't stop, Rikka twisted in her saddle to face Kytenia and raise a brow. Kytenia shook her head to discourage conversation.

They reached the castle walls in the early afternoon. The gates stood wide as if to welcome them, broad banners of vermillion trimmed with bronze fluttering against the walls to either side. A pair of guards stood beside the gateway and paid them little mind as they passed. The courtyard was empty, save the four guards beside the heavy wood doors of the castle. The men watched them without interest.

Alira drew to a halt halfway through the courtyard and dismounted. She smoothed her white robes before starting toward the castle's main doors. The girls followed.

"This doesn't look like a carpenter's shop," Rikka whispered.

Kytenia hushed her as the guards at the door crossed spears.

"State your business," one of the men said, his voice flat.

"I am Alira, Master of the House of Fire, hailing from Kirban Temple. These are my escorts." She gestured to Rikka and Kytenia. "I am here to speak to King Relythes. A message was sent by carrier pigeon with word of my coming."

The crossed spears lifted. "Proceed." The guards motioned them forward and opened the doors. One tilted his spear to offer direction. "King Relythes will receive you in the throne room, straight ahead from where you stand."

Kytenia and Rikka offered slight curtsies as they passed the men, though Alira brushed past them with her chin held high.

The inside of the castle was no cheerier than the outside, the dark interior lit with torches that made the great hall stiflingly hot. Greasy smoke clouded the open rafters overhead and stained the wooden beams with soot. They passed through several archways before the room widened, though its size barely accommodated the people crammed inside. A long table stretched nearly from the foot of the throne's dais to the archway in which the mages stood. Benches at the table's sides were packed with men and women in finery, all of them eating and drinking and laughing uproariously.

On the throne was a man who seemed too short to be kingly, balding beneath his crown. While not fat, he was certainly not as fit as he could have been. His remaining hair was cut short, most of it graying—a sharp contrast to his thick beard, which was dark and peppered with only a few white hairs. His eyes lit with delight when he saw them and he opened his arms wide. "Come, come!" he shouted, waving them forward. "There's always room for more fine women at my table!"

"King Relythes of Eastern Elenhiise," Alira called back over the noise of those who cavorted over the endless feast. "I expected more formality in our reception."

"That's the problem with you mages," Relythes laughed. "Everything's always prim and proper. No room for any fun. Come! Sit, drink! Tell me why your Archmage has sent you." He rose from his throne and gestured toward the table. A wave of his hands sent people scattering, making room for the three mages at the end nearest the throne. He descended from the dais at an easy pace and drew back the tall chair at the head of the table, easing himself down into it as Alira took a seat beside him.

Kytenia had no desire to sit near the king, but she had no choice. She settled across the table from Alira and bunched her skirts against her legs to make room for Rikka to sit.

"I was under the impression the Archmage sent word ahead to establish our meeting." Alira shook her head when someone beside her offered a goblet and decanter.

"She mentioned something, aye, but I wasn't sure if that was still the case," Relythes said. A servant deposited a full goblet into the king's hand and he swirled the wine in it absently. "Just being cautious, mind you. It's not every day a proposition like this comes along."

Alira said nothing and Relythes sank back in his chair to study her. Despite his apparent playful demeanor, his eyes were shrewd. He sipped his wine without seeming to taste it. "It seems convenient, doesn't it? The timing of it all. Between the Eldani king's solstice, the attack on the temple and your Archmage seeking my...what would you say, patronage?"

Kytenia's eyes widened, but she kept the rest of her face blank. The Giftless rulers had always treated the mages fairly in exchange for the services they could provide, but Relythes and his people had about as much involvement with the temple as a rooster had with nesting. Part of it had been stubborn pride, but Kytenia suspected just as much was an unwillingness to associate with mages sponsored by a rival king.

"In my opinion, sir, your people have a great deal to gain." Alira's expression never changed, though Relythes raised a brow at the informal way she addressed him. She was not speaking to her ruler, but his rank still demanded respect.

"Has the temple really grown so autonomous it has the power to withdraw from the man who paid to found it?" he asked, resting his goblet on the table.

Alira smiled grimly. "Until Kifel's failure to protect it, the temple was able to provide for itself. Our mages are stationed across the whole island. Cities pay for their services with goods that can be sold easily, if not used. We are not asking for endless support. We seek only what is needed to rebuild. The benefit of our service is an invaluable resource for any patron."

Relythes stroked his beard with one calloused hand. "The temple is on Eldani lands."

"Only until you push your borders forward. Or do you forget the southern lands were only held by the Eldani as a result of the temple's location?" Alira's question brought a heavy silence. Even those seated nearby stilled their revelry.

Kytenia clutched her skirts in both hands and stared down at the table so she wouldn't have to look at Alira. How could she speak of such things? Alira was Master of a House of affinity and deserved respect, but the casual way she spoke of betraying King Kifel made bile rise in the back of Kytenia's throat. She squirmed as she gulped against it.

The movement didn't go unnoticed. Relythes nodded in her direction. "You're not the first mage I've dealt with who has brought an envoy, but they don't speak. Why is that? Are they students? They aren't in uniform. Tell me, girl," he said, his gaze sharpening as it shifted to Rikka, "what purpose does your presence here serve?"

Rikka gave Alira a fleeting glance. The Master's face never changed. "Mages do not travel alone, Majesty," Rikka said. "We accomplish more in groups."

Relythes turned his eyes to Kytenia. Her stomach knotted and she was sure she looked like a startled mouse. She couldn't find her voice, so she nodded in agreement instead.

Seemingly satisfied, the king returned his attention to Alira. "I expect a benefit immediately." He lifted his goblet to swirl its contents once more. "Full chapter houses of mages stationed in every major city, instead of the skeleton crews present now. An embassy here in Alwhen and a meeting with the Archmage to discuss the possibility of relocating, rather than rebuilding. I will send an ambassador to the temple to meet with her. I shall, of course, give you time to discuss the merits of relocation amongst yourselves before expecting my ambassador's return."

"A most gracious consideration, my lord," Alira murmured.

He ignored her shift in tone. "I trust you wish to return with my response as soon as possible?"

Alira shrugged and smoothed the front of her robes. "A rest overnight would be well met, as well as new mounts to relieve our own."

"So shall it be," Relythes agreed. He raised both hands overhead and clapped twice to summon servants. They came with trays of food and flasks of wine, replenishing what stocked the table already, laying heaping platters before the king and his guests. Alira appeared to relax, accepting a goblet and drinking from it as a servant filled her plate.

Kytenia gave Rikka a tiny, knowing frown. Beneath the table, her friend patted her hand. They had to let Kifel know what they'd heard, but just how was a mageling supposed to carry warning to a king?

<hr />

TIMBERS AND ASH FILLED THE STOREROOMS, ALL THAT REMAINED OF the collapsed roof. Firal shared Master Nondar's disappointment at how much had been lost.

Most of the temple's medical supplies were destroyed. A great deal of healing could be done with magic alone but, like all magelings with a healing affinity, she knew the virtues of using herbal remedies. Too much dependence on magical healing could weaken the body. Too many weak bodies could weaken an entire country. It made sense to reserve use of magic for the most severe illnesses and injuries. It didn't harm anyone to have a case of sniffles or sneezes from time to time, and it was best to let the body work on its own to fight what it could. Symptoms could be eased with tinctures or teas.

Firal brushed grit from another bottle and her brow furrowed as she tried to make out its label. Most of Nondar's students had been set to work in the storerooms after the wreckage of the roofing was removed, but Nondar had assigned her to the ruins of the infirmary. She'd spent most of the morning alone, rooting through the mess of broken shelving and shattered glass to find what could be salvaged. As disheartening as it was to see the damage, she found some comfort in working with the familiar supplies. She'd never devoted much thought to what might come after her studies, but sitting among Nondar's supplies— even in the wreckage—she found herself more at home than she ever recalled. With the rest of her hopes shattered, knowing she still had a place among the medicine bottles gave her peace. No matter what came in the days ahead, at least she had that.

"The temple's not as big as I expected, but I didn't see you at all yesterday."

Firal jumped. The bottle in her hand slipped and she clamped both hands around it, unwilling to let anything else be wasted. She twisted where she sat and breathed a sigh of relief when she saw Vahn behind her. The temple was full of strange men and she was alone. Had it been anyone else, she wouldn't have been comfortable, but she considered Vahn a friendly face. "Ran's not here."

"I wasn't looking for him." Vahn ducked under the half-fallen shelf that obscured the doorway. "I apologize, I didn't mean to startle you."

"Perhaps you shouldn't sneak up on me, then." Firal added the bottle to the collection in a box beside her and checked the floor. Everything she'd found had been packed, so she stood and dusted her knees. The Masters had recovered several crates of clothing from the half-ruined storerooms. She'd been fortunate to find a green mageling's robe that was only a little big on her frame. On the other hand, she hadn't been fortunate enough to find sandals to replace what she'd left in the palace. Her silk slippers from the palace were made for dancing, not work, and the thin soles offered little protection. She turned in place, mindful of the broken glass scattered on the floor.

Vahn glanced about as he stepped into the storeroom. "Do you need any help in here? We've been sent to help the magelings clean. Most of the large rubble has been cleared out, so there aren't many tasks left that require brute strength." He reached for a handful of vials still standing on a shelf and his brow furrowed as he read the labels.

Firal snorted a laugh. His lithe frame made it seem unlikely he'd been chosen for anything requiring brute strength. "I appreciate the offer, but I can manage this on my own." She took a wide step to a clear space on the floor and plucked the vials out of his hands to inspect their seals. "Convenient that you'd end up wherever I am. Or were you hoping to find Kytenia in here?"

A hint of color rose in his cheeks. "I'm just trying to help," Vahn protested. "And trying to find something to do. You have no idea how boring it is here." He cringed as soon as the words were out of his mouth. "Sorry, I didn't mean it like that. I just want to help. I thought it would be better for me to work with someone I'd met before."

She tip-toed back to her box and knelt beside it to put the vials away. "I've met you, yes, but I can't say how proper it is for you to be sitting alone in a room with a girl you don't really know."

"Should I invite you to get to know me, then?"

Firal gave him a solemn look. "You're awfully forward, aren't you?"

"All right, then, let me start over, since I've clearly gotten off on the wrong foot with you." Vahn brushed dirt from his palms and swept into a bow. "I greatly appreciated your company during the ball, my lady. I would be grateful for the chance to become better acquainted with you, as you are a friend of a dear friend and we spent so little time together during the festivities."

Firal rose just enough to offer a curtsy. "If it would please my lord, you are still too forward in your advances."

The look of frustration that crossed his face almost made her smile.

"However," she continued, "I am not opposed to the idea of your company during the noon meal. That is, if you are hungry, and don't mind the presence of my friends?"

Vahn grinned. "Lunch, my lady, sounds like an excellent idea. I would welcome the opportunity to get to know some of the other mages here. Maybe then they wouldn't look at me like a weasel in a henhouse."

Choking back a laugh, she gestured toward the charred doorframe. "Lead the way, then. Has the dining hall been cleaned? I don't even know where meals are being served." She lifted her skirt just above her ankles and hopped over the grime and glass on tip-toe. Vahn offered his arm. She waved him away, stepping out into the courtyard with a swish of her soot-stained robes.

He studied the courtyard as they walked. "You know, from what I'd heard about the temple, I'd expected it would be more like its own city."

"It'd be nice if it was," Firal sighed. "There's a market a few miles away, sort of a trading outpost between Wethertree and the farms out this direction. But there's not much as far as real civilization goes."

"Why put the temple in the middle of nowhere?" He motioned for her to enter the dining hall first and she slipped in with a nod of thanks. The doors and roof were gone, but most of the tables had been salvaged with little more than the occasional scorch mark.

Firal scanned the room for her friends, but didn't see them in the crowd. She sank into a seat and Vahn settled across the table from her. "It's a matter of privacy, mostly," she said. "Learning magecraft requires a lot of focus and concentration, so they removed as many distractions as possible."

"But right on the edge of those ruins?" Vahn shuddered and leaned back so a woman could place a tray of food before him. "I wouldn't want to be that close to them. They give me chills."

"I like them, personally. I think the ruins are lovely." Firal murmured a thank-you to the maid.

"The royal gardens are lovely. I'm not sure I'd put the ruins in the same category." Vahn waited to pick up his fork until she spread her napkin on her lap.

She raised a brow. "How gentlemanly of you. Are you certain you're friends with Ran?"

Vahn laughed. "That's unfair. Ran's stubborn, not uncouth." He shoveled a forkful of food into his mouth. "And yes, I'm certain. I've known him since we were children."

"So you grew up at the palace together?" She picked at the

fish on her plate. When resources were scarce, the island relied more heavily on the sea. With the temple burned, she expected they would eat little else for some time.

"Yes. My family was relocated to the palace grounds when my father became Captain of the Ilmenhith Royal Guard. I met Ran in the gardens and we became friends right away. I didn't know then that he was the king's son." He smiled nervously and Firal was relieved to see her own uncertainty mirrored in his expression. Crowned or not, Ran was still a part of the royal family. The idea still seemed absurd.

Vahn speared more food with his fork. "King Kifelethelas is kind, though. He didn't mind his son playing with the child of someone so much lower in rank."

Firal made a sour face. "His Majesty's views of who belongs in the palace do seem to be rather liberal."

"You speak with a note of contempt." He sounded surprised, but his face expressed curiosity. "There are not many who think ill of the king for reasons other than rumors surrounding his heritage."

"He cannot help who his parents were," she replied dryly. "I'm just not certain I appreciate the way he views my relationship with Ran."

Vahn leaned back in his chair. "Relationship?"

That had been the wrong word. Firal winced and allowed herself a few bites of food before she spoke again. "I consider him a friend. Nothing else. I think the king may...assume there's something more." She couldn't fathom why else he would have bought her a dress and provided jewels for her to wear. Men did not give priceless gems to their son's friends.

Vahn did not reply immediately and when she looked up, he frowned with thought.

"Is it really that concerning?" she teased.

"No," he replied with a small chuckle. "Just gauging my chances, that's all."

She blinked. "I beg your pardon?"

Vahn flashed her a grin and pushed himself up, offering a wink that set her cheeks on fire before he took his leave.

Biting her lower lip, Firal stared down at the table and the empty plate he left behind.

Green robes swirled to a stop at the edge of Firal's vision. "What was that all about?" Shymin asked.

Firal fought back a groan. Of course someone had seen. Why would she have a single moment to herself? "You're just a moment too late." She buried her face in her hands and breathed deeply as she willed the color to fade from her cheeks.

"Oh, not too late. I heard a bit of that." Shymin grinned as she seated herself and leaned across the table to take a roll from Firal's plate. "He is a bit of a flirt, isn't he? Sounds like we might want to introduce that one to Rikka."

Firal laughed, but regained her senses enough to give her head a shake. "Lifetree's mercy, we'd be attending a wedding before the week was out. No matter. His charms won't work on me. He was just as interested in Kytenia when the two of them danced at the ball."

"And what did Kytenia think of him?" Shymin raised a brow.

"Who could say? Either way, it's probably best if her attentions are turned away from Ran. Fraternization with a Master could get her in trouble." Firal's voice softened as she spoke and she gave her friend a meaningful look.

Shymin nodded solemnly and turned her attention to the meal a maid left before her.

Knowledge of Ran's family burned on the tip of Firal's tongue, but she swallowed it back. If nothing else, at least she could speak of him wearing the white.

21

JEALOUSY

"So what exactly is the king's interest in things between you and Firal?"

Ran glanced up from the half-burned papers and books on the desk in front of him. Vahn leaned against the doorframe with his arms folded over his chest, his posture a shade too casual to be natural. Ran managed to keep from frowning at the question. He stuffed a few legible papers into a book worth keeping. "I couldn't tell you. Sending you off to fish for information, is she?"

"No, she's not." Vahn's gaze drifted the room. Most of the rubble had been removed, but old notes still covered the floor. The scattered papers were all that remained to show the room had been a Master's office.

"Why the interest, then?" Ran draped an arm over the back of the chair, stretching his legs and righting his robes. Though he preferred his custom-fitted robe, he'd changed to something from the temple storerooms for cleaning. Stained with soot and ash until it was more gray than white, the too-small robe looked ridiculous on him. He could have had something longer, but knee-length seemed more practical, even if the sleeves were short. Floor-length robes would have been a hindrance.

"I just wanted to know," Vahn said. "Curiosity. Trying to determine what's worth investing myself in."

Ran gave him an incredulous look. "You've got to be kidding."

Vahn sighed. His arms shifted tighter across his chest as he glanced over his shoulder. The courtyard behind him was empty. "Look, I'm trying to give you a chance to speak up. I don't want to turn my attention in a direction it might not be appreciated. You've known her longer than I have, and I don't know what your father's intentions are. If he's trying to groom her on your behalf, just say so."

Ran snorted as he pushed himself up and shoved his chair into place against the desk. "If I knew anything about his interests and intentions, do you think I'd be sitting here, sorting through garbage and waiting for a public coronation?"

"I'm being as straightforward as I can," Vahn said.

"And I think you're being hasty! Just because something has a skirt doesn't mean you should chase it." Ran scowled, raking fingers through his hair and tugging at his too-short sleeves. "Besides, you've only just met her! What, you think she'll be swooning for you after one dance together in Ilmenhith?"

Vahn held up his hands. "That's not what I mean! I didn't say she would." His shoulders stiffened, but he sounded calm. "There are a lot of interesting young women in the temple and I have my eye on a few I'd like to see again, but you were here first. You could have any girl you wanted falling at your feet. If she's the one you want, just say so."

Ran's closed the distance between them with slow strides. His eyes narrowed. "Firal isn't going to throw herself at anyone's feet, and if you were wise, you'd choose your words about her carefully."

Vahn stared back, lifting his chin. There was a gleam in his eyes; not quite a challenge, but a look of determination Ran had seen too many times before. "There are several girls here who are interested in you, but if you aren't going to make a move, there's no reason I shouldn't."

"Interested in me?" Ran almost choked, his face twisting with disbelief. "Blight it all! You should know better than anyone else—"

"Are you pursuing her or not?" Vahn interrupted, stepping closer. "You're not going to cow me over something when you won't even give me a straight answer about it!"

"It's not like that!" Ran snapped.

"It's fairly obvious it *is* something like that, and neither one of you seems to be aware you are yelling." Nondar's voice from the doorway made both of them start. Ran recoiled, set his jaw and turned back to the books on the desk.

"I apologize, Master." Vahn bowed, though he gave Ran a dark look out of the corner of his eye. "I wasn't aware there was anyone in this part of the temple to overhear us."

The old mage shook his head and leaned on his cane. "For as loud as the two of you were getting, it was more than just overhearing. I never would have imagined I'd find the two of you bickering like schoolboys over some girl."

"She's not just some girl," Ran said sourly.

Nondar raised one thick eyebrow.

"It was nothing, Master," Vahn muttered.

"I don't care what it was, it's over now. As for you," Nondar turned and leveled a knobby finger at Vahn's face, "you should not be meddling where mages are trying to work. Rejoin the rest of the soldiers and make yourself useful."

"But—" Vahn began. The old Master's gaze hardened. Vahn shut his mouth and bowed again. "As you wish." He gave Ran one more glance before he left.

Nondar sighed and shook his head. "And you," he said as he moved toward the desk, "you and I need to speak."

"I have nothing to say, Master Nondar." Ran replied, avoiding the Master's eyes. Though he was a court mage now, he was not in a position of power within the temple. As a Master of an affinity, Nondar was still his superior. The old man made him uncomfortable.

"I do not need you to say anything. I need you to listen, my lord."

Ran lifted his head as Nondar eased himself into the chair beside the desk. The old man's face didn't change, just as grim and condescending as ever, but the reverent tone he'd used was one Ran hadn't heard from him before. He knew Nondar didn't like him, though he wasn't sure why. Respect was the last thing he expected from the old mage.

Nondar rested one gnarled hand atop his cane and scratched his eyebrow with the other. "You must take a message to your father. I'm sure you've heard mention of Alira being sent to Alwhen."

"To Alwhen?" Ran repeated, startled. "What business do mages have in the eastern capital?"

Nondar lifted a finger to his lips. "Mind your voice. It isn't safe to ward our words with magic now. If you'll keep it down, I'll explain everything."

Ran drew back from the desk and crossed his arms, waiting for the Master to go on. He hadn't known what had compelled him to return to the temple, but as Nondar related what he knew, Ran found himself grateful he'd come.

EVENING BREEZES SWEPT CHARRED LEAVES FROM BRANCHES, FILLING the air with ash. Vahn coughed into his sleeve with a grimace. There was likely somewhere better to sit than beneath the burned trees, but the garden was the only place where he didn't feel like he was underfoot.

There were more soldiers than the mages knew what to do with. Most were working, but he saw some of his comrades standing beside doorways or crouching beside buildings, looking uncomfortable and awkward. Just trying to stay out of the way, he figured, like him. He didn't like feeling useless. It gave him too much time to think, and thinking was the last thing he wanted to do.

Vahn scrubbed a hand through his blond hair and waved as a friend walked by. "Hey, Jolim, are you busy?"

Jolim paused mid-stride. "Working, like you should be."

Pushing himself from the garden bench, Vahn stretched and motioned him closer. "Can you take a break? Sitting still is driving me crazy. How about a quick sparring match?"

"I don't know," Jolim murmured, glancing over his shoulder.

"Just a quick one, I promise. We're not supposed to leave temple grounds or I'd take a walk." Vahn scanned the trees and the ground beneath them and held up a finger in gesture for Jolim to wait.

Jolim rolled his eyes, but stayed put while Vahn scouted a pair of sticks out of the ash. Their swords would have been preferable, but the Masters had ordered the soldiers to stow their equipment in the temple's central tower.

"Catch." Vahn tossed his friend a stick and snapped a twig off his own.

Jolim snatched the branch out of the air and heaved a sigh. "All right, as long as it's fast." He twirled his stick in hand and settled into a defensive stance.

Vahn darted in with a jab.

Without moving a step, Jolim swatted his stick aside and struck him in the ribs. "Dead."

"Ow!" Scowling, Vahn rubbed his side. He shifted on his feet and adjusted his grip on his stick before moving in again.

Jolim sidestepped and plunged the end of his stick toward the side of Vahn's head. "Dead again." He slapped his companion's cheek with his stick and moved back, relaxing his stance. "Come on, Vahn, I thought we were sparring. If you're not going to fight seriously, I'm going to go back to work."

"I am fighting seriously," Vahn protested.

Jolim shot him a reproachful look. "You're too distracted. Why are we really sparring?"

Shrugging, Vahn lowered his makeshift weapon to his side. "I just wanted to clear my head, that's all."

"Too many mage girls in it?" Jolim grinned.

Vahn glared at him, his ears burning. "It's not like that."

"Well then what's it like?" Jolim pitched his stick into the charred hedges and watched ashen leaves float into the air. "Must be pretty bad if it's got you flustered."

"I'm not flustered," Vahn muttered. His hand drifted to the back of his neck. "Just distracted, like you said. I...I made a friend angry. Didn't mean to, I was just curious about something and he didn't like it being brought up."

Jolim dusted his hands against his pants and crossed his arms. "So it is about a girl."

Vahn threw his hands into the air with a growl of exasperation. "Why do you keep saying that?"

"Because there's not much that gets you flustered. One thing that does is matters involving girls. So?"

Eyeing his friend gloomily, Vahn relented and released a sigh. "Okay, fine. I was asking him about a girl."

"And?"

Vahn threw his stick aside. "And he didn't like me asking about her."

"Well," Jolim said with a shrug, "maybe you can't relate, but if there were a girl you fancied, would you like other people asking about her?"

A vision of snapping hazel eyes and neat brown curls came to mind. Vahn grimaced and shook it away.

Jolim ticked a finger at him. "And there's your answer."

"I don't think that's the same," Vahn said. "It's not like she knows I like her."

"Why not?"

"It was one night. And she's not even here, she's off on

temple business with a Master mage." Vahn scuffed the toe of his boot against the cobblestones.

"Well, that's your problem. Can't help you. It sounds like you just need some time to think." Jolim glanced over his shoulder. "But I'd better get back to work. Good luck, either way."

Vahn hooked his thumbs in his pockets and watched as his friend vanished into the central tower. Time to think was the last thing he wanted, but he suspected Jolim was right. He scratched his neck and wandered across the courtyard at a languid pace.

He wanted to be annoyed at Ran, he realized, but that wasn't fair. Trying to get Ran to admit his interest in Firal had little bearing on anything in the end. Vahn liked Firal well enough, but it was obvious Ran thought something of her, or he wouldn't have let Firal into the palace in the first place. Vahn was used to being a womanizer; Ran had always been subdued around women, even going so far as avoiding them altogether. He understood why. Ran's situation was complicated enough without adding women into the mix.

And yet Vahn couldn't help wishing his friend would act. He wasn't certain he understood the dynamic between Firal and Ran, his efforts to ferret out information rather fruitless, but it was clear his attempt to nudge his friend into action had not been appreciated. Vahn figured Firal would make a fine friend, but whatever ties she had to Ran were complicated. His thoughts were complicated enough without letting Ran's problems into his head.

Again Vahn thought of Kytenia's bright eyes and perfect curls, and his ears grew hot once more. That was something new. He was used to making girls blush, but he couldn't recall a girl making him feel flustered before. Maybe that was part of his problem. Vahn considered that as he ran his conversation with Jolim back through his head. There had to be an easier way to get his thoughts straight.

Stopping in the doorway of a ruined office, he found himself staring at an overturned shelf of supplies. An idea stole into his mind and he crept forward, taking refuge in the abandoned office and digging through the mess until he found paper, a bottle of ink, and a pen.

———

AFTER THE DOZENTH TIME SHE TRIPPED OVER HER OWN FEET IN THE dark, Firal regretted her decision to venture into the ruins. It had been hard enough to get out of the upper floors of the tower once the magelings were herded in for the night. It had been impossible to sneak past the soldiers in the lower floors.

She should have gone sooner. It had crossed her mind when she'd ventured into the courtyard, the first night after she'd returned from Ilmenhith. She'd seen him waiting. But the scent of smoke had still clung to the temple as if the fires still burned, and her feelings had been too raw. Passing on that opportunity had been a mistake, but after several days of attempting to escape, she'd finally made up an excuse about wanting to check her room for belongings. After some deliberation, the guards had let her go.

Part of her wished she had gone to the burned-out dormitory instead of the outermost rings of the ruins. She was sure the other girls would be looking for her, and she felt guilty for leaving them. Shymin and Marreli had made a point of seeking her out so they could sleep in a group, their presence a small comfort in the crowd. But Firal had put this meeting off longer than she should have, and every day she waited only made it harder to act.

With the guards roving the temple courtyard, she had not dared take a lantern or create a mage-light. Her hands roved the stone walls in hopes of finding her way. With no light, it was difficult going.

"You're late." Daemon's gruff greeting took her by surprise. She spun to face him. He crouched atop the wall of the narrow corridor, his form silhouetted by the moon.

Despite her best efforts to remain calm, anger seeped into her voice. "The temple is teeming with soldiers after what happened. But you know all about that, don't you?"

The soft violet of his eyes flickered in the dark. "You know I was nowhere near the temple when it was razed."

"You could have been anywhere. And your men, General?" She clutched the skirt of her robe. "The temple is my entire life. Everything I know, everyone I love! If any mages had been there—"

"If any mages had been there, the mage-barrier wouldn't have fallen," Daemon said. "The temple was almost empty and none of you were harmed. Do you honestly think I would burden myself the way I did, taking you all the way to Ilmenhith, just to shatter your trust like that?"

"I think I was foolish to trust an Underling in the first place." She glowered up at him. Being called a burden after the hours she'd spent training him during their travels made her seethe.

"We had a deal, mageling." Daemon dropped into the corridor. His luminescent eyes narrowed behind his mask. "One you've apparently forgotten about. You've been back, what, a week already? And you're only just now crawling into the ruins to—"

"The temple is destroyed!" Firal cried. Angry tears brimmed against her eyelashes and she blinked hard to clear them. "My home, my belongings, everything is gone. The past week has been nothing but efforts to clean up while the king's soldiers are here to help, and you want to lecture me on being late to teach you to wield a power that would let you destroy even more?"

"I told you I had nothing to do with that. I wasn't even here! You think I would have let this happen?" He thrust a clawed finger toward the sky, where the light from the Archmage's tower threw a dim, ruddy glow against the hazy clouds.

"The mask you sent me was flames." Her throat tightened and she blinked away tears again. "You were taunting me before it happened, and I was too blind to see it."

317

"Coincidence." His dismissive tone only fueled the anger burning in her chest.

"You've boasted about your rank and power among your people. You think I'd believe for a moment you didn't know they planned to attack the temple?" She fought back a bitter laugh. "And why? What does it gain you to ruin us? What benefit is it for you to anger an entire college of mages?"

"It was about a vendetta," Daemon said. "Not the temple."

"So you admit it!" A deep ache swelled behind her ribs. "You did know, and you knew why. What if it wasn't just the Archmage? What if there had been more people there? Other Masters? Other mages? What if I'd been there? What if—"

"The only person she wanted to be there was you! You really want to know why it happened? Why Lumia did it? It's because of you!" The venom evaporated from his voice, leaving only bitterness. "And because of me."

Firal drew back a step. The burning thoughts of her involvement—her guilt—returned. "She wanted...me?"

"Because I asked you to be here. Because I moved without her consent, getting you to teach me something she can't. You think she wants me to be stronger than she is?" Daemon scoffed. "The moment I make the Underlings independent, that's the moment she loses control. You think I was happy about what she did to the temple? You think I had something to do with it? I'm as angry as you are."

Then it was her doing in more ways than one. She swallowed as his words stole the heat out of her anger. Her mistake and her selfish folly had drawn the Underling queen's ire. All the more reason to cut ties. "It doesn't matter if you're angry or not. This happened because of what we've done, and it won't happen again." She steeled herself and turned on her heel.

"Where are you going?"

"I have better things to do," she snapped.

"Like frolic with that blond-headed distraction of yours?"

Firal stopped mid-stride and spun back with her mouth agape. "What?"

His eyes narrowed. "Oh, nothing. Never mind. The temple keeps you so busy, of course you can't make good on your promises. Far too busy to flirt over lunch or sit in the gardens talking to some prick-eared whelp."

Her amber eyes widened. "You...are you *jealous*?"

His breath caught and for a moment, she swore she saw him stiffen.

"Well, you're right about one thing," Firal said coolly. "I'd much rather spend my time with a prick-eared whelp than be out here with a monster like you." She tossed her head and stormed down the ruined corridor.

"We had a deal!" Daemon snarled after her.

"The deal was that I would teach you more once I got home," she called over her shoulder. "Now I practically have no home to return to."

"Firal!"

She stomped a foot. "Our deal is off!"

"If you set one foot outside these halls, you will not be welcome here again."

"You make it sound like I'd come back!" She laughed humorlessly as she rounded the corner and slipped out of sight.

The moment she escaped his illuminated gaze, it felt like a weight had been lifted.

22

TO REBUILD

FIRAL ROUNDED THE DOORWAY INTO A BURNED-OUT OFFICE AND planted her hands on her hips. "There you are!"

Shymin squealed and thumped a hand to her chest as if to catch her heart.

Giggling, Marreli hid her smirk behind the sheaf of papers in her hand. She waved Firal into the room. "I was starting to wonder when we'd see you."

Firal inspected their progress as she crept in. They had already cleaned a great deal, but as with the rest of the temple, it would be some time before the space was usable again. "I was starting to wonder the same. There were only three offices left to check. I should have guessed you'd be here."

Nondar's office was one of the most interesting, packed full of notes, scrolls, trinkets, and all manner of other things. It was also one of the offices farthest from the Archmage's tower, meaning it still contained some usable goods. Most magelings had started their own small caches of interesting and useful objects, from partially-filled bottles of ink to odd insects trapped in pieces of amber.

"We didn't pick it," Shymin said. "We were assigned. I'd

rather not sort through all of this and find my grades from our last test."

Again, Marreli giggled. "You might find Firal's. That would be worth looking at. That was the day she got in trouble for daydreaming, wasn't it?"

Firal stifled a groan. Marreli's earth affinity meant she rarely set foot in Master Nondar's classrooms. Firal had long thought those blunders were outside the younger girl's knowledge. "How did you hear about that?"

"Kytenia told us all about it," Marreli said.

Shymin coughed as if clearing her throat and turned her attention to the crates of supplies they'd already sealed. "Either way, there are plenty of things I'd rather be doing than cleaning out offices. But the Masters want us to have them all emptied by the end of the day."

"Of course they do," Firal grumbled. A stray paper caught her eye and she picked it up to peruse the childish doodles on its margins. "Brant forbid we get our bedrooms back soon."

Marreli put aside her papers and hopped over to assist Shymin with a crate. "But once they're done with the offices, they want to repair the classrooms. We'll be back to our studies in no time."

Firal laughed. "I do suppose we'll be free of housekeeping duty once classes start again. I imagine they'll have the king's men finishing the job."

"Speaking of soldiers," Shymin said, grunting as she pushed the crate beyond the door, "where did you get off to last night? We couldn't find you."

"What does that have to do with soldiers?" Firal looked between the two of them and a flush crept into her cheeks. "I just needed some fresh air. I went outside to clear my head. I don't think I can stand being stuck in that tower with so many people for much longer."

Marreli dusted her hands together and pulled a glass paperweight from a pile of ash. A crack marred its surface, catching the light and throwing dancing rainbows against the wall and floor. She dusted off the glass. "I understand. I'd like some time alone, too."

"We all would." Shymin gave Firal a meaningful glance. "Though the only place left where you'd have an ounce of privacy is the ruins."

Firal met her stare impassively. "I just went for a walk, that's all."

"In the ruins?" Marreli asked.

"Even after you said you thought Underlings did this?" Shymin gestured around the classroom. "What did you think you were going to earn by doing that? Answers? Apologies?"

"It's not like that," Firal protested. Yet, some part of her had hoped for those things. Instead, he'd been unrepentant and stubborn and had driven home how wrong she'd been. She wet her lips before going on. "There's too much to explain. I had to go out there, just one last time. I said I would meet him. We had a deal. I said I would help him, but after this...I changed my mind."

Shymin crossed her arms. "Help him with what?"

How could she answer? The acrid smell of ash burned in her nose, reminding Firal of what she had done. "Daemon is...he's Gifted."

Marreli's paperweight clunked to the floor.

"Gifted!" Shymin cried. "First, you expect us to believe in Underlings, and now this?"

"That was him, wasn't it?" Marreli tugged her braids, her eyes alight. "The man in black, who danced with you at the ball?"

Both Shymin and Firal gaped.

"Yes," Firal managed after a moment. "It was."

Shymin's features crumpled into a scowl. "Don't tell me you've been teaching him!"

"It was part of our agreement." Firal wrung the skirt of her robe between her hands. "How we got to Ilmenhith in the first place. He made me promise to show him how to control it in exchange for taking me to Ilmenhith."

Indignation burned on Shymin's face. "You're not authorized to teach."

"Aren't you listening? He's a wild mage!" Desperation crept into Firal's voice and made her chest grow tight. "You know what happens if a mage doesn't learn to control their Gift. Would you let him destroy himself? Regardless of what you think of him, or his people, or what happened here, letting him tear himself apart with his own Gift is against everything the temple stands for."

Shymin clamped her mouth shut and fumed.

"And even if it wasn't, would you really want a wild mage against us?" Firal glanced to Marreli. "Knowing no limits, not caring to preserve himself, if only because he doesn't know any better? Wild magic is more dangerous, more destructive than anything else we could face."

Both her companions shivered. Firal nodded, half to herself, half to agree with their discomfort. Wild magic was stronger than anything taught or controlled, but it was power at risk of the user's life. Natural elements, like windstorms or raging fires, could draw out a wild mage's power. With no idea how to monitor themselves, they had no way to restrain it. Some first-year magelings experienced it. Not all survived. Firal had never seen it, but the idea of a mage being seized by the very power they sought to manipulate was frightening enough.

"So I taught him basics," Firal said, softer. "The most simple things I could. Just enough to be sure he was in control of his power and not the other way around. But it doesn't matter. The deal is off." Her shoulders sank as she spoke and she rubbed her forehead as if to smooth away her worry.

"Firal, if you taught him how to wield magic, and the temple was attacked by men from the ruins..." Shymin trailed off.

"I know." For an instant, Firal felt the sting of tears. She breathed deep and it dissipated. "I made a mistake. I know. And

I've already been punished for it. The only reason I agreed to do it was because it gave me the chance to ask the court mages about my mother. And then because I did it, the only way for me to find out who she was was destroyed."

"You don't know that for sure," Shymin said.

"Yes I do." Firal clenched her fists in her robes and sank to the floor. Ashes stirred and swirled around her like snowfall. "I found them, Shymin. In the library this morning. The records from Ilmenhith. They're gone. Every single one, burned, ruined." Unable to fight anymore, she closed her eyes. Tears coursed down her cheeks, leaving pale trails through smudges of soot.

Marreli crept closer and wrapped her arms around Firal's shoulders. Firal turned her head to bury her face against the smaller girl's chest as the first sob wracked her. Shymin joined them, and together they sat among the ruins of everything Firal had ever known.

She had done it to herself, robbed herself of all she'd ever wanted. Yet some things could not be taken, and comfort came in the warmth of her friends' embrace.

Firal cried until her ribs ached, until her tears ran dry. Then, finally, she wiped her face and sat back. Heavy bands of grief still wrapped her chest and constricted her breath, but the new emptiness came with a subtle sense of peace.

"It's not your fault, you know," Shymin murmured. "You're not responsible for what other people do with power."

"We won't tell the Masters," Marreli whispered, smoothing Firal's hair.

Shymin nodded and wiped her own cheeks. "We'll help you how we can."

"Thank you," Firal choked out.

"What can we do?" Shymin asked. "What will *you* do? If you don't have the ruins, and you can't find your mother..."

Firal sniffled and wiped her face again. The tears left dirty smudges on her cheeks. "All I've ever done is study. It's all I'm good at. I wasn't certain at first, but with everything I've learned, I think...I think I'm going to teach."

"Here?" Shymin asked, surprised.

Firal nodded. "I've spent my whole life thinking of what would happen when I found my parents, of trying to be something that would make them proud. I never stopped to think about what was important to me. But I care about this. I care about learning, about helping people learn."

"The temple doesn't retain many Masters as teachers, but your grades have always been so good," Marreli said, her dark eyes shining. "I'm sure they'd keep you. You could even be the one to replace Master Nondar, someday."

"It's a good calling," Shymin agreed. "You've always been so dedicated to your studies."

"I think I'd enjoy it." Firal wouldn't say as much, but she had enjoyed her lessons with Daemon. If nothing else, at least meeting him had set her on the right path.

Marreli stood and pulled Firal to her feet. "You should go speak to Nondar about it."

"What? Right now?" Firal scrubbed her cheeks with her dingy sleeve.

"Yes, right now!" Shymin agreed. "Before you change your mind."

Before she lost her nerve, Firal suspected she meant. "But I hardly know what to say."

"Just tell him what you told us. Ask him to point you in the right direction. It'll give you something else to look forward to. Something to keep your mind off of..." Shymin cleared her throat as her eyes wandered the ruined office. "Well, you know."

Firal gulped and nodded. She was right. A distraction from the ache of loss that had settled in her chest would be welcome. "Will the two of you be all right here without me?"

"Of course we will," Marreli assured her.

Mustering a smile, Firal bowed her head in silent thanks and tip-toed back to the door. She paused once, resting her fingertips on the blackened stone and looking back.

Shymin nodded in reassurance, and Firal hurried on.

FAT GRAY CLOUDS HUNG LOW IN THE SKY AND THUNDER GROWLED IN the distance as Firal made her way to the Archmage's tower. Magelings rushed out the open double doors with oiled cloth in their hands and distress on their faces. Numerous piles of unsorted debris sat about the temple courtyard, all in need of protection from the rain. Who knew what was still there to be salvaged?

A cold raindrop hit her cheek just before she reached the tower, and Firal looked skyward. Some things never changed. She wiped away the water and slid inside.

Halfway up the tower, the high-ranking Masters had been afforded small, private offices. Though she hadn't had a reason to venture into them before now, it was not difficult to find Nondar's. The temporary office was bursting with dried herbs and bottles of medicine recovered from his storerooms. The rich, spicy scent was noticeable from anywhere on that floor.

Firal crept to the open doorway and peered inside.

Nondar sat beside the window with his back to the door, watching as the first raindrops fell. Though there was no glass in the windows, the rain did not enter. For a moment, she wondered if the old Master held it at bay.

"I did receive the letter, you know," Nondar said. "The one from Temar."

Ducking her eyes, Firal stepped into his office and clasped her hands together. "How did you know it was me?"

"Every mage bears a unique presence. No two Gifts are alike. With time, you will learn to tell them apart, too." The old Master stroked his beard in thought. Unlike the other Masters she'd seen about, his robes were stained gray with ash. Whether it was from sorting the supplies brought up to him or from searching for them in the rubble himself, she did not know.

"What did she write?" Firal asked, unsure what else to say.

"That she granted you permission to review all Ilmenhith's archives, along with the temple's private archives, if they were necessary for you to find what you sought."

Her throat tightened. The court Master had bestowed her a great gift, only for it to slip through her fingers as ash. "I appreciate that she's a woman of her word."

"You would like her, I believe," Nondar said. "Temar is a good woman. I am sure if she had the means, she would have helped you further. But she did not. And neither will the records anymore, I'm afraid."

"I know." Firal paced closer. "Thank you, Master Nondar."

"I did not realize the records had been moved to Kirban." He rested his hands atop his cane. His fingers flexed, his knuckles white. "It was not within my authority to allow you to read them before you wear white. But had I known the records were stored here, I would have tried."

A sense of comfort stirred inside her, a diffuse warmth that pushed against the ache and sadness that had cooled her heart. Firal closed her eyes and clung to it. Nondar was a good man, grandfatherly and kind. No matter how her crushed hopes hurt, she still had him. "Thank you, Master. I appreciate that. But I came to speak with you about something else."

He cocked his head and cast her curious look from the corner of one mage-blue eye.

Firal twisted her fingers, as if movement could soothe her nerves. She inched closer and drew a breath. "My whole life has been consumed by wanting to know my parents. I never thought much beyond trying to reach the white so I could impress them, whoever they were." She knelt beside his chair and rested her hands in her lap. "I suppose in some ways, I thought knowing them would help me know myself. To know what I wanted."

Nondar raised one thick brow. "And now that you've been

robbed of the chance to find their legacy?"

"I think it's time to start building my own."

He chuckled and reclined in his chair. "Who sent you?"

Her cheeks reddened. "What do you mean?"

"A life's calling does not change in the span of a week, child. Don't hurry from one to another, no matter who urges you. When the temple is rebuilt, we will speak of what you wish to do. It's best if you take this time to reflect on it."

"But what if I'm already sure?"

Nondar ticked a gnarled finger at her. "Then you will still be sure two weeks from now."

She worried her lower lip between her teeth. "Do you think the temple will be able to rebuild?"

"It has before," he said with a shrug. "Just before you were born, in fact."

Her brow furrowed. "You told me that you didn't know my mother."

"I didn't." Nondar's face softened with a smile. "But I knew you. A tiny babe, entrusted to us. The strongest Masters were certain you would be Gifted. You cannot imagine their delight in discovering you were. And strong in it, too."

Firal blushed again, this time with pride. Compliments from the old Master were few and far between. "Do you think I'm strong enough to become a teacher?"

"I believe you are strong enough to do anything you set your mind to, child. And when the temple is restored, we will know for sure."

She closed her amber eyes and savored his words. She did not feel strong; her weakness had caused grief for everyone. But she respected Nondar, and he had no reason to lead her astray. She nodded as she pushed herself up from the floor.

Nondar tilted his head as she turned away. "Where are you going?"

To forge a new life. To start again. To set her path in motion.

Firal paused at the door and smiled. "To rebuild."

GLOSSARY

Affinity – One's natural inclination in magic. There are five major affinities: Earth, water, fire, wind, and life. These provide the primary source of power a mage can draw from and manipulate. While there are smaller subcategories affinities may fall into, granting specific talents in narrow fields, they are generally related to one of the five and, as result, only the five major affinities are recognized.

Alira – (*uh-LEER-ah*) – Master of the House of Fire.

Alwhen – (*OWL-when*) – The capital of the eastern half of Elenhiise island, a region known as the Giftless Lands.

Anaide – (*uh-NAYD*) – Master of the House of Water.

Archmage – The leader of Kirban Temple, generally recognized as the leader of all mages.

Core – An underground city beneath the ruins, home of the Underlings.

GLOSSARY

Daemon – (*DAY-mun*) – An Underling soldier. His tainted magic has twisted his body into a monstrous form.

Edagan – (*ED-ah-gan*) – Master of the House of Earth.

Eldani – (*ell-DAN-ee*) – The only inhabitants of Ithilear who are known to be Gifted. Eldani are long-lived, due to their magic, and differ from humans only in their pointed ears. Diluted bloodlines are recognized by the reduced point of an Eldani's ear, which directly corresponds with their prowess as a mage.

Elenhiise – (*ELL-en-heese*) – A small island in the middle of the Lantaaran sea, generally used as a waypoint in trade between the region's northern and southern continents. The island is ruled by two factions, the Gifted Eldani and Giftless men.

Envesi – (*in-VESS-see*) – The Archmage of Kirban Temple.

Firal – (*fur-ALL*) – A green-rank mageling at Kirban temple.

Flows – The natural ebb and flow of magic, which mages are able to seize and manipulate.

Gift – The ability to use magic.

House – A subsection of mages, ruled by a particular affinity. Mages within the House of Healing, Fire, etc. may take classes together, but their education is overseen by the Master of their House.

Ileara – (*ill-ee-ARE-ah*) – The second moon. The smaller of the two, Ileara is known as The Mother and is stationary in the sky. As it is only visible in the far western regions of the known world, such as the Westkings and the Chains of Raeldan, some residents of Elenhiise and the other eastern regions do not believe Ileara exists.

Ilmenhith – (*ill-men-HITH*) – The capital of the western half of Elenhiise island, which is under Eldani control.

Ithi – (*ith-EE*) – The first moon. The larger of the two, Ithi is known as The Soldier and circles Ithilear once per day. The thirteen months of the year are framed around Ithi's phases; its cycle is 28 days.

Ithilear – (*ith-ILL-ee-arr*) – The world. The name is derived from the two moons, Ithi and Ileara. In folklore, the moons are lovers. Ithi ventures forth to patrol and protect their child, Ithilear, while Ileara remains in one place to provide a stable home.

Kifel – (*kiff-EL*) – Full name Kifelethelas Penedhionn. The Eldani king and ruler of the western half of Elenhiise island.

Kirban Temple – (*KER-ban*) – Founded by Archmage Envesi, Kirban Temple is the only school of magecraft on Elenhiise Island. A prestigious college sponsored by the Eldani crown and located near the southern edge of the ruins.

Kytenia – (*kit-teen-yah*) – A yellow-rank mageling at Kirban Temple and Firal's best friend.

Lumia – (*loo-MEE-ah*) – Queen of the Underlings.

Mageling – A mage in training. Magelings are divided into five ranks before they graduate to Master and wear robes in corresponding colors. The five ranks are gray, lavender, yellow, green, and blue.

Marreli – (*mah-RELL-ee*) – A gray-rank mageling at Kirban Temple. One of Firal's friends.

Master – A mage recognized as skilled enough to wield magic without supervision. Masters outside the temple act as healers and scholars, and are in charge of scouting Gifted children to send for training. Masters who remain within the temple are generally teachers. Master mages are the only mages allowed to wear white. Court Masters and Masters of an affinity mark their eyes with black ink to distinguish their rank.

Medreal – (*mee-dree-al*) – King Kifel's stewardess.

Melora – (*mel-LOR-ah*) – Master of the House of Wind.

Nondar – (*non-DAR*) – Master of the House of Healing, also known as the House of Life. Nondar is one of few recognized half-Eldani Masters and is unparalleled as a medic.

Ran – Full name Lomithrandel. A blue-rank mageling at Kirban temple and the only part-time student allowed. He considers Firal a friend, while she considers him a nuisance.

Relythes – (*rell-uh-THEEZ*) – The Giftless King, ruler of Alwhen and the eastern half of Elenhiise island.

Rikka – (*RIK-kuh*) – A yellow-rank mageling at Kirban Temple. One of Firal's friends.

Ruins – A sprawling labyrinth in the center of the island. The ruins fall entirely on Eldani lands.

Shymin – (*SHY-min*) – A green-rank mageling at Kirban Temple. One of Firal's friends and Kytenia's elder sister.

GLOSSARY

Tren – Full name Tren Achos. Lumia's general.

Underlings – Giftless people driven into the ruins by war, rumored to be monsters and believed to be legend.

Vahn – Full name Vahnil Tanrys. A low-ranking soldier in Ilmenhith's military.

Made in the USA
Monee, IL
20 June 2021

71809204R00204